M000197694

REVELATIONS

THE BELLE MORTE SERIES

BELLE MORTE

REVELATIONS

HUNTED
Winter 2024

CHANGES
Winter 2025

REVELATIONS

BELLE MORTE BOOK TWO

BELLA HIGGIN

wattpad books **W**

wattpad books

An imprint of Wattpad WEBTOON Book Group

Content Warning: mentions of blood, mentions of violence, language

Published in Canada by Wattpad WEBTOON Book Group, a division of Wattpad WEBTOON Studios, Inc.

36 Wellington Street E., Suite 200, Toronto, ON M5E 1C7 Canada

www.wattpad.com

First Wattpad Books edition: May 2023

ISBN 978-1-99025-949-4 (Hardcover original)
ISBN 978-1-99025-950-0 (eBook edition)

Library and Archives Canada Cataloguing in Publication information is available upon request.

Printed and bound in Canada

1 3 5 7 9 10 8 6 4 2

Cover design by Ysabel Enverga

Images © larisabozhikova © pit3dd via Adobe Stock, © Valerie_k via Shutterstock, © PitakAreekul via iStock, © Thomas Dumortier via Unsplash

For my mum, who never lost faith in me,
even when I lost faith in myself.

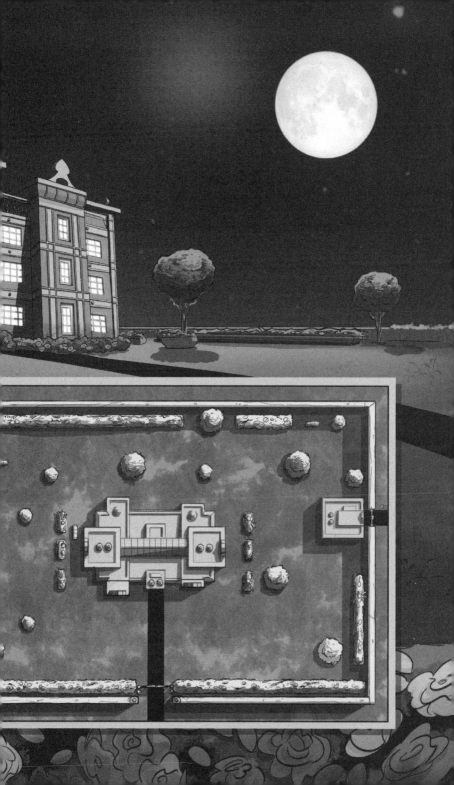

CHAPTER ONE

Renie

I drifted in darkness, blind and deaf to anything but the constant, gnawing ache in my stomach. Every so often a warm, sweet liquid slid down my throat and the hunger pangs faded, but never for long. That terrible hunger always surged back, like fire.

Occasionally, there were snatches of awareness: the sensation of cool hands touching my face; the faint murmur of a male voice. At the back of my fevered brain, I was aware that I knew that voice, *loved* that voice. But then the hunger roared back and everything was lost.

It could have been days, months, or even years before I finally cracked my eyes open. A corniced ceiling took shape above me, bright spots of light coalescing into a crystal chandelier.

Pieces of memory filtered back into my battered brain.

Belle Morte.

I was lying tangled in black satin covers in a huge four-poster bed, and the walls around me were indigo blue, much darker than the pale-gold bedroom I shared with Roux. Light from the chandelier winked off a pair of swords mounted on the wall.

I knew this room—this was *Edmond's* bedroom.

And standing by that bed was Edmond Dantès himself, the vampire I'd fallen in love with. He looked like a dark angel, all coal-black hair and ivory skin, eyes glittering like diamonds, and the breath would have caught in my lungs at the sheer beauty of him . . . but I no longer needed to breathe.

I touched my throat, then pressed my palm to my chest. No heartbeat.

Memories rushed back, making me reel: June's escape from the west wing, the attack on Belle Morte, my final attempt to help her, which had ended with her plunging a knife into my chest, and—

"Etienne," I gasped. My lungs felt rusty and my lips were dry.

The vampire who had pretended to be my friend—who'd helped me find the truth about June only to reveal that he was the one who'd killed her and turned her into a monster.

Edmond slid onto the bed next to me, as graceful and as fluid as a cat. "Hush, *mon ange*. Don't worry about that now."

I recoiled from him instinctively, and Edmond went very still.

Emotion roared in my head, making it hard to think.

I was dead.

I had died out there in the snow.

All I'd wanted when I'd come to Belle Morte was to make sure that June was okay, and now I couldn't even comprehend what the future held. I'd never grow older than eighteen. I'd never have a career. It would be years before I built up enough UV resistance to spend any real time in the sun. All the things I'd taken for granted as a human were lost to me now.

The pain of all those lost maybes caught in my throat, making my eyes burn, but no tears fell.

My palm was still pressed to my chest, vainly waiting to feel the thump of a heart that would never beat again. Probing my teeth with my tongue, I flinched when I felt the sharp points of fangs. When I'd first opened my eyes as a vampire, cradled in Edmond's arms on the snowy grounds of Belle Morte, I'd been aware of these changes, but in an abstract sort of way.

Now the reality hit me like a hammer to the brain.

I was a vampire.

For the rest of my life, I'd have to rely on human blood to survive. I'd become the very thing I'd once feared.

"What have you done to me?" I whispered.

A shadow of pain swept across Edmond's perfect face.

Nausea curdled inside me, and I clutched my stomach. The sweet liquid I remembered drinking when I was lost in the darkness, the only thing that had quelled the hunger pangs—that had been blood. I'd been drinking *human blood*.

"I'm a monster," I rasped.

Still, Edmond didn't move, didn't speak, but the look in his eyes was devastated, like something inside him was breaking.

I'd given him permission to turn me—I knew that, but I didn't know how to cope with the monumental change that had come over my body and my life. I was scared and angry, and I had no idea what I was supposed to do with myself.

An aching wave of hunger rolled over me and I groaned. My fangs pricked my lower lip, and my gums throbbed.

Ignoring my harsh words, Edmond pulled me gently against his chest. "The hunger will pass. You're almost there," he murmured.

His voice was like velvet, wrapping me in warmth and safety, and the room dimmed, blackness rushing to welcome me back. My last thought was that, despite what I'd said to him, I was glad that Edmond was here, holding me.

Edmond

Sitting on the edge of the bed, watching Renie toss and turn in a restless sleep, Edmond wished there'd been another way to save her.

He'd once told her that if he could go back in time, even if he knew all the terrible times that awaited him as a vampire, he'd still choose this life. But he wouldn't have chosen it for *her*.

Etienne's treachery had given Edmond what he desperately wanted—for Renie to stay with him. Now she would never grow old and die while he watched helplessly. They had a chance to actually be together.

But that meant nothing if Renie wasn't happy with the choice she'd made.

The door opened and Ysanne Moreau swept in, Ludovic following tentatively behind. The Lady of Belle Morte cast her eye over Renie's sleeping form, but her cool expression didn't change.

"How is she doing?" she asked.

"Better," Edmond replied, stroking the tangled mess of Renie's auburn hair, brighter than ever against her vampire-pale skin.

Ysanne knew about his feelings for Renie now, but he'd first lied to her about them, and he knew Ysanne wouldn't forget that. Their friendship had been forged through the ages, love and loss binding them together, and Edmond had hated to lie to the person who'd known him longer than anyone. But relationships between vampires and donors were strictly forbidden, and when Edmond realized that he couldn't fight his feelings for Renie, he'd had to lie to his oldest friend.

"Do you believe she's through the worst of it?" Ysanne asked. "Because the Council will be coming soon, and you can't be here when they arrive."

Edmond closed his eyes. Turning a human without permission from the Council—the collective rulers of the British and Irish Vampire Houses—was one of the most serious crimes a vampire could commit. Ysanne should have punished him immediately, but she'd stayed her hand so he could help Renie through the turn. It was not a reprieve that anyone else would have granted. But even Ysanne couldn't hold off his punishment forever, especially when she herself was in serious trouble with the Council.

Under her watch, June Mayfield had been killed and turned, but instead of waking up as a vampire, she had woken up rabid. Vampire law decreed that rabids were too dangerous to live, and Ysanne should have killed June the moment she'd found her. She hadn't. Instead, she'd hidden June in the mansion's west wing, and then she'd brought Renie to Belle Morte under the guise of being a donor, hoping that Renie might be able to help June recover her sanity.

But Renie had failed. Rabids could not be saved, and by the time Ysanne realized that, it was too late—Etienne had turned June loose on the house just as Belle Morte had come under attack from enemy forces.

The bodies of the people who'd died because of that had been removed, but the house still smelled of blood.

Edmond's illegal turning of Renie was just one of the many bleak shadows darkening Belle Morte.

"Edmond?" Ysanne prompted, and he realized he hadn't answered her question.

He gazed down at Renie again, curled up in his bed where she'd been for the last three days, her hair spread over his pillow like a shower of autumn leaves. He could tell Ysanne that he needed more time with her, but it would be a lie. Renie was through the worst of the turn—the next time she awoke, it would be as a true vampire. Edmond had helped her as much as he could, and he wouldn't disrespect the time Ysanne had given him by asking for more. He wouldn't lie to her again.

"Yes," he said, his heart feeling like a rock in his chest. He had no idea what punishment he had incurred by turning the girl he loved.

Ysanne's icy mask slipped for a fraction of a second. "*Vieil ami,* you know I have no choice."

Edmond climbed off the bed and approached her—the woman who'd first opened his eyes to the vampire world and who he'd once loved as a partner and still loved as a friend. "I would never blame you," he said. "The choice was mine, and I'd make it again, regardless of the consequences."

Ysanne kissed his cheek, a soft brush of her lips, and then the cool mask was back in place.

"It's time to go," she said.

Edmond looked back at Renie, memorizing every line of her face, every strand of her hair. He remembered the way her lips curved when she smiled at him, the way her eyes could flash with anger or glitter with laughter. He committed every part of her to memory because he didn't know when he'd see her again.

Ysanne left the room and Edmond started to follow her, but stopped when Ludovic put a hand on his shoulder.

"I'll take care of her," Ludovic said.

Edmond laid his hand on Ludovic's. "Thank you," he said.

Then, with one last look back at the girl who'd stolen his ancient heart, Edmond left to pay the price for saving her.

Renie

The next time I woke up, Edmond had gone. Ludovic and Isabeau stood close to the door, speaking in low voices. I was a vampire now, and could hear every word they said. Too bad I didn't speak French.

They both looked over as I slowly sat up, and Ludovic approached me. His face was unreadable. "How do you feel?"

"I . . . okay." The crippling hunger pangs had faded to a dull ache in the pit of my stomach.

I climbed out of bed, expecting my legs to feel shaky, but they were strong. My whole body felt strong.

This was it then. I really was a vampire.

When I was first turned, I hadn't had time to process the enormity of it; I'd literally just died, after all. In my conscious moments during the turn, I'd registered only the worst parts. Now I was calmer, more able to think about the decision I'd made.

Yes, I was a vampire, and while I was technically no longer *alive*, I would still *live*. Possibly forever. I had never imagined something like this happening to me, and it would take some serious getting used to, but the knife that June had plunged into my chest had not ended everything.

June . . .

A sharp pain sliced through my heart, and I sucked in a breath that I didn't need anymore.

"What happened?" I asked.

"How much do you remember?" Isabeau asked, clasping her hands in front of her. Her thick hazelnut curls were pulled back in a low ponytail, and her expression was solemn.

"I remember Etienne being the bastard who murdered my sister," I said in a low, hard voice. "Where is he?"

Ludovic and Isabeau exchanged a look.

"We don't know," Isabeau said.

"What?"

Ludovic took over. "After June stabbed you, she and Etienne disappeared. By the time Edmond and I reached the gardens, they'd gone. We have no idea where they went."

"Roux? Jason?" I said.

I hadn't come to Belle Morte to make friends, but my roommate, Roux Hayes, and Jason Grant, another donor who'd arrived at the same time as us, had quickly found their way under my skin and into my heart. They were the best friends I'd never expected to have.

"They're fine," Isabeau said, but something in her voice gave me pause.

"How long have I been here?" I asked.

"Three days."

"Where's Edmond?"

Another look passed between the older vampires, and Ludovic's face darkened.

"Renie, you must understand that Edmond did something very serious by turning you," said Isabeau gently.

My stomach turned to ice. Something was wrong.

"Where is he?" I repeated.

"Yesterday he was imprisoned for turning you without permission," Ludovic said.

His eyes were hard as he looked at me, and I wondered if he blamed me for what had happened. Edmond was his best friend, someone he'd survived the hell of war with, and Edmond wouldn't be locked up if I hadn't come to Belle Morte.

Then the ice in my stomach turned to fire.

No, Edmond wouldn't be locked up if *Etienne* hadn't murdered my sister.

"Did Ysanne lock him up?" I demanded.

I wanted Ludovic to say no, that it had been done by another member of the Council. Just days ago, Ysanne had had Edmond whipped with silver for defending me against another vampire; I couldn't bear to think that she'd punish him again.

"Yes, she did," Ludovic said.

I closed my eyes.

There were bigger things going on here than just Edmond and me—I knew that—but the thought of him suffering, *again*, for my sake, was almost more than I could bear.

Edmond no longer loved Ysanne romantically, but he still loved her as a friend. He still trusted and respected her. Did that count for nothing?

"Can I see him?" I said.

Isabeau shook her head. "I'm afraid not."

This wasn't fair. Edmond had only turned me to save my life. How could Ysanne punish him for that?

"I need to see Ysanne," I said.

Isabeau's expression was sympathetic but firm. "I don't think that's a good idea."

Rage suddenly blazed through me, faster than I could rein it in. "I don't *care* what you think. Maybe you blindly support everything Ysanne does because you're sleeping with her, or whatever you two are doing, but I'm not standing by while she does this to him. Not again."

Isabeau's eyes flared red and her lips pulled back from her fangs. "Watch what you say," she warned.

"What's Ysanne going to do—terminate my contract? I'm not a donor anymore."

As I spoke, I felt a strange swell of power—not physical power but something else. I was a *vampire* now, and Ysanne couldn't brush me off the way she had when I was human.

I stalked across the room and threw open the door so hard it left a dent in the fancy wallpaper.

Isabeau strode after me. The red had faded from her eyes but her face was set in hard lines. "Don't be foolish, Renie."

Her hand touched my shoulder but I shook her off. I spun to face her, my bare feet sinking into the thick carpet that lined Belle Morte's many hallways. Rage blistered inside me, so hot and fierce it felt like I would combust on the spot. My gums ached as my fangs emerged, sliding to their full length.

This wasn't just about Edmond. It was about my sweet sister dying in this house and coming back as a blood-crazed monster at the hands of a man I had trusted. It was about that man escaping justice while Edmond was punished for *saving my life*.

Isabeau regarded me, her face infuriatingly blank. If I'd hoped that becoming a vampire would mean I could better decipher what they might be thinking, I'd been wrong to.

Ludovic stood a little behind her, his eyes fixed on me. When Edmond had leaped to my defense against Adrian, the vampire who'd groped me during a welcome party for visitors from House Nox, Ludovic had made sure no one else had bothered me while Edmond and Adrian were removed from the ballroom. He'd shielded me from Adrian when the other vampire returned, and then a few hours later he'd broken Belle Morte's rules and smuggled me into the north wing, where the vampires slept and no donor was meant to go, so I could see Edmond after his beating. I wasn't sure how Ludovic felt about me at this point, but I hoped he understood that the rage I felt was on Edmond's behalf.

Pieces of memory clicked together in my head, and I remembered what I'd said to Edmond the last time I'd woken up. Some of my rage died down, replaced by scalding shame. I'd called myself a monster—and by extension, him. I'd blamed Edmond because, however horrible and unfair it was, in that moment I needed to blame *someone*. It had been a while since I'd truly thought of vampires as monsters, but when I'd felt the prick of my fangs and realized I'd been drinking human blood, my old fears had resurfaced, and had spilled cruelly from my mouth.

I had to see Edmond, and Ysanne was the only person who could give me that.

"I told Edmond I would take care of you," Ludovic said, still watching me.

"You can't stop me from going to Ysanne."

He could, but that didn't stop me saying it. And it didn't stop him from replying: "I know."

Turning my back on the two vampires, I walked off to find Ysanne. I had no idea what I'd do when I did, but I couldn't leave Edmond like this.

He'd saved me. Now I would save him.

CHAPTER TWO

Edmond

Edmond Dantès leaned his head on the stone wall behind him, Renie's words playing in an endless, savage loop through his mind.

The Belle Morte cells, hidden away so donors and most staff didn't even know they existed, were a far cry from the luxury of the rest of the mansion. They were stark stone rooms, almost medieval in their austerity, with no furniture and no amenities—nothing to break up the solid stone except for iron rings driven deep into the walls.

Edmond had been in worse prisons—the days he'd spent in the Conciergerie during the French Revolution were among the bleakest of his life—but the Belle Morte cells held one horror that the Conciergerie had not.

He was shackled with silver.

Silver manacles and chains bound his wrists to the rings in the walls, the metal burning through skin and flesh. Blood formed small puddles on either side of his body, and the slightest movement was agony.

He had no idea how long he'd be here.

The door opened and Ysanne walked in. To anyone else, she would have looked like she normally did—the icy Lady of Belle Morte. But Edmond knew her. He could see the way she moved, a little slower than normal, the way she held herself a little too rigidly, and the shadows in her eyes.

The click of her high heels echoed around the stone walls, fading to silence when she paused in front of him.

"Oh, *mon garçon d'hiver*," she said quietly. "This isn't what I wanted for you."

"I don't blame you," Edmond said.

Ysanne took off her shoes and knelt in front of him, her hands folded in her lap. For a long moment neither of them said a word.

"Renie called herself a monster," said Edmond. "After everything, she still sees us that way. I often thought about how hard it would be to watch her walk out of Belle Morte and never come back. I faced the awful reality of watching her die out there in the snow. But I never thought she'd turn on me."

"Stop it," said Ysanne firmly. "Renie is not Charlotte. This is not the same situation."

Hundreds of years ago, Edmond had confessed his vampire nature to another woman he'd loved. Charlotte's response had been to declare him a monster and gather a mob to kill him. Her betrayal had left a deep scar on Edmond's heart.

Ysanne tilted her head slightly, so her blond hair slipped over one shoulder. "I do know how it feels," she said. "A long time ago, a woman I deeply cared for turned on me in the same way when she found out what I was. But I do not believe that Renie sees you as a monster."

Edmond managed a half smile that turned into a hiss of pain as his shackled wrists moved slightly. "I never thought I'd see the day that you defended her."

"I'm not. I'm advising you to let go of the past."

"What happens to Renie now?"

Ysanne considered it. "I don't know. That depends on what happens when the Council gets here."

Edmond tried not to think about the fact that turning Renie illegally wasn't his only transgression: he'd helped Ysanne hide June, and had helped cover up June's murder along with Isabeau and, later on, Ludovic. The Council would expect answers from all of them.

"The vampires who attacked the house—they must have been working for Etienne," he said.

Ysanne's lips thinned. "That seems the most likely assumption."

"But why? What was he trying to achieve?"

Ysanne said nothing, her eyes pensive.

Edmond shifted, instinctively reaching for his old friend, then squeezed his eyes shut as a wave of agony rolled over him. Anyone else might not have been able to face what they had done to him, but Ysanne watched every second, without flinching, without apologizing. He knew that it hurt her to know that she was the cause of his suffering, but she wouldn't shy away from it. She wouldn't pretend it wasn't happening.

"For a long time you said that you'd never give your heart to anyone again," Ysanne said. "What changed? Why is Renie so special?"

"Over the last ten years, more donors have come into Belle Morte than I can remember, and they've always treated me the same way: They look at me with awe, wanting to be with me just because I'm a vampire. They try to tempt their way into my bed in the hopes that I will make them immortal. They see me as a novelty, some unattainable prize they want to claim."

"But not Renie," Ysanne guessed.

"From the moment she arrived, she refused to be starstruck by me. She was the first human girl in a very long time to treat me like an ordinary person rather than a trophy, and I wasn't prepared for that."

Renie had exploded into his life like a wrecking ball, all temper and beauty and defiance, cracking the wall that he'd spent so long building around himself, and his old, wounded heart had started to *feel* again.

He'd never wanted to fall in love again, but that's what this was.

He loved Renie.

Much as he'd tried to fight it, he'd given her his heart, one small piece at a time. She owned it—owned every part of him.

And despite Ysanne's reassurances, Edmond wasn't convinced that Renie didn't regret her decision—didn't blame him for turning her. In his centuries-long life he'd seen and done and suffered so much, but the thought of losing Renie *crushed* him.

"Why didn't you tell me about Isabeau?" he asked, trying to focus on something else.

He'd known that Ysanne and Isabeau had been a couple back in the '60s, but not once in the ten years that they'd all lived in Belle Morte had Ysanne even hinted that she and Isabeau had rekindled their relationship.

Ysanne looked down at her hands. "I didn't tell anyone."

"You don't normally keep things from me."

"Like you kept Renie from me?"

Edmond shut his eyes against another wave of pain from the silver shackles. "That's different," he said. "Renie and I weren't *allowed* to be together; we had to keep it secret."

"A fair point," Ysanne conceded. "Isabeau and I decided that our relationship should remain a secret because my priority will always be Belle Morte. The House must come first, no matter what, and I can't be seen to have favorites."

"Not even when it's the woman you love?"

A pause.

"Not even then," Ysanne said.

"It doesn't have to be like this."

Ysanne's smile was small and a little sad. "Yes, it does. If I could get away with favoring the people most important to me, then you wouldn't be locked up like this."

"I knew there'd be a price for turning Renie, and I'd pay it a thousand times over."

"You really love her, don't you?" Ysanne said, her voice soft.

"More than anything." Edmond flexed his fingers, feeling the awful burn of the silver chains. "Promise me you'll keep her safe. Etienne is still out there. We have no idea what he wants, but he's tried to kill her before, and there's nothing to suggest he won't try again."

"I won't let anything happen to her," Ysanne said.

She climbed to her feet, smoothed out her skirt, and slipped her shoes back on. "I should go before the rest of the Council arrives. We have a lot to discuss."

Edmond should be supporting Renie as she faced the Council; instead, he was stuck down here, chained and helpless. His hands ached with the urge to curl into fists, but that would only make the pain worse.

Ysanne softly kissed Edmond's forehead, and then walked out of the cells and closed the door behind her, leaving him alone.

Resting his head on the wall again, Edmond closed his eyes and thought of Renie.

Renie

As I stalked out of the north wing, I almost ran into Tamara, a donor who'd arrived at Belle Morte at the same time as me. Her eyes widened, and I wondered how many people knew what had really happened out on the grounds a few nights ago. Knowing Ysanne, she would have kept as much of it under wraps as possible, so I could only imagine the rumors that were flying around.

Tamara's heartbeat was a hammering noise in my ears, inviting my eyes to the shape of her throat, the veins beneath her skin. I was *thirsty*, I realized with a jolt of horror. I wanted to bite Tamara and drink her blood.

She shrank back, and I wondered what I looked like to her. Were my eyes shining red? Could she see my fangs? Her heart beat faster, the scent of her blood filling the air, tempting me.

I hurried past her. Would I always feel that temptation around a human, or would the urge to bite fade with time?

At the bottom of the staircase I paused, one hand clutching the banister. The last time I'd come down these stairs Belle Morte had been under attack, and I'd been rushing to the ballroom in a misguided attempt to protect Edmond. But here, in the vestibule, I'd found two bodies: a vampire I hadn't known, and Abigail, one of the donors. Her blood had been mopped up and the parquet floor was as clean and polished as ever, but I could still *see* her lying there, her arm hanging from her body by a string of sinew, her eyes staring at the ceiling, frozen wide with shock and terror.

Hot on the heels of that memory came another: Aiden lying at the bottom of the steps in the west wing, his throat ripped open, the monster that had been my sister crouched over him.

Had anyone else died in the attack?

My mind went to Melissa. She'd been June's friend, and she'd pushed for answers after she'd realized I hadn't come here to be a donor, but I hadn't been able to give them to her. She'd also been Aiden's girlfriend. He'd gone to the west wing to find the truth, and June had killed him for it.

Was Melissa okay?

I looked back up the main staircase. Maybe I should go to her first. Then I thought of Edmond again. I needed to know what was happening to him. Ysanne had the answers to everything—assuming she was willing to share them.

Her office was the likeliest place to find her, and when I got there, I walked in without knocking. It was empty. I stared around the small room, as cold and remote as Ysanne herself, all dark wallpaper and white carpet and polished black desk. The desk was empty but for a small wooden frame that I'd never seen before. I crept closer and picked it up. It was small enough to fit in the palm of my hand: a framed oil painting of a handsome man with dark hair and olive skin, smiling softly. The style of the artistry, the faded colors, and the battered frame all suggested that this painting was very old, and I quickly put it back down before I did something stupid like drop it.

The door opened behind me and I whipped around.

Ysanne's eyes went from me to the painting and narrowed. "You shouldn't be in here without my permission," she said.

I'd been so angry when I'd left the north wing, but memories of the terrible night that had ended my human life had drained the rage out of me, leaving a bone-deep exhaustion.

"Why are you punishing Edmond for saving my life?" I said.

Ysanne walked across the room, her high heels noiseless in the thick carpet. She picked up the tiny painting, and I thought I glimpsed her thumb gently stroking the frame before she placed it in one of the desk drawers.

"I'm not. I'm punishing him for breaking the rules," she said.

"Is that how you see the world? As nothing but rules to be upheld? Isn't there any room for compassion or humanity?"

"The turning of humans is a serious offense. When the Council created the donor system we agreed that turning new vampires would be an emergency-only situation."

"It *was* an emergency. I was dying."

Ysanne simply looked at me, as frustratingly blank as ever. "To vampires who have lived hundreds of years, and to the balance that exists between us and humans, the life of a single girl is not worth much."

She placed her hands flat on the desktop and leaned forward. I knew firsthand how powerful those pale, delicate hands really were.

"Humans vastly outnumber vampires, and they could wipe us out if they wanted to. Edmond has broken one of our most import-ant laws and he must be punished, both so the Council sees how seriously I am taking his transgression and so the human world realizes we are not ruled by our baser instincts."

I wasn't blind to the reality of this. Humans saw vampires as beautiful, mysterious, and immortal—somehow *more* than ordinary people. But if the human world caught a glimpse of the dangerous beast that lurked beneath the polished veneer, they might not be so enamored of vampires. And if human favor turned against them, the donor system could disintegrate and the Houses could collapse. Vampires could be driven back into the shadows.

Even so—"There are exceptions to every rule," I insisted.

"Perhaps," Ysanne conceded. "But vampires are predators; we can smell weakness. If I am seen to be weak, allowing my vampires to walk all over me, then others may be tempted to challenge me as Lady of the House." Her voice turned hard and cold. "I will not allow that to happen. It's easy for you to walk in here with your self-righteous attitude and your childish view of the world, but there is far more at stake here than you and Edmond."

My temper sparked but I shoved it back down. I pulled out one of the chairs and sat in front of the desk. Something that could have been surprise flickered in Ysanne's eyes, then it was gone, quick as a blink. She'd probably expected me to start yelling.

"Explain to me what else is at stake. What did I miss while I was unconscious? Who attacked the mansion?" I hesitated because I didn't want the answer to my next question, even though I needed to hear it. "How many people died?"

Ysanne regarded me for a moment before taking a seat herself.

"First, I need you to tell me exactly what happened with Etienne and June out in the gardens," she said.

I cast my mind back to that awful night, when the life I'd known had ended.

"I was trying to stop June from hurting anyone else. Ludovic injured her with a sword and she fled the ballroom, so I went after her. I don't know what I thought I'd do when I caught up with her, I wasn't thinking clearly. But when I followed her outside, Etienne was waiting for me."

That awful moment of betrayal sliced through me again, sharp as a blade, and I put a hand to my chest. The lack of a heartbeat still felt alien to me.

Ysanne quietly waited for me to continue.

"He told me that he was the one who'd killed June." The words tasted sour.

"Was he also the one who released her the first time you went up to the west wing?"

"Yeah. He said it wasn't personal, but he couldn't let me interfere with June. He said he'd turned her because it was necessary, but that he hadn't meant for her to become rabid, and that he was sorry but I had to die."

"Anything else?"

I swallowed a knot in my throat. "The last thing he said was that a revolution was coming and the vampire world was going to change. Does that mean anything to you?"

Ysanne didn't answer. "In response to your earlier question, we lost three members of security and two members of staff." She paused, her pale eyes boring into me. "Three other donors were killed: Aiden, Abigail, and Ranesh. You were the only one who was turned."

I was relieved that Melissa wasn't among the victims.

"Were there any vampire casualties?" I said.

"Two of Jemima's entourage that she brought from Nox were killed, along with Rosa," Ysanne replied.

Rosa had fed from me once, back when I was pretending to be just another donor, but we'd barely exchanged more than a sentence.

"There was also another casualty, from House Midnight," Ysanne continued.

"Wait, what?" I frowned. "What was someone from Midnight doing here?"

"That's the big question, and one that will need to be addressed once the Council arrives."

There was something she wasn't telling me.

"Who attacked Belle Morte?" I asked.

"I don't know." Ysanne's expression never changed, but there was the faintest hint of frustration in her voice. Ysanne Moreau didn't like not knowing things.

"But . . . I mean, what House were they from?"

"They weren't."

"I don't understand."

"Renie, you're not the only new vampire that the Council is coming to investigate. The vampires that broke into Belle Morte were *all* newly turned."

My brain couldn't quite process that. I wasn't a Vladdict, and I'd never kept up with all the vampires of the Houses in the UK or Ireland, so I'd simply assumed that the intruders had come from one of those.

"What happened to them?" I asked. Maybe if I had more of the pieces, I could fit them together in the confusion in my head.

"Thirteen were killed that night. The others . . . disappeared."

"They ran away?"

Ysanne nodded.

"They must have realized what a massive mistake they'd made," I said.

New vampires were vastly stronger than any human but they couldn't match the strength of an older vampire. Whoever those vampires were, they'd been outmatched from the moment they'd broken into Belle Morte.

Ysanne tapped one polished nail against her lip, deeper in thought than I'd ever seen her.

"Why do you think these people attacked my house?" she asked.

"I have no idea."

Ysanne paused, as if weighing how much she should tell me. "I do not believe the intruders fled because they were afraid of us. Their retreat was too organized, like it had been planned."

"They weren't trying to take over Belle Morte?"

"I don't know what they were trying to do yet."

"But it's all to do with Etienne, isn't it?"

There was another heavy pause.

"Thirteen of those newly turned vampires died that night. At least three times that many escaped. Who do you think turned them?"

"Etienne," I said at once.

"He fooled us all, I will admit that, but do you really think he could have orchestrated this by himself?"

"You think he had help."

"That is correct," Ysanne said. "The question now is whether or not the person who helped him is still inside Belle Morte."

CHAPTER THREE

Renie

I ce crept through my veins and I actually looked over my shoulder, as if I expected to see Etienne's accomplice slinking through the office door.

"Am I in danger?" I asked. "If Etienne wants me dead, then anyone helping him probably wants the same thing."

"The thought had occurred to me. I'll make sure you're never alone," Ysanne said.

"If you let Edmond go, he can protect me," I pointed out.

It was the wrong thing to say; Ysanne's eyes darkened. "That is not my decision to make," she said. "I've done all I can for Edmond."

"What do you mean?"

"He must be punished for illegally turning you—there's nothing I can do about that, but I was merciful enough to postpone his punishment until he'd helped you through the turn."

I couldn't help saying, "Do you really call that mercy?"

I expected her to react angrily, but when she spoke, she just sounded tired.

"Yes, Renie, I do. It's far more than anyone else would have given him. Do you think I don't understand why you're angry?" She shook her head, not a strand of sleek blond hair moving. "I understand far more than you think. You're the one who struggles to see past the end of your nose."

Part of me still wanted to shout and rage that she was wrong, to overturn her desk and rampage through Belle Morte until I'd found Edmond. But that wouldn't get me anywhere, and I needed to start understanding how the vampire world worked because I was part of it now.

And yet, I wasn't the only one struggling to see past the end of my nose. Ysanne was so focused on the fucking rules that she couldn't see that they sometimes needed to be broken.

I tried to speak calmly. "What do you think would have happened to the balance between humans and vampires if Edmond had obeyed the rules and let me die? There was no way he could have got permission from the Council in time."

Ysanne stared at me.

"June was murdered and turned without you knowing. Now multiple other people are dead, and the person behind it all is missing. If Edmond had refused to help me and had watched me die in the snow? That would have made this whole mess worse. You say that my life isn't worth much in the greater scheme of things—okay, fine. This situation is a colossal clusterfuck, and *you're* the one who hid June in the west wing. You broke the rules yourself, by not killing June when you first found her."

Ysanne's jaw tightened, but she didn't deny it.

"How do you think it would look if, on top of everyone else who's died, Edmond let me die, too, because you wouldn't let him save me? You can't honestly think that would help this balance you're so desperate to preserve."

For a long moment we stared at each other across the desktop.

One thing that Belle Morte had taught me was that while I had a tendency to view the world in black and white, Ysanne did too. She just didn't realize it.

"I can assure you that when the Council arrives, I will be held accountable for my mistakes," said Ysanne.

For most of my time here, I'd hated Ysanne, but now I felt a spark of sympathy. She'd locked June up and brought me to Belle Morte in the hopes that I might be able to restore June's sanity, because if I could do that, there was hope for anyone else who turned rabid in the future. It was rare, but it could happen to any vampire at any time, and Ysanne had been trying to prevent that. I might not agree with her methods, but her intentions were good.

I just wasn't sure the Council would see it that way.

"Let me talk to them," I said impulsively. "I can explain what you were trying to do."

"The gesture is appreciated, but it won't do any good. The rules are the rules."

"When will they arrive?"

"Jemima and what remains of her entourage are still here, staying in the north wing. Henry, Charles, and Caoimhe will be here within the next couple of hours." Ysanne looked me up and down. "You may wish to get dressed before you meet them."

I glanced down, for the first time realizing that I was wearing a pair of black silk pajamas that I didn't remember anyone putting on me. Part of me didn't care what the Council thought. The other part recognized that it was probably quite important to make a good impression on these people.

"What's going to happen to me?" I asked quietly, almost afraid to hear the answer.

"How do you mean?"

"If the Council decides they don't like me, can they hurt me?"

"We do not hurt people simply because we don't like them," said Ysanne, sounding faintly exasperated. "They may not approve of what Edmond has done but they cannot change it. Your life is not in danger from them, if that's what you're worried about."

"But where do I go from here? I can't go back to a normal life, can I?"

"Your future is entirely down to you. I won't force you to stay in Belle Morte."

"Would you let me stay if I wanted to?"

Ysanne scrutinized me. "Do you?"

I hesitated. *Did* I want to?

"Not such an easy decision, is it?" Ysanne said.

"I used to wonder why vampires built perfect little bubbles inside these mansions, but now I think I understand. You've all been through so much, but you don't have to worry about that as long as you're behind these walls. You can live every day in bliss and safety, and who wouldn't want that? But I've only been a vampire for three days, and I've been asleep for most of it. I don't want to be sealed off from the world the way the rest of you are. I don't know where I fit in."

"I should point out the key reason for you to stay, and that's Edmond. He lives here."

"He's in prison," I said, but I managed to say it without anger or judgment.

"That's not permanent. He'll be released in time."

"And then what?"

"That's rather up to you and Edmond, isn't it? You can't expect me to chaperone your romance. If you wish to leave Belle Morte, I won't stop you, and if Edmond wishes to go with you, I won't stop him either. But you need to be prepared for the fact that this is his home, and he might not want to leave," Ysanne said. "In any case, these are hardly decisions that you should be thinking about now. We have larger problems to contend with."

"Right," I said, glancing down at my pajamas again. I couldn't sweat now, so wearing the same thing for three days wasn't as much of a problem as it had been when I was human, but I still wanted a shower and a change of clothes.

"You should go and see your friends too. They've been worried about you," Ysanne added.

There was still so much we needed to talk about, but I got the feeling I was being dismissed. I got up and left the room.

I felt exhausted as I walked away from Ysanne's office. Nothing was as simple as I'd thought. The world wasn't black and white, but ever-shifting shades of gray, and reality was much more tangled and complicated than most people realized—myself included.

I didn't always agree with Ysanne's choices, but I didn't know the experiences that had shaped her, or the pressures involved in running Belle Morte. It wasn't just some hotel where pretty people were paid to let vampires suck from their veins—the rules were there for a reason. So much depended on humans and vampires being able to live alongside each other, and how could I possibly understand how it felt to know that the human world, which adored vampires and treated them as gods, could just as easily turn on them if that world realized there was more to these creatures than designer clothes and immortality?

What punishment would Ysanne face at the hands of the Council? Could they strip her of her leadership? What would happen to Belle Morte then? I had clashed with Ysanne before—and probably would again—but I didn't like the thought of her House being handed over to someone else.

I wished Edmond was here.

Without warning my legs gave out and I crumpled to the floor. My face felt hot and tight, and my eyes ached with the urge to cry, but my new vampire physiology made it so much harder, and I didn't understand why.

I had no idea when I'd see Edmond again.

My life as I knew it was over, and there was no going back.

I had no idea what the future held, for me or anyone else.

And Etienne, that sick fuck, was still out there somewhere. What else was he planning?

Then my stomach twisted into a painful knot, and I groaned, my mind emptying itself of everything but that sudden stab of *need*.

A shadow fell over me as someone crouched beside me and touched my shoulders. For a blinding, stupid moment, I was sure it was Edmond. I'd look up into his beautiful face and everything would be okay again—

"He really did turn you," said Jemima, and I blinked, bringing her face into focus.

The Lady of Nox stared back at me, her eyes soft and sympathetic, making her look even more like a teenager than ever.

"Surprise," I muttered. Jemima had only ever been nice to me, but I was too tired to be polite, and the knot in my stomach was getting worse.

I thought she might help me to my feet, but instead she sat down opposite me, arranging her flowing silk skirt around her knees.

"I can't tell you how sorry I am about June," Jemima said.

"Thanks. Sorry that some of your people got killed."

Jemima looked at the carpeted floor. "So am I."

"Has Ysanne told you what happened?"

"Not in detail. I believe she's saving that for the Council meeting, but I'm aware that Etienne is the one responsible for all this suffering." Jemima's lip twisted. "I'd never have thought him capable of something like this."

"You and me both." Hatred welled up inside me, hot and thick, and I clenched my hands until my nails dug into my palms.

Jemima caught my hands, her touch gentle. "He won't get away with this."

"I thought he was my friend, but he *murdered* my sister and turned her into a monster. I hate him so much."

"You're not the only one," Jemima said. "We will find him, Renie, and we'll make him pay for the lives he's taken and the suffering he's caused."

My stomach clenched again, waves of hunger pulsing through my body, and the ache in my mouth told me my fangs were emerging, pushing through my gums.

"When was the last time you fed?" Jemima asked, eyeing me with concern.

"I don't think I can," I said, clutching my stomach. The thought of sinking my fangs into another person made me feel sick.

"I know this is hard for you—remember, I've lived it—but you can't starve yourself. I'll send for a donor."

If I'd felt sick at the thought of biting someone; it was ten times worse thinking about biting someone I knew. Fortunately, Jemima wasn't insensitive enough to send for one of my friends.

She fetched Mei, whose eyes were bright with excitement. Was there some kind of prestige in being the first official donor for the first new vampire in many years? Except I wasn't the only new vampire anymore, was I? I had to remember that. There were many more out there, somewhere.

Jemima guided Mei into a kneeling position, then put her hand on Mei's chin and gently tilted her head to one side, exposing her throat. "Your fangs are sharp enough to slide cleanly through the skin, so don't bite down too hard," she instructed. "Just let your fangs do the work."

I inched closer, hypnotized by the shape of the veins beneath Mei's skin. I could hear the rapid beat of her heart, excitement kicking it into overdrive, and smell the sweet tang of her blood. My mouth watered.

"Good girl," Jemima encouraged.

I was grateful for her help, but I wished that it was Edmond here, helping me through my first proper bite.

As I leaned in, my mouth almost touching Mei's skin, a tiny shiver rolled through her. She was looking forward to this, whereas I was terrified. What if I bit her too hard? What if I tore a vein or an artery and she bled to death? My saliva had healing properties now, but that only worked on small cuts.

I would never be human again, but crossing this line would truly mark me as a vampire, and the enormity of that felt like it would crush me.

Mei swallowed, and my eyes tracked the movement of her throat. Her skin smelled faintly of lemons, although not enough to mask the delicious scent of blood pulsating from her veins.

I was so hungry that dark spots danced in front of my eyes, but I couldn't do this, and I pulled back so hard I fell backward.

"I'm sorry," I gasped. "I can't."

Jemima slid an arm around my shoulders and helped me sit up. My fangs were fully out and my gums ached with the pressure. My stomach had compacted into a tight, painful ball, and waves of hunger rolled through me, fierce and powerful.

"This isn't a choice. Blood is the only thing you can survive on now," Jemima told me.

I knew that, but this step was so huge—it was too much. It felt like everything that had made me Renie Mayfield had started unraveling the moment I'd set foot inside Belle Morte, and when I took this step, I'd lose the last shred of my humanity.

I shrugged away Jemima's arm and scrambled to my feet. "I need some space," I said.

Jemima didn't try to stop me.

CHAPTER FOUR

Renie

As I walked away from Jemima and Mei, all I could think was that I'd never eat food again. Blood was my diet now.

I thought of Isabeau carrying the blanket-wrapped corpses of small animals up to the west wing to feed June, and the desiccated remains of those animals buried among the roots of the oak tree outside. I thought of Edmond's confession that when he'd sunk into a state of selfishness and hedonism in the years leading up to the French Revolution, he'd killed two people. I thought of Ludovic murdering a wounded soldier in the ravaged trenches of the First World War so that Edmond could drink his blood and heal his own injuries. I thought of what the need for blood had turned June into.

Then I thought of the fact that I could never go out for dinner again, or stuff myself with chocolate at Christmas and Easter, or order a double-pepperoni pizza when I was having a lazy day. I'd never again cook my favorite dishes, or treat myself to ice cream on a hot day, or enjoy a steaming bowl of soup on a cold one.

I stopped, suddenly disgusted with myself. People had *died*, and I was moping over the fact that I could never eat brownies again? Where the fuck were my priorities?

This was no time for self-pity.

The Council would be here in the next couple of hours, and I needed to be ready for them. In the meantime, I was taking Ysanne's advice and going to see my friends.

As I headed up the main staircase, I couldn't help noticing how different Belle Morte felt. The blood and bodies had been cleared away but the scars of that terrible night were sunk deep into the fabric of this house. It felt quieter—more subdued but also tense, as if Belle Morte itself knew that Etienne hadn't finished whatever he was planning. I was used to seeing donors coming and going from all rooms, but by the time I reached the south wing, where the donors slept, the only person I had encountered was Amit, a boy I'd got to know a little bit before I'd become entangled in the June situation. I smiled at him, glad to see a familiar face, but Amit stared back at me with an expression caught between shock and awe. Like Tamara and Mei had.

Vladdicts and other vampire fans wanted to become the object of a vampire's desire. They wanted sharp fangs and superhuman strength and the ability to live forever. They wanted to be graceful and elegant and mysterious, adored by people the world over—that's why there was such a high donor turnover among the Houses; there were always so many people clamoring for a taste of the vampire lifestyle.

Thousands—*millions*—of people had this dream. Fan fiction sites were clogged with stories about young donors going into Vampire Houses, eventually winning the hearts of the vampires and becoming one of the undead themselves. But it had never actually happened.

Until now.

Amit and the other donors would see me as the girl who'd made that dream come true—even though the reality was pretty far from the fantasy. Edmond hadn't turned me because of some starry-eyed, romantic impulse. He'd done it because I was bleeding to death in his arms. Our love story had hardly been straightforward, and thanks to my last words to him, we still had some things to work through—as soon as he was released from prison. Whenever that would be.

I wanted to talk to Amit, to remind him that I was still *me*, but the words stuck in my throat. We passed each other without saying a single word.

When I'd first arrived at Belle Morte I felt like I hadn't quite fit in because I was the donor who wasn't completely enamored of vampires, and now I didn't fit in again, but in a very different way. I was torn between two worlds, but I didn't feel like I fully belonged to either.

I'd intended to go straight to the bedroom that I had shared with Roux, but I paused at Melissa's door. My newly sharpened vampire hearing picked up the faint sound of crying coming from inside, and my heart gave a sad little squeeze. I couldn't walk past and pretend that nothing was wrong. I knocked on the door.

"Go away," Melissa said, her voice thick with tears.

"It's Renie," I said.

There was a long pause.

Then the door opened.

The first time I'd seen Melissa I'd thought she was so beautiful she could almost have been a vampire herself, and she still was, but at the same time she was somehow faded, as if the light inside her had been snuffed out. Her eyes were swollen with tears, and there was a hard set to her jaw that I'd never seen before.

"What do you want?" she said.

"I . . . I'm really sorry about Aiden."

Anger sparked in her eyes. "You're *sorry*? You think that changes anything?"

"None of this was meant to happen—"

"But it did. My boyfriend died because you wouldn't tell me the truth about what was going on."

"I couldn't . . ." My words trailed off.

I'd come to Belle Morte because all communication from my sister had abruptly stopped and I'd worried that something was wrong. But when I'd arrived, everyone seemed to believe that June had been transferred to another House, even though that had never before happened. Even Melissa, who'd been June's friend, had refused to accept that Ysanne would lie to her House. But the harder I'd pushed and the closer I'd come to the truth, the more Melissa had started to realize that something was wrong. But when I'd finally found June, chained and rabid in the west wing, it was a secret I'd had to keep from Melissa. On the night that Belle Morte had been attacked, Aiden had had enough of seeing Melissa being so upset by me keeping the truth from her, and he'd gone to the west wing to find out what was really going on. June had killed him.

Aiden's death hadn't been my fault, but it wasn't exactly a surprise that Melissa blamed me. If I'd told her the truth, Aiden would never have gone to the west wing. And it didn't matter that I *couldn't* have told her. When I'd realized that Edmond was keeping the truth from me, I'd done the same as Aiden—I'd run to the west wing. I'd nearly died at June's hands as a result. Edmond had saved me. No one had been there to save Aiden.

"I really am sorry," I said, because what else could I say?

"Sorry doesn't bring Aiden back, does it?"

"No."

I didn't say that, one way or another, Etienne would pay for this, because that wouldn't bring Aiden back either.

"Why did Etienne do this?" Melissa said.

"How did you know he did?" I'd assumed that Ysanne would have kept the truth of that night under wraps, just as she'd hidden June from everyone.

"Amit had come out of the south wing to see what the hell was going on, and he overheard Míriam telling Ysanne. Ysanne would have never told us otherwise, would she?"

"Probably not," I admitted.

"She's clamped down on us now." Melissa's voice soured. "Security shifts are going ahead as usual, but if any of them breathe a word of this, they'll be fired on the spot. We're not allowed to write home. No one knows how long this will last."

"Neither do I, before you ask."

"Right, and I suppose you don't know why Etienne did this either."

"I really don't."

Melissa's face hardened. "I've heard that before."

"I *don't*. I have no idea why he tried to kill me, or why he turned June, or what the hell happened the night of the attack."

But I could tell she didn't believe me, and I couldn't really blame her. I'd kept too much from her in the past.

Melissa sighed and slumped against the doorframe, the anger draining out of her. "Just go away, Renie."

She shut the door in my face.

I walked to the room I'd shared with Roux, then paused again, suddenly awkward. When I was human, I would've just walked in, but this wasn't my room anymore. I didn't belong here.

Hesitantly, I knocked.

"Craig, I swear if you're sniffing for information again, I'm going to kick you in the nuts," Roux yelled from inside the room.

Craig? I turned the handle and poked my head around the door.

Roux and Jason were sitting on Roux's bed, their heads bent close together, and Roux looked up as I came in, anger flashing across her face. The color drained from her cheeks when she saw it was me.

"Oh my god," she whispered, uncoiling her long limbs. "Renie!"

Jason scrambled off the bed and across the room, throwing his arms around me and hugging me so hard that if I'd been human, it would have hurt. I buried my face against his chest. My eyes ached with the need to cry, but the tears wouldn't come. Maybe they never would again.

Jason let me go and stood to one side so Roux could hug me. But she didn't. She stood halfway between me and the bed, her hands twisting together, her expression strangely distant, as if she'd put up some sort of barrier between us.

"You're okay," she said.

"It's a huge adjustment, but I'm getting there," I said. I didn't mention my disastrous first attempt at feeding.

Roux still didn't make any move toward me. "How's the north wing?" she asked, and there was a hint of bitterness in her voice.

"I don't know. I haven't exactly had time to explore it."

"So what have you been doing all this time?" Her expression was hard and her tone sounded like she was accusing me of something.

A twinge of hurt wriggled through me. Even though I hadn't known her that long, she'd proved to be the best friend I ever had, and I didn't understand why she was being hostile now.

"Recovering," I said. "Turning into a vampire isn't easy. I'm still coming to terms with it, and to be honest, the last thing I need is you acting like this."

Roux's eyes shimmered and she pressed her lips together. She stalked into the bathroom and shut the door behind her.

Bewildered, I looked at Jason, who shook his head.

"Don't take it to heart," he said. "She's been freaking out since—" He broke off, looking awkward.

"Since I died," I finished. No point being coy about it.

"Yeah. None of the vampires are talking about what happened that night, but you and Roux were right in the middle of it, and the other donors think she knows more than she's saying. They've been hassling her for days."

"Is that why she thought I was Craig?"

"He's been one of the most persistent. Last night he wouldn't leave our room until Roux threw a shoe at his head." Jason pointed at a glittery stiletto lying near the door.

That was the Roux I knew—fiercely loyal, not the cold girl who'd stood in front of me a moment ago.

"Why is she mad at me?" I asked.

"She isn't, not really. She's been so frightened and sad these last few days, and"—Jason glanced at the bathroom door and lowered his voice—"I think she's scared that now you're a vampire you won't want to hang around with us anymore. All we knew was that you'd moved into the north wing with the rest of the vampires, and Roux thought maybe you'd ditched us."

"It wasn't my decision—Edmond took me there. I didn't even know I was in the north wing until I woke up."

"And if she was thinking clearly she'd understand that. But she saw some fucked-up stuff during that attack, she killed a vampire, she watched you die, she's been having nightmares for days, and everyone keeps pestering her for information she doesn't have."

I closed my eyes as more memories of that night flooded back: Roux had followed me to the ballroom and saved my life by beating in a vampire's head with a curtain rod torn down from this room. It hadn't been replaced yet, nor had the lock on the door, which I'd smashed with a bronze statue. I hadn't thought about how killing someone would have affected Roux, or how she must have felt when she'd rushed out to the grounds and realized she was too late to save me. The hurt inside me shifted to a different kind—hurt *for* my friend.

"Have you been with her the whole time?" I asked, noticing the small heap of Jason's clothes next to Roux's bed.

"I couldn't leave her on her own."

"You think I should talk to her?"

"I'd give her some time. This is a big adjustment for her to deal with."

"I'm the one who became a vampire," I reminded him.

He gave me a sad little smile. "Exactly."

"I don't understand."

"Roux told me how you guys planned to stay in touch once your contracts were up. Whoever got out first would wait for the other on the outside."

I still didn't get it.

"Renie, you won't be *getting* out. You're a vampire now, which means Belle Morte or one of the other Houses will be your home. When Roux's contract ends she'll leave, but you won't, and since ex-donors aren't allowed back in, Roux won't see you again."

That hit me like a slap. Vampires stayed in their mansions because it was safe for them there, but that safety meant I could lose both Roux and Jason.

"Are you okay? You're making weird faces," Jason said.

"I'm trying to cry!"

His lips twitched, and he hugged me again. "For the record, I think it's pretty cool that you're a vampire now."

I couldn't help laughing a little against his chest. He felt warm and safe and solid, grounding me when everything felt like it was spinning out of control.

"This might sound strange, but can I see your fangs?" Jason asked.

Tilting my head back, I opened my mouth. Jason's heartbeat quickened, and my fangs responded, sliding farther out of my gums. His eyes widened.

"Wow . . . that's actually really hot."

"Seriously?"

Jason's smile was distinctly mischievous. "I think vampires are the sexiest things on the planet—sue me. If you were a guy, I'd be pretty turned on by now."

I'd managed to ignore the hunger pangs, but with my fangs fully elongated, those pangs reared up with a vengeance, and I stifled a groan. How much longer could I keep this up?

"You need to feed, don't you?" Jason said.

"I can't bite someone."

"Have you tried?"

"Yeah. It was too weird."

Jason studied me, his face grave. "Why don't you drink from me?"

He tugged aside the neck of his T-shirt, baring his throat, and my eyes zeroed in on his smooth, slightly tanned skin, the pulse throbbing just beneath the surface, the juicy veins.

My mouth and stomach throbbed in tandem. I was so *hungry*.

But I backed away, edging closer to the bed that had been mine. I couldn't do this; I couldn't *bite* Jason. He didn't come after me, just watched with sad eyes.

"You have to drink. Even old vampires can't go forever without feeding, and you've only been a vampire for three days," he said.

"Do you know what they've done to Edmond? He's been thrown in prison. He should be here with me but they've locked him up."

"Okay, that's really fucking horrible, and I can't imagine what you're going through, but, honey, you can't starve yourself." Jason's voice took on a firmer note.

"I can't bite you," I said softly.

I wanted to, so very badly, but this was *Jason*. He wasn't dinner; he was my friend. Frustration surged, flooding through my arms and into my hands. Before I knew what I was doing, I whirled around and punched the bedpost.

"Whoa," Jason said, taking a step back.

I'd taken a fist-sized chunk out of the post. Large splinters protruded from between my knuckles; I pulled them out, and when tiny beads of blood bubbled up, I licked the back of my hand, sealing the punctures.

"I shouldn't even be around you until I can control this," I whispered.

I turned to leave, but Jason caught my arm. The sound of his heart-beat drummed in my ears, and the smell of his blood was driving me crazy. I shoved him against the wall, pinning him in place without needing to try.

It was no wonder some vampires thought they were above humans. We were so much weaker than them, so much more easily broken. And it was no wonder they had to try so hard not to break us.

A laugh rose in my throat and I choked it down. I was holding Jason against the wall with one hand. The smell of his blood filled my nostrils and my fangs were pushing out of my gums—and I'd *still* just thought of myself as human.

Jason's chest rose and fell with each breath, but he didn't seem afraid. My eyes latched on to his pulse, and I imagined sucking it like a piece of candy.

"It's okay," Jason said, as if he could read my thoughts.

"I can't," I whispered. "I don't know if I'll be able to stop."

I didn't know my own strength anymore; I could drain Jason dry and he wouldn't be able to stop me. That terrified me, and it should have terrified him too.

"I trust you, Renie."

"I don't trust myself," I whispered.

I couldn't—not now that I'd seen what I was capable of. I needed to get out of here and away from my friends before I did something I'd never be able to forgive myself for.

I left the south wing and made my way downstairs, heading for the exit that led out onto the grounds. The last time I'd come this way I'd been chasing June, armed with a bloody knife that I'd stolen from a dead security guard.

The last time I'd come this way, I'd still been human.

Now, for reasons I couldn't quite explain, I needed to see the place where I'd died.

Dexter Flynn, head of Belle Morte security, stood guard at the door, his hands clasped behind his back. I waited for him to tell me I needed an escort to be allowed out, then remembered I wasn't a donor anymore. I didn't need an escort. I should've been pleased, but all I could see was another way my life had changed.

"I'm sorry for the people you lost," I said.

It felt hopelessly inadequate, but I couldn't pretend it hadn't happened.

Dexter nodded. "I appreciate that. I'm sorry about your sister."

"Thanks."

"I'm sorry for you too."

Startled, I looked up. Tall and burly, his head shaved bald, Dexter was pretty intimidating physically, but there was empathy in his eyes that I hadn't expected.

"I'm luckier than everyone else who died in that attack. I got to come back," I muttered.

Dexter put a large hand on my shoulder and gently squeezed. "Vampire or not, you're still you. Don't forget that." He pushed open the door.

In the three days that I'd been asleep, the snow had mostly melted, leaving icy patches here and there, and a fading slice of moon overhead turned the frosty grass to glitter. I couldn't pinpoint the exact spot where I'd died—everything had looked different in the snow.

I gazed around the gardens, suddenly realizing I was completely alone. During my early days at Belle Morte, I'd headed here a couple of times to get away from everyone and everything, but I'd always been escorted by either security or a vampire. I'd never really had the space I needed. Now I did, and I'd only had to die to get it.

A bitter little laugh escaped my lips.

How the hell was I going to tell Mum? Oh my god, she didn't even know June was dead. When I'd found out that June was rabid, I hadn't told Mum, both because it had felt like admitting that I couldn't help my poor sister and because I honestly hadn't known how to tell her. Now I not only had to find a way but I had to admit that I'd got myself killed in the process. Although the current ban on writing home probably applied to me too. Ysanne and the Council wouldn't risk anyone leaking anything until we'd got to the bottom of this mess.

Suddenly overwhelmed with everything, I sank down under the huge oak tree that I'd once thought marked June's grave. The winter-stripped branches creaked above me, stark silhouettes against a predawn sky.

It must have been bitterly cold out here, but I couldn't feel it anymore. Leaning my head against the solid tree trunk, I closed my eyes.

Someone was shaking me awake.

I blinked and stirred. A tingling, itching feeling spread across my skin, as if millions of ants were marching all over me, and red patches appeared on my arms, spreading over my hands. The itching became a prickling burn.

Dexter stood over me. He unzipped his black jacket and threw it over my head and shoulders, shielding me.

Suddenly, I realized what was happening.

I'd fallen asleep.

The sun had risen.

Older vampires like Edmond and Ysanne could withstand sunlight for a few hours at a time. Young vampires like me could not.

Dexter pulled me to my feet, throwing his arm around my shoulders and hugging me to his chest in an attempt to cover as much of my body as possible. "Come on, let's get you inside before you ignite," he said, affecting a cheery tone.

My eyes drifted to his neck and the juicy veins just beneath the surface of his skin. The thrum of his pulse, the delicious tang of his blood—suddenly it was all too much.

The next thing I knew, Dexter was on the ground and I was straddling him, an animal growl trickling out of my throat.

CHAPTER FIVE

Renie

R enie, stop!" Dexter tried to push me back. The human me
wouldn't have stood a chance against him. The vampire me easily overpowered him.

I lowered my mouth to his throat, my fangs fully extended and
straining for a taste. His heartbeat thumped in my ears, quickened
by fear, and that was enough to make me pull back, struggling to
control myself.

When I'd walked into these gardens, Dexter had told me not to
forget who I was, and I desperately didn't want to, but the hunger
roared through me like wildfire. Even as my brain screamed at me
to stop, I couldn't keep myself from bending back over his neck,
couldn't retract my sharp, hungry fangs . . .

Someone wrenched me away.

Hunger turned to anger, and I lashed out, but an impossibly strong
hand caught my wrist. Ludovic stared down at me, a strand of blond
hair escaping his ponytail. The sun hadn't affected him yet; his face
was as smooth and pale as ever. But I'd lost Dexter's jacket during my
attack, and my skin was starting to scorch.

Ludovic dragged me through the grounds faster than Dexter
could have done and shoved me through the door, back into the
house. I stumbled and hit the carpet on my knees, shaking all over
with hunger and horror.

I'd nearly *bitten Dexter*.

Worse, I'd attacked him like a wild animal.

I doubled over, clutching my stomach.

"Jemima told me you were refusing blood, but it's not a choice. You need a donor," Ludovic snapped.

"I'll do it." The voice was so soft, so unlike its usual confident self that I almost didn't recognize it. I lifted my head to see Roux standing at the end of the hallway, her face pale but resolute.

"No," I gasped.

"You don't have a choice," Roux said, moving closer.

"She's right," Ludovic said.

A tearless sob caught in my throat. "I don't want to hurt her."

Ludovic crouched over me, coaxing me to my feet. "I won't let you."

Gently but firmly, he held both my arms behind my back. Strong as I was now, Ludovic was stronger; I couldn't break free.

Roux was standing in front of me now; I could smell her blood and hear her heartbeat, and I hated it. I hadn't bitten Jason and I couldn't bite Roux.

Only, I really *didn't* have a choice. I'd tried to hold back, and all that had happened was that I'd attacked poor Dexter.

Roux lifted her wrist to my mouth and I couldn't hold back any longer. I bit down. My fangs sliced neatly through her skin and blood rushed into my mouth. It was warm and delicious, sparking strength and energy in my limbs. My knees buckled in sheer relief.

Ludovic murmured to me the whole time, the way I imagined Edmond would've done if he'd been here, but I could barely hear his voice. All I could focus on was the sweet blood filling my mouth, sliding down my throat.

As my knees buckled farther, Ludovic guided me to the floor. Roux knelt with us, her wrist still locked in my teeth.

For a brief span of time I was lost in a sea of glorious red. Lights sparkled behind my eyes and blood tingled in my throat with each swallow. I could have stayed here forever, endlessly drinking, but Roux made a soft noise and suddenly I was catapulted back into reality. My immediate reaction was to jerk back, but I stopped myself just in time; I didn't want to slice open Roux's arm. I opened my mouth wider, sliding my fangs out of her veins. Beads of blood appeared, as bright as the ruby stud in Roux's nose.

Holding both my wrists with one hand, Ludovic pulled Roux's arm toward him and briskly ran his tongue over the puncture marks, closing them.

I'd been afraid that feeding properly for the first time would drive me into a rabid-like frenzy, but I felt better than I had since waking up as a vampire. The world around me seemed sharper, brighter, as if a veil had been lifted. I could still hear the thud of Roux's heart but it no longer filled me with the urge to bite. For now, I was sated.

"Thank you," I whispered. The red, raw patches on my skin were already fading.

"You've already seen me naked, so what's a little blood sharing between friends?" Roux joked, but when she climbed to her feet, she swayed.

"Roux?"

She waved away my concern. "I'm fine, I'm fine."

"I've taken too much, haven't I?" And both she and Ludovic had let me. I shot him a glare.

Ludovic stared back, unrepentant. "It was necessary."

Someone cleared their throat and I looked up to see Jason standing a couple of feet away. How long had he been there? I was terrified there'd be judgment in his eyes, but he didn't look at me any differently.

Ludovic clicked his fingers in Jason's direction. "Take care of her."

Jason hurried forward and slipped an arm around Roux's waist, supporting her. She swatted his shoulder.

"I can walk."

"Hush, woman, and let me be chivalrous," he said.

I waited until Jason had guided Roux away, before turning to Ludovic. "How could you let me get carried away like that?"

"I didn't. I know exactly how much blood a donor can give, and Roux was never in danger." Ludovic's face softened. "You need to trust me. I wouldn't have put her or anyone else at risk."

I raked my fingers through my hair, and my nails snagged on knots. How long did I have before the Council got here?

"You must hate me," I said.

"Why would I hate you?"

"Edmond's your best friend, and he's been locked up for helping me."

"Do you remember what I told Edmond that night?" Ludovic said.

I frowned, casting my mind back. Lying in the snow, I'd slid in and out of consciousness, the threads of my life slithering between my fingers.

"I'm the one who told Edmond to turn you," Ludovic said.

I blinked stupidly at the vampire before me. I definitely didn't remember that part. "You?"

"Yes, me."

"Why?"

"It was the only way to save you. I've known Edmond a long time and I've never seen him look at a woman the way he looks at you. I know how much he's lost in the past, and I couldn't stand for him to lose you too."

Ludovic's frank honesty caught me by surprise. I wondered if he was being so candid with me because I was a vampire now and therefore on his level, or if he simply respected me enough not to lie to me. Maybe it was a bit of both.

"However long the Council bastards want to keep Edmond locked up, he can take it." Ludovic looked steadily at me. "As long as he knows that you'll be waiting for him when he gets out."

"I'll wait for him forever if that's what it takes," I said.

Ludovic smiled then, and it transformed his face, making me notice for the first time how young he must have been when he'd died—probably about Edmond's age, just a few years older than me. It was strange to think that the creatures the world was so obsessed with were so young in so many ways.

"Good," he said. "Now, you don't have long until the Council arrives, so if you wish to get dressed, I suggest you do it now."

The Council was gathered in the dining hall, around one end of the long trestle table we used for meals. It was strange to be in this room and not be eating—to be staring at the dour expressions of unfamiliar vampires and not the friendly faces of the other donors who usually sat around me.

Jemima, sitting opposite, smiled warmly at me, but I was too nervous to smile back.

Sitting next to her was Charles Abbott, Lord of Lamia, a sturdy, square man with a head of thick curls and a nose that listed slightly to the side, making me think it had been broken when he was still human. The edges of his mouth turned down when I walked into the room.

Ysanne sat at the head of the table, and to her right sat Caoimhe Ó Duinnín, the Lady of Fiaigh, the only Irish Vampire House. I wasn't wild about seeing her here if only because she and Edmond had once been a couple, and while I wasn't normally a jealous person, Caoimhe's tumbling blond curls and cornflower blue eyes made her look like an angel. I was pretty enough to turn heads occasionally, but I felt totally inadequate compared to the Irish vampire.

The last member of the Council was Henry Baldwin, Lord of Midnight, who was handsome in an unassuming sort of way, except for his intense green eyes, which felt like lasers locked onto my face.

Ludovic and Isabeau also sat at the table, even though they weren't part of the Council. Maybe Ysanne needed the support of her friends today. It was strange to think of Ysanne needing help with anything.

Rising to his feet, Charles indicated a chair with his hand. It was farther down the table from the vampires, and probably a sign of my inferior status, but I took it without saying anything.

"So," Charles said, taking his own seat again. "We have rather a lot to discuss, don't we?"

I suddenly felt the weight of all those pairs of eyes, and I shrank back, a mouse being eyed by a bunch of hungry cats. Then I remembered I was one of them now, and I didn't have to cower. I straightened, trying to mimic Ysanne's proud posture.

"Ysanne has already told us her version of events. Perhaps you'd like to share yours," Charles said.

"Start from the beginning," Jemima encouraged, giving me another little smile.

I told them how Ysanne had found June, recently turned and rabid, in the hallways of Belle Morte, but that she thought she'd glimpsed some humanity left in my sister. I told them of her plan, to see if there was any way of reversing whatever it was that turned a vampire rabid, and that she'd brought me here to help. Charles made a noise of disgust at that. I explained how Ysanne had continued to investigate June's murder while I worked with June in the west wing, but that ultimately we'd failed. June had escaped on the same night that a horde of newly turned vampires had invaded Belle Morte, and that just before June stabbed me in the garden, Etienne had admitted to me that he was responsible for turning her.

"That's the part I don't understand," Henry said. His voice had a distinct Cockney twang, and somehow it startled me. I'd grown used to the lilting cadences of the French vampires and the cultured vowels of the English ones. Henry sounded more real than most of them.

"What?" I said.

"The rabid stabbed you? Are you sure?"

I touched my chest. There was no mark left, but I'd never forget the spot where the blade had been driven in. "Yeah, I'm sure."

The Council exchanged looks, and even Ysanne seemed pensive. I glanced at Ludovic; he was staring at the table, his forehead furrowed.

"What's wrong?" I said, turning back to the Council.

"Having seen a rabid in action, you don't need us to remind you how dangerous and out of control they are," Henry said. "That's why our rules have always been to kill them on sight. But rabids don't use weapons. The bloodlust reduces them to little more than mindless animals, and they use their fangs to kill."

Aiden's ruined throat flashed through my mind, and I swallowed. I knew exactly how much damage those fangs could do.

"But June did use a knife," I said.

"She couldn't have done," said Charles.

"But she did." I was getting annoyed now.

His expression was pure skepticism; clearly he didn't believe me. "You're also claiming that the rabid didn't attempt to drink from you? Even though rabids are entirely driven by their hunger and will feed from humans, animals, and other vampires?" he said.

"Why would I lie about this?" I said.

Charles smirked a little. "We know that you and Edmond Dantès were conducting a secret, illegal affair." He shot Ysanne a hard look. "You shouldn't have been able to get away with it right under the nose of the Lady of Belle Morte, but it seems she had too many other problems to worry about."

Ysanne's face was a marble mask, giving away nothing.

"How do we know that you and Edmond didn't take advantage of the rabid's escape and use that as an excuse for him turning you? Your alleged injury would have healed during the turn, so what evidence is there that you were stabbed at all?" Charles continued.

"Is eyewitness testimony good enough?" Ludovic spoke up. "I was in the garden with Edmond and Renie, and I can verify her story. She'd been stabbed in the chest and she was bleeding to death when Edmond made the decision to save her by turning her."

Charles's smirk didn't waver. "Ludovic de Vauban, you served alongside Dantès during the Great War. You lived together afterward, and you came to Belle Morte together. Clearly you are not a neutral party in this."

"That doesn't make me a liar."

"It makes you a man who could lie for the sake of someone very important to him."

"Roux Hayes was there too," I said. "She'll tell you—"

"Your roommate, the girl you persuaded to help you break the rules of this House, and who risked her life to save you during that attack? She's hardly a neutral party either."

"Then what about Míriam?" I'd vaguely heard the other vampire's voice when I'd been dying in the snow; she'd been out there too.

"Míriam Diaz y Centeno? One of Dantès's former lovers?" Charles gave me a pitying look.

I ground my teeth together in frustration. "What about the knife? Someone must have found it."

"According to Ysanne, no weapon was found," Charles said.

I looked at Ysanne; still her face gave away nothing.

"June or Etienne must have taken it with them when they fled," I said.

"Or it never existed," Charles said.

I wanted to punch him. I really, *really* wanted to punch him.

"I love my sister. I'd have done anything to save her, and I would *never* take advantage of what happened to her, in any way," I said, my voice trembling with barely restrained rage.

"Unfortunately, we only have your word for that."

I started to snap back, but a sharp look from Ysanne made me fall silent. The last thing any of us needed was for me to make things worse.

"Why did you put June in the west wing and not the cells?" Caoimhe asked Ysanne. Her Irish lilt was soft and warm.

Cells? My ears pricked up. Was that where Edmond was?

"I hoped that, if there was any chance of her regaining her mind, then putting her in a room that resembled the one she'd had as a donor might help," Ysanne replied.

"Clearly you were wrong," Charles said.

"It would seem so."

"How closely did the timing of the attack coincide with June's escape?" Caoimhe asked me.

"I don't know, but it must have been pretty close. When I fell down the stairs after June chased me, I only blacked out long enough for her to kill Aiden. When I came to and fled, I ran into Ludovic, and he told me the house was under attack," I said.

Ludovic nodded, and I resisted the urge to ask Charles if Ludovic's testimony counted in this case.

"By the newly turned vampires that no one has ever seen before," Charles said.

"As you're aware, they weren't all newly turned. Eric Wilson was among them," Ysanne said, her frosty gaze sliding to Henry.

I assumed that Eric Wilson was the vampire from Midnight who'd died in the attack.

"I'm really not sure what to say about this," Henry admitted.

"Can you explain why one of your vampires was here?"

"Honestly? No. The first I knew of it was when you contacted me to inform me that he was dead."

"Surely you noticed that he'd left Midnight," Charles said.

"As you're well aware, Eric has recently begun a relationship with William Harris, one of your vampires. On the night of the Belle Morte attack, Eric informed me that he was visiting William at

Lamia. It wasn't the first time he'd done so, and I had no reason to question him."

"But William didn't come with him to Belle Morte?" Jemima checked.

Charles shook his head. "Eric didn't come to Lamia that night. Whatever Eric was doing here, William wasn't part of it."

I couldn't help saying, "You can't know that for sure."

"*I* keep track of what my vampires are doing," said Charles smugly.

I wondered if Ysanne wanted to punch him as much as I did.

"Are we to assume that Eric was helping Etienne?" Isabeau asked.

"Can you think of another reason he would be here?" Charles said.

"Not yet, but I'm wary about leaping to conclusions when we have very little evidence," Isabeau replied.

"Why would Etienne turn June?" Caoimhe asked. "He couldn't have known she would turn rabid, so what was he planning?"

I hadn't even thought about that yet.

"We also haven't addressed the fact that Ysanne committed a serious offense by not killing June as soon as she found her," said Charles.

"Don't you think we should be focusing more on the person who killed and turned June in the first place?" said Isabeau.

"If Ysanne had killed the rabid immediately, then it wouldn't have escaped, and no one else would have died," Charles said.

Ysanne's face was like stone. She really had been trying to help her people, but Charles had a point, much as I hated to admit it. How much of that blame did Ysanne put on herself?

"Ysanne knows the rules, and I believe she'll accept her punishment for her role in this. However, might I suggest a temporary reprieve?" Henry said. "The rabid is out there somewhere, along with Etienne and the new vampires who escaped Belle Morte, and if we want to get to the bottom of this, we have to work together."

Jemima and Caoimhe nodded in agreement.

I closed my eyes in relief. I couldn't imagine that Ysanne and I would ever really get along, but I'd been thrown into the deep end of the vampire world, and I didn't want to navigate that alone. Ysanne didn't like me, but I was one of her vampires now, and I believed she'd honor that by protecting me the same way she would anyone else in her House.

Charles drummed his fingers on the table, bringing everyone's attention to him. "There's something else we need to discuss," he said. "We've heard Renie's and Ysanne's version of events, but they're not the only ones involved in this, are they?"

"You're welcome to question Edmond, too, assuming you won't reject anything he says the way you have with Ludovic," said Ysanne.

"I'm not talking about him." Charles looked past us, to the entry-way at the end of the room. "You can come in now."

Etienne walked into the dining hall.

CHAPTER SIX

Renie

I'd imagined seeing Etienne again, imagined turning my new strength on him, but now that he was here, I felt frozen to my chair. It was like I was back out in the gardens the night I'd died, like the cold had settled in my bones and turned my blood to ice.

How could he be here?

Ludovic shifted in his seat, and I wasn't sure if he was getting ready to grab me if I went for Etienne. I wanted to claw out Etienne's eyes, but I couldn't *move*.

At the head of the table, Ysanne had gone very still, her eyes dark with anger, her lips pressed into a thin line.

"What is the meaning of this?" she said.

Charles got to his feet and beckoned Etienne over. Etienne edged closer to the table, looking like a wild animal about to bolt.

I gripped the edge of the table until my fingers hurt, and even though my heart didn't beat now, I swore I heard it pounding in my ears.

"What's going on?" Caoimhe asked.

"So far we've heard one side of the story, but Etienne approached me after escaping Belle Morte, and he has a very different version of events that I think we need to hear."

"*Escaping?*" I burst out. "He didn't *escape*. He ran away when he realized his attack on Belle Morte wasn't working."

Etienne looked at me with sad eyes. "That's not what happened, and you know it."

"What I know is that you *killed my sister*," I spat. The ice was melting inside me, turning to fire.

"No, I didn't."

"What's going on?" Jemima asked, looking from Etienne to Charles.

I looked desperately at Ysanne, sure that she was about to surge out of her seat and show Etienne what happened to people who betrayed her, but she seemed as frozen as I was.

"Give him a chance to explain," Charles said.

"Explain *what*?" I leaped to my feet, electric with furious energy.

Isabeau and Ludovic moved at the same time, flowing out of their seats with immortal grace and flanking me. Isabeau held my wrist, and Ludovic put one hand on my shoulder.

"Don't do anything rash," he warned in a low voice.

My whole body was shaking but I let the two vampires guide me back into my seat. They sat down on either side of me.

"I did not kill June Mayfield," Etienne said.

"You *told* me you did," I shouted.

Etienne shook his head. His eyes were sorrowful, his red hair slightly disheveled, as if he'd run his fingers through it. "Renie, I don't understand why you're lying about this. I would never hurt June. I'm the one who was trying to help you find out what happened to her, remember?" He looked around at the Council. "Roux Hayes can corroborate this. She knew that I was helping Renie."

"Don't bring her into this," I spat. "You pretended to help me so that you could trick me into going to the west wing, where June was waiting for me."

"I tried to go *with* you to the west wing. You're the one who refused. Again, Roux Hayes was witness to this," Etienne said.

"You knew I wouldn't let you go with me. You were counting on it."

Etienne looked bewildered, and it was horribly convincing. I didn't dare look at the Council.

"All I ever did was try to help you. I showed you that oak tree, where it looked like a grave had been dug, and I told you I'd help you unearth it to see what was there, but you didn't wait for me. You rushed off to do it early in the morning, before I was even awake. I had no idea you would do that," Etienne said.

He lifted his gaze to the Council. "When Ysanne told us that June Mayfield had been transferred to another House but that we weren't to discuss it, I didn't believe her, and I wasn't the only one. But everyone else seemed willing to do as they were told. Then Renie arrived at Belle Morte. She was determined to find out what had happened to June, and everyone was lying to her, and I couldn't bear it. I liked June, and I wanted the truth too. I was willing to risk punishment at Ysanne's hands if it meant helping Renie get to the bottom of this. I even tried to raise my concerns with Jemima when she arrived for a visit a few days ago, but she didn't appear to be interested."

All eyes turned to Jemima.

"Is this true?" Caoimhe asked.

Jemima looked as uncomfortable as I'd ever seen her. "Well, yes," she admitted. "But he had nothing but vague concerns about a donor, and no evidence that anything bad had happened, and I had no reason to doubt Ysanne."

"Why didn't you tell me this?" Ysanne demanded.

"I meant to, but . . ." Jemima glanced at me. "If you'll recall, you held a welcome gathering for my entourage, and there was some . . . unpleasantness between Edmond and Adrian. I'm afraid it slipped my mind after that."

"I fully intended to contact Charles, Henry, or Caoimhe, and see if they would listen to my concerns, but Belle Morte was attacked before I could," Etienne said.

"If you weren't involved in any way, why did you run?" Caoimhe asked.

"Were you trying to stop June?" Jemima asked.

Etienne bit his lip. "I wish I could say I was, but the truth is I ran because I was scared."

"What were you scared of?"

Etienne's eyes slid to Ysanne.

"Everyone in Belle Morte must have known that June hadn't been transferred, but no one dared talk about it. If you think I'm exaggerating about us not being allowed to ask questions, please check with the donors. The ones who survived, anyway. Edmond Dantès is Ysanne's oldest friend, and she had him whipped with silver for hitting another vampire. Can you blame me for being afraid of her?"

"The silver-whipping was approved by me, as penance for the insult done to my House." Jemima spoke up.

I could've hugged her.

"But was it your idea or Ysanne's?" Etienne said.

Jemima shut her mouth.

"What happened that night, with you, Renie, and June?" Henry asked.

I started to protest, and Ludovic gave my arm a warning squeeze. His face was rigid but fire burned in his eyes, the same fire I felt licking along my bones.

"I have no idea what happened between Renie and June. I wasn't there," Etienne said.

"You *liar*," I shouted, unable to contain myself.

"Did anyone see me there?" Etienne asked.

"*I* did."

"Are you expecting us to accept your story without question?" Charles asked.

I didn't know how to respond to that.

"I don't know why Renie has chosen to frame me for what happened to her. Maybe it wasn't her choice." Etienne looked at Ysanne again. "But as soon as I realized she *had* framed me, I panicked. I fled Belle Morte because I didn't know what else to do."

"And you went to Lamia?" Henry said.

Etienne nodded. "I couldn't go to Nox, not with Jemima already at Belle Morte, Fiaigh is in Ireland, and Lamia is closer to Winchester than Midnight."

"You didn't think to mention any of this until now?" Ysanne asked Charles, her voice low and dangerous.

"I brought it up when I thought it was relevant," he replied.

"This is bullshit," I said. "Etienne tried to kill me. He sent me to the west wing—"

"Renie, if you truly believe that I killed June, why wouldn't I do the same to you? If I wanted you dead why wouldn't I just do it myself?" Etienne said.

I didn't know how to respond to that either. Frustration and anger clashed like a storm in my head, making it hard to think.

"You know I didn't kill June. You know I had nothing to do with the attack on Belle Morte," Etienne continued.

"I know you're full of shit."

"Did anyone besides you hear Etienne's alleged confession?" Charles said.

I clenched my hands beneath the table to stop them from shaking. "No."

"Then it's simply your word against his."

This wasn't happening, was it? Etienne couldn't be persuading them that he wasn't the murdering bastard that I *knew* he was.

"I knew that I was taking a big risk by returning to Belle Morte, but I had to," Etienne said.

"Why?" Henry asked.

"Because June's real killer is still here, and she'll get away with it if someone doesn't stop her."

"Her? You know who it is?" Caoimhe asked.

Etienne hesitated. "I believe that Isabeau Aguillon murdered June Mayfield."

CHAPTER SEVEN

Renie

Isabeau let out a soft gasp at the same time that Ysanne said, "What are you talking about?" Her voice was steady, but something dangerous lurked beneath the surface.

The atmosphere in the dining hall was tense, charged, like the room itself was holding its breath.

Etienne cowered away from Ysanne. I didn't buy it for a second, but I wasn't the one he wanted to fool.

"Do you have any evidence for this claim?" Jemima asked. She sounded cautious, but less than convinced.

"Ysanne, you told the Council that only a handful of people in Belle Morte knew the truth about June. You, Isabeau, Edmond, Ludovic, and Renie," Etienne said.

"That is correct," Ysanne said.

"Who, aside from you, was the first to know?"

Isabeau and Ysanne looked at each other, and I really wished they hadn't, because the Council was actually *listening* to Etienne, and there were a hundred ways that look could be interpreted. Guilt was one of them.

"I was," Isabeau said, perhaps to save Ysanne from having to admit it.

"You and June were close, weren't you?" Etienne said.

Isabeau blinked. "Not especially."

"I often saw you together, in the library, in the grounds."

"No, you didn't." There was a sharp edge to Isabeau's voice. "That isn't true."

"I understand that Etienne is not the only one to have witnessed your closeness with June Mayfield," said Charles. "When Etienne sought refuge at Lamia, he informed me that a member of Belle Morte security had also expressed surprise that Isabeau and June were spending so much time together. I have spoken to that guard myself, and she's informed me that she will gladly back up Etienne's statement. She's also willing to testify to the fact that she saw Isabeau and June together on the night that June was killed."

"Which guard?" said Ysanne.

"You'll forgive me if I protect her anonymity until we get to the bottom of this."

Ysanne's expression didn't change, but her hands, resting on the tabletop, tightened. Maybe she was fantasizing about punching him too.

"Whoever she is, she's lying," Isabeau insisted.

"You were in charge of feeding June while she was imprisoned in the west wing, weren't you?" Etienne said.

Isabeau gave a sharp nod.

"Did Ysanne ask you to, or did you volunteer?"

"I volunteered."

"Why?"

"To help Ysanne."

"But why you? Edmond has known Ysanne longer than anyone; why wouldn't she turn to him first?" Etienne pressed.

Neither Ysanne nor Isabeau spoke for a long moment, and the tension in the room grew even thicker. I felt like I was watching Etienne back Isabeau into a corner, but I wasn't sure how to stop it.

"Was it because of your relationship?" Etienne said.

Jemima raised her eyebrows, and Henry's mouth made a soft shape of surprise. Charles didn't react at all, so I assumed Etienne had already told him, and this didn't seem to be news to Caoimhe either.

"You and Ysanne are in a relationship, aren't you?" Etienne continued.

Isabeau's mouth opened, but no sound came out. I suddenly realized that I had no idea what the rules were for Council members. They could get married—France's largest Vampire House, De Sang, was jointly ruled by Adele Desmoulins and her husband, Anthoine, but they'd been married long before vampires revealed themselves to the world. The relationship rules might be different for everyone else, and apparently, Ysanne and Isabeau had kept theirs a secret.

"Isabeau would gladly help you cover up something like this because of her feelings for you, so would you do the same for her? Say, for example, if you knew she had killed a donor?" Etienne said to Ysanne.

"This is absurd. Do you have any actual evidence for these claims?" Ysanne snapped.

"Do you have any actual evidence for Renie's claims against me?" said Etienne quietly.

Ysanne fell silent, and my stomach plunged like a stone. This wasn't supposed to happen. Edmond should be here, helping us form a plan to go after Etienne and find June, and instead I was forced to sit and listen to this *bullshit*.

"He has a point," Henry said.

"You're suggesting that Isabeau turned June and I helped cover it up." Ysanne's voice was ice.

"You've already admitted to covering up the murder," Charles pointed out.

"And I've already explained why."

"I overheard Renie's story while I was waiting to come into the dining hall, and some things aren't adding up," Etienne continued. "Renie insists that June stabbed her, even though we all know rabids don't use weapons. Ysanne insists that she was trying to bring June back from being a rabid, even though she's been around long enough to know that's impossible."

"I've been around long enough to know that we have little understanding of rabids because we always kill them on sight," Ysanne said. "We couldn't say for sure that becoming rabid was irreversible because no one had ever really tried to reverse it."

"Also a fair point," said Henry.

"What if we accept that Renie is telling the truth about being stabbed? If I'd been out there with her, why wouldn't June have tried to kill me?" Etienne said.

"We don't know that she didn't," Caoimhe said. "You could have healed by now."

"If I'd fought June out in the snow there would've been signs of a struggle or bloodshed that wasn't Renie's. Ask Ludovic, Edmond, Roux, or Míriam if they saw *any* signs of this," Etienne said.

My stomach sank even further. There hadn't been any signs of a fight because there hadn't been one. June had been purely focused on me; Etienne might as well have not even been there.

"The question, then, is why would June use a knife against Renie?" Etienne waited a beat, looking at each of the Council members in turn. "Unless someone had trained her to. I believe Ysanne was telling the truth when she said she'd brought Renie here to work with June. But I'm not sure I believe that she was trying to restore June's mind."

"What do you think she was doing, then?" said Jemima.

"We think of rabids as animals, don't we? They're feral, they're dangerous, they have to be put down for everyone's safety. But even feral animals can be trained. I think Ysanne did see an opportunity with June, just not the one she's claiming. After Renie dug up what she thought was June's grave, she tried to get into the west wing, but Edmond and Ysanne stopped her. Ysanne had Renie and Roux

locked in their room. According to Renie, someone then mysteri-
ously unlocked their door, allowing them to leave and go to the west
wing. Doesn't that strike you as a little too convenient?"

"Unless *you* were the one who unlocked it," I snapped.

"As you'll recall, I tried to go with you to the west wing but you
asked me not to. If I'd been the one to let you out, why would I skulk
away and then intercept you a few moments later and pretend I didn't
know what was going on? Why would I not simply unlock your door
and tell you that I was helping you find the truth once and for all?

"Someone unleashed June that day, and then they did the same
thing again a couple of weeks later when Aiden Young attempted
to get into the west wing. June didn't break free. She was *released*."
Etienne looked around the table again. "Who better to release her
than the person who had the most constant, daily access to her? The
person who was alone with her. The person who was feeding her."
His eyes locked onto Isabeau.

"But Renie and Edmond were alone with June too," Jemima
objected.

"Ysanne's not stupid; if she wanted someone to release June,
she wouldn't let it be a fragile human being. She'd need a strong,
centuries-old vampire who could hold their own against a rabid.
We know it can't have been Edmond, as he was convalescing in his
bedroom at the time. If it was Ludovic, then Renie couldn't have run
into him coming the opposite way as she was fleeing from June. That
leaves Isabeau."

"Why would I release a rabid?" Isabeau said.

"Why would I?" Etienne countered. "I believe that Ysanne was
attempting to train June like a dog and you were helping her. I'm not
sure where Renie fits into this yet. Maybe she knew what was going
on, maybe she truly believed that Ysanne was trying to help."

"You're suggesting that Ysanne trained June and then turned her
on Renie? Why would she do that?" Jemima pressed him.

"I don't have all the answers. Perhaps Renie wanted to be a vampire and Ysanne knew the Council wouldn't authorize it, so she arranged a scenario in which Edmond would be forced to turn her. Perhaps Renie knew nothing about it. Perhaps she's been in on it from the start and she's framing me on Ysanne's orders. Maybe I'm completely wrong about Isabeau, and Ysanne killed and turned June. I don't know. All I know is there's a lot more to this than Ysanne or Renie are saying."

"So, what, you're saying that Isabeau turned all those new vampires too? And let them into Belle Morte?" I said.

"I know nothing about that attack, but it seems likely that it's linked to what happened to June, and therefore likely that the same person is behind both incidents," Etienne returned.

"Did you forget the part where I saved Isabeau's life during the attack? If she'd let a bunch of enemy vampires into the house, why would they then turn on her?"

"It's possible that Isabeau appearing to need your help was an elaborate ruse designed to throw us off the scent," said Jemima. She didn't look happy as she said it, her big eyes getting even wider as she looked at Isabeau.

"More elaborate than what Etienne is pulling now?" I demanded.

"At this point, Isabeau does seem a likelier suspect than Etienne. That doesn't mean we're ready to condemn her, but clearly a lot of questions need to be answered."

Isabeau's face was white, even by vampire standards. She cast an imploring look at Ysanne, but Ysanne remained silent. But I noticed how her hands gripped the arms of her chair, her knuckles turning white from the pressure.

"Isabeau didn't do this." Even as I said it, I couldn't help but feel a tiny flicker of doubt. I didn't want to believe anything that Etienne said. Isabeau had never given me any reason to doubt her—except that even Ysanne thought that Etienne couldn't have been working alone. *Someone* had to have helped him. Could I rule Isabeau out just because I liked her? Equally, what would she gain from all this?

"You told me a revolution was coming," I said, glaring at Etienne.

He just shook his head, like I wasn't worth responding to anymore. I wanted to throw a chair at his head. He couldn't get away with this.

"You realize that if Isabeau is found to be responsible for this, execution will be considered," Charles said, staring hard at Ysanne.

Isabeau was so still she might have been carved from stone. Part of me wanted to reach out to her, to squeeze her hand or touch her knee, *something*. The other part couldn't help wondering if Etienne had mixed a little truth with his lies. What if Isabeau *had* helped him, and now he was throwing her under the bus to save himself?

Jemima held up both hands. "Let's not be too hasty. The evidence against Isabeau is hardly solid. But she'll need to be interrogated. In the meantime, may I recommend that she be removed to a neutral location? If she's behind the attack, it's not safe to keep her here."

"By removed you mean imprisoned," Ysanne said.

Jemima's face softened. "Yes."

"And when you say a neutral location, I presume it's one you won't share with me."

Jemima looked away.

"This all started in your House, Ysanne, so until we can be sure that this woman"—Charles waved a dismissive hand at Isabeau—"is not responsible for the atrocity, then the location of her confinement shall not be shared with you."

"If, after she's been interrogated, we determine that she's innocent, she will immediately be returned to Belle Morte," Jemima said, and I think she was trying to sound reassuring.

A pause stretched out, tension turning the air as thick as tar. Ysanne clutched the arms of her chair, and I was sure she would leap up and defend Isabeau.

But she didn't.

"Very well," she said. "I'll arrange to have security take her away."

Isabeau's shoulders stiffened and a shadow of raw hurt flashed in her eyes, but she didn't say a word. Dexter and a small group of his security personnel were quickly summoned. Dexter's eyes narrowed when Ysanne told him to remove Isabeau, but he said nothing. He was only the hired help, after all; it wasn't his place to question Ysanne's decisions. But he clearly wasn't happy as his people escorted Isabeau from the room.

I kept expecting Ysanne to insist that Isabeau was innocent, but she didn't. Then I wondered why I expected it at all. After what she'd done to Edmond, she'd hardly change her tune for Isabeau's sake.

Then she surprised me.

"You're making a mistake," she said in a quiet voice, not looking at anyone in particular. "The evidence against Isabeau is far from concrete, and when you realize that she's not responsible, we'll all have to ask ourselves what the real perpetrator wants and why he's doing this." Her eyes bored into Etienne, still sitting quietly at the other end of the table. "And what he plans to do next."

Ysanne's words chilled me. If Isabeau was innocent, then Etienne could still have an accomplice in Belle Morte. The old rumor of secret passageways crawled into my brain, and I looked uneasily at the wood-paneled walls around us.

"We still have a lot to discuss regarding this situation," Ysanne said. "Now that the rabid is no longer here, I've had the west wing prepared for visitors. I'd be honored if the Council members stayed here while we continue this investigation."

"You're too kind." Charles didn't sound sincere, but Ysanne ignored it.

She rose to her feet, smoothing down her crisp white blouse. "Then let us adjourn. I'm sure you're all hungry, and my donors are ready to feed you. We can reconvene after we've eaten."

I didn't go with them as they left the dining hall and headed to the various feeding rooms dotted around the mansion. It didn't seem right that the donors should still be expected to provide blood after everything that had happened lately, but there wasn't much I could do about it.

Ludovic stayed behind, and I was about to tell him that he didn't have to when I remembered what Ysanne had told me back in her office. If Isabeau wasn't Etienne's accomplice, then someone in Belle Morte might still want me dead. It wasn't safe for me to be left alone.

I drifted out of the dining hall and into the ballroom, Ludovic shadowing me like a bodyguard. I was grateful that he was here, but I couldn't help wishing he was Edmond.

The last time I'd been in the ballroom, it had looked like something from a nightmare; gore had been splattered all over the marble floor and formed macabre patterns on the stucco walls. Not a trace of that carnage remained; no sign that the room had ever been used for anything but dancing.

But I'd never forget the slaughter I'd seen here.

"You don't believe Etienne, do you?" I said. My voice sounded too loud in the empty space.

Ludovic hadn't followed me all the way into the room; he lingered in the entryway, leaning one shoulder against the wall. If he was human I'd have said his posture was relaxed, but there was something watchful about him, a predator that could strike at any time.

"No," Ludovic said.

"But the Council believe him."

He said nothing to that.

I wrapped my arms around myself. "If he gets the Council on his side, we're fucked, aren't we? We can't prove anything."

"We'll find a way," Ludovic said.

"How?"

Silence.

I needed a hug. But Edmond was still imprisoned, Roux was mad at me, and Ludovic didn't strike me as the touchy-feely type. More than anything, I wanted to feel Edmond's arms around me, hear his faded French lilt reassuring me that everything would be okay.

But Edmond wasn't here, and I didn't know when he would be again.

I left the ballroom, Ludovic still shadowing me. I didn't know where I planned on going, but when I reached the parlor just beyond the dining hall, the last room before the vestibule, I stopped.

Dexter hovered close to the front door, his hands clasped behind him, his gaze trained on the floor. There was no sign of the guards who'd come with him to arrest Isabeau. Isabeau herself stood at the base of the staircase; her head was held high but her eyes glittered with fear.

How did the Council interrogate suspects?

Vampires had already demonstrated their archaic sense of justice by silver-whipping Edmond for punching Adrian, so it was easy to believe they'd torture information out of their prisoners.

Ysanne stood in front of Isabeau. For the longest moment, the two women stared at each other. Then Ysanne lifted a hand and gently laid it against Isabeau's cheek. She murmured something in French, and Isabeau's lip trembled.

"Ma belle," Ysanne whispered. "They won't hurt you."

"I didn't do this," Isabeau said.

"But someone did. The Council are scared and they're not used to it. It's been so long since any of us has been scared. They need to feel that they are doing something, even if that means imprisoning an innocent woman. They'll take you to a neutral location and question you, that's all. It cannot take them long to ascertain that you're not responsible for this. Then they'll bring you back."

"And in the meantime, the real monster goes free." Bitterness tinged Isabeau's words.

"Not for long," Ysanne said, her voice razor-sharp. "Etienne won't get away with this, I swear it."

Isabeau kissed her, pressing her mouth to Ysanne's with the force of someone about to lose something infinitely precious. Ysanne cupped Isabeau's cheek.

I turned away, not wanting to intrude on a private moment. Sometimes I thought Ysanne was pure ice; other times, I was reminded how very human she still was.

In that moment, I pitied Ysanne. As leader of Belle Morte, she had to put the well-being of her people above everything—including her own happiness. I couldn't imagine having to choose between my love for Edmond and the vampires of Belle Morte. Objectively, the right thing to do was whatever was best for the vampires, but who could honestly say they'd give up the person they loved, even if it was better for everyone else?

I wanted to hate Ysanne for separating me from Edmond, but she, too, was separating herself from someone she loved—and she had to do it voluntarily. I couldn't imagine that kind of strength.

Isabeau murmured something else in French, and I left them to it, heading back to the ballroom since I couldn't get upstairs.

Standing in the middle of the dance floor, I gazed at the lavish decor, remembering the masked ball, when I'd danced with Edmond as a human.

My life had changed so much in just a few days.

The next time Belle Morte threw a ball would I head down the main staircase with the other vampires? Would I have my own page on the vampire fan sites, my own columns in the gossip magazines? The thought made my stomach twist.

High heels clicked on the marble floor and I turned to see Ysanne flowing into the room. Her face was cold and impassive, no trace of the woman who'd just sent her lover to an unknown prison.

She stopped and looked me over, head to toe. Unease prickled my skin. I'd sassed Ysanne before because I believed my status as donor protected me. I didn't have that protection anymore. Now I was subject to vampire laws, and they weren't the same as human ones.

Ysanne had whipped and imprisoned Edmond for breaking the rules. That could happen to me too. I needed to remember that.

"Ludovic, please wait in the dining hall. I'd like to talk to Renie alone," Ysanne said.

Ludovic looked at me, and I didn't know if he was wordlessly asking if I minded being alone with Ysanne, but I nodded just in case. He left the ballroom.

"Follow me," Ysanne said, and strode toward the small door at the back of the ballroom through which the human staff would ferry silver trays of champagne to and from the kitchen.

I'd never seen the kitchen before, but I had only a moment to absorb the polished chrome appliances and wine racks filled with bottles before Ysanne opened another door, which led to a narrow, white-walled corridor.

Was this one of the secret passageways that Vladdicts speculated about?

"Where are you taking me?" I said.

Ysanne didn't answer.

"Hey," I said, stopping. "I'm not taking another step until you tell me where we're going."

Ysanne turned to face me. "For once in your life, will you do as you are told? I wouldn't do this for just anyone, you know."

"Do what?"

"Give you the one thing you truly want. I'm taking you to see Edmond."

CHAPTER EIGHT

Renie

At the end of the corridor was another door, and beyond that a small set of stairs leading down to a metal door that appeared to be set directly into a wall of rock. It was so crude and rough looking that I couldn't initially absorb what I was seeing. Everything in Belle Morte was so beautiful, and this ugly little space came as a total shock.

It became even more so when Ysanne produced a key from somewhere on her person, unlocked the door, and ushered me inside.

Despite everything I'd learned about what vampires were capable of, I was still naive enough to believe that a vampire's version of prison wouldn't be so different from a human's.

I was wrong.

Edmond was slumped against the wall of a dank stone room, his head hanging on his chest. Silver manacles were wrapped around his bloody, ravaged wrists; those manacles were attached to chains that were looped through a set of iron rings in the wall.

When June had been confined to the west wing, her constant struggles to break free had caused the chains to rub away great patches of skin on her arms—Edmond didn't need to struggle for these chains to do their terrible work. The deadly metal seared through his flesh, leaving angry, ravaged areas of bloody skin on each side of the manacles.

When I'd first met Edmond he'd been like some beautiful angel, all raven's-wing hair and ivory skin, and the sight of him brought so low sent a swift, sharp pain to my heart. It wasn't my fault that this had happened to him, but if he'd never met me, he wouldn't be here now. He'd still be enjoying a life of luxury in Belle Morte, respected and adored by humans and vampires alike. Instead, he was chained to a wall in a horrible stone room, bloodied and beaten down.

And he'd done it all for me.

I ran to him.

"You only have a few minutes, so use them wisely," Ysanne said. She left the cell and closed the door behind us.

Edmond lifted his head. His face was pale—not the beautiful paleness I associated with vampires but closer to a chalky white, like the life and strength had bled out of him. His eyes glittered, dark with pain and exhaustion.

"Mon ange?" he whispered, and the hope in his voice broke my heart.

Had he thought I wouldn't come for him?

Considering what I'd said the last time I saw him, he probably thought exactly that.

I slid my arms around him as carefully as I could, trying not to knock his injured wrists.

What happened to vampires when they didn't feed for a long time?

A hideous image flashed through my head—Edmond withering and decaying in front of me, his skin drying out and cracking, his hair turning to gray straw, the dark brilliance of his eyes turning dull. I'd never thought of vampires starving to death, but what if that was Edmond's punishment? What if he was never allowed to leave this place?

"Please," I whispered, and my voice hitched. "Please tell me that this isn't permanent. Tell me they'll let you out of here."

Edmond shifted but the movement jolted his wrists, and a hiss of pain escaped his lips.

I cupped his face with both hands. His beautiful eyes were shadowed with pain.

"If they think they can keep you down here, they're wrong. I'll break you out . . . I'll—" Anger choked me.

I might only have been a vampire for a few days, but it would take more than that pack of heartless bastards to keep me from protecting the man I loved.

"*Non, ma chérie*, you must let this run its course," Edmond murmured. His voice sounded different; the velvet timbre and curling French vowels were strained and roughened by his punishment.

"But they're killing you!"

"They won't. This is a prison sentence, not a death sentence."

Swallowing my rage, I tried to think clearly. Ysanne had told me that Edmond would be released eventually, but all rational thought had fled when I'd seen him slumped in this horrible cell.

I sank back on my heels, sheer relief burning my eyes. If I was still human, I'd be a sobbing wreck by now.

"I didn't think you'd come," Edmond whispered.

"I'm sorry," I said, placing my palm on his cheek again. "What I said—I didn't mean it. When I woke up as a vampire I was terrified. My entire life had changed—I'd *died*. You know what that's like. I was scared and I lashed out, and I'm *sorry*. I didn't mean any of it."

He looked like he didn't believe me. Maybe it'd been different for him. His human life had been so grim and bleak that waking up as a vampire must have been a blessing for him, rather than the terrifying and monumental adjustment it was for me.

"Edmond, look at me. Didn't you wonder why I broke out of my room the night of the attack?"

After realizing that Belle Morte had been invaded by enemy forces, Edmond had locked Roux and me in our bedroom, trying to keep us safe. But, terrified that he'd get himself killed, I'd smashed the lock and joined the fight. That was the night that I'd realized the full extent of my feelings for Edmond, but I'd never had a chance to tell him.

"I broke out because I couldn't bear the thought of anything happening to you," I said. "I couldn't bear the thought of losing you."

Hope sparked in the dark depths of his eyes, but it was tempered with caution.

Gently, I pressed my lips to his. Other times when I'd kissed him, it had been fiery and passionate, the feelings we'd tried to deny exploding to life with a force that left us both reeling. This time the kiss was soft, chaste, but somehow more meaningful.

"Edmond Dantès," I whispered. "I'm so completely in love with you."

Edmond

All Edmond could do was stare at Renie, because despite Ysanne's reassurances that Renie hadn't meant what she'd said, that word had gone round and round in his head ever since he'd been imprisoned.

Monster.

Monster.

Monster.

When he found words, his voice was hoarse. "Don't say that if you don't mean it."

"I wouldn't." Renie kissed him again, her mouth soft against his. "I love you, Edmond. I'm in love with you."

In that moment he forgot about the chains and the prison cell. There was only the need to hold Renie, to stroke the smoothness of her skin and run his fingers through her autumn-colored hair, but when he tried to put his arms around her, the chains held him back. Pain seared through him, turning everything white, and he suppressed a snarl.

"Don't try to move," Renie whispered, kissing his forehead. Her voice hitched with unshed tears.

"Say it again," Edmond said, because he needed to hear those three words, the ones he hadn't thought he'd ever hear again.

"I love you."

"But I've condemned you to this life." Edmond couldn't forget the awful look on Renie's face when she'd woken up, the horror dawning in her eyes when she'd realized she was now a vampire.

"You did it to save me."

"It's not the life you wanted."

Renie sat back on her heels and regarded him, her face serious. "No. If I'm being honest, this isn't the life I'd have chosen, but it's the life I have now, and I don't regret that. And I don't blame you. If it wasn't for you, I'd be dead."

"You *are* dead," Edmond pointed out. "You might be walking around, but you'll never be human again."

"You think I don't know that?"

"I think you don't know what you've let yourself in for."

Everything that Edmond had ever wanted was here in front of him, offering her heart in her hands, and part of him was afraid to take it.

Renie shifted closer to him, dipping her head so that she could look into his eyes. She was so much smaller than him; he wasn't used to looking up at her.

"Edmond, listen to me. I know that I don't fully understand everything about being a vampire. There are a lot of things I'll have to get used to, and there'll probably be some dark times ahead, but that's okay. I can handle it. I've fallen in love with you, Edmond. I don't care if I'm human or vampire, as long as I'm with you."

Edmond's old heart cracked wide open. He gazed into Renie's eyes, the warm hazel color he could get lost in, and read the hope and the fear there—the fear that he didn't feel the same way, perhaps, or the fear that her earlier words had irreparably damaged things between them.

"I swore to myself that I'd never love again," he said, and Renie stiffened. "I told myself that it wasn't worth the pain," he continued. "But . . ." Leaning forward, he rested his forehead against hers. Her skin was cool now, not warm like it had been when she was human, but every inch of it was precious to him. "It *is* worth it. It's always worth it. I didn't want to fall in love with you, but you stole my heart and I don't want it back."

Renie made a soft noise, and Edmond thought she was about to collapse into his arms, but she stopped herself, her eyes flicking to the silver manacles ravaging his wrists.

"How long do you have to stay down here?" she asked, stroking a strand of hair off his forehead.

"I don't know yet."

Her eyes hardened. "Ysanne hasn't told you?"

"She doesn't know either. It's for the whole Council to decide, and I think they've got bigger things to worry about now."

Renie didn't have a heartbeat anymore, and Edmond could no longer gauge her emotions by listening to it, but her feelings were written all over her face. Something was wrong. The shape of her mouth was too hard, a muscle twitched in her jaw, and shadows had crept into her eyes.

"What's happened?" Edmond asked.

"Nothing," Renie said, but she didn't meet his eyes.

If his hands were free he'd have put a finger under her chin and made her look at him. He hated that he couldn't touch her.

"Tell me," he said.

"The meeting with the Council didn't go very well."

"Why?"

Renie stared at the small patch of floor between them. Then she told him how Etienne had turned himself in, how he'd persuaded the

Council to doubt Renie and Ysanne's version of events, even though theirs was the truth, and how Isabeau had been taken away for questioning. By the time she finished, a fire had ignited in Edmond's chest. The bastard who'd orchestrated Renie's death was in Belle Morte, while Edmond was stuck down here, unable to protect her. He gritted his teeth and his fangs pricked his lip.

"No matter what happens, you have to stay away from him," he warned.

He still didn't know why Etienne wanted Renie dead, but if he laid a hand on her, then Edmond would kill him, silver chains or not.

"I'm more worried about you. Ludovic's got my back upstairs, but you're trapped here. What if Etienne tries something?"

"He won't."

Renie's expression wobbled. "You don't know that."

Edmond rested his forehead against hers. "Ysanne would never let him get close to the cells."

"Could you take him? If it came to a fight?" Renie asked.

That fire in Edmond's chest flared up again. "I've got a good couple of hundred years on Etienne Banville. I'm stronger than him and he knows it."

"That's what I'm afraid of." Renie touched Edmond's hand, the barest brush of her fingertips. "If he wanted you out of the way, this is the perfect time to do it."

"I'm already out of the way," Edmond said.

"But—"

Edmond stopped her with a gentle kiss.

"No matter how many lies he spins to the Council, Ysanne will not let him out of her sight," he whispered.

"She already did. She's down here with us, and he's sucking on donor necks with the rest of the Council."

"Ysanne will have made sure that security are tailing him," Edmond insisted.

"The same security that have sworn they'll testify that Isabeau was involved with June's death?"

"I don't know which guard Etienne's talking about, or why she'd help him, but Ysanne's not stupid. There are people in this house that she trusts implicitly, like Dexter Flynn." Edmond kissed the tip of Renie's nose. "Please don't worry about me."

She made a noise that was half laugh, half sob. "I'll always worry about you."

Ysanne opened the door. "Time's up," she said.

Renie squeezed her eyes shut. "I don't want to leave you," she whispered.

"You have to." Edmond kissed her once more, slow and lingering, as if he could imprint the shape of her mouth onto his. In that brief moment, he could forget the pain of the silver shackles, the burning rage at Etienne, and the gnawing uncertainty of what the future held. There was only the girl who'd come unexpectedly into his life and had stolen his heart. Then the moment ended and Renie was pulling back, her eyes bright and red.

"I don't know when I'll see you again," she said.

"I'll be out of here before you know it," Edmond said, with more confidence than he felt.

"Renie, it's time to go," said Ysanne.

Slowly, Renie climbed to her feet, her fingers lingering on the back of Edmond's hand. When she walked away, it felt like she was taking all the light with her. She looked back before Ysanne closed the door, then Edmond was alone again, with nothing but the pain and his fears.

CHAPTER NINE

Renie

W"e need to talk," I said, following Ysanne back down the corridor.

"Do we?"

"Yes."

Ysanne abruptly stopped and turned to me, her arms folded. "I'll warn you that I'm in no mood for tantrums," she said.

I struggled to rein in the emotion that had built inside me from the moment I'd seen that horrible little cell and those hideous wounds on Edmond's wrists.

"How can you cope with doing this to him?" I said. For once it wasn't an accusation; I genuinely struggled to understand.

Ysanne made a noise of irritation. "We've already discussed this. Despite the history I share with Edmond, I cannot be seen to be favoring him. He cannot get away with breaking the rules, even if I can sympathize with why he did."

"Wait, you sympathize with him?" That wasn't what I'd expected, and it overrode everything else in my head.

Ysanne stared at the floor, and something about her seemed to shift, making her appear younger and more vulnerable. I was used to her being the Lady of Belle Morte, the big bad vampire who enforced the rules of her—*our*—kind with an iron fist, and I'd never really registered that she could only have been in her twenties when she died—not much older than me. She always seemed so ageless, so endlessly powerful, but now I wondered how much of her image was a facade to protect herself.

"I know you think I'm a monster, but I've only ever tried to do what's best for my people."

"But you keep hurting the people I care about," I said quietly.

Ysanne's eyes flared. "I've known Edmond a lot longer than you have. Don't make the mistake of thinking you're the only one who cares for him."

Under any other circumstances I'd have snapped back at her, but I bit my tongue, because Ysanne's anger wasn't about me and Edmond. It was about Isabeau. Seeing Edmond locked up was like being punched repeatedly in the heart, but Ysanne was feeling that too.

"You love her, don't you?" I said.

Ysanne didn't answer, but that in itself spoke volumes. If Isabeau was just a fling Ysanne would have scoffed at my words, or made some cutting remark. But she loved Isabeau like I loved Edmond, and she'd been forced to have Isabeau arrested.

"I'm sorry," I said.

Still, Ysanne said nothing.

"Can I ask you something?" I said.

Ysanne finally looked at me, and I took that as a yes.

"When I first started working with June, you tried to stop Isabeau from helping. Edmond had to get Ludovic instead. Why?"

"I didn't want her involved."

"But she was already *feeding* June. Isn't that far more dangerous than standing guard outside the door?"

"Isabeau is nothing if not stubborn. From the moment she found out about June she insisted on doing everything she could to help. When I allowed Ludovic to act as your backup instead of Isabeau, it was because I was trying to limit her involvement. I thought if I did that, I could cut her out of the situation altogether. But she refused to be brushed aside."

So Ysanne did try to protect the people she loved when she could. But it hadn't worked. Ysanne must have realized that Isabeau would not be elbowed out of anything, and had reluctantly allowed her to carry on helping as much as she could.

Now that was being used against her to condemn Isabeau.

Standing in that corridor with her, I had no idea how I felt about Ysanne. I'd been so angry with her in the past, but I was starting to understand what she had to deal with and why she made these decisions. And I was starting to see how heavily some of these decisions weighed on her.

I wanted to reassure her that the Council had no evidence against Isabeau, so they'd have to release her sooner or later, but the words stuck in my throat. At the back of my brain, a nasty little voice whispered, *What if Etienne's telling the truth about her?* Etienne was a liar, but mixing a little truth with his lies could make them that much stronger.

I kept my mouth shut and walked down the corridor, the click of Ysanne's heels following me.

I expected the kitchen to be empty when we went into it, but Dexter was there, pouring himself a mug of coffee. He didn't react as we came in, but I was so stricken with shame that I froze on the spot.

Dexter had been the first person I'd met when I'd arrived at Belle Morte, and though I knew little about him, he'd always seemed like a nice guy. I'd attacked him like a wild animal out in the gardens, and I hadn't even apologized.

"Uh, Ysanne? Could I have a moment alone with Dexter?" I said.

Her eyebrow twitched, not quite a lift, but close. She didn't say anything, though, just quietly walked out of the kitchen and left me alone with the man I'd almost killed.

Suddenly the kitchen seemed huge, a mile of space separating me from Dexter, and I had no idea how to cross it.

"I'm so sorry," I blurted.

"It wasn't your fault."

"Yeah, it was. I'd had two opportunities to feed before I went outside and I turned them both down. If I'd fed, I wouldn't have lost control."

"You screwed up." Dexter shrugged broad shoulders. "It happens."

"How can you be so calm about this?"

"Because no one was hurt. I don't see the point in making a big deal over a mistake."

"I could have really hurt you," I said.

"But you didn't. I'm okay, kid. I was a bodyguard before I took this job, and getting banged up came with the territory. It'd take more than one teenage vampire to put me down."

I tried to smile but it wouldn't come. "I should just have fed when Jemima told me to."

Dexter added a teaspoon of sugar to his coffee, tasted it, then added more. "I get why you didn't. You may be a vampire now but your mind's still human, and it's natural that you're not comfortable with drinking blood."

"It feels like everyone's making excuses for me." I sighed.

"Maybe they wouldn't have to if you'd stop being so hard on yourself." Dexter patted the countertop. "Come on. You look like you could use a friend."

I edged farther into the room. I could still hear Dexter's heart beating, but it was a muted thump now—something I was vaguely aware of rather than something that resonated throughout my whole body and coaxed my fangs from my gums.

"Why are you being so nice to me?" I asked.

"You've been through a lot."

"So? That's not your problem." I didn't mean to throw his kindness back in his face, but he was head of security, not an advice columnist for confused new vampires.

"True." Dexter sipped his coffee, and little spirals of steam wafted around his face. "I suppose when I look at you, I think of my daughter. I'd like to think that if she was ever in trouble there'd be someone willing to help her."

"I didn't know you had a daughter."

"You wouldn't, would you? Although if you live in Belle Morte long enough, you'll end up meeting her; she's determined to follow in my footsteps as head of security."

"Really?" It seemed like an odd aspiration for a young girl in this day and age—most of them were too busy planning how to become donors. They wanted to mingle with vampires, not guard them.

"She's only thirteen, so she's got a long way to go, but she's already started training."

"But this is dangerous. Surely you don't want your kid mixed up in this kind of life."

Dexter gave a rueful chuckle. "If you ever meet my Nikki, you'll understand. Once she's got it in her head to do something, there's no stopping her."

"I bet her mum loves that."

The laughter faded from Dexter's eyes. "My wife passed away when Nikki was very young."

"Oh god, I'm so sorry."

"You weren't to know." Dexter's words were breezy but his eyes remained troubled. He reached beneath his T-shirt and pulled out a small gold locket. It was an antique, feminine piece of jewelry, totally out of place around the neck of the muscle-bound, fortysomething head of security. Dexter used his thumbnail to open the locket, then leaned forward to show me the tiny pictures inside—a woman with a head of thick curls, and a chubby-cheeked baby.

"They're beautiful," I said.

Dexter grinned proudly. "It's just me and my girl now, us against the world." He closed the locket and tucked it back beneath his shirt.

"But you spend so much time here. Who takes care of Nikki?" I asked.

Dexter's smile slipped and he ran a hand over his shaved head. "A neighbor does a lot of babysitting for me. It's not ideal, I know, but I want to set aside enough money for my girl so that she never has to go without anything. The more I work, the more I earn, the more I have to set her up for the future."

I didn't point out that maybe Nikki would rather have her dad around than the promise of financial stability further down the line. Instead I said, "Maybe this isn't my place to say, but you could have been injured in that attack, and I could have really hurt you this morning. Maybe that's a sign that you should think about retiring from this gig."

I waited for him to tell me to mind my own business, but Dexter just chuckled. "You may be right. And I suppose I'm not getting any younger."

I didn't know Nikki Flynn, but I hated the thought that the vampire world might strip her dad from her like it had stripped June from me.

Ludovic opened the kitchen door. "The Council is reconvening," he told me.

Dexter drained his coffee and left the mug in the sink. I guessed that the staff in charge of kitchen duties were still here then, same as the donors. How long did Ysanne think she could keep the attack and the people who'd died hidden? Maybe that was what the Council planned to discuss next.

I followed Ludovic back into the dining hall, Dexter bringing up the rear. The Council had already reclaimed their seats around the table, and Etienne sat slightly farther up, his eyes downcast.

Charles gave me a cold look. "Not her," he said to the other vampires gathered around the table.

I stopped.

"We feel that we need some time to discuss everything we've learned without non-Council members," Jemima said. At least she sounded apologetic, unlike Charles, who'd sounded like he couldn't wait to see the back of me.

"That goes for you too," Jemima said, looking at Etienne.

Etienne didn't protest. He didn't react at all, and it made my skin prickle, because I had no idea what was going through his head, and I hated the thought of him roaming around Belle Morte like nothing had happened.

Ysanne obviously thought the same, because as Etienne headed out of the dining hall, Ysanne caught Dexter's eye and gave him a tiny nod. Dexter patted my shoulder, then followed Etienne.

"Come on," Ludovic said to me in a low voice.

He was trying to keep me away from Etienne, I realized, with a warm rush of gratitude.

As we left the dining hall, I looked back at Ysanne, but her back was to me, as she faced the Council. I couldn't read a single emotion on any of their faces. I'd never liked that about vampires, but it made me especially uneasy when there was so much at stake, so much that I couldn't control.

In the vestibule, I paused. Dexter and Etienne had already disappeared, but two security guards in black uniforms stood by the front door, and that made my skin prickle all over again. Security patrolled the grounds all around the house and guarded the back exit so no donor could go outside without permission, but I'd never seen them guarding the front door until today. I knew why it was necessary, but it felt wrong, somehow.

A faint noise came from outside, and I tilted my head, listening. It sounded like voices—lots and lots of voices.

"What's going on?" I asked Ludovic.

"About half an hour ago people started gathering at the gates. We're not sure who they are yet, but we have to consider the possibility that someone in Belle Morte has leaked information about everything that's happened."

"But they're definitely human?"

"It's daylight outside. No new vampire could withstand the sun for this long."

"Maybe they're the families of the people who died in the attack," I said. There were no computers in Belle Morte and donors weren't allowed phones, so their only way of communicating with friends and family was via letters. Since only three days had passed, it was unlikely that any of the dead donors' families knew that anything was wrong yet. But what about the families of the staff and security guards who'd been killed? They went home at the end of their shifts, so surely someone had missed them by now.

"I don't know what Ysanne's done about that," Ludovic admitted. "But we have next of kin on record for everyone who comes into Belle Morte, and no one at the gates today is known to anyone inside this house."

"They're random strangers? Doesn't that seem weird to you?"

"Protestors have gathered at our gates before. Not everyone likes vampires," Ludovic said. He gestured to the staircase on our left. "Maybe you'd feel better if we went to see your friends?"

"I'm not so sure about that," I muttered, remembering how Roux had reacted last time. Then again, she had let me feed from her.

I gazed up the stairs, thinking of the two wings where vampires and donors slept. "What do I do while Edmond's locked up? Am I supposed to stay in his room?"

"It's where you've been these last three days," Ludovic said.

"Yeah, but I don't remember any of that."

"Do you feel uncomfortable staying there?"

I tried to find words to describe how I was feeling. "Not *uncomfortable*, exactly, but it doesn't feel right when he's not there. Does that make sense?"

Ludovic nodded, his eyes shadowed. "We do have a spare room now, if you'd prefer that."

"Whose—oh."

Rosa had been one of the casualties, and even though I hadn't known her, I felt a pang in my chest for the vampire who'd never again return to her room.

"I can't do that," I said.

The only thing worse than taking over Edmond's bedroom while he was imprisoned would be moving into the room of a recently murdered woman, whose friends were probably still coming to terms with her death.

"You know you can't stay in the south wing anymore, don't you?" Ludovic said.

I scuffed the carpet with my foot. I couldn't go back to my old room even if vampires were allowed to sleep in that wing—Jason had moved in now. When their contracts were up, he and Roux would leave Belle Morte, and I wouldn't. Becoming a vampire meant I had a real future with Edmond, but it also meant I could lose my friends, and even thinking that made my chest ache.

"I'm having a hard time working out where I belong," I muttered.

Ludovic awkwardly patted my shoulder, like he wasn't used to doing it. "Why don't we go to Edmond's room and see if you can get used to it?" he said.

"Actually, can we go to the library?" That had always been my favorite room in the house, the place where I'd felt calmest.

"Of course."

Edmond

How long would he be down here? At some point would the monotony override the pain?

Closing his eyes, he thought of Renie. He'd suffer this a thousand times over and worse if it meant she was safe, and once he was free, all the pain would be worth it. Then he could hold her, kiss her, start a life with her.

Somewhere inside the mansion a scream broke out, and Edmond's eyes flew open. The voice wasn't Renie's, but fear was an icy blast inside him nonetheless—something was seriously wrong inside Belle Morte, and Renie was up there.

Another scream rang out, a deep male voice this time, and a moment later Edmond heard the faint crash of breaking glass. Was Belle Morte under attack again?

He threw himself against the chains, fighting them with every bit of strength he had left. They gnawed through the flesh of his wrists, and the pain was like fire; blood streamed down his arms, splattering on the stone floor around him. But he couldn't break free.

Edmond screamed with fury and frustration, his fangs bursting from his gums.

He'd accepted his punishment when he was thrown down here, knowing it was the consequence for turning Renie, but now she was up there alone, facing who knew what, and he was trapped down here, powerless, helpless.

Without these chains, he'd have ripped through a thousand enemies to protect Renie.

But right now he wasn't even strong enough to protect himself.

CHAPTER TEN

Renie

I was sitting on one of the library's plush sofas, idly picking at a cushion and wondering what to say to Ludovic, who hovered by the bookshelves like a bodyguard, when the screaming started.

Before I could even react, Ludovic moved in front of me with predatory grace, ready to shield me from anything that might come through the door.

"What the hell is that?" I said, clutching the back of the sofa.

"I don't know."

I jumped up but Ludovic grabbed my arm before I could take another step.

"Don't even think about going out there," he warned.

"But someone's in trouble."

Ludovic's grip on my wrist didn't relax. "I promised Edmond I'd take care of you."

"Listen—"

Ludovic stiffened and swung back to the door, still keeping me behind him.

"Someone's out there," he said.

My heart climbed into my throat.

"I won't let anything happen to you," Ludovic said. His voice was low and hard, and edged with violence in a way I'd never heard before.

I remembered what Edmond had told me about how he and

Ludovic had met, fighting side by side in the blasted trenches of the
First World War, and almost felt a pang of pity for whoever was stupid enough to cross him. Ludovic looked like he was ready to rip
someone apart.

The library door burst open and Roux and Jason stumbled in,
both of them wide-eyed and breathing hard.

"You're okay," Roux cried.

She ran to us and shoved Ludovic out of the way so she could hug
me. Ludovic blinked at her.

"What's going on?" I said.

Jason closed the library door and hurried to join us. "They're
back," he said.

"Who?"

He looked at the door and lowered his voice to a frantic whisper.
"The vampires who attacked the house a few days ago."

Ludovic went very still, his eyes flickering red.

"Are you okay? Are you hurt?" I said, scanning Roux and Jason
for injuries.

"We're fine. We heard the screams and we came looking for you,
and . . ." Roux trailed off.

"Someone let them in," Jason said. "The back door's wide open, no
guards, and there are vampires *everywhere*."

"How many?" Ludovic asked.

"I have no idea. Just . . . a lot."

"But they didn't try to hurt us," Roux chimed in. "They *saw* us, but
it was like they didn't care that we were there."

A chill rushed over me. "Is this about me? Is Etienne sending them
to finish the job?"

"That's *not* going to happen," Roux said fiercely, clutching my
hand.

"But people are getting hurt. We all heard the screams so—"
Realization slammed into me like a freight train, and I swayed on the

spot. Ludovic caught my elbow. "Oh my god," I whispered. "Etienne told me that a revolution was coming, and what does a revolution do? It gets rid of the leaders."

Ludovic's eyes widened. "The Council," he said.

I ran for the door before he could stop me. At the back of my mind a voice screamed at me to stop, wait, because the last time I'd done this I'd got myself killed, but I couldn't hide in the library while Etienne went after the Council, especially not when most of them didn't seem to realize he was the bad guy.

Ludovic caught me before I reached the end of the hallway, and clapped a hand over my mouth. I wasn't stupid enough to fight him. "Just wait," he said.

A scuffle sounded from somewhere around the corner, the thud of a body hitting a wall or a floor, a strangled cry, and an awful wet noise that sounded like someone smashing a melon with a hammer.

Roux whimpered and clutched Jason's arm.

Despite Ludovic's promise to keep me safe, he couldn't ignore that something bad was happening around that corner. He took his hand from my mouth, the hard look in his eyes warning me to keep quiet. Then he crept down the hall, keeping close to the wall; I copied him, Roux and Jason close behind. Newly turned vampires couldn't compete with older ones when it came to strength, so none of them could take Ludovic one-on-one, but they could probably overpower him with sheer numbers. I guessed Ludovic hadn't survived a war by being reckless.

He looked around the corner. His whole body tensed, and he swore under his breath; I peeked around him because I had to. I was too tangled up in this to be shielded now.

Ysanne stood halfway down the hall, her pencil skirt and silk blouse a patchwork of blood and gore. Several bodies were strewn at her feet, and five snarling vampires surrounded her, trying to box her in so they could land a blow. Charles lay close by, his eyes fixed sightlessly on the ceiling, his chest looking like a small bomb had gone off behind his ribs. Just outside the fray, Dexter leaned against the wall, one hand pressed against his side. Blood seeped through his fingers, and his face was gray.

A black-uniformed guard rushed toward them from the vestibule, brandishing the silver-coated knife that all members of Belle Morte security carried, and my heart lifted, because the guard would reach Ysanne before we could.

He did.

Then he plunged the knife between her ribs.

Ysanne snarled and staggered, her eyes flashing with pain, and the guard pulled the knife free, preparing to stab her again.

Ludovic got there first.

He streaked down the hall like lightning and grabbed the guard by the throat. The guard slashed with the knife but Ludovic easily dodged, and the blade sailed harmlessly by his face.

Ludovic slammed the guard's head against the wall and he dropped like a stone. Two of the vampires turned on Ludovic; one of them aimed a punch and Ludovic grabbed the man's arm and snapped it like a dry twig. The vampire screamed and fell to his knees.

I was as strong as those vampires now. I should help Ludovic. But having vampire strength didn't mean I knew how to use it—I'd never thrown a punch in my life, and I was terrified to leave Roux and Jason.

While I dithered, two of the vampires shoved Ysanne hard against the wall, trying to pin her down, and she should have handled them easily, but her clothes were soaked with blood from her wound—the silver blade would have done far more damage than a regular one.

I had to help her.

But Dexter got there first.

With a roar, he launched himself at the nearest vampire and tackled him to the floor in a sprawl of limbs. Light flashed off the silver blade of his knife as he plunged it into the vampire's chest.

Ludovic grabbed the second vampire and broke her neck with a loud crack. It wouldn't kill her, but it took her out of the fight.

The three remaining vampires hesitated, torn between Ysanne and Ludovic, and Ludovic moved before they could decide. One devastating punch sent a man to the floor, his jaw horribly dislocated. Another punch sent a woman reeling into Ysanne. Ysanne promptly stabbed the woman with the knife she'd picked up from the floor.

The final vampire was smart enough to run, and Ludovic didn't give chase. He turned to Ysanne and gripped her elbow with one hand, supporting her as she leaned against the wall, her eyes bright and flashing with pain.

Dexter gave a hoarse gasp and slumped to the floor beside the vampire he'd killed.

"Dexter?" I ran to him.

Blood steadily pulsed from a wound on the left of his stomach; his T-shirt was soaked through. His eyes were wide and unfocused and his breath rattled in his lungs.

"Oh god, hold on." I pressed both palms against his wound but he shook his head.

"Run. Save yourselves," he gasped.

"I'm not leaving you."

Dexter grasped my hand with blood-slicked fingers. "It's okay."

"No, it's not."

I realized with a jolt of horror that I could hear the frenzied flutter of his heartbeat in his chest. It was weak, irregular, and I *knew* that he was dying. My eyes burned.

"Please," I whispered.

He tried to shake his head, but even that movement made his face scrunch with pain. "My ticket's punched."

With a shaking hand he pulled the little gold locket from beneath his T-shirt. Only minutes had passed since he'd shown it to me—how was that possible? It felt like days. Dexter slid the locket over his head and pressed it into my hand. His fingers left bloody imprints on my skin.

"Give this to my daughter," he whispered.

"I promise." I slipped the necklace into my pocket; it didn't feel right to wear it.

Dexter managed to smile, and then the light faded from his eyes, the glassiness of death stealing over them. I actually heard his heart stop, and I let out a wretched cry, but there was no time to grieve now. Belle Morte was crawling with enemies, and the most precious thing in my world was still chained and helpless down in the cells.

"Edmond," I whispered.

CHAPTER ELEVEN

Renie

Ysanne batted Ludovic's hand away. Her other hand was pressed tightly against her ribs.

"It's a scratch," she said, but the pain in her voice and the blood spilling between her fingers told a different story.

Ludovic looked up and down the hallway, checking for more attackers. We could hear people shouting and the occasional crash but there were no more screams, and I had no idea how to interpret that, nor did I care at that moment. If Etienne wanted to take Edmond out, now was the perfect time, when Edmond couldn't fight back. I had to get to him first.

"Have you got the key to the cells?" I asked Ysanne.

Ysanne reached into a pocket in her skirt that I hadn't even known was there and pulled out a tiny key with bloodied fingers.

I reached out to take it but she pulled it back.

"We can't go through the dining hall. There are too many of them," she said.

"I have to get to Edmond."

Ysanne shook her head. It was the first time that I'd seen her sleek blond hair look disheveled, and that was almost as wrong as seeing her covered in blood. Ysanne was always picture-perfect, no matter what.

"There's another way," she said. "Follow me."

She strode past me, her high heels stabbing into the carpet, and if it wasn't for all the blood, I'd never have known anything was wrong. But how long would that last?

Ysanne had lived for hundreds and hundreds of years, but no vampire was invulnerable to silver.

She led us back the way we'd come, but before we reached the corner that turned off toward the library, she veered right, into a short stretch of hall that led between two feeding rooms.

Directly ahead of us was the meditation room, the door left open to show a glimpse of white walls and a white floor, with pastel-colored mats rolled and stacked in one corner.

Ysanne held up a hand and we all stopped, pressed flat against the wall. Two vampires I didn't recognize ran past, and farther down the hall I heard voices.

"Did you find her?" someone said.

"Not yet. She's here somewhere. Keep looking," said another voice.

I glanced at Ysanne. Were they talking about me or her?

Ysanne kept her hand raised until the voices moved away from us, then she made a beckoning gesture. We hurried into the meditation room, and Ludovic closed the door behind us. Ysanne led us across the room, blood dripping from her wound, creating a macabre Pollock painting on the white floor. Anyone who opened the door would know we'd been here. At the back of the meditation room, a door led into a small feeding room, with mint walls and a carpet of palest gray, furnished only with a chaise longue and a large painting of a woman in Elizabethan dress on the farthest wall. I'd never been in here before. There was still so much of Belle Morte I didn't know, and it made the thought of living here permanently seem even stranger.

Since making our escape, Ysanne had carried herself as if she wasn't even injured, but now she braced herself on the chaise longue, leaving a bloody handprint on the ivory velvet, and a soft sound of pain hissed between her teeth.

I'd seen Ysanne angry, seen her torn, even seen her grieving, but I'd never thought I'd see her so vulnerable. She looked terribly young, like all her power and agelessness was bleeding out of the wound between her ribs.

"I will kill Etienne for this," she said.

"The rest of the Council?" Ludovic asked.

Ysanne's face hardened. "Jemima and Henry died first. Caoimhe broke one of the windows in the dining hall and escaped. I don't know what happened to her after that."

I felt a stab of regret for Jemima, who'd always struck me as the nicest member of the Council, and then Dexter filled my head, and I slipped a hand into my pocket, curling my fingers around the hard shape of the locket. No matter what, I'd find Nikki Flynn and tell her that her dad had died a hero.

"What are we doing in here?" Roux asked, looking around the room.

It was only then that I realized there were no doors other than the one that had led us here from the meditation room. I looked at Ysanne.

She leaned on the chaise longue a moment longer, her fingers digging into the padded upholstery, then she straightened and walked across the room to the painting on the wall.

"Ludovic," she said, beckoning.

He went to her, and she wiped one bloody hand clean on his shirt. Ludovic frowned but didn't say anything. Ysanne ran her hand along the bottom of the frame, then paused and pressed on something with her thumbnail. A small section of the frame swung down on a hinge, revealing a tiny keypad. Ysanne tapped in some numbers, and with the faintest click, the painting swung away from the wall, revealing a dark passageway.

"No way!" Roux exclaimed.

Silently, I echoed the sentiment. I'd dismissed the myth of Belle Morte's secret passageways, but they were, unbelievably, real.

Ysanne clipped the section of wooden frame back into place, hiding the keypad. "Let's go," she said.

We followed her into the passageway. Once we were all in, Ysanne pressed a small button on the wall and the painting swung back into place with another click, sealing us in total darkness. I could still see—one of the perks of being a vampire—but Roux put her hand on my shoulder so she didn't trip. Jason did the same to her.

"Will this take us to the cells?" I asked.

"Not directly. It leads to another feeding room at the back of the house, and from there, we can get to the cells," Ysanne replied.

"Who else knows about this?" Ludovic asked, and his tone of voice led me to understand that he hadn't known.

"Just Isabeau and Dexter."

"Not even Edmond?" I said. She'd trusted him with the truth about June, so I was surprised she hadn't done the same with this secret.

"No."

"How come Dexter got to know?" Jason asked.

Ysanne made a noise that could have been pain or irritation. "Because someone had to teach me how to use the keypads."

She probably wouldn't have admitted that if she hadn't been injured.

We came to the end of the passage, and Ysanne pressed a button on her left, opening up a section of wall that led into another feeding room. I didn't recognize this one, either, and I felt a quick stab of panic when I realized that I had no idea where in Belle Morte we were, or how far we were from Edmond.

"There's another passage in here?" Roux asked, scanning the walls.

"Not in here. Next door," Ysanne said.

We'd emerged from behind another huge painting, and as Ysanne pushed it back into place, she paused, one hand on the frame, the other pressed against her ribs, a muscle twitching in her jaw, like she was clenching her teeth.

Ludovic moved closer to her and murmured something in French.

Ysanne shook her head. He tried to take her elbow, and she knocked his hand away.

"We need to keep moving," she said.

She left another trail of blood droplets behind her as she strode across the floor and opened the door that led into one of Belle Morte's many hallways. The coast must have been clear, for she gave us a small nod.

One by one, we slipped out of the feeding room and into the one next door, which looked much the same as the first, only this time instead of a painting on the wall we were faced with a bookcase stacked with leather-bound titles. Ysanne pulled a couple of books from the middle shelf, revealing another tiny keypad. She tapped in the code and the bookcase swung open to reveal another black passageway.

Roux caught my eye, and if the situation had been less dire, I think we'd have laughed. All the Scooby-Doo jokes we'd made, and this kind of thing was straight out of the old cartoon. But there was no intrepid team of plucky young heroes and their dog to unravel this mess—only a battered group of friends fighting to escape the over-run mansion they'd formerly called home before anyone else died.

As we made our way through the passageway my nerves felt stretched to breaking point. What if Etienne beat us to the cells? Chained in silver, Edmond couldn't protect himself, and the thought of him so vulnerable made my stomach lurch. I had to believe he was still safe in there, that Etienne's priority would be to take out immediate threats.

The floor dropped into a series of narrow steps. We must be almost there, and my heart jumped into my throat.

I'm coming, Edmond.

The passage came to an end, and as Ysanne opened up another section of wall, I pushed past her and into the cells. Edmond was crouched by the wall, his fangs out and his eyes blazing red.

His arms were a mess of bloody, ravaged flesh where he must have tried and failed to break free.

"*Dieu merci,*" he whispered when he saw me.

"There's no time to explain properly, but we have to get out of here," I said.

Ysanne produced the key from her blood-drenched pocket and unlocked Edmond's cuffs. The metal had burned so deeply into his skin that I had to pry them away, bits of his skin and flesh clinging to the bracelets. Every time he hissed with pain I winced and bit my lip. I barely felt the pain in my own fingertips where the silver scorched them.

Slinging his arm around my shoulders, I tried to get him to stand, but he sagged against me with a stifled moan. Ludovic quickly took his other arm.

"He needs blood," Jason said.

I'd have offered up my own in a heartbeat—if I'd still had a heart-beat—but my vampire blood was no good to him.

Jason nudged me aside. "Let me." He peeled his collar down, exposing his neck.

"You should drink too," said Roux to Ysanne.

"I'm fine," Ysanne said.

"It wasn't a suggestion."

"You've already fed Renie today, and you gave more than a donor usually would," said Ludovic. "You can't give any more."

"That's my choice—"

"If you collapse from blood loss one of us will have to carry you, and that will only slow us down more," he said.

Roux held his gaze for a moment then looked away. "Fine."

I supported Edmond while he leaned in and sank his fangs into Jason's throat. To fully heal, he needed more than Jason could give, but anything was better than nothing. Ludovic shifted Edmond's full weight to me, then crossed the room to the door—to stand guard, I guessed.

He was halfway there when the door flew open.

Six vampires marched into the cells; they stopped dead when they saw us.

My stomach plunged. Etienne *had* sent his minions after Edmond, and if we'd been even a minute later, it could have been too late.

Ysanne raised her chin, her eyes burning red like fire. An animal-like growl trickled out of her throat, and Edmond slipped an arm around my waist, pulling me back.

The Lady of Belle Morte launched herself at the vampires who'd invaded her home. Even with her injury, she smashed through our would-be attackers like a hurricane, unleashing the full power of the beast that lived inside her, practically rabid in her fury. Blood sprayed across the floor and up the walls, drenching Ysanne like rain.

Ludovic moved quickly to guard Ysanne's back, and when one of the vampires took a swing at him, Ludovic lifted the man off his feet and crushed his throat.

It was all fast, and so strangely *quiet*. Aside from the wet sound of blood and thicker things spilling across the floor, or the horrible crunch of breaking bones, none of the new vampires had a chance to scream.

Somehow, seeing Ysanne like this was more terrifying than June in full bloodlust. June had barely looked human, a monster wearing a girl's skin, but Ysanne still looked like a woman—one painted with blood. The juxtaposition of human and monster chilled me.

"What do we do now?" Roux asked. She stared up at the ceiling, probably to avoid seeing the carnage.

I looked at our little group. Ysanne had made short work of the new vampires, but now her face was drawn tight with pain, and when Ludovic offered her his arm, she leaned on him without complaint. I was still supporting Edmond. Roux and Jason were human, which made them incredibly vulnerable, and I knew as much about fight-ing as I did about rocket science. That left Ludovic, and he couldn't take on all of Belle Morte's enemies single-handedly, especially not when he was keeping Ysanne on her feet.

"We have to leave Belle Morte," I said.

"No," said Ysanne at once.

"Etienne's already assassinated most of the Council, and now he's after you, and probably me too."

Edmond's head whipped to me. "The Council's dead?"

"Later," I said. "Ysanne, we can't stay here. We're completely out-numbered, and we still don't know what we're dealing with. We don't know how many vampires Etienne has brought. We don't know what he wants. We don't know who we can trust because obviously some of your security guards are working for him."

Ysanne straightened as much as she could while still leaning on Ludovic. "I will not abandon my house."

"Do you have a better suggestion?" I snapped.

"Etienne can't just take over, though. Aside from you guys, there are fifteen other vampires in Belle Morte, and they won't let him do this, right?" Roux said, still staring at the ceiling.

"Unless they're on his side too. Someone in Belle Morte has helped him. He can't have done all this by himself," I said.

"Can we get out of here while we're deciding?" Jason said. "Someone could come looking for—" He glanced at the bodies scat-tered on the floor and swallowed hard.

Ysanne moved away from Ludovic and approached the wall that hid the entrance to the secret passageway. I didn't see where the key-pad to open it was; at that moment, Edmond made a muffled noise of pain and I glanced up at him, my heart twisting in my chest. I'd seen him badly hurt before—the bloody mess of his back after his whipping was something I'd never forget. But this was different. Then, I'd lain in bed with him, and we'd both known that the whipping was over and nothing else would happen. Now, I was responsible for keeping him on his feet, and we had no idea what we'd be hit with next.

The section of wall swung open, and Ludovic took Ysanne's arm again, letting her lean on him as they went into the passage.

No one spoke as we made our way back to the feeding room, but I was keenly aware that we were moving a lot slower than before. Ysanne had surged to life again while she'd been fighting the vampires in the cells, and now she was flagging. Edmond's blood soaked into my clothes as he leaned on me.

"Is there another passage that will get us out of the house?" Roux asked, once the bookshelves had swung back into place behind us.

"There are several passages all over Belle Morte, but none that lead out of the mansion," Ysanne said.

"Okay, then we have two options. We're about halfway between the front door and the nearest back exit. We have to go out through one of them."

I hadn't even realized there was more than one back exit.

"Perhaps you didn't hear me the first time," said Ysanne coolly. "I'm not abandoning my house."

"No one's asking you to *abandon* it," said Roux. "But Etienne wants you and Renie dead, so the very least we need to do is get you both out of Belle Morte. We can plan our next move once you're safe."

"She's right," Edmond said. "We can't stay here."

Ysanne pressed her lips together until they were a bloodless line. "This is my house," she said, very quietly.

"I know. But we have no choice."

"So which exit are we aiming for?" Roux asked.

"The front door would get us closer to the street, whereas the back door will only take us to the grounds, and they're probably crawling with Etienne's vampires," I said.

"Unlikely, at this time of day," Jason pointed out.

"Going out of the front doors means going through the gates, and they were blocked by people earlier. We don't know if they're involved with this either," said Ludovic.

I hadn't thought of that. I'd assumed the possible protestors were friends or family of the dead, but maybe Ludovic was right and they were just another cog in Etienne's machine. But why hadn't he turned them like he had all the new vampires?

"We'll take the back exit," Ysanne said. "It's closest to the garage, where we keep vampire-proofed vehicles. We can use those to get away."

Belle Morte had a garage? It must be on the other side of the grounds, where I hadn't had time to explore yet.

"Are the keys for all the vehicles in the garage?" Roux asked.

Ysanne nodded.

"Then let's go," I said.

The blood that Edmond had taken from Jason wasn't nearly enough, and I didn't know how much longer he and Ysanne could stay on their feet.

We crept out of the room and down the hallway. No one had screamed since the Council's assassination, but I could hear running feet coming from what sounded like every part of the mansion, and so much frantic activity was *wrong* inside Belle Morte. At the end of the hallway, we turned left. Farther up, a right and then another left would take us to the back exit that I knew. We were so close—

"Stop. Go back," said Ludovic urgently.

Too late, I realized the sound of running feet had grown closer. Vampires surged around the corner, more than I could count—we had no hope of getting through them and reaching the exit.

We had to retreat. If we could get back the way we'd come, maybe we could barricade ourselves in that feeding room, take the secret passageway back to the cells, and try to escape from there.

More vampires appeared behind us, spilling from the short hallway that led to the meditation room. One of them grabbed Roux's arm, trying to pull her in, and she screamed.

Ludovic snapped the vampire's arm with a single jerk of his hand,

and he let Roux go, but by then both Ludovic and Roux had moved past the hall that led back where we needed to go, and were in the long stretch of hallway that led to the vestibule and the front door.

The enemy vampires were thinner there, and as they tried to mob Ludovic, he lashed back with the full force of an older, stronger vampire. Behind us, Etienne's minions pushed forward, and panic felt like a firework in my chest because we were outnumbered and I didn't know what to do. Then the panic sharpened to cold determination: I'd fought to protect Belle Morte before; I could do it again.

I lunged forward and seized a vampire who was trying to get her arm around Ludovic's neck. When she spun to face me, a snarl on her lips, I hit her, a solid punch straight to the jaw that sent her reeling back.

Another vampire caught my hair and yanked me back, and I swung into the movement, my fist already raised for another punch. This blow only grazed his jaw, but with my new vampire strength, even that was enough to make my attacker stumble and let go of my hair.

Edmond surged to life. He grabbed the nearest vampires and smashed their heads together so hard that I heard their skulls break. He kicked another vampire in the chest, sending him flying back and knocking over the people standing behind him, then he delivered another kick to the knee of a vampire stupid enough to get close to him. The man's leg wrenched sideways with a horrible popping sound, and he screamed.

"Go," Edmond said, pushing me.

Ludovic had cleared the hallway ahead—any vampires not dead at his hands had fled.

But we couldn't keep this up for long. Edmond's face was drawn tight with pain and his jaw was clenched, Ysanne's wound was still bleeding, and Roux and Jason didn't have vampire strength. We had to get *out* of here.

We fled down the hall, Etienne's vampires following at a cautious distance, and for a soaring moment I thought we'd make it.

As we reached the vestibule, I heard a snarl overhead, then something leaped down the stairs and landed in a crouch in front of us.

"June," I whispered.

The thing that had been my sister stared back at me, her eyes bright red, her fangs jutting like daggers, looking just as she had right before she'd killed me. Fresh blood soaked her tattered clothes.

Edmond pushed me behind him, but June was no longer looking at us. Her red eyes were fixed on Ysanne.

I glanced over my shoulder. Etienne's minions had caught up, fanning out behind us and blocking off the hallway. More vampires emerged from the parlors on the left and right of the vestibule, cutting off our access to the front door and the hallway on the other side of the staircase.

"Oh, this is bad," Roux whispered.

I scanned the faces surrounding us. Most of them were strangers, but I recognized Míriam among them, her forehead creased with confusion.

"What the hell is going on?" she demanded.

"Why isn't it attacking?" said another voice, and I craned my neck to see Phillip, the vampire who'd whipped Edmond on Ysanne's orders.

Dread trickled down my spine.

Why wasn't June *doing* anything?

"I told you." The voice I hated most rang through the vestibule, and the vampires parted to let Etienne through. Edmond pushed me farther behind him, trying to shield me from even seeing the man who'd murdered my sister.

"Ysanne has been experimenting on the rabid and she's trained it to obey her." Etienne spread his arms, indicating his assembled minions. "It's why she turned all these people too. Imagine the power she'd have if she could create rabids, and control them too. No one would dare stand against her."

I waited for Ysanne to deny it but she didn't, and when I looked back, she was leaning on Ludovic again, her face pale. Blood continued to leak between her fingers, pressed against her wound.

"She turned June Mayfield and lied about it to everyone. When I found out what she was doing, she framed me for June's murder. But I didn't do it. I tried to warn the Council, and Ysanne assassinated them for it," Etienne said.

A few gasps went up, probably from the Belle Morte vampires mingled with Etienne's minions.

"You don't actually believe this, do you?" I said, looking at the faces I could see—Míriam, Phillip, Gideon, Deepika, Benjamin. "Etienne turned all these vampires and unleashed them on Belle Morte. People *died*."

"That's not true," said one of the new vampires, a young woman whose blond hair was sticky with drying blood. "Ysanne turned us so she could study us and see if she could control us. She forced us to attack Belle Morte three days ago, to take out anyone who was getting too close to the truth. Etienne found us after we escaped the house. He helped us."

"They *killed* the Council," I shouted.

Ysanne's vampires weren't listening to Etienne's bullshit . . . were they?

"That wasn't us." The blond vampire pointed at June. "Ysanne and the rabid killed the Council. We all saw it."

"Ysanne has always pulled the strings of our world," Etienne said. "She's the one who dragged us out of the shadows, and she's controlled us ever since. But she can't be allowed to get away with this."

Míriam moved forward, and June swung to her, softly growling. Míriam froze.

I had no idea how old Míriam was, but clearly she had no wish to take on a rabid.

June prowled forward, her body hunched over, her hands like claws, and fear flickered in Míriam's brown eyes. But she didn't back down. June sniffed the air and cocked her head to one side, and she was so like a wild animal that it made me feel sick. How had I ever thought there could be anything left of my sweet sister in this monster?

June suddenly lunged, her hand swinging at Míriam's face, and Míriam recoiled, but she wasn't fast enough, and the ragged tips of June's nails gouged her cheek. Blood welled up, ruby red against the warm brown of Míriam's skin.

"No," Ysanne cried, and pulled away from Ludovic.

June stopped dead.

My heart turned to ice.

June wasn't obeying Ysanne, I *knew* that, but to everyone watching, it looked like she was.

Míriam touched her bleeding cheek. "Ysanne?" she said, and there was doubt in her voice.

Close by, Gideon's eyes were narrowed.

"Your lover and accomplice has already been arrested. Now it's time for you to hand yourself over. All of you," said Etienne, gazing at us. His voice was soft, his forehead wrinkled with false compassion. "You'll be treated fairly, I promise."

A couple of Etienne's minions edged forward, but a savage snarl from June made them shrink back again.

My mind raced. Etienne wanted Ysanne and me dead, and probably the others too. If we let him arrest us, it would be the last thing we ever did. But his minions were blocking off every exit, except . . .

The staircase.

I grabbed Edmond's hand and squeezed, and when he looked at me, I flicked my gaze at the staircase. It was a split-second look, hopefully too fast for anyone else to see, and I wasn't sure that

Edmond would understand. He dipped his head in the tiniest nod. I looked behind me, to where Ysanne was again leaning on Ludovic, and Jason and Roux huddled together, their faces pale.

"No matter what happens, stay with me," I said.

Roux gave a shaky nod.

I gave Edmond's hand another squeeze.

Then we ran.

I tore up the stairs, still holding tightly to Edmond's hand, my friends hot on my heels. Etienne hadn't expected us to go up, and I hoped like hell that there were hidden passageways up here too; otherwise we were running toward a dead end.

As we reached the top, Edmond pulled me in the direction of the north wing. I caught a quick glimpse of donors gathered farther down the hallway, having emerged from the south wing to see what was going on. Melissa was among them, and for a brief moment, her eyes locked with mine.

We passed three doors in the north wing before Edmond kicked one open and pulled me inside. Roux and Jason were next in, with Ludovic and Ysanne bringing up the rear—and how in the *hell* was she still wearing high heels?

Ludovic strode across the room, grabbed the four-poster bed with both hands, and dragged it in front of the door as if it weighed nothing.

"That will buy us seconds at the most," he said.

"Is there a passageway in here?" Jason asked, scanning the walls.

There couldn't be, I realized. Edmond hadn't known the passageways existed, so he definitely didn't know which rooms they were in, and it was too much to hope that he'd just happened to pick the right one.

But he hadn't brought us here for no reason. I trusted him.

So did Ludovic. "What's the plan?" he said, looking at Edmond rather than Ysanne.

Edmond walked to the windows, sealed from the outside by UV-blocking shades. "We jump," he said.

"Really?" There was a definite note of panic in Jason's voice.

"Vampires can jump from higher than this and walk away," Edmond said.

"Yeah, but Roux and I aren't vampires!"

"And you and Ysanne are injured," I said, touching Edmond's arm.

"We can handle it," said Ysanne curtly.

The door rattled, and I startled.

"Time to go," Edmond said.

"We'll have to carry the humans," said Ludovic, and swept Roux into his arms. She gave a startled squeak.

"Wait, how are we—" I couldn't finish the sentence before Edmond backed up, broke into a short run, then launched himself at the window, his arms crossed over his face to protect it. Glass shattered and the shades burst apart, and I couldn't hold back a sharp cry because even though I knew Edmond could survive the jump, there was something truly horrible about watching the man I loved throw himself out a window.

"Go," Ludovic ordered me.

Wood scraped on wood as the vampires outside the room pushed on the door, and the bed slid across the bare floorboards.

I slung Jason over my shoulder, closed my eyes, and jumped.

Wind rushed around me, coupled with a fleeting rush of very human fear, then I hit the ground in a crouch. Shock waves reverberated up my legs, and my teeth clacked together.

Ludovic landed neatly beside me, Roux's face buried in his shoulder, and Ysanne followed half a second later, her high heels clutched in one hand. She swayed as she landed, her jaw clenched tight, fresh blood splattering the grass, then put her shoes back on as if she hadn't just jumped out a window.

I set Jason down. Almost immediately, he gave a yell of warning, and I spun around to find a man charging at me. His heartbeat thundered with adrenaline—he was human. He was also about to attack me, and was a lot bigger than me, and in the panic of the moment, I forgot about my new strength.

I slapped him.

It was an open-handed slap, nothing that should have caused a guy of his size any damage. But I was a vampire now, and his jaw shattered beneath my palm. He fell to the ground with a choked scream, and my stomach lurched.

But there was no time to wallow in the horror of what I'd just done, because he wasn't the only one charging at us.

The gates that sealed Belle Morte off from the world hung open now, and it was so *wrong* to see that; those gates usually only opened to admit or release donors or guests, not a crowd of complete strangers. But they'd spilled into the grounds just as Etienne's minions had spilled into Belle Morte.

"Come on, the garage is this way," Jason cried.

Two more men tried to corner us but Edmond got to them before I could, and punched them out cold faster than I could blink.

"Move," he ordered.

The rumble of an engine sounded and I tensed, bracing for whatever else Etienne had up his sleeve. A black van veered around the corner, smashing over the regimented flower beds and taking a chunk off the corner of an ornamental stone bench. A man sat behind the wheel—I vaguely recognized him as a Belle Morte guard.

"Get in," he yelled, leaning out of the window.

I hesitated.

A guard had stabbed Ysanne—could we trust this guy?

But we were completely outnumbered, and my skin was starting to redden from the winter sun. I needed to get under cover before I burst into flames.

"We can trust him," Ysanne said, as if she could read my mind.

I wrenched open the doors at the back of the van and threw myself inside, where I huddled in the farthest corner, away from the sun. Roux and Jason clambered in behind me, then Ysanne, Edmond, and Ludovic. Two men grabbed the back of Ysanne's blouse and tried to pull her back out, and Ludovic kicked one of them in the face, smashing the guy's nose and spraying his teeth across the lawn. The other guy was smart enough to let Ysanne go. Ludovic slammed the doors shut, sealing us in darkness.

The van jolted as it hit something, and I heard voices yelling, but they faded away as we drove through the gates and away from Belle Morte.

Padded benches were on either side of the van's interior, and Ysanne sat opposite me, her hands clenched in her lap. She looked crumpled and exhausted and very, very young. So many people had lost something thanks to Etienne, but Ysanne had lost everything, and maybe it was a trick of the shadows, or maybe exhaustion was making me see things, but I thought I saw the reddish shimmer of tears in her eyes.

CHAPTER TWELVE

Edmond

He couldn't remember the last time he'd felt exhaustion like this. It wasn't just the pain of his injuries—it was the realization that everything vampires had built over the last ten years was in danger of crashing down. Until Ysanne had brought them out of the shadows, most vampires had lived solitary, lonely lives, unable to stay too long in one place before the people around them noticed that they never aged or ate human food or couldn't be out in the sun for more than a short period of time. Revealing themselves to the world had changed that, and for the first time in centuries, many vampires had found themselves with a proper home—Edmond among them.

Now a dark shadow had fallen over them. They'd been safe in their houses. Their days of running had finally been over. Why had Etienne taken that away?

Edmond had often thought that he shouldn't let the decadence of Belle Morte go to his head—he'd gone down that road before, hundreds of years ago, and it had cost two people their lives—but now he realized that he'd grown used to living in luxury, to having fresh blood at his beck and call. He'd grown soft at Belle Morte, and he couldn't be soft now—not only for his own sake, but because, for the first time in a long time, he had someone to protect.

Renie slumped on the bench beside him, her head on his shoulder, and Edmond wanted to put his arm around her but his ravaged wrists hurt too much. He needed blood.

"What do we do now?" Roux asked in a small voice. She sat close to the van doors, tucked under Jason's arm. The piercing in her nose looked like a drop of blood, and Edmond tried not to look at it.

"I had a safe house planned for an emergency such as this, but now I'm afraid it's been compromised," Ysanne said.

"Yeah, we can't risk that," Roux agreed.

Ysanne hadn't actually answered the question, and from the way Renie, Roux, and Jason looked at her, Edmond suspected they'd noticed too. They were used to Ysanne being in charge, ruling her house with an iron fist, and it must be hard for them to grasp that even she didn't know what to do or say in this situation.

Edmond met her eyes across the span of floor between them, and she stared bleakly back.

"Who's the guy driving the van?" Jason asked. His voice was steady, but the way he held Roux made Edmond think it was as much for his comfort as Roux's.

"Andrew," Edmond answered, when Ysanne stayed silent.

"Are you sure we can trust him?"

Edmond looked at Ysanne again. He couldn't answer that for her.

"Yes," said Ysanne at last.

She touched her injured side, as if she still couldn't believe one of her own guards had stabbed her. Edmond was struggling with it himself. Anyone who applied to work at a Vampire House was very carefully vetted, and many of them had worked there since Belle Morte had been built. They should've been loyal.

Edmond leaned his head on Renie's and closed his eyes. "What are we going to do?" she whispered, and he honestly didn't know how to answer.

Something crashed onto the van roof.

Everyone looked up, and Roux squeaked, clutching Jason's arm.

"I think someone wants to join us," Ludovic said. He was already on his feet, red flickering in his eyes, and Edmond's mind flashed back more than a century to when he and Ludovic had fought side by side in the blood-soaked, shell-blasted trenches. They'd kept each other alive during that terrible time, and despite the fact that Edmond was exhausted to his bones, despite the pain in his wrists that made it hard to think, he stood up, too, preparing to face this new threat.

His friends needed him.

Renie needed him.

Ysanne rapped the partition that separated the back of the van from the cab. "Stop," she commanded.

Andrew obediently braked, and movement shifted across the roof. It had to be a vampire—a human would have fallen when the van stopped.

Ysanne's eyes burned fiery red and her fangs were fully extended. She stalked across the floor and kicked open the doors with a stilet-toed foot.

Renie started to get up but Edmond held out a hand. "You need to stay here," he said.

She started to protest, and Edmond silenced her with a kiss. "It's not safe," he said. "Stay with Jason and Roux."

He climbed out of the van and looked up.

Caoimhe crouched on the roof, like a hunting cat, the winter sun casting a pale halo around her. She straightened up and smiled when she saw him, but Edmond couldn't smile back.

A long time ago, he and Caoimhe had been lovers, and he considered her a trusted friend, but Ysanne had said that Caoimhe had escaped the dining hall when Etienne's vampires massacred the Council. It pained Edmond to suspect Caoimhe, but he had to consider the possibility that she'd escaped because she'd known the attack was coming.

He glanced at Ysanne. There was no welcome in her blazing eyes.

Caoimhe leaped down from the van, landing neatly on both feet.

Ysanne edged back, not because she was afraid, Edmond knew, but because a little distance made it harder for the pair of them to rip each other's throats out.

"Ysanne?" Caoimhe cocked her head to one side, looking genuinely puzzled.

"Stay where you are," Ysanne warned.

Caoimhe took a step forward. "But—"

"I said *stay*," Ysanne snarled.

Slowly, Caoimhe lifted both hands. "I'm not your enemy, you know that."

"Do I?" Ysanne's words were pure ice.

Caoimhe's eyes searched Edmond's face. He stared neutrally back. Trusting the wrong person had cost Renie her life. He wouldn't let anything like that happen again.

"How did you get out of Belle Morte?" Ludovic asked.

"I escaped, the same as you." Her forehead scrunched up in a frown. "Why are you all looking at me like this?"

"You and I were the only Council members who managed to escape. Henry, Jemima, and Charles are dead. Etienne and his newly turned vampires have seized control of Belle Morte, and I cannot believe he accomplished this without help," Ysanne said.

"Are you accusing me of helping him?" Caoimhe asked.

"I'm questioning the fact that you escaped so quickly and without injury."

"I'm very old and very strong, but I've lived long enough to recognize a losing battle when I see it. We were completely outnumbered, and as fond as I am of Belle Morte, I had no wish to die there. I fled to save myself and I feel no shame in that," said Caoimhe hotly.

"How did you know we were in the van?" Ludovic asked.

"I didn't. But I know what Belle Morte vehicles look like, and when I spotted this one, I guessed it had escaped the mansion. I guessed right, didn't I?"

Ysanne's frigid expression didn't waver.

Caoimhe turned to Edmond, her blue eyes beseeching. "You know I'd never jeopardize our way of life. I don't know who helped Etienne, but it wasn't me."

Edmond searched her face. He probably knew her better than anyone else here; before today he'd have laughed at the thought of her betraying them. But he'd never have thought Etienne was capable of this either.

"If I was working with Etienne, I'd have come with backup, and I'd have killed you all as soon as you'd stopped the van," said Caoimhe, irritation creeping into her voice.

"Etienne's minions wouldn't be much good as backup. They're all new vampires," Renie said from inside the van.

"Eric Wilson wasn't," Caoimhe pointed out. "He shouldn't even have been in Belle Morte when he was killed, so shall we assume that was random, or was he involved with Etienne? If so, we don't know how many more people in Midnight have been compromised. We don't know if the other Houses are compromised too."

Edmond hadn't considered that, and it chilled him. For the first time in a decade there was no one to run most of the Vampire Houses in the UK. Caoimhe could return to her own House in Ireland, but Nox, Lamia, and Midnight were now leaderless—which must have been Etienne's plan all along.

"If Eric was working with Etienne, why is he dead now? The new vampires wouldn't have killed him," Renie observed.

Edmond glanced back at her. Her face was a pale moon haloed with autumn-colored hair in the darkness of the van, and her forehead was wrinkled with worry. He gave her a reassuring smile, which she returned. If Caoimhe was a threat, Edmond would die before he let her get near Renie.

"Rosa or the two Nox vampires who died might have done. We don't know what really happened that night," Caoimhe said.

"What if you're trying to trick us into trusting you so that you can lead us right back into Etienne's hands?" Ludovic asked.

Caoimhe gave him a withering look. "I fought like a demon to get out of Belle Morte, and I have no intention of going back. We're all victims of Etienne's treachery, and we should stick together."

Edmond looked around at their little group. Ysanne's posture was poker straight, trying to hide any weakness, but she couldn't go on much longer without blood. Edmond couldn't either. Jason's donation had taken the edge off but it wasn't enough, especially not after several hours chained with silver and without a single drop of human blood.

Renie wasn't hurt, but new vampires needed blood more regularly than older vampires—sooner rather than later, she'd need to feed too. Roux and Jason couldn't fight vampires, and Ludovic couldn't protect the whole group single-handedly. They could use another ally.

But this wasn't just about strengthening their numbers.

It was about whether or not he could trust an old friend.

Caoimhe had never lied to Edmond or given him any reason to doubt her.

Etienne's betrayal had shaken everyone, but Edmond had no history with Etienne. He did with Caoimhe, and now that he thought about it, *really* thought about it, he couldn't believe that she was involved with this.

"I trust her," Edmond told Ysanne.

Ysanne held his gaze, her jaw rigid, then she nodded. "And I trust you," she said. She pinned Caoimhe with a cold, hard look. "But if I find out that you're lying, I'll snap your neck."

Anger flickered across Caoimhe's face, but when she spoke, her Irish lilt was as calm and measured as ever. "I swear on my House that I speak the truth. I am your friend, Ysanne. I am no friend of traitors and murderers."

"Then we're all in this together." Ysanne gestured to the van. "Shall we?"

Renie shuffled back as Caoimhe and Ysanne climbed into the van, but Ludovic put a hand on Edmond's arm before he followed them.

"Are you sure about this?" he said.

"I have faith in her."

"And if you're wrong?" Ludovic pressed.

Edmond's fangs slid out. "If I'm wrong, then I'll kill her myself."

CHAPTER THIRTEEN

Renie

Wene need to decide where to go," I said, as the van started moving again.

If Caoimhe had found us, Etienne could too. We had no idea how far his reach extended or what resources he had.

"Fiaigh is isolated and fortified; it's probably the safest option," said Caoimhe.

I thought back to the research I'd done before applying for Belle Morte. I couldn't remember seeing pictures of the other houses across the UK and Ireland. Maybe I had, but I hadn't been paying attention—understandable considering that Belle Morte had been my main priority.

"Doesn't this seem suspicious to anyone else?" I couldn't help saying. "She wants to take us to her own house—hello, trap?"

"If I was your enemy, I wouldn't bother taking you all the way to Ireland. I'd gather my forces and kill you now," Caoimhe pointed out.

I wasn't entirely convinced, but Edmond knew her better than I did, and I'd follow his lead. Still, I made sure that I sat between her and my human friends.

The van was quiet as everyone mulled over Caoimhe's offer.

"Is Fiaigh really the safest place we can go?" Jason asked, looking around at the Belle Morte vampires.

"It seems so," said Ysanne, but she didn't sound entirely happy about it. I couldn't tell if it was because she still wasn't convinced by

Caoimhe's claim of innocence or because she didn't want to go to another house while her own was in enemy hands.

If Etienne was after us—and I couldn't believe that he'd let us go—we had to put as much distance between us and him as possible and hunker down somewhere he couldn't easily sneak up on. Whether I liked it or not, Fiaigh fitted the bill.

"I guess we're going to Ireland, then," said Roux. She didn't sound happy about it either.

Suddenly I sat bolt upright, my shoulder knocking Edmond's. "We need to get to a phone," I said.

"Why?" Ludovic asked.

I gestured to Roux and Jason. "We need to call our families."

"Right," Jason said. "Pretty soon the whole world will know that something bad has happened at Belle Morte, and we need to let our families know we're safe."

"That's not what I'm worried about," I said grimly.

Jason frowned, not catching on.

Roux got it, though. "All our personal information is on our donor applications, including our addresses and family members. All those applications are filed away inside Belle Morte, and since vampires don't use computers, all Etienne has to do is go through the house's paper files until he finds ours. Then he'll know how to get to our families."

Jason paled. "You think he'll go after them?"

"Do you want to take the risk?" I said.

"We could pick them up and take them with us to Ireland," Caoimhe suggested.

"Thanks, but there's no way I'm bringing my mum into this. I need to contact her to tell her to get the hell out of the house."

Not to mention, my mum lived in Southampton, which, depending on traffic, was a good thirty minutes' drive from Winchester. Roux and Jason lived in Winchester, but it would take too long to drive to all our homes and warn our families in person.

"I don't suppose Andrew has a phone?" Roux said.

Ysanne shook her head. "Only select staff members are allowed to carry phones."

"You and Ysanne need to feed too," I said to Edmond.

He gave me a tight smile. "I'll be fine."

"You're not fine. You need blood," I insisted.

Gently, he took one of my hands and turned it over. "So do you."

I stared at my fingers, blistered red where I'd removed Edmond's cuffs. I'd barely noticed the pain at the time. I turned my hand over again so I didn't have to see the damage.

"Phone first," I said.

Through the partition, Ysanne told Andrew that we needed to find somewhere with a phone, and I felt the van turn a corner, then another. I had no idea where we were. We drove a little longer, putting more distance between us and Belle Morte, then the van finally came to a stop.

I heard the driver's door slam, and the sound of footsteps walking around the side of the van. Ysanne had said she trusted our driver, but as the doors opened, I found myself tensing. Etienne's betrayal had cut deep.

"Have you found a phone?" Ysanne asked.

Andrew pointed to something that I couldn't see. "Someone in there will have one."

I crept to the open doors and peeked out. Pre–Belle Morte, I'd never been to Winchester, and I knew nothing about the city outside the vampire mansion. Andrew had taken us to a narrow street, where Regency and Elizabethan bow-fronted shops were crammed together on either side, surrounding a small traditional pub almost directly opposite us. Bright sprays of flowers spilled over boxes fixed beneath the second-floor windows, and hung in baskets on either side of the entrance. The name of the pub—The Bishop—was spelled out in large gold letters along a black background that bisected the pub's facade.

"You're sure?" Ysanne said.

"You're in the human world now, and almost every single one of us carries a phone," Jason said. He patted Ysanne's shoulder as he climbed out of the van, and she shot him an icy look that he completely ignored.

"All we have to do is persuade someone to let us use theirs," I added.

Edmond started to get up from the padded bench but I put both hands on his shoulders to stop him. "You can't come," I said.

His dark eyebrows drew together. "Why not?"

"Look at yourself, Edmond. You can't walk in looking like that." I looked at the other vampires. "None of you can. Even if you weren't covered in blood, you're all too famous. Until we know what's really going on at Belle Morte, I think we should try to keep this under wraps." My gaze fastened on Ysanne. "There's a balance to maintain, after all."

Everything Ysanne had done so far, including her treatment of Edmond, had been to preserve the balance that humans and vampires had forged. For a long time I hadn't got that, but now that I'd crossed the line from human to vampire, I was starting to understand.

Vampires were dangerous. You could dress them up in pretty clothes, parade them in front of the cameras, and talk about them like they were rock stars, but they were still predators. The average human simply didn't understand that. For vampires to survive in a world in which humans were the dominant species, they needed to hide the darker, deadlier aspects of their nature. If humans no longer trusted vampires, then the empire that vampires had built to protect themselves could come crashing down.

Assuming it already hadn't.

Ysanne slowly nodded. She was looking at me as if she'd never seen me properly before, or as if I was some sweet but dim animal that had just done something surprising.

"Donors are generally quite well known, too, especially in the city that's home to the UK's most famous Vampire House," Andrew pointed out. "Maybe I should go alone. No one takes notice of what security looks like."

Roux fluffed up her pixie cut with one hand and managed a smile. "No offense, but strangers are more likely to lend their phone to a pretty girl than a random guy."

"Fair point."

Thick banks of cloud had slid across the sun, but I could feel the lethal light itching along my skin like a thousand ants. It was a good thing the pub was so close.

Roux glanced up at the sky, too, and bit her lip. "Maybe you should stay behind, too, Renie. You'll be safer in the van."

I shook my head.

"We could call your mum for you, if you give us the number—"

"She won't listen to some stranger calling and telling her to jump on the first train out of Southampton in case enemy vampires come after her. If she doesn't hear it from me, she'll think it's a prank call."

"Okay, then." Roux whipped off her black silk blazer and held it over my head like a parasol. "We'll get you there and back safely."

I gave Edmond's hand a quick squeeze before heading across the street.

When I walked into the pub, Roux and Jason on either side of me, I was immediately hit with a clash of smells: the tang of beer, the tantalizing whiff of grease drifting from the kitchen, the fainter notes of perfume and cologne underscored by the occasional sourness of body odor. The murmur of voices and the beat of many hearts packed into one room was a loud drumming in my ears, and I paused in the doorway, struggling to steady myself.

Set against the opposite wall, the bar was a thick slab of polished wood intermittently lined with gleaming brass beer taps and leather-topped barstools. Behind it stood a thirtyish woman in a dark-blue shirt.

"I'm going to need to see some ID, kids," she said as we approached.

"We're not here to drink. We just need to use a phone," I said. I could see a cordless one on the bar behind her, tucked next to the till.

"Sorry, not for customer use."

"Please," I said, as pathetically as possible. "We're desperate."

The woman's expression wasn't unfriendly, but she also didn't look like she'd cave. Dressed in Belle Morte's finest, Roux and Jason looked like a couple of rich kids who probably had the latest model of phone.

"Please," I said again. "We're in trouble and we just need to call home. We'll be five minutes. I'm begging you."

Behind me, Roux let out a very convincing sob, and the woman's face softened.

"Okay, but be quick," she said, and handed over the phone.

I let Roux and Jason call their families first, while I wrestled with what I'd say to my mum. Sooner or later I'd have to tell her that June was never coming home, and I might not be able to either, but dumping that on her now would be more than she could handle. The important thing was getting her out of Etienne's reach.

My mind flashed to Nikki Flynn, and I was suddenly very aware of Dexter's locket in my pocket. I wished I could contact her; the poor girl had no idea that her dad was lying dead inside Belle Morte.

Jason handed me the phone and I dialed my home number. Mum never remembered to charge her cell phone.

Just stay calm, I silently told myself. I needed to stress the importance of her leaving without frightening her too much.

But when the phone picked up, it wasn't my mum's voice.

It was Etienne's.

CHAPTER FOURTEEN

Renie

Shock turned my knees to water. "How . . . ?" I couldn't finish the sentence.

This wasn't supposed to happen.

"Never underestimate me, Renie." His voice was poison in my ears.

I forced myself not to grip the phone too tightly or I'd break it. "You bastard," I breathed.

Roux and Jason shot me alarmed looks.

"I know," said Etienne. "Now, Renie, this is the situation. I'm at your house, and it'll be a lot better for your mother if you get here before she does. I have no particular wish to hurt her, but I will if you don't do as I say. And it won't just be her. I know where Roux and Jason live, and I have a few friends willing to visit their families. Do you understand?"

"Yes." I almost choked on the word.

"Are you still in Winchester?"

"Yes."

Roux was making frantic hand gestures, but I couldn't meet her eyes.

"Go to Canon Street," Etienne said.

"I don't know where that is," I whispered, fear and panic making my throat burn.

"It's close to Winchester Cathedral." Etienne's voice sharpened. "You're smart enough to find your way there, so don't waste my time, and don't tell your friends where you're going."

"What happens when I get there?"

"That depends on you. Be quick." Etienne hung up.

The phone slipped from my hands and thudded on the floor.

"What happened?" Roux cried.

"I have to go," I said.

"Wait, who was on the phone?" Roux was getting frantic now.

But I couldn't tell her. If Etienne knew where I was, he'd have sent someone after me by now, but if I didn't do what he said, he'd kill my mum like he'd killed my sister. He'd have Roux and Jason's families killed, and then he'd *still* find a way to get me where he wanted me.

I snatched the silk blazer from Roux's hands, threw it over my head, and ran from the pub.

"Renie, wait," Jason shouted.

I didn't slow down. I had to get away from the pub before Edmond saw me, because he'd never let me go alone, and I couldn't let him risk himself. He was already injured; he couldn't take Etienne on until he had healed.

The second I was out of the pub, I turned left, running in the opposite direction of the parked van.

Where the hell was Winchester Cathedral? My mind raced. I knew nothing about the city, and without a phone, I couldn't pull up a map. It could be miles away.

Think, Renie.

I veered around a corner, and hope soared in my chest. At the end of the street, a black taxi idled by the curb. A woman climbed out of it, pulling a suitcase, and I put on an extra burst of speed.

I reached the taxi and threw myself into the back seat. "How far away is Canon Street?" I cried.

"What?" The driver twisted to look at me through the plastic partition separating the front and back seats.

"Canon Street! Where is it?"

"About a mile from here—"

"Please take me there."

He frowned, eyeing the blazer I still held over my head.

"Are you okay? Are you in trouble?" he asked, his voice softening.

"*Please*. I'll pay double. Just drive."

I had to get out of here before Edmond or anyone else came after me.

The driver sighed and shook his head, but he wasn't about to turn down a double fare. He pulled away from the curb.

I looked through the rear window and saw Ludovic round the corner, his blond ponytail streaming behind him. He was fast but the taxi was faster. A whimper rose in my throat. I *had* to do this to protect the people I loved, but I was fucking terrified. Etienne had admitted that he wanted me dead, so why did he now want me to hand myself over alive? Why not just order his minions to kill me when I arrived at Canon Street? What was the evil bastard planning now?

With the blazer draped over my head, I couldn't see anything out of the window, and the next few minutes passed in a blur of suffocating fear and anxiety. I tried not to think about what Etienne would do to me, but June's bloodied, savage face played on a loop through my head. I couldn't forget what that man was capable of.

"Are we nearly there?" I said.

"About a minute away," the driver replied.

I didn't have a penny on me; the promise of double fare had been a complete lie. But I couldn't wait until we'd arrived to tell him that— getting mixed up with Etienne's bullshit might cost the poor guy his life. That only left one choice.

I threw open the door and bolted.

"Get back here." The driver's voice roared after me, but I was gone before he'd undone his seat belt.

I found Canon Street by peeking at street names from under the blazer draped over my head, and though I couldn't see the faces of the few people I passed by, I could imagine the strange looks I was getting. At least no one tried to stop me.

Canon Street was a narrow strip of road flanked on both sides by terraced redbrick houses. It was mostly cast in shadow, and I crossed to the darkest part of the street, trying to get some relief from the itching on the backs of my hands.

At the end of the road, a dark-gray car was parked by the curb. Two human men stood by it—one was of average height and build, with thinning hair that formed a wispy island above his forehead; the other was large and bearded, shifting his weight from foot to foot. He nudged the balding man when he saw me, and my steps faltered.

The balding man checked his watch. "You got here quick. Etienne will be pleased."

The thought of pleasing him made me want to throw up. "What happens now?" I said.

The bearded man opened the door and gestured to the back seat. "Get in."

"Why are you helping Etienne?" I asked. I could guess why he hadn't turned them into vampires—he needed minions who could go out during the day. But what was in it for them?

"Do you want to play question time, or do you want to get to Etienne before he hurts anyone you care about?" the balding man asked.

Rage boiled in my chest, the predator inside me surging to life. My hands curled into fists, and I felt the ache of my fangs sliding out. There was nothing menacing about either of these men, and neither of them stood a chance against me now that I was a vampire. But they held the power here, and we all knew it.

I approached the car.

Part of me still desperately hoped that Edmond would suddenly charge in to save me, even though I'd have to run from him if he did. But no one came.

The bearded guy moved without warning. I saw his arm flick in my periphery, and something encircled my neck. I didn't feel the pain at first, and then it suddenly hit, white-hot fire racing through me and turning my blood to acid.

A silver chain was looped around my neck, sucking the strength out of me. I clawed at it, but the metal corroded the tips of my fingers, which were already raw and peeling under the light of day.

I didn't know if being a new vampire meant that silver hurt more, or if this was what Edmond had endured while he was locked in Belle Morte's cells—all I knew was that agony was eating me alive. I couldn't even scream; it was as if my voice had been cauterized.

I fell to my knees, helplessly scrabbling at the chain with bloody fingers.

Someone threw a coarse sack over my head, muffling me in darkness. Metal cuffs were clamped around my wrists and ankles, and fresh fire flooded me—the monsters had chained me head to foot with silver, and it was scorching like acid. My stomach heaved and churned, but vampires couldn't be sick. Blood streamed down my neck and pooled between my breasts.

Two pairs of hands lifted me off my feet and tossed me into the back of the car. The doors slammed and the engine started, softly rumbling through my bones.

I had no idea where they were taking me or what the hell would happen next.

It was almost a relief when unconsciousness sucked me under.

Edmond

"We should get back in the van," Ludovic said, looking up and down the street. There were only a couple of people about, and they were too busy hunching over their phones to pay any attention to their surroundings, but that could quickly change.

Edmond didn't want to take his eyes off the pub where Renie was, but if they were trying to keep what had happened at Belle Morte quiet for now, they couldn't risk anyone spotting them.

Ysanne swayed suddenly and braced her hand on the van's back doors, still hanging open. Edmond moved to her side.

"You need blood," he said.

A muscle twitched in Ysanne's jaw. "It'll have to wait until we get to Fiaigh."

"We don't know how long that will be," Edmond cautioned.

Andrew appeared around the side of the van. "I can feed you," he said, holding up his wrist.

The offer was for Ysanne, but Edmond's fangs slid out, straining to bite Andrew, to drink his warm, delicious blood.

Ysanne shook her head, but Edmond touched her arm. "You should do it. We have no idea if we'll reach Fiaigh without running into trouble."

Ysanne stared at him, and for just a moment, Edmond felt catapulted back in time, hundreds of years ago, to the night he'd met Ysanne. She'd been stabbed then, too, after being attacked by robbers on the road, and after killing them, she'd turned to the frightened peasant boy hiding nearby, and had asked to drink his blood so she could heal her wound. Edmond had fed her then, but he couldn't feed her now.

Andrew offered her his wrist again, and Edmond sensed rather than saw her relent.

"We should do it in the van," she said. "We don't want to draw any attention to ourselves."

She climbed into the van, Andrew following, and they sat on the left bench in the darkest corner.

"You need blood too," Ludovic said to Edmond.

He tilted his head in the direction of the pub. A middle-aged man had stumbled out and, judging by the way he was leaning on the wall and struggling to light a cigarette, he was already very drunk. The drunker someone was, the less likely they were to remember being bitten by a vampire.

"Before you protest, consider that the stronger you are, the more you'll be able to protect Renie," Ludovic added.

Edmond allowed a rueful smile. Ludovic knew exactly how to get to him.

"Stay here and keep an eye on the pub," he said.

Ludovic nodded.

As the drunk man headed down a narrow side street, Edmond went after him. It felt strange to be doing this again. For centuries he'd hunted humans from the shadows, taking as much blood as he could without hurting them and then disappearing until it was safe to hunt again. The donor system had changed all that. He'd grown used to donors offering up their veins in the luxury of Belle Morte, and there was something very jarring about suddenly being forced to revert back to how things used to be.

The man moved slowly ahead of Edmond, his feet shuffling over the ground, cigarette smoke wafting over his shoulder.

Smoking was banned at Belle Morte because it affected the taste of the blood, and most vampires didn't like feeding from drunk people for the same reason, but Edmond couldn't afford to be picky.

He waited until the man stopped to stub out his cigarette, then slipped up behind him, silent as a ghost, and sank his fangs into the man's neck. His blood was bitter and unpleasant, but Edmond gulped down as much as he could without hurting the man. It wasn't enough to heal his injuries but it gave him a much-needed boost of energy. He'd be strong enough to fight if it came to it.

The man leaned against the wall, his eyelids fluttering with the unexpected ecstasy of Edmond's bite, and Edmond slipped away as quietly as he'd come.

As soon as the pub and the van came back into view, he realized that something was wrong. Roux and Jason stood by the van, Roux frantically gesturing while she told Andrew something. Ysanne was still in the van with Caoimhe, but there was no sign of Ludovic or Renie.

Edmond's blood ran cold.

He ran to the van and grabbed Roux's arm. "What happened?" he said.

Roux's face was pale, her eyes huge and shocked. "I think Etienne has Renie's mum. She phoned home but someone else answered, and whoever it was freaked her out, but she seemed to know them, so it has to be Etienne, right?"

"How could Etienne have got to her house already?"

"Southampton isn't that far away from Winchester. If he went straight there after we escaped the mansion . . ." Roux trailed off.

Ludovic jogged toward them, his face grim. "Renie got in a taxi. I don't know where she went, and I couldn't catch up. I'm sorry."

Edmond struggled to control the icy wave of fear rising inside him. "If Renie thinks that Etienne has her mother, she'll go home."

But Roux shook her head. "We couldn't hear his side of the conversation but Renie definitely said that she didn't know where somewhere was, and she asked what would happen when she got there. I don't think Etienne was telling her to come home."

"Where the hell else would he send her?" Edmond's hands curled into fists.

"I don't know."

Edmond punched the side of the van, and Roux jumped. "This is my fault. I shouldn't have left her," he said.

He should have learned from the last time—when June had killed her. But apparently he hadn't learned a damn thing, and now she'd slipped through his fingers.

"Hey," said Roux, pointing at him. "This is Etienne's fault, not yours, and there's no time for a pity party. We need to decide what to do."

"We have to go to her house," said Jason. He slumped against the van, staring at his feet.

"But she's not there," Roux said.

"Her mum is, though, and so's Etienne. He's already killed June; we can't let him kill Renie's mum too."

Roux bit her lip, her eyes bright with unshed tears. "But that means we can't go after Renie."

Edmond resisted the urge to punch the van again.

"We already can't go after her," said Caoimhe, poking her head out. "We have no idea where she is, and no way of tracking her."

"I'm *not* abandoning her," Edmond growled.

"I didn't suggest you should. But Etienne knows where she is."

Roux's expression cleared. "And we know where Etienne is."

A grim sort of calm settled on Edmond, quieting the surging waves of fear and anger. "Then I'll make him talk."

"You think this could be a trap?" Jason asked.

"Etienne almost took Renie from me a few days ago. If he thinks he can do that again, he's wrong. I'll peel the skin from his skull if it means finding her," Edmond said.

Jason swallowed. "Okay then."

"Does anyone actually know Renie's address?" Roux said.

Ysanne climbed out of the van. "I do. I memorized the addresses of every current donor."

"Then let's go," said Edmond.

As everyone climbed into the van, Edmond looked back at the pub where he'd last seen Renie. "I'll find you," he whispered. "No matter what it takes, I'll find you."

CHAPTER FIFTEEN

Renie

My senses trickled slowly back to life. I was being dragged along a hard floor; the cloth sack was still over my head, the coarse fibers scraping my face. I could hear two heartbeats—I guessed from the guys Etienne had sent to kidnap me—and when I strained my ears even further, I detected the faint sound of running water.

Was I still in Winchester or had Etienne's minions taken me somewhere else? How much time had I lost while I was unconscious? Enough for Edmond to realize I'd gone. My heart twisted sharply.

My captors hauled me into a chair, and the pressure of the cuffs around my wrists and ankles momentarily eased as someone undid them. Then they cuffed them again—my ankles to the chair legs and my wrists behind the chair so I couldn't move my arms.

Maybe I should've pretended that I was still unconscious, but when the bag was ripped off my head, I couldn't keep from reflexively gasping.

I was in a small wooden structure with boarded-up windows and an uneven concrete floor, broken here and there by clumps of weeds. Etienne stood in front of me, flanked on either side by my kidnappers. Rage boiled through me.

"What the fuck is wrong with you?" I cried. "Do you know what this sick son of a bitch has done? Why are you helping him?" They'd removed the silver chain while I was unconscious but my voice still felt ravaged.

The bearded man swallowed, drawing my eyes to his throat. My stomach throbbed with the sudden need for blood.

"Because he's going to help us," Beardy said, gazing at Etienne with what I could only call hero worship. It was the same expression I'd seen on Vladdicts as they cooed over their latest vampire crush, on the faces of every single person who'd got swept up in the vampire mania of the last ten years.

"Help you? He'll *kill* you," I snarled.

"Yeah, and then he'll turn me."

My eyes shot to Etienne but his face gave away nothing. *Bastard.*

"He's going to make us immortal," said the balding man, and his face suddenly twisted with anger. "All my life I've been a loser, and pretty girls like you never even look at me, but when I'm a vampire, that will change. People will notice me. They'll *respect* me."

"Of course they will," Etienne said.

I stared at the man I'd thought was my friend, and something else surfaced among the hunger for blood and the burning anger—the bitter sting of betrayal.

"I trusted you," I said softly.

Etienne glanced at his human lackeys. "Give us a moment," he said.

They all but bowed to him before hurrying out of the building.

Etienne fetched a chair from a corner and positioned it in front of me. Then he sat, not close enough that I could reach him if my arms had been free, but close enough that we could look into each other's eyes, read each other's faces.

"Renie, please believe me when I say this isn't personal. You're a nice girl, and if there was another way around this, I really would take it."

His voice was sincere, and I hated him for that. I'd rather he was a cackling Bond villain, rubbing his hands together in gleeful anticipation of my death, than sitting there with a sympathetic stare, telling me that he was sorry I had to die.

"Why did you kill my sister?" Even if I was going to die here, I had to know.

"Because she asked me to."

His answer was the last thing I'd expected, and the words hit me like a punch; I actually recoiled.

"What did you say?" My voice came out in a whisper.

"June is not some blameless victim in all this. She *wanted* to be turned."

"She didn't want to be a monster!"

"No," Etienne agreed. "But I didn't know that would happen. It really wasn't my intention."

"Then what was?"

Etienne's eyes bored into me, and I hoped that every ounce of the hatred I felt for him was reflected in my own stare.

"I needed her," he said.

"Why?"

"Because the vampire world needs to change, and I can't do it alone."

I struggled to think back to that night in the snow, when June had killed me. "You said a revolution was coming."

Etienne nodded.

"What the fuck does that have to do with June?"

"The donor system isn't working, and the only way we'll ever change it is to tear it all down. I couldn't do that under the Council's iron grip, nor could I overthrow them without help. June was my accomplice inside Belle Morte."

"You're lying. Belle Morte was June's dream, she'd never do *anything* to hurt the House."

"Yes, she would, if there was something she wanted more." Etienne waited a beat. "June was in love with me. When I told her that I'd grant her greatest wish and make her immortal so we could be together forever, there was nothing she wouldn't do for me. But first we had to overthrow Ysanne. The Lady of Belle Morte, with her rigid rules and antiquated ideals, would never have let us be together."

"No." I shook my head so fiercely that my hair whipped against my eyes. "June wouldn't do something like that."

"June would have done anything for me." Etienne's voice was strangely neutral—he didn't sound regretful or smug, and that made me angrier.

"You're *lying*," I shouted, my eyes burning with unshed tears.

"Wouldn't you do anything to prove your love for Edmond? Or is there a limit?" Etienne asked.

"Of course there is."

"What is that limit? What would you not be willing to do to be with him?"

Words died on my tongue—how the hell did I know?

"Exactly. It's very easy to pass moral judgments when you're not in that position."

"It's easy to pass judgment on a guy who kills people to get what he wants," I snapped.

"Really?" Etienne leaned back in his chair, looking amused. We could have been in any feeding room in Belle Morte, except that I was chained and bleeding. "How much judgment have you passed on Edmond? I'm willing to bet he killed plenty of people during the three wars he fought in. Or are you going to tell me that's different?"

"It *is* different."

"Why?"

"Edmond didn't fight those wars for his own benefit. He was trying to help make the world a better place."

"That's exactly what I'm trying to do—for vampires. Unfortunately, that means some sacrifices have to be made. Edmond has plenty of blood on his hands, and you've overlooked that because of your feelings for him. You have no moral authority here, Renie, and neither does Edmond."

"You never loved June, did you?" I knew the answer but I had to hear him say it.

"No. We needed her, and I used her accordingly." His voice was soft now, talking to me like he thought I'd understand.

The emotion inside me was like a tornado, a surging force of rage and grief and confusion, but in spite of that, my ears pricked up at the word *we*.

Please, don't let it be Caoimhe, I thought.

"Who are you working with? Who was twisted enough to help you?"

Shadows flickered in Etienne's eyes. "Besides your sister, you mean?"

My cuffed hands curled into fists behind the chair. "Just tell me."

"No one was helping *me*. The whole thing was her idea," Etienne said.

"*Whose?*"

It didn't make a difference now—if it was Caoimhe then I couldn't stop her. But I had to know.

The door at the end of the room opened. "I'm afraid it was mine," said the figure who stepped inside.

My heart skittered. I *recognized* that voice, but it couldn't be . . .

As the figure walked forward, the shadows in the room fell away, revealing a vampire I thought I'd never see again. Her blond hair was pulled into a high ponytail, drawing attention to her delicate features and making her look more like a little china doll than ever.

"Jemima?" I whispered.

CHAPTER SIXTEEN

Renie

The Lady of Nox stared back at me, as healthy and beautiful as ever.

"But . . ." I faltered. "You're supposed to be dead. Ysanne said—"

Jemima's lips tipped up in a little smile. "Yes, I performed a very convincing death scene."

Her betrayal was a drop in the ocean compared to Etienne's, but it added to the growing pressure inside me, the anger pushing against my chest. I'd trusted Jemima too—*liked* her, even. I'd even thought she was a better lady than Ysanne; How could I have misjudged her so badly? A few kind words, a smile or two, and I'd been suckered into thinking she was some sort of angel.

"Why are you doing this?" I said. "I just . . . I don't understand. Vampires have everything they could ever want and more—why are you trying to destroy that?"

She actually seemed surprised. "Is *that* what you think I'm doing?"

"You assassinated the Council, slaughtered innocent humans and vampires, and took over Belle Morte. Did I miss the part where that *doesn't* destroy everything that vampires have worked to build?"

"We've built prisons," Jemima snapped. "Yes, we have our pretty houses, our designer clothes, and our hordes of fans, but we're trapped inside gilded cages. We don't have any *freedom*. We're completely subservient to the fear of humans turning on us, subservient to the Council and their laws, and I'm tired of it."

"You have no idea what it's like to be a vampire," Etienne said to me.

I started to protest, but Jemima cut me off with a slash of her small hand. *"Don't,"* she warned, her eyes glittering. "Do not insult us by pretending that the few hours you've been awake as a vampire is remotely comparable to those of us who've lived for hundreds of years."

"Some of us want more than the life that the Council allows us. We want the freedom to come and go from our houses whenever we want, not whenever the Council permits it. We want the freedom to have relationships with humans, and feed as often as we feel like it. We want to be able to choose the course of our own lives, and not have to answer to the Council all the time," Etienne said.

"You didn't have to assassinate them for that," I said.

"Do you think they'd have listened to me? Do you think they'd have ever agreed to change the system?"

"I don't know," I cried. "But you could have *tried*. You didn't have to jump straight to murder."

"This world needs to remember what we're capable of," said Jemima. "We're not just pretty things to look at. We're the beasts that stalked the night before their ancestors were even born, and we deserve more respect than mere stardom."

"So what—you'll remind people that vampires can be killers? How does that benefit anyone?"

"It will remind them we are the gods and goddesses of this world. I don't want us to live in fear of them; I want them to live in fear of *us*."

"Again, how does that benefit you? It flatters your ego, sure, but it won't help vampires. If people are scared of you, they won't want to be donors."

"Of course they will. Humans are remarkably stupid. They're drawn to beauty—even beauty that's capable of killing them. Even if they fully understood what we're capable of, they'd still choose to see our glamorous side. They'd gloss over the danger and focus on the clothes and the luxury and the thrill of the bite. Everyone wants to be famous and everyone wants to live forever, and vampires have both. People will always adore us."

"I never wanted that," I said.

"Excuse me?"

"I never wanted to be famous or to live forever."

A smile curled the corners of Jemima's mouth. Her face was cold and porcelain. "And isn't it ironic that you're the one who will."

I remembered how she'd spoken in my defense at the Council meeting. The lying bitch had poured the charm on nice and thick, and I'd fallen for it. I hated her.

"What exactly did June agree to do for you?" I asked Etienne. I couldn't process the awful revelation that she'd helped him until I had all the pieces.

He didn't respond.

"Please," I said, my voice breaking. "I need to know."

Etienne glanced at Jemima; she gave a small shrug in response. He seemed to take that as a yes.

"The most important step in shaping a new world was to get rid of the Council. Ysanne was the obvious first step. June wanted to be a vampire, and I offered to turn her if she then accused Ysanne of the crime."

"And June agreed."

"Yes."

I closed my eyes for a long, painful moment, trying to reconcile the sister that I'd loved with the parts of her that I'd obviously never known.

"I never imagined that she'd wake up rabid," Etienne reiterated.

"But when she did, you saw an opportunity. That's why you didn't kill her."

"I didn't kill her because I was afraid it would get messy, and that would risk creating evidence that could link me to her death," Etienne said.

"So you just left her?"

"Yes."

"Even though you knew that she could have killed someone?"

"I turned her in the west wing, so she was away from the donors and other vampires."

"Right, like that would have stopped her," I snapped.

"When Ysanne found her, I was sure that she'd kill June. But she didn't, and that made me suspicious. So I visited June after Ysanne had secured her in the west wing. You can imagine my surprise when she seemed to respond to the sound of my voice."

Pieces in my head started shifting toward each other—June killing me with a knife rather than her fangs, the way she'd seemed to respond to Ysanne earlier today.

"She does what you tell her, doesn't she?" I said.

"Ysanne and I think more alike than either of us realized. I know now that she brought you to Belle Morte in the hopes that you could turn June into a normal vampire. I approached the subject a little differently. I've never thought that a rabid could be restored—they're little more than feral animals. But, as I explained to the Council, even feral animals can be trained. When I realized that June appeared to recognize my voice, I wondered how far I could take that, whether or not I could train her to obey me."

"She's my sister," I said. The way he talked about her made me want to claw his face off.

"No, she's not, and she hasn't been since she died."

"Since you *killed* her," I spat.

Etienne inclined his head.

"That's how you made it seem as though Ysanne was controlling her at the mansion. But you didn't even say anything—how is she obeying you?"

"You don't really think I'm going to tell you that, do you?" said Etienne pityingly.

"You were controlling her in the grounds that night, weren't you? You made her stab me."

"I did."

"She could easily have ripped out my throat. Why the knife?"

"It was a test, to see what I could get her to do."

I looked at Jemima but her face gave away nothing.

"Why do you two want me dead?"

"When you arrived at Belle Morte, it quickly became clear that Ysanne had brought you there in connection with June. Why else would she allow you constant access to the west wing, where she was secretly hiding a rabid? But I didn't know what you were doing with June, or whether or not it would interfere with my training of her. Unfortunately, I couldn't take that risk. I had June kill you because you were in the way, that's all," said Etienne.

"Then why am I here now? Why go to so much trouble to kidnap me?"

"Ysanne wouldn't have fled Belle Morte unless she had somewhere to go. With the house in our hands, we have access to all the private information secured in her office, including the locations of two potential bolt-holes. But I don't believe Ysanne will be foolish enough to flee to either of those now, so she must have somewhere else that we don't know about. You're going to tell us where it is," said Jemima.

"I have no idea," I said.

Jemima's expression hardened. "I'm in no mood for games."

"I'm not playing."

Jemima put a hand on the back of my neck and tapped her fingernail against my skin. "I'm not a cruel woman, and I don't hurt people unnecessarily, but I haven't come this far to stop now. I'll get the information I want out of you, even if it means spilling blood."

I swallowed the knot of panic in my throat.

Torture.

She was talking about torture.

I locked eyes with her, refusing to show even a speck of the fear that threatened to choke me. "You can do whatever you want, but it won't make any difference, because I *do not know a thing*."

She didn't believe me.

I hadn't expected her to.

I'd thought that either Jemima or Etienne would be in charge of my interrogation, but instead they handed the job to a vampire I'd never seen before—another one of their minions. He'd got his hands on one of the silver-coated knives carried by Belle Morte security— probably taken from either a dead guard or one who'd turned traitor.

It was hard to imagine the black-uniformed, stoic security person- nel being as enamored of vampires as the donors were, but maybe that was why they worked at Belle Morte. They didn't get the lavish life- style, luxury clothes, and thrill of being bitten, but they also weren't on limited contracts. They could work there and be around vampires for as long as they wanted. Maybe some of them *were* secret Vladdicts, but could never be donors because of their age. Young blood tasted the best, so donors were usually between eighteen and twenty-four. Most of the security personnel at Belle Morte were older than that.

Or maybe Etienne and Jemima had simply paid them off.

The reasons why they'd done this were largely irrelevant now, because they *had* done it, but focusing on it helped distract me from what was happening.

Jemima's lackey dragged the tip of the knife across my inner arm; the silver scorching through my skin was more painful than the sharpness of the blade. A hiss squeezed through my tightly clenched teeth.

"Is your memory coming back yet?" the vampire asked.

"Fuck you."

I didn't even know if Ysanne would go to Ireland now or if she'd consider it as compromised as her previous bolt-holes. Roux and Jason weren't stupid—they'd have figured out that Etienne had answered the phone. If Ysanne thought there was even a slight chance that I'd blab to Etienne, she wouldn't go near Fiaigh.

The vampire cut me again, the blade slowly slicing through my skin. He'd already assured me that once he finished with my right arm, he'd move on to my left, and then he'd get started on my legs.

And then my chest.

And then my face.

I should have been terrified.

But all I could think was that, no matter what happened to me, at least my friends would be safe. Without knowing where I was, they couldn't come after me, and even if they did still intend to head for Fiaigh, I really would die before I betrayed them. They were more than my friends; they'd become my family.

I wasn't afraid to die for my family.

The vampire sliced my arm again, deeper this time, and it burned like fire. I wrapped the edges of my mind around myself, sinking deep inside my own brain. I'd die here—I was sure of it—but I'd die happy as long as my friends were safe. As long as Edmond was safe. I just wished we'd had more time together.

When I thought about him, the beautiful vampire I'd fallen so helplessly and unexpectedly in love with, the pain didn't seem as bad.

Edmond

Andrew drove as fast as he could, but to Edmond it still felt like forever until they reached Southampton. His hands were curled into tight fists the whole way. His chest felt like it was full of thorns. They ran into traffic almost as soon as they left Winchester, and the journey that Andrew had assured them would only take about thirty minutes was closer to an hour. To Edmond, every wasted minute was a knife twisting in his ribs. If it wasn't for his lingering injuries, he might have jumped out of the van and run the rest of the way.

Mon dieu, but he'd forgotten about this. Loving someone was giving them your heart—when someone hurt Renie, they hurt Edmond too. He feared for her more than he feared for himself, and that fear was an icy wave that crashed into him, making him feel like all his vampire strength had been stripped away.

What use was superior strength when he couldn't use it to protect the woman he loved?

The van finally stopped on Thirlmere Road, where Renie lived, and Edmond managed to restrain himself from throwing open the doors and running to her house. They had no idea what they were walking into; they needed to be careful.

"Renie lives at number nine," Ysanne said.

How had he not known that already? Edmond wondered.

He climbed out of the van, with Ludovic, Roux, and Jason following. Ysanne and Caoimhe stayed with Andrew, who would have to be ready to make a quick getaway if necessary. It also wasn't safe to leave him alone when the place could be crawling with Etienne's vampires.

Renie's house was an end-of-terrace property, with chipped brickwork and grubby windows, through which Edmond glimpsed tattered net curtains. It was a sad-looking little place, and Edmond felt a different clench in his chest at the thought of Renie living here. He'd always known that she didn't have money, but he'd grown used to seeing her in Belle Morte—dressed in expensive clothes and surrounded by expensive decor.

Edmond shook his head, suddenly disgusted with himself. He

really had been sucked into the Belle Morte lifestyle. He really had started to grow soft and pampered.

This was what Renie would have gone back to if she'd left the mansion as a human. It may be small and run-down, but it was her home.

Ludovic broke away from them and jogged down the street.

"How are we doing this?" Jason asked, eyeing the house.

Edmond silently debated it.

When he was at full strength, he wouldn't have hesitated to take Etienne on, but his injuries weren't fully healed. Caoimhe and Ludovic were more than capable of tackling the bastard in a fight, but none of them knew what Etienne had said to Renie on the phone. The most obvious leverage against her would be the life of her mother. If Etienne was holding her hostage in that house, then charging in could put her in even greater danger.

Assuming that Etienne hadn't already killed her.

Ludovic rejoined them. "There are no signs of lookouts anywhere."

"That seems sloppy," Roux commented.

Edmond narrowed his eyes, the urge to fight coiling through him like a waking beast. "Unless Etienne's not here anymore."

Ludovic caught Edmond's arm even though Edmond hadn't moved, as though he knew Edmond was about to stalk down the front path and kick in Renie's front door.

"Easy," he warned.

Roux tilted her head to one side as she regarded Renie's house. Winter sunlight winked off her nose stud. "I don't know why Etienne wants Renie so badly, but if he's left Belle Morte and come all this way to lure her into a trap, she's obviously important to him, and surely he wouldn't screw this opportunity up. He rightly predicted that Renie would call home to warn her mum, which is why he came here. Since Renie ran from us, we can assume Etienne told her to come alone. But he knew that Renie was with us, and he must know that we'd never abandon her. Since we don't know where he told

Renie to go, the logical next step would be for us to come here, the last place we knew Etienne was. There's no way he'd face Ysanne, Edmond, and Ludovic alone, so if he doesn't have backup, then it suggests he's not here anymore."

"His backup could be in the house," Jason said.

"I don't think so," Edmond said. "If Etienne wants everyone to think that he was wrongly accused of June's murder and he's just an innocent victim of Ysanne's schemes, then he has to tread very carefully. The vampires he turned can't be out in sunlight long enough to fight us older vampires, and his human lackeys wouldn't stand a chance either. But more importantly, everything he's done so far has been contained to Belle Morte. He's not stupid enough to try kidnapping or killing all of us in broad daylight, in the middle of a residential street. That would turn the attention of the human world on him and Belle Morte, and I'm not sure he's ready for that. I think that's why he set this trap for Renie rather than sending his forces after us when we escaped. Once he knew that she was going wherever he's told her to go, he'd have left this house."

"But what about Renie's mum? Do you think he's let her go?" Jason said.

He didn't voice the alternative, the thing that had gnawed at Edmond during the whole drive here. Etienne had killed June. He'd tried to kill Renie—more than once. He wouldn't hesitate to kill their mother too.

Roux lifted her chin. "There's only one way to find out."

Before anyone could stop her, she strode up the path and knocked loudly on the door.

"Do you think that was a good idea?" Jason said, looking at Edmond and Ludovic.

"It's too late to worry about it now," Edmond said, and followed Roux.

She stood in front of the door, and even though Edmond could hear her heart beating too fast, her back was straight and her shoulders were squared, refusing to show her fear. She might be as breakable as any human, but the fire that burned at her core was pure steel.

Roux knocked again, louder this time, but there was still no answer, and she bit her lip. "What do we do if he's killed Renie's mum?" she whispered.

Edmond didn't know how to answer that.

He tried to open the door but it was locked, so he smashed the lock with the flat of his hand and the door swung open to reveal a tiny hallway and a narrow staircase.

Wait here, he mouthed to Roux, then he went into the house.

The carpet was faded to a dull gray, worn through to bare boards in places, and the air was heavy with the smell of cheap food and cheap laundry detergent. It made Edmond's nose itch. But there was no smell of blood, nothing to indicate that anything bad had happened.

"Well?" said Roux, peeking inside.

"No one's here," Edmond said.

"We should search the house anyway, just to be sure," Roux insisted.

It was small, so it wouldn't take long. Edmond went through the shoebox-sized kitchen with the cracked linoleum floor, minimal appliances, and cabinet with a missing door; the equally small living room, furnished with a threadbare sofa and a television; and the narrow slice of bathroom, featuring a tiny plastic shower that an adult would barely fit into.

He headed upstairs, Roux following closely behind.

The second floor was no better than the first: just two small bedrooms with single beds, peeling wallpaper, and ragged carpets.

Renie had never really bought into the Belle Morte lifestyle, but Edmond could understand why June had been so keen to get away from this—why the decadent vampire world had sucked her up. She really had been living a dream.

She'd died for a dream, too, he soberly reminded himself.

"Do you think Etienne kidnapped Renie's mum too?" Roux asked, slumping against the wall.

"Perhaps. Or perhaps whatever he said to Renie on the phone had nothing to do with her mother," Edmond said, but he wasn't sure he believed that. If Etienne wasn't planning on killing Renie, then using her mother as a hostage would guarantee her good behavior.

Roux shivered suddenly.

"What?" Edmond said.

"Sorry, it's just . . . you look kind of scary right now, like you want to kill someone."

"I do," he said honestly.

"Considering what Etienne's done, I guess I can't blame you." Roux's mouth wobbled. "Edmond . . . what do we do now? We have no idea where Renie is."

Edmond gazed around the bedroom that had been Renie's. She must have shared it with June, judging by the two beds and the several pairs of shoes suggesting two different tastes in fashion that were scattered across the floor. But the room held little life or character, and the few bits of shabby furniture revealed almost nothing of the intriguing girl he'd fallen in love with.

A photo pinned to the wall above one of the beds caught his eye. He moved into the room to get a closer look. Renie and June, with their arms around each other, smiled out of the picture. They only looked about twelve and thirteen, their faces still full of childish innocence. When he thought about what had happened to these sisters, Edmond's dead heart ached. It would've been better for both of them if they'd never come to Belle Morte.

Roux crept into the room. "It feels like a tomb in here," she whispered.

Edmond knew what she meant. There was something heavy about the silence in the small house, something stifling and oppressive.

"But it's not," he said. "We're not losing anyone else to Etienne."

Roux nodded, but her lip trembled. "I'm so scared that he'll hurt her."

Her words cut through Edmond's determination, and suddenly he was hit with an overwhelming sense of doubt. What if he was too late? What if Etienne killed Renie before Edmond could find her?

In terms of strength and endurance, vampires were superhuman. Their bodies could recover from terrible injuries and weather conditions that no human could. As long as they weren't injured, they could last longer without blood than a human could without water. They survived wars, revolutions, and other social upheavals, and all the ways the world had changed over the years. So this feeling of helplessness came as a shock to Edmond. It reminded him of how it had felt to be human—constrained by all his human weaknesses and frailties. It made him feel out of place in his own skin.

He closed his eyes. "Before I met Renie, I swore that I'd never love anyone again, but now, if I lose her, I'll lose everything."

"Hey," said Jason, appearing in the doorway. "One way or another, we're getting our girl back."

"Edmond?" Ludovic's voice came from downstairs, and there was a quiet urgency in it that made Edmond bolt from the bedroom and leap down the stairs like a cat, landing in a fluid crouch.

Ludovic stood inside the doorway, pressed against the wall so he couldn't be seen from the outside. Edmond adopted the same position.

"A car just drove past the house. Nothing to worry about normally, but something about it didn't feel right. It moved too slowly, like the driver was looking for something," Ludovic murmured.

"Could you see inside?" Edmond asked.

"The windows were tinted but it looked like there were two men inside. I'm assuming human since they weren't wrapped up against the sun."

"They must have seen the van."

"Ysanne and Caoimhe were inside when the car arrived, but the inhabitants may still have recognized it as a Belle Morte vehicle."

Edmond risked a look outside. The van was still parked outside, the back doors shut now, Andrew waiting at the wheel.

"There's nothing on the van that specifically marks it out as Belle Morte property," he said.

Ludovic started to reply, then stopped at the sound of an engine.

Edmond carefully listened. It sounded as though the car was moving slowly, inching down the street in their direction. "What do you think the chances are it's the same car coming back for a second look?" he said.

"I'd say very likely."

"So would I."

"What do you want to do?"

Edmond ran his tongue across the points of his fangs. "I want to find out who's in that car."

They waited until the car sounded as if it was crawling past the house. Neither of them needed to speak—years of fighting side by side had made them attuned to each other in a way that Edmond couldn't explain. They moved in tandem, flowing out of the house and down the path. The car picked up speed the second the driver saw them, but Edmond had already reached the vehicle. The back door was locked; Edmond smashed the lock and wrenched the door open.

"Shit, *shit,*" the driver cried as Edmond climbed into the back seat, and the car picked up speed again, as if that would help.

Edmond leaned forward and wrapped one hand around the man's throat, not hard enough to choke, but hard enough to make the man's pulse jump frantically beneath his palm.

"Stop the car," Edmond said.

"Don't do it," cried the man in the front passenger seat.

Edmond tightened his grip a little more, and the car started to slow.

"Stop the car or I'll break your neck," Edmond said.

"You—you can't. You'd cause a crash," the driver said, his hands clutching the steering wheel.

"I'm a vampire, I can walk away from a crash." Edmond cut a sharp look at the passenger. "Your friend can't."

The door on Edmond's other side suddenly wrenched open and Ludovic climbed into the car. He smoothed down his ponytail with one hand, as if chasing down a moving car was nothing more than a minor inconvenience.

Edmond leaned forward and put his mouth close to the driver's ear. "Stop. The. Car," he said, his voice low and lethal.

This time, the driver did as he was told.

As soon as the car stopped, the man in the passenger seat threw open his door and tried to bolt, but Ludovic calmly grabbed a handful of his hair and hauled him back.

The driver swallowed, his throat bobbing desperately against Edmond's hand, but Edmond didn't relax his grip.

"You're going to answer some questions for me, or I'm going to make things very unpleasant for you. Do you understand?" he said.

The driver nodded.

"What's your name?"

The driver relaxed a fraction, as if he'd expected Edmond to ask something less benign. "Sully," he said. "This is Lee." He indicated his passenger, whose hair Ludovic was still holding.

"Do you know who I am, Sully?" Edmond asked.

"Yes."

"Do you know who Renie Mayfield is?"

"Y-yes."

"Good. Where is she?"

"I don't know."

Edmond heard the quickening of Sully's heartbeat—that was almost certainly a lie.

"I don't believe you," he said, and Sully trembled. "What does Etienne want with Renie?"

"I don't know!"

That felt like the truth, though it was hard to be sure when Sully's heart sounded like it was about to pound right out of his chest.

"Why did he send you here?" Edmond said.

Sully looked at Lee, and suddenly Edmond had the feeling that he'd missed something.

"He didn't," Lee said. He tried to move his head, then winced because Ludovic absolutely was not letting go of his hair.

"What are you talking about?" Ludovic said.

Sully swallowed hard. "Etienne didn't send us, okay?"

"Then who did?" Edmond growled.

A pause.

"Jemima Sutton," said Sully.

Even though he didn't need to breathe, it felt like the air had just been knocked out of Edmond's lungs. He sagged in his seat, his grip finally loosening on Sully's throat. Sully took the moment to suck in a gasp of air.

Edmond looked at Ludovic. His expression was neutral but his eyes churned with shock, doubt, and anger.

"Jemima's dead," Ludovic said.

Lee shook his head, then winced again. "No, she's not."

Edmond's mind raced. Jemima was alive? Worse, she was *involved* with this?

"Are Etienne and Jemima working together?" he said.

"I don't know," Sully replied, but his pulse stuttered.

Any other time Edmond might have threatened him again, tried to scare the man into giving up what he knew, but Renie's life hung in the balance, and this spineless, quivering sack of bones was Edmond's only link to her. There was no more time for threats.

He reached around the seat, grabbed Sully's smallest finger, and pulled it straight back until it snapped. Sully screamed, and Edmond put a hand over his mouth to muffle it. His other hand stayed on Sully's throat, applying just enough pressure to remind the man that Edmond could break his neck as easily as his finger.

"Are Etienne and Jemima working together?" Edmond repeated, moving his hand from Sully's mouth.

"Yes," Sully sobbed, tears rolling down his face and pooling where Edmond's fingers gripped his neck.

"Why?"

"I swear I don't know."

"Why are you here?" Ludovic asked. "Has Etienne kidnapped Renie's mother?"

"No," Lee said. He slumped in his seat, as if resigned to his fate. "We don't know what Etienne or Jemima want with Renie, but as far as we know, he only threatened Renie's mum to lure Renie into a trap. He's never even met the woman, and the moment Renie gave herself up, Etienne left her house," Lee said.

At least that meant Renie's mother was safe, which was one less thing to worry about.

"So what are you doing here?" Ludovic asked.

"Jemima doesn't want Etienne to bank whatever he's doing solely on Renie. She thinks Etienne should have waited for Renie's mum to come home and then taken her as leverage."

That was what Edmond had feared Etienne would do. He was glad he'd been wrong.

"Jemima sent you two to watch the house and seize Renie's mother if you could," he guessed.

Lee nodded.

Sully was still crying.

A possible rift between Jemima and Etienne's visions of . . .

whatever they were doing was an interesting piece of information, but Edmond filed that away for now. Renie came first.

"Where have they taken Renie?" he said.

Sully swallowed, his blood thrumming below the surface of his skin. "Please," he whispered. "She'll kill us."

"*I'll* kill you," Edmond snarled, and twisted Sully's broken finger.

It had been a long time since he'd hurt anyone—a long time since he'd *wanted* to. But the thought of Renie suffering brought the darkest parts of himself roaring to the surface, almost blinding him with rage.

Sully sagged in his seat, tears streaming down his face, and Edmond felt a hot wave of contempt for the man. Apparently, he was happy to work for vampires until he saw what they were capable of, and he was happy to kidnap an innocent woman and hand her over to the people who'd murdered her daughter, but dissolved into a quivering wreck when confronted with the repercussions of that.

"What will you do to us if we tell you?" Lee asked, his eyes downcast.

The dark part of Edmond wanted to kill them both. They didn't seem to care if Etienne or Jemima killed Renie or her mother, nor did they seem to care about all the people who'd already died. Why did they deserve mercy when they'd had no intention of showing it?

But he'd taken lives before, due to his own carelessness, and it had haunted him for a long time. He would kill to protect himself or the people he loved, but if he killed Sully and Lee, it would be in cold blood. Not everyone would have seen a difference, but Edmond did.

"Tell me what I want to know, and I'll let you live," he said. "Lie to me, and you'll end the day in a shallow grave."

Sully whimpered again but Lee nodded, his face set. "Do we have your word on that?"

"You do," Edmond said. "Now tell me where she is."

CHAPTER SEVENTEEN

Renie

Consciousness rushed back in a red wave of pain. I could hear my own blood *drip, drip, dripping* on the floor. I tried to cling to the image of Edmond, the memories that had helped me through the torture, but they slipped between my fingers.

With an effort, I lifted my head. My arms were cut to ribbons but my torturer hadn't moved on to my legs yet. He must have given up when I'd passed out.

A shape moved in front of me, and I blinked the exhaustion out of my eyes. Etienne gazed down at me with a sympathetic expression, and I wondered if I was strong enough to rip his head off. If I ever got free, maybe I'd find out.

"Oh, Renie," he said, positioning a chair in front of me again.

It sounded like genuine regret in his voice, and I managed enough strength to spit at him.

He didn't blink.

"Why the fuck do you think I know where Ysanne's going? We're not exactly friends," I said.

"Ysanne trusted you with secrets that she wouldn't share with most of her House. Are you trying to tell me that even though you and Ysanne escaped Belle Morte together she's refused to tell you where your runaway group is going?"

"Why didn't you go after any of them?"

"Roux and Jason have little value as bargaining chips, and they can't withstand interrogation the way you can. Whatever injuries you get will heal, and then we can start again. I can't do that with a human," Etienne said.

There was more to it than that, I was sure. My mind turned over the pieces, trying to fit them together.

"You took me because you knew I'd give myself up to save my mum, and to protect Roux and Jason's families, but also because you know that you can now use me as leverage to get Edmond to give himself up. That's what you meant by bargaining chips, isn't it? This isn't just about hunting Ysanne down, it's about getting leverage over Edmond, because you're too chickenshit to face him in a fair fight."

Etienne looked amused. "I'm not afraid of Edmond Dantès."

"Bullshit." Another piece clicked into place in my head. "When Adrian groped me at Jemima's welcoming party, that wasn't just him being a douche bag, was it? Jemima told him to do it."

Etienne reclined in his chair, shrewdly eyeing me. "Why would she do that?"

"Because you both knew there was something between Edmond and me. You knew he'd break the rules to defend me, and you knew Ysanne would have to punish him for it. You needed him out of the way when you released June and let your minions rampage through the house because you are afraid of him, and you didn't want him involved. Or maybe you were hoping to kill him while he was recovering in bed? Is that why you came to his door that day?"

Etienne said nothing, but something dark glittered in his eyes.

"I'm right, aren't I?" I said, a surge of triumph momentarily overwhelming the pain.

He smiled again, sharper this time.

I tried to visualize the whole picture.

"You want to tear down the donor system, and you manipulated June into helping you. She was supposed to frame Ysanne, so when you brought the Council to investigate, Ysanne would be removed from her position as Lady of Belle Morte. I'm not sure what your next step after that would have been, but it doesn't matter, does it, because June ruined everything by turning rabid. You couldn't use her to frame Ysanne because she can't talk. You expected Ysanne to kill her, but when she didn't, you decided to investigate. You couldn't find out what she was doing, but when she brought me to Belle Morte, you knew it was connected to June and you tried to kill me to keep me from interfering with your plans.

"Once it was time for Jemima to visit, you got Edmond out of the way and then you set June free. I don't know how long you've been turning people into vampires, and I'm guessing Jemima's helped with that, but once you had enough forces, you set them on Belle Morte. That's why they ended up fleeing that night—not because they were overwhelmed but because that attack was never about seizing the house. If you couldn't immediately frame Ysanne as June's killer, you needed to paint her as completely incompetent by making sure that staff and donors died on her watch.

"You wanted everyone in Belle Morte to lose faith in her, so that, if she survived the Council assassination, it'd be easier to turn the House against her. Tricking everyone into thinking she was controlling June was just the icing on the cake, wasn't it? I bet you also used that first attack to thin out security, so it would be easier for a bloodless takeover the second time."

Etienne wasn't smiling anymore. His eyes were as cold as Ysanne's had ever been. "Very clever," he said.

"What happens now? You'll install your new vampires in every House? What happens to the humans you've manipulated into helping you? Will you actually turn them, or did you only turn people so they'd be meat shields for your attack?"

"Does it matter?" Etienne said. He was leaning forward now, and I was horribly reminded of all the times I'd talked to June while she'd been chained up in Belle Morte's west wing. Now I was the one in chains.

"Yes," I said.

"Why? I sent two humans to kidnap you and turn you over to me. They knew exactly what they were doing, and what I had in store for you, and they didn't hesitate. Why does their fate concern you, in light of that?"

I didn't know how to answer that. The door opened and Jemima came in. "Is she talking yet?" she asked.

"Not about anything useful," Etienne replied, leaning back.

I looked at Jemima.

"Where does this end?" I asked. "Have you thought about the European Vampire Houses? De Sang? Dans l'Ombre? Blutrausch? Di Notte?" I wished I could remember more, but I was too exhausted. "What about the Houses in the US and Asia? Sooner or later they'll learn what's happened—do you think they'll just accept you two seizing control of every House in the UK?"

"The rulers of Vampire Houses across the world are more concerned with their own affairs than what goes on in this little island. They'll find out eventually, but even if they suspect foul play, do you really think they'll start a war over it? Like Ysanne, any vampire in charge of a House knows that the balance between humans and vampires must be maintained at all costs. Starting a war hardly helps that balance," Jemima said with blithe confidence.

"Right, until you decide that the UK isn't enough and you want to seize other Houses."

Jemima made a dismissive noise. "I have no interest in overseas Houses."

"Bullshit," I snapped, and her eyes narrowed. There was no flare of red yet, though, so I obviously wasn't getting under her skin enough. "You were on the Council; you had the power to argue for change. Instead, you chose to destroy everything. Maybe Etienne really does think he's helping the vampire world, but you just want power. You weren't happy ruling only Nox so you decided to seize all the UK Houses, and once you're established in them, you'll want more. People like you always do."

In the flash of silence that followed my words, I saw Etienne shoot Jemima a speculative look.

Jemima's face hardened, her eyes turning cold. There was nothing left of the woman who'd spoken kindly to me, who'd defended me during the Council meeting. Had that part of her been a complete lie?

"Whatever happens in the future, you won't be around to see it," she said.

"That doesn't give me much incentive to talk."

"Then consider what will happen if you don't tell us what we want to know. We lured you into a trap—do not think we can't do the same to your friends. Would you rather it was Roux Hayes in this chair? Or Jason Grant? Unlike you, they won't heal."

I wanted to snap back that Jemima had no way of getting to my friends, but I didn't *know* that. I had no idea how far her reach extended or how many steps ahead of us she still was.

"What happens when Edmond gives himself up to save you? Because he will," Jemima continued. "Perhaps you can stay silent to save yourself, but that will change if it's Edmond's life on the line." Her voice was completely flat as she spoke—she wasn't relishing this, but that emptiness only made her threats worse. "We will kill you, Renie, and Edmond, too, but the nature of that death is up to you. If you wish it to be as painless as possible, that can be arranged. If you wish to continue playing games, I'll make you watch as I rip out Edmond's eyes. I'll make him beg for death, and you'll see every second of it."

I looked into Jemima's eyes, cold and blue, and knew that she meant it. She was prepared to destroy the entire donor system and

risk the lives of vampires worldwide if it helped build the future she
wanted; she wouldn't hesitate to torture Edmond.

My resolve crumbled. I'd coped with the pain until now because I
knew that I was protecting my friends. But if protecting them meant
watching Edmond die slowly and horribly in front of me? I didn't
know what I'd do in that situation, and I *really* didn't want to find out.

I looked up at Jemima and clenched my fists, feeling the cuffs bite
into my skin. Blood dripping from my wounds was the only sound
in the room.

"If you hurt Edmond or my friends, I'll kill you," I said.

Jemima laughed. It was a sweet laugh, like a bell, and it matched
the teenage prettiness of her face. "You have no idea what it means to
kill someone, Renie, so you'll forgive me if your threats don't make
me tremble with fear."

I spat at her.

She responded with a backhand that rocked my head on my shoulders. Pain exploded through my jaw and the coppery taste of my
own blood filled my mouth. I spat at Jemima again, and my blood
made a bright splash across her pale face.

Etienne quietly regarded us both, his eyes calculating.

Jemima turned and pointed a polished fingernail at him. "Make
her talk," she said, an edge of anger in her voice. Maybe I'd finally
started getting under the bitch's skin.

Jemima stalked out of the room, and though she didn't slam the
door, she shut it harder than she had before.

"It would be easier for everyone if you'd just talk," Etienne told me,
watching as blood continued to drop from the gashes that ran up and
down my arms.

"Okay, you've swayed me. Come here and I'll whisper it into your
ear." I bared my fangs.

Etienne chuckled. "I never lied about liking you, Renie. If I could
do this without killing you, I would."

"I'm flattered," I snapped. "I trusted you, Etienne. June trusted you. And you betrayed us both. I'll get you for what you did to my sister."

I expected him to laugh, like Jemima had done, but Etienne leaned back in his chair and studied me as if he was taking me seriously. He'd said this whole mess was Jemima's idea, but I couldn't help wondering if Etienne was the bigger threat.

"Jemima wasn't bluffing. If you think you're hurting now, you have no idea how much worse it will get." Etienne patted my knee. "Take some time to think about it."

Etienne left after that, but Baldy and Beardy took his place, standing on either side of the door and watching me with hard eyes. Etienne's words felt like tiny blades wriggling around under my skin, cutting right to my deepest fears.

I'd kept quiet so far, but if what Jemima said was true, they were only just getting warmed up—maybe they wouldn't even *need* Edmond to make me talk. I wished I could stay strong enough to withstand anything, but the reality was that I might not be. If they broke me, if I talked, then it might cost the people I loved their lives. Maybe my information was useless anyway, maybe Ysanne had changed her mind about going to Ireland, but I couldn't take that risk.

I had to get out of here.

I strained against the cuffs, but the only result was a sickening burst of pain. The humans watched, blithely confident that I was helpless. They were right. I couldn't break the silver cuffs—not when they were sucking the strength right out of me—and the only way I could slip them off would be to crush every bone in my hand. Maybe if I waited long enough, Jemima would do that for me—

I froze, my mind racing. I could heal from injuries now, so a crushed hand wouldn't cause permanent damage. My legs were cuffed to each chair leg, so I couldn't run with the chair still attached, but if I could get the cuffs off my hand, I could break the legs off the chair.

I gave my hands another experimental flex, biting back a cry at the sharp scorch of pain.

"Fuck," I whispered. This was going to *hurt*.

I'd need my right hand to rip the cuffs off, so I stuck my left hand out behind me, my fingers stiff and straight, and closed my eyes, drawing on every good memory I had of Edmond and my friends to give me strength. Then I rocked my chair in a sharp, violent motion, throwing my weight back with everything I had. The chair toppled over. Blinding pain lanced through me as my thumb and middle finger splintered and smashed against the concrete ground beneath me. I screamed, black spots dancing in my eyes as I hovered on the cusp of passing out.

"Oh shit," said a voice from the door—Baldy, I thought.

I had seconds before they either rushed over to me or went for help, so I gritted my teeth against the blinding waves of pain and wrenched my damaged hand as hard as I could. Shattered bones ground together, blood slickened my skin, and my hand slipped free of the cuffs.

A fresh wave of agony roared through me, and I curled the fingers of my good hand into the floor, trying to ground myself so I wouldn't black out.

The roof blurred in and out of focus above me, then Baldy's face appeared, peering down at me. His mouth was moving, but everything was going fuzzy around me, and I couldn't hear what he was saying. The only thing I could hear was a steady *thump-thump-thump*, which seemed to be getting louder and louder. My fangs slid out with a faint sting that I barely noticed.

I needed *blood*.

Baldy reached for me, and pure vampire instinct took over.

My hand shot out and grabbed his neck. I couldn't get a decent grip because of my smashed thumb, so I curled my good fingers into the veins and arteries that pumped below the surface of his skin, then used the last shreds of my strength to rip out his throat.

Hot blood gushed over my face, and I yanked the dead man closer so his blood poured into my mouth. Fresh energy flooded me, strength infusing my muscles, and I let out a little moan.

I could have drained every drop from his body, but I had to get out of here; even with fresh blood rejuvenating me, I couldn't hold my own against Etienne or Jemima if they came back.

I tossed Baldy to one side, then smashed the chair to splinters, freeing my other hand and my legs. I could get the cuffs off the chair legs but not off my legs—not unless I wanted to smash up my feet. My only option was to run with the cuffs still attached and pray that they didn't suck the strength out of me before I could get away.

I clambered awkwardly to my feet. The cuffs around my ankles were too tight—the metal had sunk through skin and flesh. Every step would be agony, but I clenched my teeth and bore it.

Beardy was on his knees, huddled in the farthest corner, practically catatonic with terror as I approached. I could only imagine how I looked: blood drenched, red eyed, my fangs jutting out.

The man's lips moved, and I realized he was praying, stumbling frantically over the words as if they'd save him. I didn't want to kill him. He'd helped my enemies in return for immortality, but so had June.

Equally, I couldn't leave him able to raise the alarm.

I hit him with the back of my hand, and he crashed into the wall before sliding into a senseless heap on the floor.

Stepping over him, I opened the door and slipped outside.

CHAPTER EIGHTEEN

Renie

The sun was still up so I hobbled as fast as I could for the nearest patch of trees. In the summer, a roof of leaves would have sheltered me, but in January, I could only crouch beneath the thickest branches and cling to the shred of protection they offered. It wasn't much and it wouldn't last long.

My legs felt like they were being dissolved in acid, fire licking all the way up to my skull.

The strength I'd got from Baldy's blood was already fading, leeched out of me by the bastard silver cuffs. My fingers were still twisted and broken, and I could barely stay on my feet. Hunger pulsed in my stomach, hot and sharp.

I couldn't tell where I was. The building I'd been kept in was little more than a large shed; there were no signs on the walls or any other indication of what it was. Trees ringed the building in small clusters, branches clutching each other like crooked fingers, but when I peered past the thick trunks all I could see were lines of hedges and more trees, and the spread of fields between them.

We were somewhere in the countryside then—hopefully on the outskirts of either Southampton or Winchester. As long as I wasn't far from either city, I should be able to find my way back to civilization.

I staggered through the trees, and every step sent fresh bolts of agony shooting through me, but I gritted my teeth and plowed on.

The sound of running water reached my ears—there was a river nearby.

I paused, turning my head this way and that, trying to pinpoint where the river was. I still wasn't used to this kind of sharp hearing, and the pressure in my head—the near-blinding rush of pain from my injuries—made it difficult to properly focus.

There—the river was on my right, I was sure of it. I staggered in that direction. It probably took less than a minute to reach it, but every step felt like a hundred years.

The river materialized through a knot of trees. It was a wide, crystal clear ribbon of water, and the clumps of vegetation poking up along the riverbank still gleamed with frost that the winter sun hadn't completely melted.

The river would be freezing, but what choice did I have? I couldn't go much farther on foot, and it wouldn't be long before Jemima or Etienne realized I'd escaped and came after me. The river would carry me faster than I could run, and it wasn't like I could freeze to death.

Closing my eyes, I slipped into the water.

Edmond

He glimpsed a building through the knots of trees—a shabby wooden shack, all alone in the swaths of countryside that hugged the edges of Southampton. The ground was littered with twigs and natural debris, but Edmond sidestepped it all with the natural grace of a vampire. Ludovic and Caoimhe flanked him, equally silent.

They'd left the van behind about half a mile ago. It was too dangerous to drive it to the rural hideout that Sully had told him about—any vampire would hear it coming. Going on foot was the best way.

Roux and Jason had wanted to come, but this time Edmond had

refused. He didn't know what he was walking into, but it was too dangerous for Renie's friends.

He crept closer to the shack, his ears pricked to every sound around them, and when he heard snatches of conversation, he paused and raised a hand. Ludovic and Caoimhe both froze.

"They're talking about Renie," Edmond whispered, his hands curling into fists. The humans inside the wooden building hadn't mentioned her by name, but there was only one girl they could be talking about.

". . . could you let her escape?" one voice barked, and Edmond felt a fierce burst of joy in his chest. He should've known that Renie would find her own way out of this mess—that it would take more than Jemima, Etienne, and their gang of puppets to keep her captive.

A proud smile curled his lips, only to vanish a split second later when he picked up a scent he knew only too well. Renie's blood—and there was far too much of it.

Edmond's unbeating heart clenched.

Renie was out here somewhere, wounded and defenseless against the sun. Edmond and the two vampires with him were old enough to withstand direct sunlight—Renie wasn't.

He had to find her.

"Ludovic," he whispered, beckoning.

Quiet as a ghost, Ludovic moved to his side.

"Renie's escaped, but she can't have been gone for long. Can you track her?" Edmond said.

Every vampire that Edmond had ever met had lived much of their lives alone, but Ludovic had once taken things further and completely isolated himself from humans. Forced to drink animal blood to survive, he'd learned how to track prey, how to read bent blades of grass and disturbances in fallen leaves—if anyone could find Renie, it was Ludovic.

Ludovic nodded, his eyes already scanning the ground. "This way," he said, pointing.

Edmond soon realized that he didn't need Ludovic to track Renie, because once they moved away from the shack and headed into the ragged patches of trees that dotted the area, the trail became obvious. Wet red splatters of blood stood out on the brown leaf mold carpeting the ground, and fresh rage flared in Edmond's chest.

What had Etienne done to her?

Had she collapsed out here, overcome by her injuries? Was she still trying to run, not realizing that he had come for her?

Emerging through a patch of trees, Edmond found himself on the bank of a wide river. Renie's trail abruptly stopped, and he knew in an instant what she had done.

"She's gone into the river," he snapped, breaking into a run.

"The scent's fresh, she can't have gone far," Ludovic said, drawing level with him.

That didn't ease the tight knot in Edmond's chest. Renie wouldn't freeze to death in the wintry water and she couldn't drown, but if she lost consciousness, there was no knowing how far the river would take her or what would happen if someone else found her—and that was if the sun didn't get her first.

He ran for half a mile before he saw her, and then he was hit by a wave of fear so strong it almost sent him to his knees. If his heart still beat, it would have stopped then.

Renie floated facedown in the middle of the river, her limbs splayed around her, softly bobbing with the movement of the water. He *knew* she couldn't drown, but she was so still, so fragile looking that Edmond couldn't fight off the cresting panic threatening to suck him under.

He leaped into the river.

The water wasn't deep, and he easily waded through it until he reached Renie and gathered her into his arms. Her face was porcelain white and her eyes were closed, but they fluttered open when he grabbed her. Droplets of icy water clung to her eyelashes like tiny diamonds.

"Edmond," she whispered.

Silver cuffs were on her wrists and ankles, leaving angry gouges all around, and partially healed cuts lined her arms, and Edmond bit back a snarl of fury. He wanted to charge back to that wooden shack and tear apart every single bastard who'd hurt her.

"You shouldn't be here," Renie whispered. "You should have gone to Ireland without me."

"Never!" he said fiercely.

"I hate to interrupt the charming reunion, but we need to get away before Jemima and Etienne come back," said Caoimhe from the bank.

She was right. Edmond's blood burned with vengeance, but Renie was injured, he himself hadn't fully healed, and Ysanne hadn't recovered from her stab wound. They were in no state to fight.

Cradling Renie, Edmond waded out of the river. She moaned and turned away from the sun, pressing her face against his chest.

"Here," said Ludovic, pulling off his shirt and handing it to Edmond.

Edmond draped it across Renie's head and shoulders, covering her as best he could. "Hold on, mon ange," he whispered, and her shirt-covered head moved in a nod.

Edmond ran.

Renie

I sat in the back of Andrew's black van, leaning against Edmond's chest. He hadn't taken his hands off me since pulling me out of the river.

I knew that vampires couldn't drown or catch hypothermia, but could they go into shock? It felt like there was a block of stone wedged in my chest. Everything that Etienne and Jemima had told me went round and round in my head, taunting me.

June had fantasized about a vampire falling in love with her. She'd watched all the vampire romance films, obsessively stalked every fan site, and read fan fiction until her eyes ached. In the end, she believed she'd achieved her dream. Only it had ended up killing her.

While Caoimhe crouched at my feet, examining the cuffs, Edmond gently lifted my injured hand. The bleeding had stopped, thanks to Baldy, but I hadn't taken enough of his blood to knit the broken bones back together. An image of Baldy staring down at me as I ripped out his throat flashed through my head, and I squeezed my eyes shut, as if that would block the memory.

I'd killed someone today.

I didn't know how to process that.

"Who did this to you?" Edmond asked, his voice low and savage, still looking at my hand.

"I did," I said, flinching away from the memory. "It was the only way to get out of the cuffs."

Approval flared in Caoimhe's blue eyes. "You're tougher than you look."

"Thanks?"

"You'll have to be tough again now, because without a key, the only way to get these cuffs off is to break them, and that's going to hurt."

"Can't you pick the lock?" Roux asked.

Caoimhe looked blankly at her.

Roux rolled her eyes and fumbled in the tufts of her hair until she found a hairpin. "Please tell me someone's done this before."

"I have," Jason said.

"You've had to pick your way out of handcuffs?" Roux tried for a light tone, but I heard the strain in her voice. This day was weighing on all of us.

"If you're really lucky, I'll get drunk and tell you about it sometime," Jason replied.

He took the hairpin from Roux and twisted it into the shape he wanted. It was dark enough in the van that he had to pat his way down my leg until he found the cuff on my ankle. Even the slightest pressure of his fingers sent fresh pain shooting through my system. I hissed and clutched Edmond's arm.

"Sorry, honey, but Caoimhe's right. This will hurt," Jason said.

It did, but I buried my face in Edmond's chest, inhaling the smell of him, and using his body as a buffer to absorb my sounds of pain. Even in the dark, Jason worked quickly, unlocking first one cuff and then the other, before moving to the one on my wrist.

Roux peeled the metal bracelets away from my skin, wincing and whispering sorry every time I whimpered.

When the cuffs were finally off, and that awful feeling of burning wasn't quite as bad, Roux held her wrist to my lips. "Don't even think about refusing," she said fiercely, and shot Ludovic a hard look.

I was too exhausted to protest, and this time, Ludovic didn't say anything.

I sank my fangs into her wrist, and warm blood rushed into my mouth, making me moan, but I only took a few mouthfuls before sealing the wounds with my tongue. As long as I was strong enough to stand, I could wait until we arrived at Fiaigh to feed again.

Assuming we were still going there.

"How did you know where to find me?" I asked.

"Jemima sent a couple of her human lackeys to watch your mother's house. They turned out to be quite talkative," Edmond said.

"Did you kill them?" If they'd threatened my mum, I didn't care if they were dead, but at the same time, the memory of my fingers curling into Baldy's throat, the sensation of his blood pouring over me, made me feel ill. I was tired of death.

Edmond glanced at Ludovic. "No. We tied them up and left them in the trunk of their own car. Someone will find them eventually."

"What about my mum? How am I supposed to keep her safe?" I said.

"I don't think she's in any danger now. There's no point in Etienne going after her again, not when he doesn't know where any of us are or how to get a hold of us. A hostage is only good if he can use them," Roux said. "But I did leave your mum a note, telling her to leave Southampton. It was all I could do—you can't risk calling home again."

"Are we still going to Fiaigh?" I said.

Nobody answered. Ysanne sat in the corner, her shoulders slumped, her hands loose in her lap. She'd already known about Jemima's betrayal by the time Edmond had found me, and it had cut a lot deeper than Etienne's.

"We have to," Caoimhe said. "If Etienne doesn't know I'm with you, there's no reason for him to suspect you'd go to my house."

"Is it safe for us, though?" Roux objected. "If Etienne and Jemima have supporters in other Houses, how do we know we're not walking into another trap?"

"Ysanne, Edmond, and Renie need blood, and my donors can provide that. We all need rest, and Renie needs to be somewhere safe for new vampires. My castle is the best place."

"Unless it's been compromised," Roux said.

Caoimhe pursed her lips. "Even *if* that's the case, which I think is extremely unlikely, Fiaigh's location makes it impossible for anyone to sneak up on it. That's one of the reasons we decided to go there in the first place. If Etienne learns that we're there, he won't take us unawares, and if the worst should happen, and we're forced to run again, then at least we'll have time to prepare first. If you have a better suggestion, I'm open to hearing it."

Roux sighed. "I don't."

"How do we get there, though?" Jason said.

"Ferry?"

"None of us have passports or money."

"Vampires don't have passports," Caoimhe said.

"We still need money. Or are you counting on free tickets because you're famous?" Jason asked.

Caoimhe's expression suggested that was exactly what she expected.

"Even if you could get free tickets, do you think it's a good idea to go somewhere as public as a ferry port?" Roux cautioned.

"Surely that's the perfect place," said Caoimhe. "Etienne won't risk making a move with so many witnesses."

"Maybe not, but you guys will get recognized, and if that info makes its way back to Etienne, he'll guess we're running to Ireland. If Fiaigh is safe for us, we can't risk jeopardizing that."

"Could we steal a boat?" I asked.

"You mean a speedboat or something? Does anyone here know how to pilot one?"

No one answered.

"I was thinking more like a rowboat," I said.

"Sweetie, do you have any idea how long it would take to row to Ireland?"

"No," I mumbled. "But vampires can row faster than humans . . ."

I trailed off because Roux was looking at me like I'd just said something incredibly dumb. Which I probably had.

"Even if vampires row twice as fast as humans, we're talking hundreds of miles. We'd be stuck in a rowboat for days," Roux said.

"Oh." Unexpected tears prickled my eyes. I was so *tired*. Lack of blood had made my stomach squeeze into a hard knot, and my gums ached where my fangs wanted to emerge. Pain from my injuries had filled my head with fog, making it hard to think, and the horror of everything that had happened today—the attack on the house, the torture, the fact that I'd *killed* someone—was lurking below the surface of that fog.

"Then we only have one choice." Caoimhe looked up at the roof of the van. "We fly."

"Wait, do you mean . . . you guys can't actually *fly*, can you? You haven't been keeping that secret all this time?" Jason said.

"In a plane," Caoimhe said.

Jason rubbed his eyes. "Sorry, it's been a long day."

"And it's not over yet," I muttered.

"There's a private airport at Lee-on-the-Solent, only half an hour away from here," said Caoimhe.

Ysanne spoke for the first time since my rescue. "Tell Andrew to take us there." She didn't look at anyone, and there was a hollowness in her voice that I'd never heard before.

Caoimhe knocked on the partition, and Andrew obediently braked. The Irish vampire moved to the van doors, then paused and looked back at me.

"Even once I get us a flight, it'll take a couple of hours to reach Fiaigh. Will you be all right until then?" she said.

I tried to smile, but it felt like more of a grimace. "I don't really have a choice, do I?"

"No."

Caoimhe climbed out of the van and closed the doors behind her, sealing us in darkness. A few moments later, we started moving again.

I closed my eyes and rested my head on Edmond's chest, trying not to think about how much everything hurt.

"What do we do if Fiaigh *isn't* safe?" said Jason in a small voice.

Even Ysanne didn't have an answer for that.

—

We reached the airport within half an hour.

"Wait here," Caoimhe said, and stood up, fluffing her blond curls with one hand.

"What are you doing?" Roux asked.

"Getting us a flight."

"With no money?"

Caoimhe smiled. "Let me worry about that."

She climbed out of the van, giving us a glimpse of the airport. The sun was starting to set, spilling red light across the sky. It made me think of the man I'd killed, the way it had been so easy to rip the life out of him and drink the blood that had poured onto my face. I looked away.

Caoimhe closed the doors again.

Roux still looked troubled, her forehead wrinkled, her teeth nibbling her lower lip.

"Caoimhe is one of the most famous women in the world. Don't underestimate the influence that celebrity can bring," said Ysanne.

"Influential enough that she can charter us a private plane at the last minute, with no money?" Roux said.

"Yes."

Roux still didn't look convinced, but whatever Caoimhe did worked—within twenty minutes she was back to inform us that a small private plane was willing to take us to Ireland.

I was barely aware of the journey across the sea. I spent part of it huddled under Andrew's T-shirt, shielding myself from the dying sun, and even once the sunset faded into slate-gray evening and I came out from under the shirt, I couldn't focus on anything. The sea rushed by beneath us, but I hardly saw it. I didn't even realize we'd landed in Ireland until Edmond kissed my forehead and told me we'd arrived.

We'd been forced to abandon the van back in England, and I thought that Caoimhe would work her Irish magic again, but instead Andrew stole one, and before I knew it, we were driving along the N22 to Killarney, a town in County Kerry, in the southwest of Ireland.

I had no idea what time it was, but the sky overhead had darkened to indigo, studded with stars and a grinning slice of moon. Now that the sun was no longer a threat, Andrew had swiped a van with windows, and I was glad; the new van was no bigger than the old one, but the windows made it feel less claustrophobic.

Fiaigh was located on the outskirts of Killarney National Park—a magnificent sprawl of lakes, mountain peaks, and woodlands of oak and yew. The road leading to the house was carved into the countryside for the convenience of tourists who didn't want to hike too far to catch a glimpse of the only Vampire House in Ireland.

Caoimhe visibly brightened as we drew closer to Fiaigh, and it made me think how hard this must have been for her. Not only had she lost friends, but she'd been stranded in another country, separated from her home by miles and miles of land and sea.

Fiaigh was more of a castle than a mansion. It soared up from the wild, rugged landscape, a huge building of gray stone, with many wood-shuttered windows, and chimney stacks protruding from turreted roofs. Two round towers flanked the main building; one was crenellated, the other capped with a small pointed roof like a witch's hat. The only resemblance it bore to Belle Morte was that the building was surrounded by a stone wall, broken only in the middle by a large gate. Unlike the wrought-iron gate leading into Belle Morte, Fiaigh's was a slab of solid black wood. I could see nothing of the house below the top of that gate.

"It's beautiful," Roux murmured, mashing her face against the window.

It was, but at the same time there was something bleak about the grayness of the stone and the cluttered shapes of turrets, chimneys, and roofs cutting a silhouette against the sky. All the way out here in the wilderness, it seemed like the sort of stereotypical castle that traditional vampires of fiction were expected to live in. I could imagine Dracula, dressed in a sweeping black cape, lurking in one of the upstairs rooms.

Caoimhe leaned forward—there was no partition in our new ride—and tapped Andrew on the shoulder. "Stop here," she said.

Obediently, he braked a short distance from the gate. Caoimhe climbed out and approached her house. Almost immediately, the huge wooden slab swung open and two men strode down the path that led to the castle.

They were both dressed in similar uniforms to the Belle Morte guards, only these were olive green rather than black, and each bore a silver brooch engraved with Celtic knotwork—a ring pierced through with a long, straight pin. They wore polished brogue shoes with silver buckles, and green caps on their heads. Black radios were clipped to their belts.

"Lady Caoimhe," the taller man said, executing a small bow. "We weren't expecting you back so soon, and . . ." His voice trailed off as he looked at our van.

"Seamus," Caoimhe said, "I'm afraid a lot has happened since I've been away. My friends will be staying with us for the foreseeable future."

Seamus nodded, and I wondered if he was head of security here—the Irish Dexter Flynn. Thinking of Dexter brought a pang to my chest.

"Gather the donors," Caoimhe instructed. "My friends need to feed."

The entrance to Fiaigh was less grandiose than Belle Morte's; in fact, I almost didn't see the small door that led into the castle, until Seamus opened it with a flourish, bowing as we passed.

The door led into a stone vestibule, which was brightened by tapestries hanging on the walls. Suits of armor occupied all four corners; they'd have looked foreboding if not for the tapestries.

Directly ahead was a stone staircase, wider than the one at Belle Morte, which led up to a wall—hung with another huge tapestry—before bisecting off into two separate staircases, one to the left and one to the right.

A cluster of donors in expensive pajamas appeared from the left staircase. Architecturally, Belle Morte and Fiaigh didn't have much in common, but when it came to fashion, their ruling women shared the same tastes.

Caoimhe swept over to them, as graceful and imperious as Ysanne had ever been, and spoke quietly with the donors standing on the lowest step. They all looked at me, and I lowered my eyes to the floor. Edmond's arm tightened around my waist, trying to silently reassure me, but for once it wasn't enough. I felt sharp all over, like my skin didn't fit properly, like I was completely out of place here.

I didn't even look up when Caoimhe came back over to us.

"Jennifer will escort you to the guest bedrooms, then I'll send some donors up," she said.

At Belle Morte, the west wing was where visitors stayed, so before Ysanne had hidden June there, I guessed it had been out of bounds for donors. Were donors normally allowed in vampires' rooms in Fiaigh, or was Caoimhe bending the rules because of the circumstances? I was too tired to ask.

Footsteps approached—Jennifer, I assumed—but I still didn't look up. I wanted to lie down on the floor and go to sleep, and pretend that none of this was happening.

Edmond touched the small of my back. "Mon ange?" he said, his voice gentle.

Finally, I lifted my gaze from the floor. Edmond's eyes were shadowed with worry, his dark brows pulled together, and a knot of emotion threatened to choke me. I wanted to believe we could achieve anything now we were together, but everything was so fucked-up, and love alone couldn't fix that.

"Come on," Edmond murmured, putting his arm around my waist so I could lean on him. But I still didn't say anything as Jennifer led us away.

CHAPTER NINETEEN

Edmond

He'd never known Renie to be so quiet.

Jennifer led them past the throng of staring donors, then up another set of stairs to the third floor and down a wide hallway, whose stone-flagged floor was softened by a woven runner, before turning left. At any other time, Edmond would have been interested in exploring Fiaigh—this was the first time he'd visited—but the only thing he could focus on was the girl at his side, huddled against him as if he was the only thing keeping her on her feet.

There were questions written all over Jennifer's face, but perhaps Caoimhe had warned her not to pry, because she didn't ask anything.

"Do you need one room or two?" she asked.

"One," Edmond replied, surprised that Caoimhe hadn't already said this to Jennifer.

"This feels really weird," Renie said.

"What does?" Edmond said.

She listlessly gestured to the doors on either side of them, leading to Fiaigh's guest rooms. "The first night I came to Belle Morte, Gideon led me, Roux, and Jason through the south wing until we got to our rooms. Now I'm doing that again, but everything's different this time. I was human then. Now I'm a vampire, my sister's dead, and we're on the run from the person who killed her, a person I trusted and considered a friend."

Jennifer looked back at them, her forehead wrinkled in a frown.

Edmond wondered if Caoimhe was planning on telling her House everything that had happened, or if she thought it was better to keep them in the dark. For everyone's sake, he hoped it was the former. Ysanne had lied to Belle Morte about June, and though it had been with the best intentions, the results had been devastating. Caoimhe couldn't be foolish enough to make the same mistake.

Jennifer stopped in front of a door and opened it. "The donors will be along shortly," she said.

"Thank you," Edmond said, guiding Renie into the room. He closed the door behind them.

"Do you know her?" Renie asked, wrapping her arms around herself.

"Jennifer? No. We've only met once, ten years ago when we were coming out of the shadows."

"Are we safe here?"

It would be so easy to feed her a soothing lie, but Edmond had lied to Renie before, about June, and it had torn her up inside. He wouldn't lie to her again, not even about this.

"I really don't know, but I'd like to think so. At the very least we can rest and heal and plan our next move," he said.

"What the hell *is* our next move?" Renie said.

Someone knocked on the door before Edmond could answer. He opened it to find eight donors standing outside, looking uncertain and a little scared. Edmond supposed that was hardly surprising. Life in a Vampire House was supposed to be luxurious, relaxing, and predictable. Vampires and donors from other Houses weren't supposed to arrive unannounced, covered in blood, and looking like they'd been through hell.

"Lady Caoimhe said you'd need all of us?" said the tallest donor, tucking a strand of dark hair behind her ear.

Edmond nodded. Renie's injuries had been bad, and fully healing them would require more blood than any one donor could safely give. But Renie wouldn't know how much to safely take yet, so Edmond needed to supervise her feeding.

"Renie?" he said.

She was staring at the floor again, her arms still wrapped around herself, looking sad and lost, but she raised her head when he said her name.

"Do you want to sit down for this?" Edmond asked.

Renie glanced at the bed, then shook her head.

On the drive to Southampton Ludovic had told Edmond that Renie had struggled with the reality of drinking blood to survive, but she didn't hesitate this time; when the dark-haired donor approached her, Renie took the girl's wrist and bit down.

Edmond watched her drink, her throat bobbing as she swallowed, until he gauged she'd taken enough, then he put a hand on her shoulder. Renie pulled back, her eyes gleaming red. Edmond ushered the next donor over while he swept his tongue over the fang marks on the first girl's wrist, sealing them. He'd drink when he was sure that Renie had had enough, not before.

Renie took more from five of the donors than a vampire would on a normal day, but her body needed it. The donors she'd drunk from wouldn't be able to feed any other vampires for a while, but Caoimhe would know that. Edmond had known her long enough to appreciate that she wouldn't put her donors at risk.

Then it was his turn. He drank quickly from the remaining donors, then escorted them all from the room without another word.

Renie looked down at herself, and her face crumpled. The blood had washed off her skin and hair when she'd jumped into the river, but her clothes were still black with it, and suddenly it was all Edmond could smell.

"I killed someone today," she said quietly.

"You didn't have a choice." Even as he said it, Edmond knew that made little difference. He'd had no choice about taking lives in times of war, but it had still taken him a long time to stop seeing the faces of the people he'd killed in his nightmares.

"I'm proud of you for fighting back and doing whatever was necessary to free yourself," he added.

Renie picked at her blood-crusted clothes. "I need a shower."

"Renie—" Edmond started, but she held up a hand to cut him off.

"I just . . . I think I need some time alone," she said.

He didn't want to leave her like this, exhausted and broken, but if it was what she needed, he had to do it.

Hot anger flashed in his chest. Renie's physical wounds had healed, but drinking blood couldn't repair the emotional damage. The man she'd thought was her friend had murdered her sister, been instrumental in causing many other deaths, had threatened her mother, her friends, the people she loved, and then had kidnapped and tortured her. She'd killed because of him, and Edmond had no idea how long she'd carry the weight of that.

If Etienne were here now, Edmond would kill him with his bare hands.

Renie disappeared into the bathroom, and as the shower started running, another knock came at the bedroom door. Caoimhe stood on the other side. She'd changed into clean jeans and a crisp white blouse, and her blond curls spilled thickly around her shoulders. She was still one of the most beautiful women that Edmond had ever seen. But she no longer stirred him the way she had when they'd been together, all those long decades ago, and the spark he'd once felt for Caoimhe then was nothing compared to the fire he felt for Renie.

"Can we talk?" she said.

Edmond beckoned her into the room but Caoimhe shook her head. "Not here."

She led him to an empty room three doors down the hallway, and when they were inside, she leaned against the closed door.

"What's going on?" Edmond asked.

"Have you given any thought to where we go from here?" Caoimhe asked.

"We've only just arrived," Edmond pointed out. "I was hoping we could take some time to rest and recover before doing anything else."

"But how much time do you think we have?"

Edmond studied his old lover carefully. "Is there something you're not telling me?"

Caoimhe took a moment to answer. "Etienne doesn't appear to know that I'm with you, but he knows that I'm still alive, and since I'm an eyewitness to the fact that Ysanne did not orchestrate the assassination of the Council, he'll want me out of the way. Coming to Fiaigh was the right thing to do, but Etienne's not stupid. If he hasn't already guessed that I'd run here, he soon will."

"You said he couldn't launch an invasion on us here."

"He can't, but he's been ahead of us the whole way, and it would be foolish to assume that we're safe here simply because he can't repeat what happened at Belle Morte."

"What are you suggesting?" Edmond asked.

"I honestly have no idea. But we'll need to address this sooner rather than later."

"Have you brought this up with Ysanne?"

"Not yet."

"Why come to me instead of her?"

"Ysanne is one of the strongest women I've ever met, but she's just lost her House, her leadership, her people, and the woman she loves. I thought she needed some time to come to terms with that before being reminded that we're not even close to being out of the woods yet."

Edmond closed his eyes and tried to think. Getting to Fiaigh had been their goal, but Caoimhe was right—they couldn't stay here forever. But where else were they meant to go?

"I'm not saying we need to formulate a plan right now, or start packing to go on the run for good, but we need to be aware of the reality of our situation," Caoimhe said.

"We can discuss it properly tomorrow. Everyone needs this night to rest," Edmond said, thinking of the bleak look in Renie's eyes.

Caoimhe smiled, but it was wan. "At least this finally made you come to Fiaigh."

"I always meant to," Edmond said.

"But you never did."

He couldn't deny it. Caoimhe would never again be his lover, but she'd always be his friend, and he should have made more effort. During the early years of the donor system, Edmond had stuck by Ysanne's side to make sure that everything ran smoothly, and though he'd had every intention of visiting Fiaigh, somehow it hadn't happened.

"I'm sorry," he said.

Caoimhe smiled again, and it was warmer this time, more real. "Maybe when this mess is all cleared up, you'll find time to visit more often."

Edmond couldn't smile back because they both knew that Caoimhe's words were hollow. There was no guarantee that any of this *would* be cleared up, or how Etienne's actions would reshape their world.

"I assume that Renie will come with you?" Caoimhe said.

"She will."

"You really are in love with her," Caoimhe said.

"I am."

"You once told me that you didn't ever want to fall in love again."

"And you told me it wasn't something I had any control over."

Caoimhe looked expectantly at him.

"You were right. Is that what you wanted to hear?" Edmond said.

"Absolutely."

Edmond laughed.

Caoimhe smiled. "I like Renie. I think she'll be good for you."

"She already has been."

Renie

I sat under the scalding shower water, my arms locked around my knees, my exhausted mind going over and over the events of the day. I saw the face of the man I'd killed, the fear and desperation in his eyes, felt his blood pouring over my face, remembered the taste of it in my mouth. I'd scrubbed my skin and my hair until there was no trace of it left, but I imagined I could still feel it—sticky and drying—still smell it, still taste it.

My stomach felt hollow, snarled with sickness and guilt, but I was angry too—at myself for feeling this way, and at that man for *making* me feel this way. He'd kidnapped me and handed me over to someone he knew would brutally torture me. No one had forced him to do it. I didn't want to feel a shred of guilt over killing someone who'd done that to me, but I couldn't help it.

The bathroom door opened and Roux peeked in. "You okay?" she said.

I tried to say yes, to pretend, but all that came out was a choked sob.

"Oh, sweetie!" Roux rushed into the shower, crouched down, and hugged me.

"You're getting wet," I mumbled, trying to push her away.

"I don't care."

We sat like that for a while, as the water rained down on us, until I felt strong enough to pull out of Roux's hug. I shoved my wet hair off my face.

"Edmond said he was proud of me for killing that guy because it meant I'd fought back," I said.

"I agree with him. You had no other option. Not to mention, you didn't just do it to protect yourself. You were protecting us, weren't you? If Etienne had made you talk, he'd have come after us."

"I hadn't thought of it like that," I admitted.

Roux gave my bare back a soothing rub. "Do you think you're ready to get up?"

I nodded.

Roux fetched a towel from the rack on the wall and wrapped it around my shoulders. "Let's get out of here," she said.

She led me out of the bathroom, then sat on the bed while I dried off. This was the first time that I'd actually taken note of the room that Caoimhe had given us. It was bigger than the room Roux and I had shared at Belle Morte, with a polished wooden floor and burgundy walls that flowed up to an arched ceiling. The four-poster bed was draped in white silk, the wardrobe along the nearest wall was large enough to practically be a room in its own right, and the space was dotted here and there with fat red candles on tall iron holders.

Keeping my towel tucked around me, I rummaged through the wardrobe until I found a pair of silk trousers and a cream fine-knit sweater that looked about my size.

"Does Caoimhe keep the guest rooms stocked with clothes for when people come to stay?" I asked.

"I guess so," Roux said.

"How does she know what size—" I paused partway through pulling the trousers on.

"Problem?" Roux said.

"Donors have to give their measurements to their assigned House before going there, so their clothes can be provided for them. Do Houses do the same for vampire visitors?"

Roux shrugged. "Maybe? Why does that matter?"

My throat felt like it was full of thorns. "What if these are Jemima's clothes? We're about the same height."

After everything Jemima had done, the thought of wearing her clothes made me feel sick.

Roux gave me an appraising look. "You're curvier than Jemima, and that outfit looks like a pretty good fit, so I doubt they're hers.

Plenty of vampires have stayed here over the last decade—those clothes could be for anyone. Besides, unless you want to walk around in a towel, you don't have much choice."

She had a point. I got dressed, then pulled my wet hair into a loose knot on top of my head, and studied my friend. In the short time that we'd known each other, Roux had become one of the most important people in my life, but I hadn't forgotten how she'd reacted when I'd become a vampire.

"Are we okay?" I asked.

Roux looked startled. "Why wouldn't we be?"

I gave her a pointed look, and Roux's expression wobbled.

"You're talking about me being a bitch when you came to see me in the south wing, aren't you?" she said.

"You weren't being a bitch, but you were mad at me, and I don't understand why," I said.

Roux looked away, her hands twisting in her lap.

"Roux? What's going on?"

"I don't have many friends outside Belle Morte," Roux confessed.

"You're kidding," I said. Roux had sacrificed her once-in-a-lifetime experience in a Vampire House to help me uncover what had happened to June, she'd stuck by me every step of the way since then, and she'd risked herself to save me when Etienne's mob had first attacked Belle Morte. She was kind and smart and compassionate, and I couldn't imagine anyone not adoring her the way I did.

"This isn't the time for a pity party, but I really don't have many friends, and none that I truly trust. You and Jason mean the world to me, and I was scared that turning into a vampire would make you all snooty and stuck-up, like so many of them are."

"I thought you liked vampires."

"I do." She sniffled. "But that doesn't mean they're not assholes sometimes."

I hugged her. "I'm still me, Roux. That won't change because I have fangs now."

Dexter Flynn had said something similar to me, and my chest twisted a little as I remembered the light fading from his eyes. Then I remembered something else.

I ran back into the bathroom and sifted through the bloody clothes I'd abandoned in the corner until I found the gold locket that Dexter had given me. I still had no idea how I'd find his daughter, but I'd find a way to keep my promise.

Sadness swept across Roux's face when she saw the locket.

"How long do you think we'll stay here?" she asked, looking around the room.

I didn't know how to answer that. We couldn't stay forever, which meant that, soon enough, we'd all have to sit down and discuss our next move.

"What's your room like?" I asked, changing the subject.

"Not as big as yours." Roux reached up and touched the silk canopy draped around the bed. "My bed's less fancy, too, but it's big enough for me and Jason, and that's all that matters."

"I didn't realize you guys were sharing a room." Jason had taken my place as Roux's roommate at Belle Morte after I'd become a vampire, but Caoimhe didn't know that. I'd assumed she'd given them separate rooms.

"We weren't at first, but it took Jason about two minutes to knock on my door and ask to move in with me."

That didn't surprise me. We were in a strange castle in a strange country, mostly surrounded by people we didn't know, with no idea what had happened to everyone we'd left behind at Belle Morte. I had the man I loved to help me through it. Jason and Roux needed each other.

Footsteps sounded outside, a soft tread that I knew well, and I couldn't keep a smile from breaking across my face.

Edmond opened the door.

Roux looked from me to Edmond and back again, and a mischievous gleam crept into her eyes. "I'll just leave you two to . . . explore your room."

She slipped out.

For a long moment Edmond and I stared at each other across the few feet of floor that separated us.

"How are you feeling?" he asked.

I thought about it. "Calmer," I said. "I'm still processing everything that's happened, and I'm still not okay, but I'm not going to fall apart."

"If you do fall, I'll always catch you."

"I know."

I gazed at the vampire who'd stolen my heart, studying each line and angle of his face, his obsidian-black hair, and the sharp glitter of his eyes, and then I rushed across the room and threw myself into his arms.

Our lips collided. Edmond's arms slid around my waist, crushing me to him, and I twisted my hands in his hair, kissing him like I was trying to drink him down. His fangs grazed my lip and I let out a little moan.

My own fangs slid out, so quickly that it stung. "Ow," I complained, leaning back and pressing a hand to my mouth.

"Your fangs react to any kind of heightened emotion. Hunger, anger"—Edmond's voice dropped a notch, vibrating along my skin—"excitement."

"Maybe I'm a bit nervous," I said.

"Nervous? You're not . . ."

"A virgin? No, but I can't compete with the number of lovers you must have racked up."

"It's a good thing it's not a competition," he teased.

"It's not that. You've got so much experience and I'm scared of disappointing you."

"How do you know *I* won't disappoint *you*?" Edmond said.

"You've got several hundred years' experience on me, Casanova."

He chuckled, his hands gliding up my arms. The sweater I wore absorbed most of the sensation, but still I shivered.

"I'll answer any question. What would you like to know?" he said.

"Can I ask how many people you've slept with?"

Edmond was silent for a moment. A lock of hair fell over his face but I didn't brush it away; I loved the stark contrast of that inky hair against his pale skin. "If I could tell you, I would," he said.

"But?" I prompted, because a but was obviously coming.

"But I don't remember."

I hadn't considered that, but it made sense. It was easy to keep track if you were sexually active for a human's lifetime, less so when you'd lived for hundreds of years.

"Do you remember when I told you about my life leading up to the French Revolution? During those years of selfishness and indulgence, I don't remember everything I did. I took whatever I wanted, whether that was blood or sex. I took a lot of women into my bed, but I don't remember how many. I couldn't recall their faces if I tried, and I rarely knew their names."

Well, I had asked.

"What's the longest you went without sex?" I asked.

"Sixty years? Maybe more."

"Oh wow. That's a *lifetime*."

"I haven't been celibate any time recently, but it has been a very long time since I slept with anyone I truly cared about. I didn't think I could feel that way about anyone again."

"And now?" I asked, though I already knew the answer.

Edmond studied my face, his glittering eyes absorbing every feature. "I have lived a very long time, and I've loved a number of women, but you, ma chérie—you *undo* me," he whispered.

Everything inside me seemed to burn and clench at the gentle beauty of his words. I kissed him like I couldn't stop, one hand twisting in his hair, the other flat against his chest, over his heart. Edmond pressed his hips against me, and even through his clothes I could feel how hard he was.

In my most private fantasies, I'd imagined what Edmond would look like naked, imagined the way his hands and mouth would feel roaming over my body. Now we were getting close to that, and my tongue was dry with anticipation, and though my heart didn't beat anymore, I swore I felt an echo of it, frantically thumping in my chest.

"We don't have to do this now," Edmond murmured against my mouth.

"Yes, we do."

We had no idea what was coming next or how long we'd be safe at Fiaigh, and I wanted to take this time with the man I loved while we still could.

Edmond gently pulled my damp hair out of its knot and let it spill around my shoulders. His eyes flared red with desire.

"Kiss me," I whispered.

A fire had started beneath my skin, and when Edmond's lips found mine again, when he started pulling at my clothes, I felt like I was about to combust. Edmond dropped my sweater to the floor. I wore nothing underneath, and the look in his eyes made me feel like something rare and precious.

I put both hands on my hips, posing for him, and gave him a wicked smile that Roux would have been proud of. I'd always been confident in my own skin, and the way Edmond gazed at me only bolstered that.

"Mon ange," he breathed.

With my eyes locked on his, I reached for the button on my trousers, flicking it open with deliberate slowness. Edmond watched every movement, his eyes as red as melted rubies. I shimmied the trousers down and kicked them out of the way. Edmond's gaze traveled slowly up my body, and everywhere he looked, I swore I felt the imprint of his hands and lips.

But that wasn't enough.

I wanted the real thing.

I pulled off Edmond's clothes with none of the slowness I'd employed for my own, but when he stood naked in front of me, all I could do was stare. He was more beautiful than any man had a right to be. My eyes trailed over the pale perfection of his chest, skin stretched tight over every line of muscle, and then moved down . . .

"Mon ange." His voice was a wicked caress. "I do believe you're blushing."

"Vampires can't blush."

He responded with a slow grin that made me tingle. When he walked toward me, I thought we would take things slow, so it caught me by surprise when he suddenly scooped me into his arms and slung me onto the bed. He braced his weight on his forearms so his body hovered above mine, perfectly aligned but not quite touching.

I drew my knees up on either side of Edmond's hips. His eyes burned even hotter, scorching trails across my skin. His hands followed the path of his eyes, shaping themselves around my breasts and hips, gliding between my legs to touch me where I wanted him the most. My whole body jumped in response, electricity zipping through me.

"Tell me you love me," Edmond whispered, nipping at my ear, his tongue tracing the lobe. "I need to hear you say it."

"I love you. Edmond, I love you so much."

His hands were gentle at first, bringing me closer and closer to a place where only bliss existed, then he sheathed himself inside, and I let out a little cry, my nails digging into his shoulders. His mouth found mine, urging my tongue into a desperate dance, as his hips moved into a desperate rhythm.

Whenever I'd fantasized about sex with Edmond, I'd always imagined it to be pretty damn spectacular. The reality blew the fantasy away. Edmond slid an arm beneath my waist, pulling my lower body tighter against him as he thrust. My hands roamed over him, feeling the places where the smoothness of his skin gave way to the ridges of scar tissue on his back, wounds he'd received as a human, and down to the shrapnel embedded in his side. Even though I didn't need to breathe, my breaths came quick and fast, my lips shaping his name at the end of every cry.

The pressure inside me wound tighter and tighter, coiling through every muscle, every nerve ending until I felt like I was drowning in sweet fire, like I was going to snap. And then I did snap, pure pleasure exploding throughout my body, Edmond's name forming a scream on my lips.

I slumped back on the bed, tiny electric shudders still rippling through me. Edmond's nose brushed mine, his black hair hanging like a curtain around us. "I'm not done with you yet," he whispered, his voice husky.

He was still rock-hard inside me, and the muscles in his arms bulged where his entire weight rested on them. My whole body had gone limp in the wake of a blistering orgasm, but when Edmond lowered his head and nibbled the line of my throat, his fangs gently scraping my skin, every muscle coiled again in delicious anticipation.

"I want to see that look in your eyes again," Edmond murmured, his tongue tracing the shape of my useless pulse. "I want to see you come apart again."

The words were barely out of his mouth before he was moving, his hips meeting mine with greater force. His eyes never left my face, watching every gasp and moan I made as our bodies melded together.

When I came again, it was with a hoarse scream, and this time Edmond joined me, gasping out my name before his mouth crashed down on mine, drinking my lingering cries as aftershocks shuddered through my system.

"I didn't think I'd ever do this again," Edmond whispered, kissing my shoulder. I lay naked in his arms, my back against his chest, our legs tangled together, the hard edges of his body against the soft curves of mine.

"Have sex?" I said.

"Lie with someone in my arms like this."

I jabbed a playful elbow into the hard muscles of his stomach. "What do you normally do—wham, bam, thank you, ma'am? Don't let the door hit you on the way out?"

Edmond stroked the curve of my hip. "I never thought I'd lie in bed with someone I truly loved again."

I laced my fingers with his and pulled his arm around my stomach. He leaned over to kiss me, and I twisted my head back, giving him better access.

"Immortality is not always what people believe it is," he murmured. "A vampire's life can be long and lonely, and I don't ever want you to regret making this choice."

"I won't," I whispered. "Your life was lonely because you *were* alone. But I won't be, because I have you."

"Tu es ma raison d'être," he said.

"What does that mean?"

He lifted a handful of my hair, watching the auburn strands trickle through his fingers. "You are my reason for being."

"Smooth talker."

"Tu es si belle."

"Hey, Frenchy," I teased. "I don't know what you're saying."

"I said you are so beautiful." A languid smile curled his lips. "Don't pretend you don't like it when I speak French to you."

It would be pointless to deny it—I loved the way his voice took on a foreign lilt, the way it curled around the French vowels like he was tasting them.

"Say something else," I said, snuggling against him.

Edmond murmured to me in French, and I had no idea what he was saying, but the sound of his voice made me feel safe.

CHAPTER TWENTY

Renie

Edmond fell asleep before me. Much as I'd liked lying naked together, I'd persuaded him to put some pants on before we settled down for the night—despite Caoimhe's assurances that Etienne couldn't sneak up on us, I was terrified that he'd find a way. If we suddenly had to go on the run again, we weren't doing it naked.

Every time I closed my eyes I saw Etienne's face, his eyes soft with sympathy as he told me that he was sorry that I had to die. He wouldn't stop coming after us, and I had no idea how to stop him.

I sat up, pushing my hair off my face. Edmond didn't stir. I looked down at him as he slept, his hair spilled across the pillow like ink, and the knot of tension in my chest eased. We *would* get through this. Etienne would not win.

Gently, I ran my thumb along the dark brushstrokes of Edmond's eyebrow, and along the edge of his cheekbone. He opened his eyes and smiled at me, soft and sleepy. I traced the shape of his mouth, and he kissed my fingertip. Then he frowned.

"What's wrong?" I said.

"I can't tell you how much I've wanted us to share a room like this, but it's not supposed to be here," Edmond said. He muttered something sharp in French. "It's meant to be at Belle Morte. That's our home."

I wasn't so sure it was *my* home, but Edmond had lived there for more than half my lifetime. It was home to him, and I wished I knew what to say.

Suddenly Edmond went very still, like a panther about to strike.

I started to speak, but he put a finger to my lips and shook his head. *Someone's outside the door*, he mouthed.

That shouldn't have come as a surprise—Fiaigh was bigger than Belle Morte and I didn't know how many people lived here—but something about Edmond's body language made my skin prickle with warning. He thought something was wrong.

What do we do? I mouthed.

Edmond put a hand on my chest and gently pushed me down. I assumed he wanted me to pretend I was sleeping—the last thing I wanted when a threat was lurking outside our door.

But I trusted Edmond.

I closed my eyes.

A few moments passed, and my whole body felt as tense as a wire, and then the bedroom door quietly opened. If I was human, I wouldn't have heard it, or the near noiseless footsteps on the wooden floor. There was no heartbeat, no breathing, so our intruder was a vampire. Etienne's face flashed through my head again, and I had to fight not to leap out of bed.

The footsteps drew closer, and the urge to run became so strong I could almost taste it.

There was a pause, as if the intruder was trying to decide what to do, then the footsteps moved to Edmond's side of the bed. I heard the faintest whisper of metal on metal, and fear gripped my throat like a fist. But still I didn't move.

Edmond struck like a snake. I heard the *crack* of breaking bone, and a sharp cry, then I scrambled out of bed and ran for the light switch on the wall, momentarily forgetting that my vampire vision was good enough to see in the dark.

A vampire I'd never seen before knelt beside the bed, Edmond standing over him. Edmond had twisted the vampire's left arm up behind his back with one hand; his other hand had a tight grip on the vampire's throat. The vampire's right arm dangled at his side. It looked badly broken. About a foot away, a long knife gleamed on the floor where the vampire must have dropped it.

The door flew open behind me and I leaped back, my eyes frantically scanning the room for a weapon in case the strange vampire had backup.

Ludovic and Ysanne stood in the doorway. Ysanne's eyes blazed red and her fangs were like sharpened daggers. The vampire on the floor shrank back, and I didn't blame him. Edmond might have broken the guy's arm but Ysanne looked like she was about to rip him apart.

"What happened?" she said, and her voice was so cold, I half expected frost to creep up the walls.

"Eoghan tried to stab me in my sleep," Edmond said, giving the vampire a little shake.

"He wasn't alone," said an Irish lilt, and Ludovic and Ysanne moved out of the doorway. Caoimhe stood behind them, and beside her was a tall blond man wearing the green uniform of Fiaigh security.

"Tadhg, you *betrayed* me?" Eoghan cried.

The guard looked at the floor, his shoulders hunched.

"He didn't mention you, actually. You were just stupid enough to go after an older, stronger, faster vampire," Caoimhe snapped, her eyes sparking red.

Eoghan tried to lunge forward, and Edmond slammed his head against the side of the bed. Vampires were made of sterner stuff than humans, but blood still trickled from the split skin on Eoghan's forehead and dripped onto the wooden floor.

"Anyone want to tell me what the fuck is going on?" I said, looking from Eoghan to Tadhg, and then to Caoimhe.

"I think we need to take this downstairs," Caoimhe said.

"What about him?" Edmond asked, giving Eoghan another shake.

Eoghan tried again to pull away, and Edmond twisted his arm at an even sharper angle. "I'll break this one too," he warned.

Eoghan muttered something in what I assumed was Gaelic.

I heard footsteps on the floor outside the room, and then Seamus appeared in what was now a very crowded doorway. His uniform was askew and his hair a bit wild, as if he'd woken up and dressed in a hurry, but his expression was alert. I didn't miss the look of disgust he gave Tadhg.

"There have been no other disturbances. All the donors are safe and sleeping," he reported.

Caoimhe nodded. "Cuff him."

Seamus pulled a pair of handcuffs from his pocket and approached Eoghan. Edmond held the other vampire steady while Seamus snapped the cuffs onto his wrists, and from the hissing noise Eoghan made, I guessed the cuffs were silver.

I knew exactly how painful that was, and for a split second I felt a flicker of sympathy for Eoghan. Then I remembered that he'd tried to kill Edmond, and that sympathy was promptly snuffed out.

"To the cells?" Seamus asked Caoimhe.

"Yes. Maeve and Fion will help escort him there." Caoimhe walked over to the knife that Eoghan had dropped. She picked it up and tilted it so the light overhead played off the polished blade. Her eyes were icy cold when she looked at Eoghan. His own eyes blazed with anger, but he dropped his gaze first.

Seamus hauled Eoghan to his feet and pushed him to the door. I still expected him to fight back, despite his broken arm and the silver cuffs, but apparently even he wasn't that stupid. Silently, he let Seamus march him out of the room.

"Caoimhe," Tadhg started, but she silenced him with a slashing motion of her hand.

"Dining room. Now," she said.

I sidled around the bed and took Edmond's hand, but he didn't look at me. His eyes were fixed on Caoimhe, and his expression was chilly. Caoimhe glanced at him, looked away again, then stalked out of the room. Tadhg scurried before her, and Ysanne and Ludovic followed.

"Edmond?" I said. I was missing something here.

He shook his head. "We need to get to the dining room."

Being led to the guest room earlier had felt like going back in time to my first night in Belle Morte, so there was something jarring about leaving it and seeing polished wooden floors instead of thick carpets. Paintings still hung on the walls, like they did in Belle Morte, but they weren't the paintings I was used to. Instead of the occasional Belle Morte statue, Fiaigh had suits of armor, and the wall space between pictures was occupied by mounted swords and daggers.

I'd been keen to get out of Belle Morte as soon as I'd found out what had happened to June, and I'd never thought that I'd come to think of the place as home—I still wasn't sure I did, but I did miss it.

Belle Morte was where I'd lost my sister, and where I'd lost my own life, but it was also where I'd met Roux and Jason, and where I'd fallen in love with Edmond.

Caoimhe led us down two floors to the dining room. The space was as big as Belle Morte's dining hall but the ceilings were higher, crossed here and there by rafters, and the walls were lined with sideboards, each one topped with a vase of flowers, some antique pottery, or a piece of armor. Rather than featuring a long trestle table, the room was occupied by six smaller tables, each edged with hammered copper and surrounded by chairs with padded velvet seats. One of the farthest tables was covered with photos and old newspapers.

Caoimhe pulled out a seat at the nearest table and pushed Tadhg into it. He sat, shoulders slumped, his heartbeat thundering in my ears.

"I assume you're going to tell us what's going on?" Ysanne said to Caoimhe, taking a seat opposite Tadhg.

Caoimhe placed Eoghan's knife on the table. "One of my vampires attempted to assassinate Edmond in his sleep. At the same time, Tadhg was supposed to assassinate me."

Tadhg winced.

"You knew this was going to happen, didn't you?" Edmond said, his eyes still locked on Caoimhe.

I tensed, looking around the room to see how many exits there were. If Caoimhe had betrayed us, then we needed to run. As if he knew what as I was thinking, Edmond's hand brushed mine, a silent reassurance.

"Not for certain," Caoimhe said.

"But you suspected," Edmond pushed.

"Yes."

Sparks of red danced in Edmond's eyes, and Ysanne's hands curled into fists.

"I do hope that I'm misinterpreting this, Caoimhe," she said, her voice as sharp as a broken icicle.

Caoimhe spread her palms. "Will you let me explain?"

Ysanne gave a curt nod.

Caoimhe gestured to the chairs around the table, but I stayed standing. I no longer trusted her. Edmond and Ludovic didn't sit down, either, and the tension in the room was thick enough to carve with Eoghan's knife.

"There were a few things that didn't make sense to me when the Council gathered at Belle Morte to discuss June Mayfield and the attack on the house. But with the revelation of Jemima's treach-ery and everything that Renie had learned from her and Etienne, we now know that they wanted to take control of all the Vampire Houses in the UK and the Republic of Ireland. As the Lady of Nox, Jemima already has control of that House. If the plan to assassinate the Council had been successful and Jemima had been the only survivor, then she would have had the right to appoint someone to run Belle Morte."

"Etienne," I said.

Caoimhe shook her head, blond curls bouncing. "I don't think so. Even though you couldn't prove any of your allegations against him, putting him in charge of Belle Morte could have been too suspicious. But she and Etienne have planned this carefully, and they would have made sure that they had supporters to step into the Council's shoes."

"There are other Belle Morte vampires involved with this," I realized, my stomach turning over.

"I believe Jemima and Etienne have been planning this for longer than any of us realized," Caoimhe replied. "Eric Wilson from Midnight died during that first attack, and Henry had no idea that he'd been in Belle Morte. Since Henry clearly wasn't helping Etienne and Jemima, it seems likely that Eric *was*, which means they've built support in Belle Morte, Nox, Midnight and probably Lamia, without anyone knowing. Ever since Renie told us what she'd learned, I've suspected that Fiaigh was probably compromised too."

"Then why the hell did you make us come here?" I burst out.

"Because you, Edmond, and Ysanne were injured and you needed blood and time to rest. The humans among us were exhausted. We couldn't have gone on much longer."

"So you decided to bring us to a place you knew wasn't safe. Brilliant." I slumped into a chair and folded my arms.

"I decided to draw out any traitors that may have been under my roof."

"By using us as bait," I snapped.

Caoimhe didn't deny it. I wanted to kick a chair at her face.

"You gambled with Renie's life," Edmond said, in a low, dangerous voice.

"No, I didn't. Renie is no threat to Etienne or Jemima. Ysanne's hopes that Renie might have some influence over June have proved entirely fruitless, so Etienne doesn't have to worry that Renie can subvert the training he's put June through. She cannot match him or Jemima for strength or speed, and she doesn't know the other Houses and their inhabitants. Etienne and Jemima need me and Ysanne out of the way, both because we're Council members and because we're strong enough to be a physical threat to them. You, Edmond, are older than Jemima, and Etienne will especially want you out of the way because of what Etienne has done to June and Renie. Therefore, it stood to reason that if anyone was going to attempt to help Etienne by assassinating his enemies, they'd go after the ones who were actually a threat to him."

"You gambled with *Edmond's* life then," I snapped.

"Even after a decade in the lap of luxury, I trusted that his survival instincts were finely honed enough that no would-be assassin would be able to sneak up on him," Caoimhe said.

"You had no right to make that decision."

She offered a graceful shrug. "Perhaps not, but I can't change it now." Seamus came quietly into the room, offered Caoimhe a small nod, then leaned against the nearest wall.

"Can we go back a few steps?" Ludovic asked. "You didn't know for sure that Etienne had supporters in Fiaigh?"

"No," Caoimhe said.

"Then how did you know they'd attempt to kill anyone rather than contacting Etienne and betraying us?"

"I made an educated guess," Caoimhe said. "Even if anyone in Fiaigh managed to contact Etienne or Jemima, they're still in England, while we're in Ireland. They may hold England's four Houses now, but their grip is tenuous and I don't believe they'd jeopardize their position by leaving Belle Morte and Nox and traveling all the way out here. Even if they did, they couldn't breach Fiaigh without us knowing about it in advance. They can't take all their newly turned vampires on a ferry, can they? One sniff of something like that and the media would be all over them. Therefore, I concluded that if Fiaigh was home to traitors, they'd either contact Etienne and Jemima, who'd probably tell them to kill as many of us as they could, or they'd kill us and tell Etienne and Jemima about it afterward."

"That's a lot of assumptions to make," Ludovic said.

"Educated guesses," said Caoimhe again. "I expected there'd most likely be an attack on myself or Ysanne, or both. That's why I returned to my own room rather than joining you in the guests' quarters—I was trying to make myself seem accessible to anyone who might want me dead."

"And this is the person who came for you," Ysanne said, pinning Tadhg with an icy glare.

"Actually, no. Tadhg did come to my room, but to confess his treachery, rather than continue with it."

"Why?" I said, suspiciously eyeing Tadhg.

"Jemima promised she'd make me a vampire," Tadhg said. "It's all I've ever wanted, and I thought that working security at a Vampire House was the closest I'd ever get to it. Eoghan knew I was a Vladdict, and he recruited me a year ago. Jemima and Etienne hadn't yet started turning new vampires, but Jemima promised to turn me when the time came."

"You knew they were planning to kill people and you helped them anyway," I said, disgusted.

Shame colored Tadhg's face. "Yes," he admitted. "I became Etienne's main point of contact inside Fiaigh. He has Belle Morte guards in his pocket who relayed his instructions to me and relayed anything from me back to him."

"His main point of contact or his *only* one?" Caoimhe asked.

"His main point."

"So you and Eoghan aren't the only traitors under my roof. Who else?"

"Siobhan," Tadhg said. From the low noise Seamus made, I guessed that Siobhan was another guard.

Caoimhe glanced at him, her face steely. "She's not working tonight, is she?"

Definitely a guard, then.

"No, her next shift starts tomorrow evening. Should we send someone to her house?" Seamus asked.

Caoimhe mulled it over, then shook her head. "That'll attract too much attention. As long as she doesn't know what's happened here, she's no real threat to us. But I want her in handcuffs the second she arrives tomorrow."

"Consider it done."

"What exactly was your role here?" I asked Tadhg. "What did Etienne want you to do?"

"I was supposed to find out which vampires and guards could be persuaded to join Etienne, and to be ready to act when Etienne eventually came for Fiaigh," Tadhg said.

"And by that, you mean assassinating anyone he wanted you to," said Caoimhe.

"I don't know. My instructions were to wait until Etienne had contacted me, and then he would relay the next step."

"Whose idea was it to try to kill me?" Edmond said.

"Eoghan's," Tadhg said.

I still wasn't sure I could tell if a human was lying, but none of the older vampires reacted, so I assumed Tadhg was telling the truth.

"When you arrived here, he wanted to prove himself by taking out Etienne's opponents," the guard continued.

"Let me guess, Eoghan was hoping that Etienne would name him Lord of Fiaigh after Caoimhe's death," I sneered.

Tadhg's silence was answer enough.

"Why didn't you go through with it?" Ludovic asked.

Tadhg darted a look at Caoimhe, then swallowed, licked his lips, and swallowed again.

"I couldn't. I want to live forever, but not at the cost of Caoimhe's life," he said.

"You're in love with her," Ysanne said.

Tadhg gave Caoimhe another look, desperate and full of longing. "Yes," he whispered. "Humans and vampires aren't allowed to be with each other, but I thought I might have a chance when I became a vampire. But I could never hurt her. When she returned here this evening and told us what had happened, I realized that I couldn't be a part of this."

My throat felt ragged, like I'd swallowed something sharp. Etienne had manipulated Tadhg, just as he'd manipulated June, playing on their love to turn them into weapons that he could wield. Tadhg had realized when things had gone too far, and he'd chosen to give himself up. June hadn't.

"Just to clarify, Etienne and Jemima still don't know we're here, do they?" Ludovic said.

Tadhg shook his head. "I told Eoghan that I'd reach out to my main Belle Morte contact to see if Etienne had instructions for us, but I never did."

"Why didn't you say anything *before* Eoghan tried to kill me?" Edmond asked.

Tadhg gave a shuddery sigh, and tears glinted in his eyes. "I was scared. I hoped I'd have more time to decide what to do, but then Eoghan told me his plan, and I realized I'd run out of time."

"Do you know who else is helping Etienne and Jemima?" Edmond asked.

"I know some names, but I'm not sure if Etienne told me all of them."

"Tell me the ones you *do* know," Ysanne commanded.

Tadhg sighed again. "Kenneth, Pat, and Brinda."

"Which of them is your main contact?"

There was a noticeable pause.

"None of them," Tadhg admitted.

Ysanne leaned forward. "Then tell me who is."

Tadhg scrubbed his hands over his face and softly groaned. "What'll happen to her?"

"That's no longer your concern. Give me her name."

There was another pause.

"Susan Harcourt," Tadhg said.

The name meant nothing to me, but Edmond and Ludovic both reacted, and Ysanne's nostrils flared. Her lips were thin and pale.

"Who's that?" I asked.

"Susan's been with Belle Morte almost from the beginning. Only Dexter worked there longer," Edmond said.

Ysanne had probably trusted her above newer staff members then, which explained why she looked so murderous. Betrayal after betrayal.

"Why do I get the feeling that Susan Harcourt is also the guard who was prepared to testify on Etienne's behalf and frame Isabeau for June's murder?" Ludovic said.

Edmond finally took a seat in front of Tadhg. "Why is Susan helping them? Did they promise to turn her too?"

"Yeah. I don't think you understand how many people want what vampires have, and what they're willing to do to get it," Tadhg said.

June flashed through my mind again, and my chest knotted. I might never come to terms with the role she'd played in this.

"Susan was responsible for helping Etienne find people to turn," Tadhg said.

"How many people?" Ysanne said.

"I don't know. Susan recruited people online then brought them to a location in Winchester so Etienne could turn them. He knew the rotation of guard patrols at Belle Morte so it was easy for him to avoid them and sneak over the wall every now and then."

"The walls of Belle Morte were supposed to keep intruders out. I never imagined they'd keep traitors in," Ysanne muttered.

"Susan lured people to somewhere in Winchester, Etienne turned them, and then what? He stashed them away until he was ready to use them?" I said.

"Yes," Tadhg said.

"How did he manage to hide away so many vampires without anyone knowing?" I demanded. "This smells like bullshit."

"He hid them at Bushfield," Tadhg said, like that meant anything to me.

"Which is?"

"It's an abandoned army camp about two miles outside Winchester," Ysanne supplied.

"So . . . plenty of space for Etienne to hide his minions," I realized.

"Why were so many people willing to help him?" Ludovic asked.

"Because people don't understand the reality of being a vampire," I said, thinking of June sitting on the floor of our little bedroom, surrounded by glossy vampire magazines. "They don't think about having to watch the people you love turn to dust or drinking blood every day. They only see the fame and the glamor and the mystery. Some people have dreamed of becoming a vampire ever since you guys revealed yourselves to the world. Some people have dreamed of it even before they knew vampires really existed. Etienne offered to make that dream a reality."

The room was silent for a couple of minutes.

"There's something that Etienne doesn't know," Tadhg said.

"What?" Ysanne said.

"Susan has worked hard to recruit people for him to turn. She's been loyal to him since long before he even knew the names of those people, but most of them have become vampires and she hasn't."

"Presumably because Etienne still needs her inside Belle Morte," Ysanne said.

"I guess so." Tadhg shoved his fingers through his hair. "Look, I didn't think things would go this far, and I can't change it now, but I might be able to help you stop it from going any further."

"How?"

"First, I want to know what you're planning on doing with me," Tadhg said.

I looked around at the older vampires, but they all had their blank masks on. For the first time I really considered how vampire law worked alongside human law. If vampires were subject to the same laws as humans, then Etienne had murdered June and killed everyone that he'd turned, and Tadhg and Susan were accomplices to that. But if most of those people had *chosen* to become vampires, was it still considered murder? Was it legally considered killing at all, considering that Etienne's victims were still living, even if not technically *alive*? None of these questions had ever been addressed before, because nothing like this had ever happened.

If Ysanne had her way, then Etienne and Jemima would be subject to whatever punishment was appropriate according to vampire law, but what would happen to Susan and Tadhg and any other corrupt guards in other Houses?

Ysanne tilted her head, like a cat sizing up a mouse, trying to decide if it was worth killing. "What do you think?"

"You probably want to kill me," Tadhg said.

Nobody denied it.

Tadhg nodded. "If I help you, I want guaranteed immunity. I can't stay at Fiaigh, I get that. I'll move, get another job, and none of you ever have to see me again, but I want your word that I can walk away from this unscathed."

"Do you know how many deaths are on Etienne's hands? You knew he was killing and turning people and you knew he was planning to take over the other Houses. You could have stopped this a long time ago but instead you helped cover it up and now you think you can walk away?" I said, my voice shaking.

"I have information that you can use against Etienne, something he doesn't know about. If you want that information, the price is my guaranteed safety," Tadhg said, but he couldn't meet my eyes.

Anger boiled inside me. This wasn't right. Tadhg had helped to destroy so many lives and he shouldn't be allowed to get away with it. But if we didn't make a deal with him, then Etienne *would* get away with it.

Caoimhe looked at her guard with utter contempt. "There's another way of getting the information out of you," she said, resting a hand on the hilt of Eoghan's knife.

"True," Tadhg agreed. "But how long will that take? Do you have the time to waste?"

Caoimhe and Ysanne exchanged looks, and something wordless flowed between them. Ysanne gave a little nod, but her jaw was tight.

"Very well," Caoimhe said, turning back to Tadhg. "You have your guaranteed immunity. No one in this house will lay a finger on you, and when this is over, you'll be free to walk away and live your life however you see fit, completely free of any consequences from your actions."

I gritted my teeth and reached for the reassurance of Edmond's hand. It wasn't fair that Tadhg would get away with this, but life *wasn't* fair. If Tadhg getting off scot-free meant we could nail Etienne, that was the price we'd have to pay.

"Tell us what you know," Ysanne said.

"Susan understood why Etienne couldn't turn her right away, but she's asked him again and again for a time frame, and he always avoids the question. When we spoke a month ago, she told me she was wondering if he actually *did* plan to turn her or if he was just bullshitting her to get what he wanted."

"Either's possible, knowing that bastard," I muttered.

"Susan decided she needed leverage. She may be enamored of vampires, but that doesn't mean she'll take shit from them. On the days when she wasn't working at Belle Morte she sometimes went to Bushfield, to help Etienne feed everyone."

"She let them feed from her?" said Edmond.

Tadhg frowned. "Not that I know of. She never mentioned it, and as far as I know, Etienne relied mostly on animal blood to keep his vampires fed."

"No wonder they were nearly out of control the first time they attacked Belle Morte," said Ludovic darkly.

"Susan helped him source that animal blood," Tadhg said.

"How?" I asked.

"She didn't say and I didn't ask. It wasn't my business. But she told me that, on one of the nights she was there, she'd secretly filmed Etienne feeding his vampires. She was going to use it against him if he refused to turn her."

"And you have a copy of this video?" Edmond said.

"No, only Susan has, and she'd never give it to me, if that's what you're thinking. But if you can get to her, you can get to that video. It proves that Etienne is in charge of the newly turned vampires."

"It doesn't incriminate Jemima though, does it?" I said. She had to pay just as much as Etienne did.

Tadhg shook his head. "I can't help you there."

"Can you tell us anything else?" Caoimhe asked.

"No."

Caoimhe ran her fingers through her blond curls. Throughout everything we'd been through she'd kept her vampire poise, but now I could see signs of exhaustion creeping in. She held herself a little less carefully, and her eyes were a little more vulnerable. It wouldn't have been noticeable to most people, but I'd seen similar, tiny, signs in Ysanne.

"What happens now?" Tadhg asked, glancing at the knife.

"You'll be confined to a spare room until we know that we don't need you anymore. When this is over, you'll be free to go." Caoimhe's lip curled. *"Unscathed."*

Tadhg stood up, and Caoimhe rose a second later, as fluid as a cat. "I'll escort you," she said.

"That's not necessary," he protested.

The smile that Caoimhe gave him was razor-sharp and ice-cold. "You gave up any right to my trust, Tadhg. As long as you remain under my roof, you will damn well do as you're told."

"What about us?" I asked.

Caoimhe's gaze roved over us. "I suggest we adjourn for the night and reconvene in the morning, when we've all had some proper rest."

CHAPTER TWENTY-ONE

Renie

I woke up nestled against Edmond's chest, his arm wrapped protectively around me.

"Good afternoon," he murmured, and I tilted back my head to look up at him. He was propped against the pillows, his hair spilling around his shoulders, and his eyes soft and warm in the way he seemed to reserve just for me.

"It's the afternoon?" I said.

Like in Belle Morte, the windows were all shielded; it was impossible to tell what time of day it was.

"It's just past two thirty," Edmond said.

"I slept for *fourteen hours*?"

"Is that so surprising, considering everything that happened yesterday?"

I scrubbed my hands over my eyes. "Did all that really happen in a day? It feels like a week."

Edmond made a soft noise of agreement.

I stretched, the curve of my body pressing harder against Edmond's, and even though we were only here because we were on the run, I shut out everything but the man I was lying in bed with.

"What time did you wake up?" I asked.

"I didn't go to sleep."

"What?" I sat up.

Edmond lifted one shoulder in a graceful shrug. "Just in case

Tadhg and Eoghan weren't the only traitors in the house."

"You didn't have to do that."

He tucked a strand of hair behind my ear, his fingertips brushing the curve of my cheek. "Twice now I haven't protected you when I should have done. I'm not taking any chances."

"Then you definitely should have woken me up earlier."

I reached up and curled my hand around his neck so I could pull him down for a kiss. I could feel him pressing against my leg, hard and eager, but before our kiss could become something more, there was a loud knock at the door.

"Guys, are you up?" said Roux.

Edmond lifted an eyebrow. "In more ways than one," he murmured, and I stifled a giggle.

"Yeah, we're awake," I called.

"Good, get your pants on. Ysanne wants to see everyone in the dining room," Roux said through the door.

"Our pants are already on."

"Then I'm very disappointed in you. You should be getting as much naked time as possible with your sexy vampire."

"I *can* hear you," Edmond said.

"I know," said Roux, laughter in her voice.

Edmond shook his head, smiling.

"I'll see you downstairs," Roux said.

I climbed out of bed. "I'll grab a quick shower." If Ysanne was going to tell us it was time to go on the run again, this could be my last chance.

I was almost at the bathroom when I heard the rustle of bedcovers and a blur of movement behind me, then Edmond scooped me into his arms.

"That shower looks big enough for two," he said, nipping at my earlobe.

His fangs weren't fully out, and the feel of the points pressing against my skin sent a shiver through me. Sometimes it was hard to remember that I'd once been repulsed by them.

Edmond carried me into the bathroom and kicked the door shut.

Twenty minutes later, we made our way down to the dining room.

Jason and Roux sat at a table near the shuttered windows: Jason was sipping a mug of coffee and Roux was nibbling an apple, while Ludovic studied a tapestry hanging on the opposite wall.

Caoimhe and Ysanne stood at the far end of the room, by the table covered in photographs and newspaper clippings. Ysanne held a photo in one hand, and there was a deeply vulnerable look in her eyes, like her icy armor had cracked open and I could see through to the softest parts of her. I thought back to the tiny oil painting in her office. I'd seen a flicker of vulnerability then, too, but in a different way, and I wondered what was in the photo she held.

"Is she safe?" Ysanne asked. She didn't seem to have noticed Edmond and me coming into the room.

Caoimhe's blue eyes filled with sympathy. "She's no threat to Etienne or Jemima now, and they're unlikely to kill her in case they need her as a bargaining chip further down the line."

Ysanne said nothing, but her nostrils flared ever so slightly.

"Are we interrupting?" Edmond said, and the women looked up.

"No," Caoimhe said. "I was just explaining that while I know where Isabeau has been imprisoned, we can't get to her now. We have to focus on our enemies and what their next move will be."

Ysanne put the photo down. For the first time I noticed that she was wearing slim-legged trousers and a knit sweater—similar to the outfit I'd donned yesterday—and while everything she wore looked elegant and classy, it was the first time I'd ever seen her out of form-fitting dresses and skirts and skyscraper heels. I'd never realized how small she was without them, and for just a moment she didn't look like an ancient, deadly vampire used to ruling her empire. She looked like a woman not much older than me, who'd lost everything and simply didn't know where to go from here.

Despite the animosity that had defined most of our relationship, my heart went out to her. Etienne had betrayed me, killed my sister, and ended the life I'd once had, but I had Edmond to lean on. The woman Ysanne loved had been taken from her and locked up somewhere, and, judging from what Caoimhe had said, there was nothing any of us could do about it.

I joined Ysanne and Caoimhe at the table and looked down at the photos.

"Wow, is that you?" I said, picking up the picture that Ysanne had put down.

It looked like it had been taken inside a club—in the left corner a small slice of stage and a hand holding the neck of a guitar was visible, and people thronged around the stage, most of them clutching drinks, their bodies reflected in the mirrored walls.

In the middle of the crowd two women were dancing. One was Isabeau, her arms held high, her head flung back, her eyes closed as she laughed. The other was Ysanne, looking simultaneously the same as she did now but also completely different. Her hair was slightly less sleek than usual, as if Isabeau had just run her fingers through it, and her usual tailored, designer clothes had been replaced by a tight miniskirt. I'd never in my wildest dreams thought I would see Ysanne in a miniskirt. But the biggest difference was the look on her face. Her lips curved into a soft, small smile, and she gazed at Isabeau as if she was the most incredible thing Ysanne had ever seen.

"That was where we met. The Marquee Club," said Ysanne, taking the photo from me. "It doesn't exist now."

"How long have you been together?" I asked.

I didn't expect her to answer—she wasn't exactly the sharing type—but her armor was still open, and she didn't shut me down like she normally would.

"We met in 1965," Ysanne said.

"Holy crap, that's decades ago," I blurted. I was still coming to terms with the reality of living as long as vampires did.

"We weren't together all that time. We parted ways during the '70s, and I didn't see her again until 2009." Ysanne abruptly put the photo down, and I sensed her closing herself off again.

"What's all this anyway?" I asked, shuffling through the photos.

"It's a project I've been doing," Caoimhe said. "I've been tracking down photos, newspapers, or anything else that has vampires in it. Much of our history was before the invention of the camera, but I'd like to document as much as possible of the last couple of centuries." She held up a black-and-white photo of women in long dresses and large hats, carrying placards proclaiming VOTES FOR WOMEN, and tapped two faces in the upper right corner. I peered closer. They looked vaguely familiar, but the picture quality was grainy and I couldn't put names to the faces.

"Sarah and Esther," Caoimhe said. "They live at Midnight." She picked up another photo, a bombed street, where men and women picked through heaps of blasted rubble and a blank-faced child was being carried away by a uniformed firefighter. "Here's Isabeau again," she said, pointing, and I leaned forward.

Isabeau was crouched at the top of the biggest rubble pile, her face smeared with soot, her hands digging through the bricks and debris.

"World War II," Caoimhe said.

Roux, Jason, and Ludovic drifted over. "This is amazing," Roux said, examining the suffragette photo. She put it down and pulled another from the pile. "Is that Gideon?"

That got Jason's attention. While we'd lived in Belle Morte, Jason had made no secret of his Jupiter-sized crush on Gideon, but Gideon had shown no sign of reciprocation until the night of Jemima's welcoming party—before we learned what a treacherous bitch she really was—when I was sure I'd noticed a spark between them.

We crowded around the photo. It was even older and grainier than the one of the suffragettes, featuring a throng of people in a large room packed around a makeshift boxing ring, and most of the faces were an indistinguishable blur, but the man in the middle of the ring, his clenched fist raised, was clearly Gideon. Dark spots spattered his face, and though he was clearly the victor, he was looking down and away from the cheering spectators. There was no happiness or triumph on his face, just bleakness.

"During the late 1800s Gideon was a champion bare-knuckle boxer," Edmond said.

"Really? That's hot," Jason blurted.

We all looked at him.

He blinked innocently back at us. "Bad timing?"

"Do you have any photos of Edmond in here?" I asked, giving him a sideward look under my lashes.

Caoimhe grinned and riffled through the photos until she found what she was looking for. "I particularly like this one," she said.

Eight soldiers sat in a muddy trench, rifles propped against the earthen wall behind them. Three wore hard helmets, and one was spooning something into his mouth from a battered tin. Two of them held lit cigarettes, and smoke formed wispy wreaths around the others.

Edmond and Ludovic sat in the middle of the group, but I didn't immediately recognize them.

"Oh my god, you have short hair," I cried, looking up at Edmond, then back at the photo.

"Military issue," he said.

"I've never imagined you with short hair."

"Do you prefer it?"

"It's . . . different."

"That's not an answer."

"Edmond Dantès, I would find you gorgeous even if you shaved your head," I told him.

A slow smile crept across his lips.

"Although I hope you don't, because I love your hair," I added.

"Should we give you two some time alone?" Roux teased.

Ludovic took the photo from me. His eyes had gone very dark, and his mouth was a hard line. Edmond hadn't moved, but something about his body language was tenser and more aware than it had been a moment ago. He watched Ludovic like he was a dog that might suddenly bite.

"Ludovic?" he said, as Ludovic continued to stare at the photo. He didn't seem to have heard Edmond.

Edmond gently took the photo, and Ludovic blinked, like he was waking up.

"You're not going to break my nose again, are you?" Edmond said, and there was humor in his voice, but Ludovic didn't smile.

Ysanne rapped her knuckles on a tabletop, and we all looked up. "Perhaps we could save the reminiscing for another day?" she said crisply.

None of us pointed out that she was the one who'd looked at the photos first.

We took seats at the various tables, facing Ysanne. Her eyes lingered on Roux and Jason, and I thought she'd tell them to leave. They were still donors, after all, and Ysanne wasn't in the habit of including donors in important vampire business. But maybe she recognized that they were as much a part of this as any of us, for she didn't say anything.

Instead, she recounted the assassination attempts that had taken place a few hours ago.

Roux made a soft noise and clutched Jason's hand.

"Are we safe here?" Jason said.

"Both of the would-be assassins have been taken care of," Ysanne said.

"That's not what I asked."

My eyebrows went up at that. Even if Jason hadn't been a Vladdict, I'd never have imagined him challenging Ysanne. From the speculative look she gave him, neither had she.

"The reality of our situation is that we probably aren't safe anywhere. Not for long, anyway," Ysanne said.

Jason nodded, as if that was the answer he'd expected.

"So, technically, we have concrete evidence against Etienne, if we can get the Bushfield camp video from Susan Harcourt," Roux said, tapping her index finger against her lip. "The problem is getting it, right?"

"Do we know where she lives? Can't we send someone there to wait for her, like Etienne did to Renie's mum?" Jason said.

"I know where every member of my staff lives, but I don't believe that will do us any good. Etienne's position at Belle Morte is still precarious. Sooner or later the outside world will realize that something has gone wrong. Etienne's lies were enough to make my vampires doubt me, but I don't believe they've all turned against me. Etienne needs his closest supporters now more than ever, and it would be foolish to let them leave Belle Morte. I don't believe Susan herself would be foolish enough to leave when we're all still on the loose," Ysanne said.

"Somehow we've got to get back inside Belle Morte then," said Roux, as if it was the most obvious thing in the world.

"Do we know who else is helping Etienne and Jemima? In any of the Houses?" Ludovic asked.

"I had a little talk with Eoghan after we took him to the cells. I wanted to be sure there were no more traitors under my roof," Caoimhe said. From the cold gleam in her eyes, I suspected that her "little talk" had mirrored the one that Etienne and I'd had after he'd kidnapped me. The bloody, painful kind.

"What did he tell you?"

"He insists that he and Tadhg are the only ones. He's given me the names of corrupt guards in Midnight, Nox, Lamia, and Belle Morte, but he was unclear about which vampires in those Houses might have been swayed to Etienne's side."

"Which means that even if we could get back into Belle Morte, we have no idea who we can trust," Edmond said.

"Correct."

Roux blew out a long sigh and leaned back in her chair. "Let's think logically about this. Twenty vampires live at Belle Morte."

"Nineteen," Ysanne corrected. "Rosa was killed during the first attack."

"Okay. Rosa's dead, Edmond, Ludovic, and you are here, Isabeau's in prison somewhere, and Etienne's a lying scumbag. That leaves fourteen vampires still in Belle Morte. Do you have any gut feelings about who we can or can't trust?"

There was a long pause as Ysanne considered the question. In my own mind, I ran over the other vampires of Belle Morte, even though it was useless because I barely knew them. Even after I'd learned why Ysanne had really brought me to Belle Morte, I'd had to pretend I was a normal donor, which meant I'd had to keep letting vampires drink from me. I'd been bitten by Rosa, Hugh, Deepika, Stephen, and Phoebe, but we'd barely exchanged more than two sentences. The other vampires I only knew by face.

"Isabeau and Gideon were always close, but he also has history with Jemima," Ysanne said.

"What kind of history?" Jason asked.

"They knew each other before vampires revealed ourselves to the world. Gideon rarely mentioned it, just that they'd had a habit of running into each over the decades."

"Why did he come to Belle Morte, and not Nox?" I asked.

"Isabeau wanted to live in Belle Morte, and Gideon wanted to be with Isabeau."

"So whatever friendship he'd had with Jemima, when it came to choosing between her and Isabeau, he chose Isabeau," I pointed out.

"Isabeau always said he was the person she trusted most, after me," Ysanne said.

"Does anyone else in the house have history with either Jemima or Etienne?" Roux asked.

"Phoebe and Jemima knew each other but they weren't close, hence why Phoebe chose my house instead of Jemima's," Ysanne said. "But Phillip and Catherine could be a problem. Their history with Jemima runs deep."

"In what way?" I asked.

"I first met Jemima in 1814, in a little village in Devon. A vampire was running wild there, turning people and abandoning them. I helped Jemima track him down and kill him, but I had nothing to do with the abandoned vampires after that. Jemima took them into her own home and cared for them."

"Seriously?"

"It may sound hard to believe in light of what she's done now, but the Jemima that I used to know cared deeply about our kind, and only wanted what was best for us. She saved Phillip and Catherine, and Amelia, too, who now lives at Nox."

"Why didn't they go to Nox with her?" I asked.

"Because Phillip had fallen in love with Rebecca Anderson," Ysanne said.

Rebecca was another Belle Morte vampire I only knew by face, a tall, striking woman with thick red hair and a generous smile.

"Rebecca chose Belle Morte, and Phillip chose to follow her," Roux guessed. "What about Catherine?"

"When vampires first gathered to discuss the possibility of coming out of the shadows, Catherine was one of the shyest women I'd ever met. I don't know if her feelings for Phillip were romantic, but she lived very much in his shadow. It didn't surprise me when she followed him to Belle Morte rather than going to Nox with Jemima. Phillip's romance with Rebecca didn't last, but since neither he nor Catherine ever requested to transfer to Nox, I assumed they were happy at Belle Morte," Ysanne said.

"But now you're not so sure, are you?" I said.

"No," Ysanne admitted. "I don't know how much loyalty they still feel for Jemima."

"Surely that comes second to common sense, though. Jemima and Etienne are destroying everything," I argued.

"Because they believe they can build something better from the ruins," Jason said. "Isn't that what Etienne told you?"

"But they're not making it better. How can anyone not see that?"

Jason bit his lip. "I'm really not trying to be a dick, but all the stuff Jemima told you? She kind of has a point."

"Excuse me?" Ysanne's voice dripped ice.

"Just hear me out," Jason said. "Jemima told Renie she was doing this because the current system has become a prison for vampires. She said that vampires are controlled by the Council and by human perception of them, and they don't have any freedom, right?" He looked at me.

I nodded.

Jason looked around the room. "Is she wrong?" His eyes rested on Ysanne. "For the last year, a hot piece of Vladdict gossip has been whether there's something going on between Benjamin and Alexandra."

My mind flashed back to the pair, to when I'd seen them dancing together during a charity ball at Belle Morte. I hadn't heard any of that gossip until Jason had told me, but the way the two vampires had looked at each other had been far from platonic.

"If the rumors *are* true, what would happen if Benjamin and Alexandra wanted to transfer to a different House? What if they didn't want to live in a Vampire House at all? What if they just wanted to get married and give up a life of fame? Or maybe they still want the fame, but they want to go solo?" Jason continued. "Would they be allowed to do that?"

"The Council is not in the habit of forbidding marriages," said Ysanne crisply.

"Yeah, but I bet they'd have to ask the Council first, wouldn't they?"

Ysanne was silent.

"Exactly," Jason said. "This is the twenty-first century. We're supposed to be at a point where grown-ass adults don't have to ask anyone's permission to get married. But vampires still do. How does that make sense?"

I glanced up at Edmond, but his face was unreadable.

"That famous vampire in Japan, the one who used to be a samurai? Toyotomi Kenshin? Did he have to ask the Lady of Kurayami for permission before he became a consultant for movie companies? Or could he do it because that's what he wanted to do?"

"He had to ask permission," said Edmond, when Ysanne still didn't answer.

Jason turned to me. "When Renie and Edmond fell in love, they had to hide it from the rest of Belle Morte because vampires and humans aren't allowed to have relationships. Maybe the Council thought that was in everyone's best interests, but Renie is eighteen, and Edmond is"—Jason paused, and frowned—"actually I have no idea how old Edmond is, but the point is they're both old enough to make their own decisions. They don't need to have their love lives micromanaged by any kind of governing body."

Edmond laced his fingers through mine.

"What if *you* wanted to get married?" Jason said to Ysanne. "Would you have to ask permission or are the rules different for you because you're a Council member?"

"I've been married twice before, I have no wish to do it again," Ysanne snapped.

"You're avoiding the question," said Jason quietly.

Silence fell on the room.

Ysanne stood as still as marble, her eyes the color of frost, her lips a bloodless line. She looked ancient and predatory, the human mask slipping away.

Jason was only nineteen, and until recently had been more interested in hairdressing than vampire politics, but he stared the Lady of Belle Morte down like she wasn't capable of snapping him like a dry twig.

I wasn't sure whether to be scared for him or impressed by his sheer balls.

"Council members are not supposed to be above the rules," said Caoimhe at last. "If one of us had wanted to get married we'd also have needed approval from the other lords and ladies of the UK Houses."

"So back to my original point—Jemima wasn't exactly wrong, was she?" Jason said. "Vampires revealing themselves was meant to be about freedom, but in some ways you guys are less free now than when you had to hide from the world. Has anyone on the Council ever *asked* the vampires of their Houses if they're still happy with the current system?"

"No, we haven't," said Caoimhe.

"If vampires were allowed to have relationships with humans, Etienne would never have got this far. If everyone knew that he and June were a couple then he'd have been the first suspect when she was killed. He couldn't have manipulated her into helping him by telling her they could only be together if the Council was overthrown. Tadhg might not have been so willing to betray his House to finally have a chance with Caoimhe."

Jason ran his hands through his blond hair and sighed.

"I'm not excusing all the shit that Etienne and Jemima have done. I hope you guys end up punishing the absolute fuck out of them, but if you don't look at *why* this happened, it'll happen again," he said.

Ysanne looked like she'd been frozen. She was the one who'd pulled vampires out of the shadows, who'd spearheaded the donor system, and now everything she'd built was crumbling. I couldn't imagine how that felt.

The tension in the room felt like a physical weight pressing down on me.

"Jason's right," said Edmond.

Ysanne's frosty gaze flicked to him.

"Ysanne, I've known you longer than anyone, but the Council's unyielding rules meant I had to lie to you about Renie. I doubt I'm the only one who's been in that position. Etienne's methods are dangerous and destructive, but the future he's offering may appeal to other vampires who are starting to feel constricted by our rules. Stopping Etienne and Jemima isn't enough," Edmond went on.

I didn't realize Ysanne had bitten her own lip until a bead of blood welled up, ruby red against her skin. Her expression was rigid, like she was trying to hold herself together, and her hands gripped the edge of the table.

"Was this all my fault?" she asked, and I'd never heard her sound so small, so *lost*.

Caoimhe moved to comfort her, but Ysanne's hand shot up, warning her off.

"Excuse me," Ysanne said. She walked out of the room, and her pace was quicker than normal, as if she was fighting not to run.

"Should someone go after her?" I whispered.

"No. Give her some time," Edmond replied.

"Will she be okay?" I'd never imagined that I'd care, but I did.

"One thing that Ysanne can't stand is to show anyone that she's vulnerable. In about an hour she'll have collected herself, and she'll be the icy ruler that used to get under your skin so much," Edmond said, kissing my forehead.

"What do we do until then?"

Belle Morte was Ysanne's House—it didn't feel right to discuss our next move without her.

Edmond leaned in closer, until his lips brushed my ear, and despite the serious situation, a tingle shot through me.

"Would you like to explore Fiaigh?" he whispered.

I wasn't sure if Caoimhe had instructed her donors to stay in their rooms while we were here, but Edmond and I didn't encounter anyone as we drifted up and down the hallways and stone staircases that made up the castle's interior. Fiaigh had a *lot* of staircases.

I paused in front of a pair of swords mounted on the wall. "The night that June escaped, Ludovic defended me and Roux with a sword." I remembered the night vividly.

"Does that surprise you? Don't forget how many of us come from a time when swords were commonplace," Edmond said.

"A gun might have been more useful."

Shadows flitted through Edmond's eyes. "Ludovic doesn't like guns."

"Because of the war?" I thought of the look in Ludovic's eyes when he'd seen the photo of him and Edmond in the trenches.

Edmond nodded.

"But swords are okay?" I pressed.

Another nod.

"He definitely seemed to know what he was doing."

"He always was good with a sword," Edmond said.

I studied the swords again. Each one was comprised of a long steel blade, a wide cross guard, and a leather-wrapped hilt leading up to a pommel that featured the same Celtic design as the brooches worn by the Fiaigh guards.

"Are *you* good with a sword?"

Edmond gave me a wicked smile. "Who do you think taught Ludovic?"

He reached up, lifted one of the swords down, and gave it an experimental swing. Even through his clothes, muscles bunched in his arms. I remembered those muscles flexing on either side of my head as he moved in me, and a bolt of heat shot through me.

"You're sexy when you do that," I said.

He gave me a heated smile and swung the sword again. I tried to picture him in the fashions of the various time periods he'd lived in. Maybe one day I'd ask him to dress up like that, so I could see it in the flesh.

"Can you teach me some moves?" I asked.

Edmond's smile faltered. "That's not a good idea."

"Why not? It might be useful next time I'm face-to-face with Etienne."

Real anger passed across Edmond's face, turning his eyes red. "I won't let him hurt you again," he growled.

"Much as I love this protective streak, don't you think I should learn how to defend myself?"

"Not with a sword. It's not a skill you can master quickly, and going up against Etienne with a sword that you don't know how to use is far too dangerous."

"Even for a vampire?" I was teasing, but Edmond's serious expression didn't change.

"We can heal from almost any injury, but we cannot regrow limbs. If you chop off your own leg while swinging around a sword, it won't grow back."

Well, that was good to know. There was the chance I'd been starting to feel the teensiest bit cocky about my newfound invulnerability, and Edmond's words brought me back down to earth.

"Besides," Edmond said, "I doubt I'd be much of a teacher these days. François was an expert swordsman and he trained me well, but it's been a long time since I properly wielded a blade. My skills are decidedly rusty."

"They don't look it," I said as Edmond swung the sword again. I pinned him with a mock-offended look. "I think you don't want to teach me because you know I'll look incredibly sexy with a sword in my hand and you won't be able to cope with my overwhelming sexiness."

"Is that so?"

Lowering the sword, Edmond approached me. He backed me up against the wall, placing his arms on either side of me. The first time he'd done that I'd felt—not intimidated exactly, but not quite comfortable either. This time breathless excitement sizzled in my veins as he crowded me with his body.

"I wish we had time to go back to our room, but that's probably not a good idea. We have to focus on what's going on with Belle Morte," I whispered.

"You're probably right." His lips grazed mine, soft at first, and then demanding. My tongue touched the hard points of his fangs and my own slid out in response, sharp and eager.

"I never thought I'd say this, but I'm actually going to miss being bitten by you," I said.

Etienne had been the first vampire to bite me, and I'd hated it. Unlike every other donor in the mansion, I hadn't been able to relax, and rather than the sweet bliss that most people experienced, I'd felt only searing pain. Even Edmond's bite had hurt until I'd finally learned to relax, and then his bite had transformed into something almost orgasmic.

Edmond nipped my lower lip and I shuddered in the most delicious way. "Vampires can still bite each other," he murmured.

"Wait, seriously?"

Edmond kissed along my jawline until he reached my ear, then he trailed soft kisses down my throat, to the place where he'd bitten me when I was human. His fangs brushed against my skin, and my eyes fluttered shut.

"There are so many places I'm looking forward to biting you," Edmond said, and kissed the spot where my pulse had once beat.

Footsteps interrupted us, and we broke apart as Roux appeared at the end of the hallway. I expected her to give us a knowing wink or make a comment about what we'd obviously been doing, but her face was grave, and my stomach plunged.

"What?" I said.

"There's something you need to see."

CHAPTER TWENTY-TWO

Edmond

He kept his hand on Renie's back as they followed Roux downstairs, both to reassure her that they'd face whatever this new development was together and to reassure himself. Renie's physical injuries had healed but he would never forget the way she'd looked—limp, pale, bloodied—when he'd pulled her from the river. He'd never forget that Etienne was responsible for that.

"I thought it would be a good idea to check online to see if anyone knew anything about what's happened—"

"Wait, you got online?" Renie interrupted Roux.

She sounded as surprised as Edmond felt. Many vampires struggled with how fast modern technology changed, and for as long as Edmond had known Caoimhe, she'd found it particularly hard. He'd once told Renie that Caoimhe would choose candlelight over electricity if she could, and though Fiaigh proved she hadn't, the thought of Caoimhe having internet access in her castle was almost more than Edmond could believe.

"Yeah, Caoimhe keeps a private laptop in her office," Roux said.

"A laptop," Edmond repeated.

"I thought I was grasping at straws when I asked her, but she said she's had one for a while, even though none of the donors know about it."

"Does she know how to use it?" Edmond asked.

"Not really."

She hadn't changed that much, then.

They reached the ground floor, and Roux led them through an entryway on their right, then a left, down a stone hallway.

"Are you going to tell us what's going on?" Edmond asked.

"It's Etienne," Roux said, which explained nothing.

Even the sound of the bastard's name made Edmond curl his free hand into a tight fist. After Renie had escaped from Etienne, she'd told them her suspicions that Etienne had manipulated the events that led to Edmond being whipped with silver so Edmond would be out of commission when Etienne released June. Renie was convinced that Etienne hadn't wanted to risk ever facing Edmond in a fair fight. But he'd failed there, because one day he *would* have to, and when that day came, Edmond would pull out Etienne's spine.

"What's he done?" Renie asked.

"It's better if I show you," Roux answered.

They stopped in front of a brass-studded wooden door, and Roux knocked. "It's us," she called.

Caoimhe opened the door and beckoned them in. There was something furtive about it, as if having a laptop was the kind of illicit activity she needed to hide from the world. At any other time, Edmond would have been amused.

Caoimhe's office was nothing like Ysanne's. The furniture was all heavy oak; iron candle holders, like the ones in Renie and Edmond's room, stood in the corners. Jason, chewing on his thumbnail, occupied a chair close to the door. A wide desk dominated the room, and sitting on top, looking out of place among all the oak and iron, was a slim silver laptop.

"And there was me expecting a PC from the Stone Age," said Renie.

Roux sat down behind the desk but Caoimhe stayed standing, eyeing the laptop with vague suspicion.

"Will that be me one day?" Renie whispered, looking up at

Edmond. "Technology is only getting more advanced—will I be able to keep up or am I going to end up like you guys?"

Edmond kissed the tip of her nose. "You might find you don't *want* to keep up."

Renie didn't look convinced.

Suddenly, Edmond had the feeling that even if Etienne and Jemima hadn't seized Belle Morte, things would have changed in the mansion. Renie wasn't like the other vampires. She was from the twenty-first century, and if he knew her, she'd want to drag Belle Morte into the modern world, whether Ysanne liked it or not. But maybe that was what they all needed.

"I didn't know if Etienne had managed to keep everything contained, or if anyone had recognized us at the pub or anywhere else," Roux explained, tapping away at the laptop.

Edmond had no idea what she was doing, but her fingers moved impressively fast.

Jason got up and joined Roux at the desk, his face grim.

"This is what we found," Roux said, standing to one side so there was room for Edmond and Renie.

Edmond almost didn't want to look. Whatever was on that screen would make everything worse. But he had no choice.

Roux tapped another button on the laptop, and the picture on the screen started playing.

Etienne's face filled the small window, and Edmond fought the urge to put his fist through the screen.

"I cannot express the shock and disbelief that Belle Morte is suffering," Etienne said. His expression was somber as he stared at whoever was filming, his voice as subdued as if he was at a funeral. "But we will not hide the truth from the world. Ysanne Moreau, the Lady of Belle Morte, has been secretly killing people and turning them into vampires. She kept them half starved so they were easier to control, but that backfired on her when she attempted to integrate them into Belle Morte and they lost control.

"Our head of security died trying to stop her, along with two more guards, two members of staff, and three donors. Two more donors have been illegally turned into vampires, with Ysanne's approval. Renie Mayfield was turned by Edmond Dantès, and I believe that her sister, June Mayfield, was turned by Ysanne herself.

"When the Council arrived at Belle Morte to investigate these crimes, Ysanne attempted to have them assassinated. She was partly successful. Lord Henry of Lamia and Lord Charles of Midnight have been killed. Lady Caoimhe of Fiaigh fled the mansion, which leads me to suspect she is involved with this. When Ysanne's own vampires confronted her, she attacked us and escaped Belle Morte, along with Edmond Dantès, Ludovic de Vauban, and Renie Mayfield. They also took two human hostages, Roux Hayes and Jason Grant. We can only assume these hostages will be acting as donors, willing or not, and I fear that their lives are in serious jeopardy.

"If anyone knows where Ysanne is, if anyone has seen her, please report that sighting to the police, but do *not* approach her. For the time being, Jemima Sutton, the only other survivor of the Council massacre, has appointed me Acting Lord of Belle Morte, and I promise you all that we will not let these killings go unpunished."

The video abruptly cut off. The room was silent but for Roux's and Jason's breathing.

"Is there any more?" Edmond asked.

"That's a clip from the statement that Etienne released to the public two hours ago. This clip alone already has a million views, and there are more every second. Social media's going into meltdown talking about it," Jason said.

For the first time Edmond wished that he'd paid closer attention to the evolving modern world. Etienne clearly had, and now he was using that against the vampires who hadn't.

Renie slumped against the wall and hugged herself. "Fuck," she said softly. "Etienne knew how hard it would be to track us down once I escaped, so now he's using the whole UK to flush us out."

"Can't we release our own press statement countering all the bull-shit?" Jason suggested.

"No," Edmond said. "Right now, Etienne has all the advantages. He and Jemima have control over Belle Morte, Nox, Lamia, and Midnight. They've convinced our friends that we're their enemies, and they still have June to use as a weapon when necessary."

Renie flinched.

"The only real evidence that can exonerate us and implicate Etienne is Susan Harcourt's video, but if we make it public, he'll kill Susan and destroy that evidence," Edmond continued.

"Then we don't mention the video," Jason said. "Caoimhe and Ysanne can testify that Etienne and Jemima were behind the Council's assassination. Renie can testify that Etienne killed June, then tried to kill her."

"But without any evidence, it's our word against his, and Etienne looks more credible right now. We all fled Belle Morte when he accused us, and he managed to make it seem as though Ysanne was controlling June. His accusations appear to have weight behind them. Ours would just be words," Caoimhe said.

"Then what the hell *do* we do?"

No one said anything for a long moment.

"I guess we can kiss good-bye any chance of breaking back into Belle Morte to get that video," said Roux glumly.

"No," said Renie, lifting her head. Her eyes blazed with the fire that had burned through Edmond's walls and stolen his heart. "We *have* to go back. It's the one thing that Etienne won't expect and won't have prepared for, especially in light of his press statement."

"But how the hell are we supposed to get back inside?" Roux said.

"I don't know yet, but we'll find a way. That piece of shit is *not* getting away with this." Renie's eyes flashed red.

Edmond felt a fierce surge of pride. Etienne had taken more from Renie than anyone. She was still adjusting to being a vampire, to having taken a life yesterday, and she'd never before been in a situation like this. Some people would have given up and broken down; Renie would not. She'd fought with everything she had to free herself from Etienne before, and now she'd continue to fight to stop him from hurting anyone else.

Roux nodded and squared her shoulders. "Where do we start?"

"We need to find Ysanne," Renie said. "Belle Morte's still her house."

"Do you know where she might have gone?" Roux asked Caoimhe.

Caoimhe shook her head.

"She wouldn't have gone after Etienne on her own, would she?" Jason asked, his eyes widening.

Caoimhe looked at Edmond. He didn't even need to think about it.

"No," he said. Ysanne was vulnerable and hurting, but he'd seen her in darker, more painful places, and he knew that she wouldn't have done anything stupid. She was still in Fiaigh, somewhere.

As he cast his mind back, hundreds of years into the past to another night when he and Ysanne had been forced to flee the place they'd called home, he realized where she might be.

"Wait here," he said.

The grounds of Fiaigh stretched out in an oblong block behind the castle, four large lawns separated by stone paths—very different to the way that Belle Morte's grounds sprawled all the way around the mansion. A wall fringed the lawns, but it was barely visible behind thickly clustered fir trees.

Edmond found Ysanne sitting under one of those trees, her head bowed, her hair like silver under the moonlight. He sat beside her, and, for the briefest moment, he wasn't in Ireland in the twenty-first century; he was back in France, slumping to the ground a short distance from Paris, the bloody reek of the guillotine's victims still clinging to his clothes.

"Running from Belle Morte—it felt like that night, didn't it?" Ysanne said quietly.

"Yes."

"I left Giovanni's portrait at Belle Morte," Ysanne said. "The only thing I saved from the Revolution, and now it's gone."

Edmond gripped her hand. "It's not gone. This isn't over."

Ysanne looked up at him, her eyes shadowed and weary. "My dear winter boy," she murmured. "Is this my fault?"

"*No*," said Edmond fiercely. "You've always tried to do what's best for your House—"

"And I've failed. Maybe it would have been better if I'd never told the world about us."

"If you hadn't, someone else would have. We couldn't have stayed hidden forever, not in this modern world. You made the right decision," Edmond insisted.

"But look where it's led us."

"You didn't do this. Etienne and Jemima did."

Ysanne shook her head. "I helped create an environment in which they *could* do this. I'm not blameless."

"You didn't know this would happen."

Ysanne stared down at their clasped hands. "Did you ever resent me for not letting you and Renie be together when she was human?"

"I don't know that I had a chance to," Edmond said.

"But what would have happened if she'd left Belle Morte and you'd never seen her again because of the rules that I upheld? Would you have resented me then?"

"I don't know. Maybe," Edmond admitted.

"You can't deny there's some merit to Jason's points. All this time I thought I was keeping my people safe, and instead I was trapping them inside a gilded cage. I brought us out of the shadows, and then I took everyone's freedom."

"We're vampires. We've never had completely normal lives, and that wasn't going to change once humans knew about us."

Ysanne's head was tipped forward again and her hair, normally pushed back in a sleek sheet behind her shoulders, hung around her face like a curtain. For Ysanne, this was practically disheveled.

"I don't know what to do," she said, her voice small and soft, and more vulnerable than Edmond had heard in a long time.

"You help us take Belle Morte back," said Renie, and both Edmond and Ysanne looked up, startled. They'd been so focused on each other that they hadn't heard Renie approach. She stood on the lawn opposite, on the other side of a stone path. Shadows from a sculpted hedge darkened her auburn hair and cast strange shapes on her face, and she looked more vampire than she ever had before.

Ysanne stiffened. The moments of vulnerability that she showed around Edmond were something he'd earned over the hundreds of years that they'd known each other, and he wasn't sure how she'd react to Renie seeing her like this.

Renie crossed the path and paused a foot or two away from Ysanne and Edmond. Away from the shadows, her skin was like porcelain, her hair spilling brightly around her shoulders, and she was so beautiful that Edmond couldn't take his eyes off her. He wanted to make love to her under the stars.

"Okay, you've made mistakes. So has everyone else. But Belle Morte is *your* House, and the Ysanne Moreau I know wouldn't sit around moping while someone stole it out from under her," Renie said.

There was a pause. Ysanne said nothing.

"What Jemima and Etienne are doing is a bigger threat to the human/vampire balance than anything. The world they want to create won't be good for anyone," Renie continued, undeterred by Ysanne's silence.

A chill wind blew through the grounds, making the fir trees *shush* together, and lifting Renie's hair until it fluttered like a flag.

Edmond's heart clenched with pride and love. He'd never imagined he'd see the day that Renie would make impassioned speeches about the safety of the vampire world to Ysanne, but her words were having an effect, even if she didn't realize it. Ysanne was sitting a little straighter, and her eyes were a little brighter. The pure steel running through her had been battered and bent, but it hadn't broken.

"Your House still needs you, Ysanne, and I know you won't let it down. Just think about it, okay? We'll be in Caoimhe's office whenever you're ready," Renie said.

She started walking back to the castle. Edmond went after her.

"Why did you come after me? I told you to wait in the office," he said, curious rather than angry.

Renie shoved her hands into her pockets. "I was scared."

"Of what?"

"I didn't know what mood Ysanne would be in. I thought she might hurt you."

Renie's fears weren't entirely unfounded. Back when she'd been human, Edmond had helped her dig up what she'd believed was June's grave on the grounds of Belle Morte. When Ysanne had found out, she'd attacked Edmond in a rage. She'd done the same thing centuries earlier, driven by rage and despair. Edmond hadn't blamed her either time. Isabeau might be the woman who'd claimed Ysanne's heart, but Edmond was still her oldest friend, the person who knew her best in the world.

Edmond took hold of Renie's hands and kissed her knuckles. "So you came to my rescue?"

Renie gave a little shrug.

"How long were you there?" he asked.

A smug smile touched her lips. "I finally managed to sneak up on you, huh?"

Edmond tapped the end of her nose. "Don't get used to it."

"Too late."

"How much did you hear?"

Renie looked away. "Ysanne said that running from Belle Morte felt like 'that night.' What was she talking about?"

"The French Revolution," Edmond replied. Again, those terrible memories flashed through his head—the blade hoisting high and coming down, again and again and again, until the streets of Paris ran black with blood, until the bodies were stacked in the hundreds. He'd seen so much death and horror over the span of his life, but some memories were seared deeper than the rest.

"Was she talking about the night you two escaped Paris?" Renie said.

Edmond nodded. "We weren't alone. Ysanne had fallen in love with a man called Giovanni, and they were living together in the city. We all fled a bloodthirsty mob together, but only Ysanne and I made it out. Giovanni sacrificed himself to the mob, giving us the chance to get away."

"Shit," Renie murmured.

"Some loves leave deeper scars than others. When I first met Ysanne, she was still grieving the loss of two husbands, but losing Giovanni . . ." Edmond trailed off, remembering the way Ysanne had attacked him, mad with rage, when they were outside the city, and how she'd then collapsed, sobbing, in his arms. He wasn't sure even Isabeau had ever seen Ysanne cry.

"Is she still in love with him?"

"I believe she's in love with Isabeau, even if she hasn't admitted as much. But the memories of the people we've loved and lost, they stay with us. They can be hard to shake, especially if that person has given their life for you."

"She still has a picture of him in her office."

"You've seen it?" That surprised Edmond. He'd thought he was the only one who'd known about it.

"It was on her desk. I just got a glimpse of it."

"Before we escaped Paris, the mob burned Ysanne's home to the ground. All her memories, everything she had to remind her of everyone else she'd loved, went up in smoke. Giovanni's portrait was the only thing she saved."

"And now Etienne has it." Renie shook her head. "No wonder she's upset."

Edmond stopped suddenly and pulled Renie into his arms so he could kiss her. He meant it to be brief—they really did have more important things to do—but when Renie twisted her fingers in Edmond's hair, as her soft body pressed against him, all other thoughts fled Edmond's mind. He kissed her until her eyes went red and her knees went weak.

"Thank you," he murmured.

"For what?" Renie blinked dazedly up at him.

Edmond traced the line of her jaw with his thumb. "For caring about Ysanne despite how much you two have clashed in the past. For trying to get her back on her feet, and for being willing to fight for Belle Morte even though it's taken so much from you."

"This is bigger than me and how I feel about Ysanne or her House," Renie said, stroking Edmond's cheek.

"I love you, mon ange," he said, and kissed her again.

CHAPTER TWENTY-THREE

Renie

I wasn't sure my speech had had any effect on Ysanne, until Edmond and I made it back to Caoimhe's office and found she'd beaten us there. The moment we walked into the room, I knew the old Ysanne was back. She stood behind Caoimhe's desk, her head held high, fresh fire blazing in her eyes.

Once I'd hated her imperiousness. Now it made me smile.

Ludovic and Seamus had also joined us; Ludovic leaned against the wall in a corner, and Seamus sat near the desk, twisting his green cap in his hands.

"I'll cut to the chase," Ysanne said, her voice sharp and clear. "I want my House back. I want everyone to know the truth of what happened, and I want to avenge all the people who've died to further Etienne and Jemima's twisted vision."

Out of the corner of my eye, I saw Jason make a tiny fist pump.

"Roux has shown me Etienne's televised statement and explained everything that was discussed in my absence. I agree with Edmond that releasing our own statement would be pointless at best, danger-ous at worst. I also agree with Renie that returning to Belle Morte is the move Etienne least expects, and therefore it's the move we must make." She spread her palms. "Now we need to discuss how to do that."

Maybe the old Ysanne wasn't entirely back. The old Ysanne wouldn't have cared about the opinions of donors or new vampires;

she'd have made the decision that she thought was best and then expected everyone to go along with it. This could be the dawn of a shiny new Ysanne.

"I can bolster our numbers by bringing some of my vampires and security personnel with us when we return to England, but I can't leave Fiaigh unprotected," Caoimhe said.

"Anyone you can spare will be appreciated," Ysanne said. "May I suggest that you send your donors home for the time being? None of us know how this will play out, and if anything goes wrong, if Etienne's vampires do come for Fiaigh, it would be better for your donors if they weren't here."

"Etienne will never take Fiaigh," Caoimhe said.

"Even so, your donors will be safest in their own homes."

Caoimhe inclined her head. "I'll make arrangements for them to leave once this meeting is over."

"Won't that look suspicious? Even if the donors aren't allowed to talk about anything, it won't take the press long to realize they've all been sent home. What if that alerts Etienne?" Roux said.

"I intend to be back in England by the time the press realizes anything," Ysanne said.

"Besides, even if anyone questioned it, a Fiaigh representative could just say it's in response to Etienne's statement," I chimed in.

"Good point," Roux said.

"It may even work in our favor," I said, thinking. "If Fiaigh sends all its donors home, Etienne and Jemima may come under public pressure to do the same thing to the donors in Nox, Midnight, Lamia, and Belle Morte. If they refuse, people will start asking questions, especially since it'll look like Fiaigh is acting independently of any collective decisions.

"But how will Etienne and Jemima's supporters act if their donors are taken away? No one wants to get rid of the donor system, they just want to change it. One thing Jemima said to me was that vampires wanted to be able to take blood whenever they felt like it, rather than being restricted to tiny amounts once a day. If that's one of the reasons she and Etienne have supporters, those supporters won't be happy when their entire donor supply gets cut off. Anything that undermines those two bastards is a good thing. Also, newly turned vampires need more blood than older vampires, so Etienne will struggle to keep his minions fed with no donors."

"That's assuming that Etienne *will* let them go," Edmond said.

He was right—we had no guarantees.

Roux's forehead scrunched up with worry. "If he doesn't, those donors are in danger, aren't they? There aren't enough of them left to feed the remaining Belle Morte vampires, let alone all the newcomers. And what's happened to June?"

The sound of her name brought a hard knot to my throat. I would never stop loving my sister or grieving for what had happened to her, but I was so *angry* with her too.

"If Etienne has turned her into a weapon, he'll want her to be close by, right?" Roux looked around at us.

"Do you think she's still in Belle Morte?" Edmond asked.

"I have no idea what happened to her after we escaped the mansion, but Etienne won't have let her run wild. He needs her too much."

"Surely he can't have hidden her in Belle Morte without anyone knowing about it?" I said.

"Ysanne did."

I glanced at Ysanne. "No, when Ysanne hid June in the west wing, everyone knew something weird was going on, they'd just been forbidden to question it and everyone obeyed Ysanne. Etienne doesn't have that kind of authority. Not yet, anyway."

"Jemima might," Jason pointed out.

"Every vampire in Belle Morte who isn't working for Etienne—and I have to assume his supporters are still in the minority—know that rabids are supposed to be killed on sight. June has proven how dangerous she is. I can't imagine the bullshit Jemima would have to spin to convince everyone that she needed to let June live.

"Equally, she won't have killed her. Like Roux said, June's too valuable. But if she is still in the mansion, then everyone is at risk. No one has ever trained a rabid before, which means no one knows how much control Etienne has or whether it'll last. If he loses control, June could turn Belle Morte into a bloodbath. Even if she's under control, Tadhg believes that Etienne fed his minions on animal blood, which isn't the same as human blood, is it? How are all those vampires going to react now that they're living inside a house with so many human food sources? Can Etienne can control them all? We don't just need to get that evidence from Susan Harcourt. We need to get the rest of the donors out of Belle Morte."

"How are we supposed to do that?" Seamus asked, still twisting his cap.

"Not a clue. But even if June isn't in Belle Morte, we have to get the donors out. I believe that most vampires in the mansion will be loyal to Ysanne once they learn the truth, but we don't know how many supporters Etienne and Jemima have, and we don't know how many people Etienne turned. For all we know, he's turned more since we've been here.

"And he's still got all those human supporters, remember? Those people flocked to him because they want what vampires have, and they're not giving that up without a fight. Even if every single one of the Belle Morte vampires comes back to our side, we're still not getting that house back without it getting bloody. When that happens, the donors can't be there. We can't let anyone else get killed in the cross fire, not only because they're completely innocent but because the higher the human body count, the harder it'll be for the vampire way of life to survive this. Stopping Etienne and Jemima isn't just about getting Belle Morte back. It's about preserving everything that vampires have spent ten years building."

Maybe changes *did* need to be made, but tearing down everything wasn't the way to make them.

Roux sighed loudly and shoved her fingers through her hair, making the short strands stick up. "So, somehow, we have to break back into Belle Morte, find our corrupt guard, get her phone with the video evidence, *and* sneak twenty-four donors out, all without anyone knowing."

It sounded hopeless when she put it like that.

"Breaking into the mansion itself isn't the problem," Ysanne said.

"How come?"

"Because I have an emergency set of keys hidden on the grounds."

"Really?" Edmond said. He sounded as surprised as the rest of us looked.

"It seemed prudent," Ysanne said.

"You never told me."

"I never told anyone."

"Then there's no way Etienne or Jemima could know about this?" I said.

"No," Ysanne replied. "But the problem remains that we need to get onto the grounds to reach the keys."

"Why don't you have an emergency key to unlock the gates?" I asked.

"When we built the donor system, Charles proposed that all the lords and ladies should have a set of keys for each house, in case anything went wrong. I think he was still afraid of the human world suddenly turning on us," Caoimhe said.

"Why didn't you do that?"

"Because I vetoed it," Ysanne answered. "There was always the chance that one of us would be challenged for the leadership position, and I wasn't comfortable knowing that anyone could access Belle Morte without my permission."

"They wouldn't have got very far though, would they? Not with the guards patrolling the grounds," Roux pointed out.

"At the time of the decision our security teams were very small. We were still ironing out various practical issues with the donor system, and I believe that my choice made sense at the time. Perhaps we should have revisited the subject once the donor system was fully established, but it never seemed important. I'd already hidden keys on the grounds, and I hoped I'd never need to use them."

"But if you didn't have a key to the gates, how were you supposed to get onto the grounds to find the key to the house?" I asked.

"I would have climbed over the wall. I know the rotation of the guards and the least patrolled areas."

"Why can't we do that?"

"There's a big difference between one vampire sneaking over the wall and all of us doing that. Besides, even if Etienne didn't think to change the guards' rotation, Jemima will have done."

"Okay, let's circle back to that," Roux said.

"How would we even get everyone back into England? Thanks to Etienne, we're wanted criminals," Jason said.

Caoimhe waved her hand dismissively. "Let me worry about that. In this country I have contacts who'll help us, whether we wish to charter another plane or take a ferry."

"Okay, let's say we pull all this off. What then? What do we do with Susan's evidence?" Jason said.

"Good point," Seamus said, looking at Caoimhe. "Even if we make it public, there's very little internet access inside a Vampire House. It wouldn't be hard for Etienne and Jemima to prevent anyone from knowing what was going on."

"But how long can they keep that up?" Roux said.

"I don't know."

"This would be a lot easier if you guys just let people have phones inside the house," Jason grumbled, slumping in his chair.

Ysanne and Caoimhe glared at him.

"How about a big projector screen?" he suggested, unfazed by their cool stares. "We could rig it up on the street outside Belle Morte and play Susan's video on a loop."

"The windows of Belle Morte are all shuttered. No one would see out," Ysanne said.

"Is the house soundproofed?"

"No."

"Then the guards patrolling outside would see the screen, and the ones working inside would hear it."

"Some of them are in Etienne's pocket, don't forget," I said.

"Yeah, but not all of them. If we broadcast Susan's video to the world, then eventually the guards still loyal to Belle Morte will hear about it. They have to. Etienne can't keep them at the mansion forever. At some point, they've got to go home," Jason said.

"He won't do that any time soon," Ysanne said.

"Again, though, how long can he keep that up?" Roux said.

"Potentially long enough to find a way to counteract our evidence," said Ysanne darkly. "One thing that we don't want is for this to become a war. I don't want to hurt any of my own vampires who've been tricked into thinking that I'm their enemy. I don't want any more of my security team dying to protect Belle Morte from the wrong person."

"What about the secret passageways?" Ludovic spoke up. "Etienne and Jemima don't know where they are, do they?"

"No. Until yesterday, Isabeau, Dexter, and I were the only ones who knew their location, and that information was stored inside our heads. Whatever else Etienne finds in my office, he won't find where the passageways are, nor the codes needed to access them. Sadly, that makes little difference since they're all inside Belle Morte. There's no passageway extending outside the house."

"Why not?" Roux said.

"They were built as a precautionary measure—I never thought

I'd actually have to use them. I considered it too dangerous to have an unguarded entryway out there that could lead directly into Belle Morte. Ironically, I always thought that if Belle Morte should encounter enemies, it would not be prudent to have a secret entry into the house that our enemies might use to take us by surprise."

Roux pulled a face. "That kind of backfired, didn't it?"

Now it was her turn to be on the receiving end of an icy Ysanne glare.

We batted ideas back and forth for the next hour, but none of us could settle on anything concrete. Finally, it got to the point where, tempers frayed, we were all just bickering with each other, and Caoimhe called a time-out.

"Arguing isn't helping anyone," she said.

"We don't have time for a break," Ysanne snapped.

"We all need to clear our heads, because we're certainly not getting anywhere at the moment," said Caoimhe firmly.

Ysanne didn't raise further objection, though the tight line of her mouth suggested she wasn't happy with the situation. Caoimhe was right, though—we all needed a break so we could clear our heads and regroup in a better mood.

Besides, the need for blood was starting to knot up my stomach. I needed to feed.

Like last night, a donor was sent to my room, though only one this time. Edmond stayed with me, watching me drink and advising when I'd taken enough. I wondered how long it would take me to learn how to recognize that on my own.

After the donor left, I flopped back on the bed and stared at the ceiling. I had no idea what time it was, and despite the fresh energy flooding my body, I felt tired and wrung out. The passion that I'd felt about reclaiming Belle Morte had dimmed in light of the many obstacles in our way.

"I know Etienne's younger than you, but how old's Jemima?" I asked.

"She was turned in 1682, but she's never told anyone how old she was when she died," Edmond said, sitting on the bed next to me.

"Wait, she's younger than you?" I propped myself on my elbows.

"Only by eleven years in vampire terms."

"Yeah, but still younger. I guess I thought she was at least as old as Ysanne."

"Ysanne's the oldest member of the Council."

Even more so now that two of them were dead, I thought. "Aren't there any really ancient vampires out there? Like Vikings, or Romans, anything like that?"

Edmond trailed his fingertips down the line of my throat. "There were once, but not anymore."

"What happened to them?"

He gave a graceful shrug. "Roman vampires died as soldiers or gladiators. Viking vampires died during invasions. We're not invulnerable. Human history is a litany of butchery—vampires died in the Crusades, the Roman-Persian Wars, the Napoleonic Wars, the Crimean Wars, the World Wars, Vietnam, and every war in between. We died during the Spanish Inquisition. We were hunted as witches. We lost our heads to the guillotine." His hand moved down from my throat and settled on my stomach. His eyes grew a shade darker, but with sadness rather than heat. "Living forever is harder than most people realize, especially during the times when people would kill us if they knew what we were. For some of us, the loneliness became too much to bear. I'm far from the only vampire to consider taking my own life."

I quietly absorbed that.

"Why did you ask?" Edmond said.

"I was trying to work out how much of a threat Jemima is."

Edmond smiled, sharp and cold. "Ysanne can handle her, and I can handle Etienne."

I gripped his hand and squeezed it tight. I'd thought before, with grim satisfaction, of what would happen if Edmond ever got his hands on Etienne, but now the thought of it scared me. Who knew what other nasty tricks Etienne had up his sleeve?

"Mon ange? What's wrong?" Edmond kissed the frown between my eyebrows.

"Nothing." I shoved those fears away. If nothing else, I had to think positive.

Edmond leaned on one elbow, looking down at me, and even though I didn't need to breathe, it felt like I *couldn't*, like pure emotion had knotted up my chest and my lungs. It was almost scary. How could one person make me feel this complete? How could I love Edmond this much? But I did. I felt my love for him in my heart, my soul, my very bones. He was under my skin, and I wanted him to stay there for the rest of our lives, however long that would be.

"How long do you think we have before we have to be back in the office?" I whispered.

Edmond's eyes sparked red. "What did you have in mind?"

"What do you think?" I nibbled his lower lip.

The red in his eyes flared brighter. "I think we have time."

Forty minutes later, we made our way back downstairs. I felt as languid as a cat, and Edmond looked particularly smug.

"We should take breaks like that more often," I said.

"Just say the word."

We turned into the hallway that led to Caoimhe's office, and almost ran into Roux, who was coming the opposite way.

"There you guys are," she said. She looked like she was about to say something else, then stopped and eyed my hair.

"What?" I said.

Her lips twitched. "You look like you had fun."

Quickly, I smoothed down my hair, which did feel a little wild.

I glanced at Edmond, but he was as sleek and perfect as ever. Of course.

"Anyway." Roux clasped her hands. "There's something else you need to see."

Edmond and I exchanged looks, and my postsex glow faded. "Something bad?" I said.

"Not exactly. Come on."

We followed her to the office, where the others were waiting. Jason now occupied the chair at the desk, while Caoimhe and Ysanne stood behind him, staring suspiciously at the laptop.

"Jason had the idea of checking the usual Vladdict sites to gauge what people think about Etienne's statement. Then he found this." Roux turned the laptop toward us.

A paused video filled the screen—a young girl sitting on the floor with her back against her bed. I'd never seen her before, but the username beneath the video was one I knew.

Nikki Flynn.

"Oh," I said, because I couldn't find any other words.

Now that I knew who she was, I could see something of Dexter in her face—they had the same chin, the same warm eyes, but where Dexter's head had been shaved smooth, his daughter had a thick crop of dark curls, like the woman in the locket. She was only thirteen, but there was something utterly determined in the set of her jaw, and I remembered Dexter saying that once Nikki got it into her head to do something, she wouldn't be persuaded otherwise.

Roux pressed Play on the video.

"By now you've probably all seen the video that Etienne Banville put out this morning," Nikki said. "I'm here to tell you that he's full of shit. Ysanne's been secretly turning vampires and driving them to near starvation? Give me a fucking break. Ysanne's the one who revealed vampires to the world, and she helped shape the rules that all vampires have to live by—including the really obvious one about *not turning humans*. Why, after ten years, would she randomly start breaking her own rules? What the actual hell would she gain from assassinating the Council?"

Nikki moved closer to the camera, her eyes flashing with anger. "My dad is head of security at Belle Morte, and he's always told me he'd trust Ysanne with his life. She trusts him too. They've worked together since the Vampire Houses were created, and she'd never hurt him. *Ever*. I don't know what's going on inside Belle Morte, but it's not what Etienne says. He's lying. Don't listen to him. Demand the truth."

The video ended.

"She's still talking about Dexter in the present tense," I said.

"I noticed that too. If she thinks Etienne's lying about everything else, she probably thinks he's lying about her dad's death too," Roux said.

"That's the one thing he's *not* lying about."

"I know." Roux's voice was sad.

"How many people have seen this?" Edmond asked.

"Nikki only has a tiny following on social media, so initially almost no one saw it. But half an hour ago, the video got picked up by some bigger Vladdict sites, and it's spreading. It hasn't got as much attention as Etienne's, but it hasn't been up as long."

"What does this mean?"

"It means that this is a variable Etienne didn't consider," Roux replied. "He's not stupid enough to think he can keep Belle Morte on lockdown forever—that's why he's publicly accused you guys. Even though he doesn't know there's any evidence against him, he won't risk letting any of us live. My guess is he'll kill Jason and me, blame it on you guys, and then kill you guys as punishment. Alternatively, he'll kill us all at once and claim that we died trying to escape justice. The point is, he's hoping to flush us out within a few days. He absolutely could keep Belle Morte locked down for that length of time, and then open it back up when he was sure the truth had died with us. But Nikki may have just thrown a wrench in his plans. If people start questioning Etienne now, he's going to lose his window of opportunity."

"Assuming that anyone takes her seriously. She's a child, after all," Ysanne said.

"The Vladdict sites that reposted her video have millions of followers. Even if only a fraction of them believe Nikki, that's enough to cast doubt on Etienne's accusations and pressure him to address what Nikki's saying."

"But how will Etienne know that Nikki's said this? I can't see him using social media," I objected.

"If he wants people to report any sightings of us, then he has to keep on top of what's happening outside Belle Morte. Susan or another corrupt guard is probably helping him with that. They'll hear about this," Roux said.

"Doesn't that put Nikki at risk?" said Jason, frowning. "Can't Etienne find out where she lives?"

"Dexter's address is in my office," Ysanne admitted.

"Shit." I looked again at the girl on the screen, and thought of the pride and love in Dexter's eyes when he'd talked about her. We couldn't let Etienne get to her. "We have to warn her."

"We could message her, but I get the feeling she wouldn't believe it." Roux tapped her finger on the desktop. "I know it's risky, but I think we need to speak to her face-to-face."

"It'll be hours before we can get back to England. What if it's too late by then?" Caoimhe said.

"I meant in a video call," Roux explained.

"We can talk to her through the machine?" Ludovic spoke up. He didn't sound convinced.

"Oh, honey, of course we can." Roux pointed to the top of the screen. "You see this teeny, tiny circle? That's a webcam."

"I have no idea what you're talking about," Ludovic told her.

"I know, and it's adorable." Roux turned to me. "When this is all over, you really need to bring these vampires up to date on the modern world."

I gave her a salute.

Roux's fingers flew over the keyboard, her nails making little clacking sounds. "Right, I've messaged Nikki, so now we play the waiting game. She's probably getting loads of messages from people, so it could take a while to hear back."

"She might not message back at all," Jason pointed out.

"She will," I said, sliding my hand into my pocket and curling my fingers around Dexter's locket. "She wants the truth as much as anyone, especially considering what Etienne said about her dad."

"We get to be the ones who tell her Dexter really is dead. Lucky us," said Jason glumly, slumping in his chair.

"I'll tell her," I said.

I was the last person Dexter had spoken to. I was the one he'd given the locket to. I'd promised him that I'd give it to Nikki. This wasn't how I'd imagined telling her, but it was still my responsibility.

The waiting game didn't last for long. Within half an hour Roux had received a reply.

"Okay," she said, scanning the message. "The bad news is that she's not convinced she can trust us. The good news is she's willing to have a video chat."

"I assume you know how to do that?" Caoimhe said.

Roux gave her an *oh please* look.

Despite the determination I'd seen on Nikki's face during her video, I still found myself expecting someone nervous, maybe even frightened. I should've known better.

Nikki Flynn glared at us onscreen. Both arms were folded and her hair was puffed up around her head like that of an angry poodle.

"Hi, Nikki," I said. "Do you know who I am?"

Her glare grew even darker. "Am I supposed to?"

I'd assumed that, with her father being so heavily involved in the vampire world, she'd have some interest in following them and their donors, but perhaps not.

"I'm Renie Mayfield, the donor who was illegally turned into a vampire."

"Prove it," Nikki snapped.

"Will you take my word for it?" said Ysanne, moving into view of the webcam.

Nikki's expression faltered for just a moment, and then the glare slammed back into place.

"Where are you?" she said.

"It's safer not to tell you that," I said.

Nikki accepted that with a nod.

"It might not be safe where you are either," said Roux, pushing her face close to mine so Nikki could see her. "Etienne knows where you live, and he really won't like that you posted that video."

She snorted. "I'm not afraid of him."

I flexed my hand beneath the desk, remembering the awful pain of bones splintering. "Don't underestimate him."

"Are you all there? Everyone Etienne said went on the run?"

"Yes, but not because—"

"Where's my dad?" Nikki interrupted.

I'd tried to rehearse what to say while we waited for her to respond to Roux's message, but now words failed me.

But I'd promised Dexter, and Nikki deserved to know the truth. I knew exactly how it felt to be kept in the dark about the fate of someone I loved, and I wouldn't put this poor kid through the same hell.

"I'm so sorry, Nikki, but Etienne wasn't lying about that. Your dad didn't make it," I said.

My words sounded horribly loud in the office. I expected Nikki to crumble, but she kept the same stony expression.

"I don't believe you," she said.

I almost wished I couldn't prove it. I held up the locket.

Nikki's tough facade cracked. "Why do you have my dad's locket?" Her voice trembled slightly, making her sound her age for the first time.

She may have already started training to follow in her dad's footsteps as head of security, but she was still a kid who'd lost the only parent she'd had.

"He asked me to give it to you," I said. "I was with him when he died, and he was a hero. He went out protecting the people who relied on him."

"Of course he did," Nikki snapped, tears shimmering in her eyes. "He was my dad, that's what he did."

"I'd have given anything to save him, but I couldn't, and now you're in danger too."

Nikki swiped away her tears with a shaking hand. "I want to know what really happened."

I told her.

"That lying piece of shit," she said when I'd finished.

"She's not wrong," Jason mumbled.

"If you can get back inside Belle Morte, you can prove that Etienne and Jemima are responsible for this?" Nikki said.

"We hope so." I couldn't promise anything.

"Will they be punished?"

"You have my word on that," said Ysanne.

"Except you don't know how to get back into Belle Morte." Nikki chewed on her thumbnail.

"Not yet, but that's nothing you need to concern yourself with," Ysanne said.

"My dad's dead because of them. I'm involved with this whether you like it or not," Nikki told her.

"You're thirteen."

"I don't give a shit."

In my periphery, Edmond lifted a dark eyebrow. I tried not to smile. It looked like I wasn't the only one willing to mouth off to Ysanne.

"Dad always said you were the strongest vampire he'd ever met. Can't you break the lock on the gates?" Nikki said.

"Yes, but the whole point of this is that we want to get the donors out and find Susan before anyone knows we're there. If we break down the gate, the guards on patrol will see us. Etienne will know we're coming before we even reach the mansion," Ysanne said.

"What you need is a distraction," Nikki said. Her eyebrows pulled down in a dark V, and her mouth scrunched up. "I've got an idea. Don't do anything until I get back in contact."

"Nikki, wait," I cried, but she was already gone.

"I don't think I'm entirely happy with the fate of my House resting in the hands of a child," Ysanne said, glaring at the laptop as if it was to blame.

I wasn't, either, not only because Nikki was thirteen and shouldn't be mixed up with all this blood and death, but because we owed it to Dexter to keep her safe.

"We have to trust her. She's Dexter's daughter, she won't do anything stupid," I said.

Ysanne didn't look convinced.

I slipped the locket back into my pocket. We couldn't stop Nikki from doing whatever she had planned, and maybe she really would be able to help.

When I'd first arrived at Belle Morte, I had likened it to some huge glittering spiderweb, sucking unsuspecting donors in. Now it truly was a web, and Jemima and Etienne were the spiders crouched at the top of it.

They needed to be stopped.

They needed to be crushed.

CHAPTER TWENTY-FOUR

Renie

It was almost midnight when we heard back from Nikki, and my nerves were stretched to a breaking point. All I could think about was Etienne finding her or sending some of his goons to abduct her, like he'd done to me. I'd healed from the torture they'd inflicted—Nikki wouldn't.

Once again, we gathered around Caoimhe's desk, while Roux read her message from Nikki.

"Oh wow," she said softly.

Nikki had taken everything we'd told her about Jemima and Etienne and given it to the Vladdict sites who'd shared her video. She didn't have any evidence, but that had never stopped rumors from taking shape. She hadn't released the names of the dead, instead hyping up that multiple people had been killed inside the mansion and no one knew who they were yet, not even their families. She urged the families and friends of donors, staff, and security, and anyone else who doubted Etienne, to demand answers by going to Belle Morte tomorrow night and protesting outside the gates until someone told them what was going on.

Social media was on fire with people discussing the validity of Nikki's claims. Unsurprisingly, plenty of people dismissed her as being full of shit, but many more were taking her words seriously.

"Was this a good idea?" Jason said.

"Yes," I said, realizing what Nikki had done. "This is exactly the distraction we need. If a big enough mob gathers at Belle Morte, we can hide among them."

"I think the mob might recognize some of the most famous vampires in the world," Jason pointed out.

"Then we'll have to disguise them somehow. Look, if we want to get inside the gates, this is the perfect way to do it. We can blend in with the crowd, and if there's enough of a commotion, no one will notice who breaks the lock on the gates."

"It's more than that," Edmond said. "A big enough crowd will draw the guards off their regular patrol to investigate, and when we break through the gates, that crowd will come with us. If Etienne has changed the guard rotations, we won't know how many to expect or where they'll be. But if they're all drawn to the gates, the grounds will be more or less free. We can reach the emergency keys and get in through one of the back doors uninterrupted. No matter what lies Etienne has fed them, Belle Morte's security detail won't assault civilians."

"Even if they've broken in?" Roux said.

"Not in this situation. The people Nikki is encouraging will be scared and confused—they're coming for answers, not because they're a threat to Belle Morte."

"What if the guards on patrol are the ones working for Etienne?" Jason said.

"They still won't risk killing innocent civilians. Jemima and Etienne don't have the numbers to hold the Houses purely by force— that's why they need to kill us and the truth. At the moment, they're passing themselves off as survivors of Ysanne's machinations, but that'll collapse the second they start killing people. They can't risk that," Edmond said.

"Besides, the press will have got wind of this by now. They'll be at the gates along with everyone else, and there's no way anyone will commit murder on film," Caoimhe said.

"But Jemima *wants* to show people the darker side of vampire nature," I said.

"Not like this," said Ysanne. "She still needs the support of the majority of vampires in the House, and they won't support her if she starts killing the donors' families."

Roux looked troubled. "This still seems very risky."

"Do you have a better idea? Especially now that Nikki has set all this in motion?" Ysanne asked.

"No," Roux mumbled.

"We'll never break in by force. Belle Morte is too well fortified to be taken in that manner."

"But it did get taken."

"That was through no fault of the House," Ysanne snapped. "It was my fault. I became complacent with my balls and television shows and adoring masses, and I was confident that no one would ever strike against me. I assumed that the Council all wanted the same thing and that we would all work to achieve it. I never anticipated anyone betraying us." Her voice took on a harsh, raw note. "My arrogance caused the downfall of my House."

Nobody said anything. Roux and Jason gaped at Ysanne as if they'd never seen her before. To them, she was the ice queen of Belle Morte, the cold, marble-hard woman who ruled over donors and vampires alike, and there was something very disconcerting about seeing her come apart like that, even if only for a moment.

If Ysanne had been anyone else, I'd have comforted her, but I knew her well enough now to understand that was not what she needed. To Ysanne, grief and comfort were things to be shown in private, not in front of everyone else.

"What's the plan for when we get inside?" I said, picking up the discussion as if Ysanne hadn't spoken.

"First, I have to show you where the passageways are," said Ysanne. She had to share the information with us or we couldn't help her, but her discomfort was evident in the rigid way she held herself and the hard shape of her mouth. Ysanne was a very private woman, and she kept her secrets close to her chest, especially where the safety of her House was concerned. She couldn't take this information back. Okay, she could change the codes on the keypads, but she couldn't change the locations of the passageways themselves.

Ysanne sketched out a couple of rough floor plans, one for each floor of Belle Morte, and used a red pen to mark Xs on the entrances and exits of each passageway.

"Seamus will stay outside with a team, to keep any Belle Morte guards from realizing what's going on, to keep the crowd from spilling too far into my grounds, and to escort the donors to safety once we get them out," she said.

"Are we taking them out of the back door too?" Roux asked.

"*You* won't do anything. You're not coming," Ysanne said.

"Excuse me?" Roux straightened up.

"You and Jason are human."

"So are Andrew and Seamus, and you're not leaving them behind," Roux argued.

"They're trained members of vampire security. You and Jason aren't. It's too dangerous," Ysanne said.

Roux folded her arms, a steely glint in her eyes. "Etienne's told everyone that you kidnapped Jason and me so that you could use us as donors. If you show up at Belle Morte without us that adds weight to his accusations. If we're with you, we can refute them. Also, can you imagine the fear and confusion those donors are feeling right now? Jason and I are still donors, like them, and they're more likely to trust us than you."

Ysanne's nostrils flared slightly.

"She has a point," Caoimhe said.

"I've failed enough donors already. Don't ask me to put two more in danger," Ysanne said, staring down at the floor plans.

"We're not asking you, though," Jason piped up. "We've come too far to be left behind now. We're both aware of the risks, and you're not responsible for us."

Ysanne's mouth tightened, and I was sure she'd refuse. I was just as sure that Roux and Jason wouldn't take no for an answer.

"Very well," said Ysanne in clipped tones. "Once we're inside Belle Morte, we shall separate into three teams. One will be in charge of getting the donors out. The other two will find Susan Harcourt and retrieve that video."

"Why three teams and not two?" I asked.

"The passageways give us an advantage over Etienne and Jemima, but we must not become complacent because of this. I won't make that mistake again. If this goes wrong and we get caught, it would be prudent if we're not all together," Ysanne explained.

I noticed that she didn't seem annoyed with my question, whereas once she would have been. Had I earned a higher level of respect from her because I was a vampire now, or because I'd proved myself worthy of it?

"What if Susan's one of the guards patrolling outside?" I said.

"I don't think she will be. If she's played as big a role in this as Tadhg says, then Etienne will keep her close by." Ysanne looked around at us. "I won't lie to you. There's a good chance that this won't work. There may not be enough of a crowd tomorrow night to provide us with the necessary distraction. We may not be able to reach the donors or Susan Harcourt without getting caught. Even if we do find Susan, she may have moved past her misgivings about Etienne and disposed of her evidence against him. Or her evidence may not be enough to convince everyone that he's lying. I just don't know."

"There's another thing we have to consider," said Edmond. "Donors are supposed to be under the protection of whichever House they're assigned to. Nothing bad has ever happened to a donor until now. Even if we can prove that Etienne and Jemima are responsible for these deaths, even if we bring them both down and take back our House, it may be too late to save the donor system. We can beat Etienne and Jemima, and yet still lose our way of life. We need to be prepared for that."

That hadn't even occurred to me, and a chill of fear prickled my skin. Ysanne had told me before what might happen to vampires if the human world ever turned against them, but I realized now that I hadn't absorbed what she was saying. It had seemed so abstract to me because it didn't affect me. But now it would. If the donor system collapsed and vampires lost their Houses, they'd have nowhere to go. *I'd* have nowhere to go.

"We have to have hope," said Roux quietly.

My mouth felt suddenly bitter. Hope wouldn't shield us from the sun or give us blood to drink. But none of this was Roux's fault, and snapping at her would achieve nothing. She was only trying to help.

"It's going to be a long wait until tomorrow night," Jason said, resting his head on Caoimhe's desk.

"At least it gives us time to arrange for my donors to be sent home, and for me to arrange transport for us back to England," Caoimhe said.

"Are you sure we'll be safe? None of your contacts will report us to the police like Etienne wants?" Roux said.

"I trust them."

"Yeah, and Ysanne trusted Etienne, Susan, and Jemima, and look how that turned out," Roux said.

Ysanne gave her a withering look.

"No offense," Roux added.

"Unless you have a better idea, then my contacts are the only way," Caoimhe said.

"Fair enough. What can we do to help?"

"Nothing, but I appreciate the offer," Caoimhe said.

"You guys should get some sleep," I said to Roux and Jason.

Humans needed more sleep than vampires, and Jason in particular looked like he was about to drop off where he was sitting.

"Yeah, that's a good idea," Roux said.

There was an anxious look in her eyes, and I thought I knew why. None of us knew how tomorrow would play out, but Ysanne was right. We might lose and Etienne might win. If that happened, we'd be on the run again, and I wasn't sure we'd be able to go back to Fiaigh. For all we knew, tonight was the last chance we'd have to sleep in a proper bed. I wanted to think positively, like Roux had said, but I also had to be prepared for reality.

Edmond and I went back to our room. Edmond needed sleep after having been up most of the night, and there was nothing else we could do until tomorrow.

As I walked into the room, an icy fist of fear gripped my throat. I'd pushed for us to go back to Belle Morte, but Etienne wanted us all dead, and we were going to walk right into his web.

Everyone I'd fled to Fiaigh with had become part of my life—even Ysanne—and the thought of losing any of them was almost more than I could bear.

But the thought of losing Edmond?

My hands started to shake.

"Are you all right, ma chérie?" Edmond asked, closing the door.

I couldn't find words. My blood felt like it was turning to ice.

"Renie?" Edmond clasped my shoulders with both hands.

"I'm scared," I whispered. "I'm so fucking scared, Edmond."

Edmond didn't murmur any meaningless platitudes, which I was grateful for. Instead, he put his arms around me and held me tight against his chest, and I closed my eyes and rested my head over his unbeating heart.

"Aren't you scared?" I whispered.

"For myself? No. But for you?" He ran gentle fingers through my hair. "Always."

Of course he wasn't scared for himself, not after his experiences at war. I touched the shrapnel buried in his side, and traced the edges of it with my fingertips.

"I'll kill Etienne if he tries to hurt you again," Edmond said, his voice low and hard, almost a growl.

"What if he hurts you?"

"I can handle it."

I gazed up at him, my heart clenching and twisting with love and fear. "Take me to bed, Edmond," I whispered.

We made love with the delicious slowness of two people still getting to know each other's bodies. Last time had been almost frantic, both of us overcome with passion and desire and the need to be with each other. Now we savored every single second, drawing out every touch, kiss, and movement, until the coiling pleasure inside me broke free and lights exploded behind my eyelids.

"Oh my god," I breathed when I could talk again. "Can we please do that every day for the rest of our lives?"

Edmond smiled, showing off a hint of fang. His eyes still shone red with lingering passion. "That's a lot of sex, mon ange."

I smirked. "I know."

He propped himself on one elbow, trailing a finger from my lips down my throat and between my breasts. "Vampires do have more stamina than humans."

"I noticed."

Edmond's tongue traced the path his finger had taken, stopping just above my belly button. I wanted him to go lower, but then I wouldn't be able to think straight.

"I used to wonder if becoming a vampire made people prettier too," I commented.

"It doesn't work like that," Edmond said, kissing my stomach.

"But you're all so hot. It's not normal," I teased.

Edmond walked his fingertips back up my body, pausing to smooth a palm over each of my breasts. "Traditionally, vampires only turned the beautiful."

"Seriously?" I half sat up, and Edmond's hand fell away from me.

"I know it sounds shallow now, but in the past it was a survival tactic. We didn't have donors at our disposal—we had to hunt for blood, and the reality was that pretty faces were better for luring potential prey."

There was a certain logic in that, but his explanation still made me feel prickly.

"I didn't say it was *right*, I said it was necessary," Edmond said, studying my expression. "Protestations won't change that. That's also why most vampires were young when they were turned. We used youth as bait, just as we used beauty."

I thought again of Jemima, who looked even younger than me. There was still so much about vampire history that I had to learn. At least I had forever in which to learn it—assuming tomorrow went according to plan.

I lay back down and snuggled into Edmond's arms.

"I know you're worried, but I genuinely believe we can do this," he murmured.

"I hope so, but Etienne and Jemima have come too far to go down without a fight."

"Maybe so, but they *are* going down." Edmond's voice was hard as iron, and red flashed in his eyes. I wondered how he'd handled that at war. Hadn't anyone noticed his eyes turning to fire when he got angry? Or maybe in the heat of the battle, no one cared.

"What about June?" I asked.

Edmond stared down at me for a long moment, his face shadowed with sadness. "Go to sleep, mon ange," he said at last, and kissed my forehead.

I knew why he wasn't answering because I knew exactly what his answer would have been. I just wasn't ready to hear it.

The next morning, we fed from the donors for the last time. Later in the afternoon, unmarked Fiaigh vehicles would ferry them all home. They'd been assured that their contracts were still in place and that they could perhaps return within a few days, as long as they kept quiet about what they'd seen. Anyone who leaked anything would have their contract terminated immediately. Maybe the donors of Belle Morte wouldn't have minded that, after all the fighting and kill-ing they'd seen, but the Fiaigh donors still didn't really know what was going on.

I worried that, once they got home and caught up with the news that we were practically wanted criminals, they might be willing to breach their contracts and tell everyone where we were, but Caoimhe assured me that she'd considered that. We'd leave Fiaigh shortly after the donors. If all went to plan, then we'd clear our names and start the process of putting everything back together. If we failed, then we'd go on the run for good, somewhere other than Fiaigh.

For me, the day passed in a state of constant dread. Roux and Jason took it in turns to monitor the various social media chan-nels that had first shared Nikki's video; even though they reported how much attention it had generated, and how many people were talking about going to Belle Morte tonight, I was aware that words were cheap. There was no guarantee that any of these people would actually turn up, and if they didn't, we wouldn't get farther than Belle Morte's gates.

I just wanted to get this over and done with, but then late after-noon crept in, and it was time to leave Fiaigh, and suddenly I wished we'd had more time, because my stomach felt like I'd swallowed lead, and my head was a knot of fear and emotion. I was afraid to go back to Belle Morte, afraid to drag the truth into the light, afraid to see Etienne and Jemima again, afraid of June, but there was no way in hell I could stay behind and let my friends go off without me.

Caoimhe had arranged a flight for us to return to England, but not from the same airport where we'd arrived in Ireland, just to be on the safe side. Instead, we split into small groups and traveled in a staggered convoy to a private airport several miles north of Fiaigh. Eight of Caoimhe's vampires and six members of her security team came with us. I'd hoped for more. We weren't going to Belle Morte to start a fight, but that didn't mean it wouldn't happen, and with all the vampires that Etienne had turned, he and Jemima still had the superior numbers.

Three minivans with blacked-out windows waited for us at the airport in England; I had no idea how Caoimhe had arranged that, but I was too tense to ask. It was dark enough for me to shed some layers, and I did so before climbing into a minivan. If we needed to run, I didn't want anything slowing me down.

Barely anyone had spoken on the flight over, and the tense atmosphere only grew worse once the minivans set off for Belle Morte. We were all aware of the many, many ways this could all go wrong.

I thought of the first time I'd made this journey, as a normal girl determined to find out what had happened to my sister. So much had happened to me since then. Some of it was terrible. But—I took Edmond's hand—some of it was beautiful. Perhaps one could not exist without the other.

We parked a short distance from Belle Morte—if Nikki's plan failed then we'd need to make a quick getaway before any of the guards realized we were there.

A light rain had begun to fall while we were on the road, and it misted down around us until the world seemed like it was shrouded in a grayish veil. But that veil wasn't enough to hide what was happening in front of Belle Morte.

Edmond made a soft exclamation in French.

"Holy shit," I whispered.

Hundreds of people were crowded in front of the gates, packed tight across the road and pavement, far more than I'd imagined. Nikki had done one hell of a job.

The second minivan pulled up behind ours, followed closely by the third. Andrew climbed out, holding two large bags. "Everyone take a hat and scarf," he said.

Roux pulled a black ball cap from one of the bags and jammed it on her head. "Can't have anyone recognizing us," she said, giving me a wink.

The memory of the first night I'd met her—driving up in a limo as brand-new donors—hit me so strongly that tears stung my eyes. It felt like a lifetime ago.

Edmond lifted out another black cap and held it gingerly, like it might bite him.

"Not quite your usual style, is it?" I said. I took the cap from him and set it on his head, pulling it down so the brim obscured his face, and then took the scarf that Roux handed me and wound it around his neck.

Vampires didn't move quite like humans; they had a fluid, elegant grace about them that at times became predatory, and that no human could replicate. But I doubted anyone would notice that in this crowd.

Ysanne joined us. To stay incognito, she'd ditched her usual tailored clothes for a pair of jeans and flat-heeled boots, and with a cap and scarf covering most of her face, I'd never have known I was standing next to the Lady of Belle Morte.

"No matter what happens, I don't want anyone risking their lives," she warned, her voice slightly muffled through her scarf. "If this goes wrong, you get out of the house. Understood?"

We all murmured agreement.

Edmond took my hand. "Are you ready?" he said.

I wasn't, but I nodded anyway.

As we approached the crowd, we split into pairs and small groups so we could integrate with everyone else without attracting too much attention. Edmond stayed with me, holding my hand. I wasn't sure if that was for my benefit or if he was trying to assure himself that Etienne would never take me away again.

Dozens of cameras flashed around us, and I instinctively recoiled, but Edmond pulled me close against him. "It's all right," he whispered.

The cameras weren't aimed at us, I realized. The first time I'd come here, the paparazzi had been shouting to get my attention, frantically snapping shots as I headed toward Belle Morte. This time, no one spared me a second glance.

The crowd shifted and swelled around us as we pushed our way through, and the tension in the air was so thick I could practically feel it, sucking at my skin like tar. Hundreds of voices shouted questions, demanded answers, and it occurred to me that this situation could turn very ugly, very quickly.

I caught a glimpse of Belle Morte's wrought-iron gates, and five men in black security uniforms standing on the other side, looking uneasy. There were usually two kinds of groups that might flock to the gates of a vampire mansion—Vladdicts and other fans, desperate for a glimpse of the vampires they idolized, and the fringe movements that hated vampires and sometimes came to the mansions to hurl abuse. The crowd that Nikki had gathered didn't fit into either category, and from the looks on their faces, the guards didn't know how to handle this. If Dexter was alive, he'd have taken charge of the situation, but maybe Etienne hadn't got around to appointing a new head of security.

"You got someone in there?" asked a middle-aged man on my right side.

"My sister," I said.

"Yeah, my niece is one of the donors. We got the whole family down here when we saw all that stuff online. You think it's true?"

"Every word of it."

He nodded, his face settling into grim lines. I edged away from him and moved farther into the crowd, trying to push to the front without drawing any attention to either me or Edmond.

Someone grabbed my arm, and I turned to see a small figure standing beside me, bundled in a thick coat with a knitted cap pulled low over their head, making it hard to see their face. Then the figure looked up, and I gasped.

"Nikki? What are you *doing* here?"

"Helping, duh," she said.

"You shouldn't be here," I hissed.

We were in the middle of a potentially volatile situation, and Nikki was just a kid. Why hadn't I considered that she'd come? Maybe it wouldn't have made a difference even if I'd thought of it, because I couldn't have stopped her, but that didn't make me feel any better.

"Too bad. I'm not going anywhere," Nikki told me.

I turned a panicked look on Edmond. He lowered his head so he could whisper in my ear.

"We'll have to lose her as soon as we're through the gates," he said.

Nikki narrowed her eyes. "What did he say?"

"Nothing," I said.

She didn't look like she believed me.

Before I could forget, I pulled Dexter's locket from my pocket and handed it to her. Nikki's tough facade cracked again, the grief of a kid who'd lost her dad flashing through. Then she hung the locket around her neck, tucked it beneath her T-shirt, and her expression solidified into pure determination.

"Let's get on with this," she said.

CHAPTER TWENTY-FIVE

Edmond

No one in the crowd had recognized him. No one meant him harm. And yet Edmond felt horribly tense, every muscle primed and ready to either fight or run.

The vampire who'd made him, François, had been hacked to a bloody ruin in his own home by an angry mob. Charlotte, whom Edmond had once loved, had summoned a mob to kill him when she'd found out he was a vampire. A bloodthirsty mob had tried to kill him and Ysanne after Edmond had escaped the guillotine.

The predator in him felt backed into a corner, and for the first time in a long time, he had to fight to keep his fangs retracted.

Someone knocked into Renie, and she clung tighter to his hand so she didn't lose her balance. Edmond drew her closer to him, shielding her from the jostling elbows and shifting feet that surrounded them. No matter what discomfort he was feeling, he wouldn't let her see it. She was scared enough already, especially now that Nikki was involved.

A few feet away, he caught Ludovic's eye. Ludovic gave him a little nod. Roux and Jason were huddled close to him, but Edmond couldn't see where everyone else was.

"What now?" Renie asked, when they were almost at the front of the crowd.

Edmond scanned the five guards on the other side of the gates. He knew them all, and none of them were among the names that Tadhg had given them. Normally there were ten to fifteen guards patrolling the grounds, both day and night, so either Etienne had reduced the patrol, or the distraction wasn't yet big enough to draw the other guards from their positions.

"It's not enough, is it?" Renie said, reading his expression.

Edmond didn't get a chance to answer.

The second Nikki heard Renie's question, she spun around and shoved back through the crowd.

Renie started to call after her, but Edmond gave a warning shake of his head. If Etienne or Jemima got wind that they were here, this could be over before they'd even got through the gates.

"She's thirteen," Renie hissed.

"I don't like this any more than you do, but we have to trust that she won't do anything stupid," Edmond said.

Even so, when Nikki was swallowed up by the throngs of people, Edmond felt a sharp pang of concern.

For a minute or two nothing happened, and then Edmond spotted Nikki's small shape breaking free of the crowd. She ran to the nearest parked car and climbed onto the roof.

"What is she *doing*?" Renie said.

"What she came here to do—give us a distraction," Edmond said.

He wasn't happy about Nikki being here, but he had to admire the girl's courage and determination. Dexter would have been proud.

"Why won't they tell us the truth?" Nikki screamed. "Who really killed those donors?"

Faces turned toward her, and Edmond nudged Renie to do the same. They had to pretend to be here for the same reason as everyone else.

"Why won't they tell us who died? What if they're lying? What if they've killed *all* the donors and now they're trying to cover it up?" Nikki cried.

With her curls covered, and her knitted hat pulled down to her eyes, Edmond doubted that anyone recognized her as the girl from the video, but all that mattered was that they were listening to her. Not all of them, but enough.

"Our families are in there. They have to tell us the *truth*," Nikki went on.

A few voices roared in agreement. Edmond glanced over his shoulder. Seven guards were there now, talking anxiously among themselves; one of them gestured to the mansion, and Edmond felt a small spike of alarm. They'd thought they finally had an advantage over Etienne by creating a situation he hadn't prepared for—but what if he *had* prepared? What if he had fresh lies to feed these people?

"If they won't give us the answers, we have to *take* them," Nikki yelled, punching the sky.

Renie grabbed the gates with both hands and rattled them. "Let us in," she shouted.

The energy of the crowd shifted again, becoming darker, more violent, people turning away from Nikki and back to the gates, jostling and shouting, and Edmond's skin prickled. These people were one lit match away from turning into an explosion. As much as they needed the distraction to get into Belle Morte, no one was supposed to get hurt.

More people started rattling the gates alongside Renie, and two more guards ran from the left side of the house. One of them dropped a hand to the sheathed silver knife on his hip, and Edmond's lip curled. Kenneth Foster—he was one of the people Tadhg had said was working for Etienne.

Edmond would deal with him once they got through the gates.

Renie looked up at Edmond, and her eyes were still shadowed with fear, but there was so much trust in her gaze too. He wished he had time to kiss her. Instead he swore to himself that nothing would keep him from revealing the truth of Etienne's lies and keeping her safe. Renie would not live her life on the run. Ysanne had warned them not to risk themselves, and Edmond had agreed, along with the others, but he'd risk anything for the girl standing at his side.

He grabbed the gates with both hands, testing the strength of the lock. A younger vampire couldn't have broken it, but Edmond could. It wouldn't be easy, though—these gates had been designed to keep out vampires, even the older, stronger ones. A pale pair of hands settled on the gate alongside his, and he turned to see Ludovic standing beside him, smiling faintly beneath his black cap.

"Once more unto the breach," Ludovic murmured.

A soldier in the trenches had said that to them once, just seconds before a hail of bullets had reduced him to bloody meat. Going up against Etienne and Jemima wasn't the same; it wasn't a war, but Edmond and Ludovic had seen and survived so much together, and it felt right that they stood together again now, facing a new kind of enemy.

Edmond braced himself, standing almost shoulder to shoulder with Ludovic, the crowd shouting and shoving around them, and *pushed*.

The gates creaked, groaned, resisting the two vampires, and Edmond gritted his teeth and pushed harder, until there was a huge screech of metal as the lock broke and the gates swung open.

The swell of the crowd surging forward slammed into Edmond; he'd have been knocked off his feet if he was human. He hooked an arm around Renie's waist and hoisted her out of the crush of bodies as they spilled into the grounds of Belle Morte.

"Shit, do you think we took it too far?" she said, as the crowd swarmed up to the house and started battering the doors and the shuttered windows. Edmond noticed that the dining hall window was still broken from where Caoimhe had made her escape, and he briefly considered entering the house that way, before dismissing it. Anyone who saw him make that jump would know he was a vampire, and if the guards knew other vampires were here, they'd radio inside and warn Etienne. Edmond couldn't risk it.

"They won't get inside the house. Once we bring the donors out, the crowd will calm down," he said.

Roux ran over to them, her cap askew. "Almost got lost in that," she said breathlessly.

Ludovic, Jason, and Ysanne followed her. Ysanne's eyes were the color of fire and blood.

A moment later, Caoimhe flowed up, followed by the people she'd brought from Fiaigh. "You three stay out here and help keep the crowd under control," she said, signaling to her guards. "There's no point getting the donors to safety if their families get trampled in the process."

Edmond wasn't sure how many of these people actually were families of the donors, but Caoimhe's point still stood. They were here to *stop* anyone else from getting hurt.

"Let's go," he said.

The crowd was too focused on the mansion itself to notice the group in dark caps and scarves making their way to the left side of the grounds. Edmond saw Ysanne wince as her flower beds and rosebushes were trampled underfoot. Better the flowers than the people, though.

Kenneth Foster had separated from the other guards and was speaking urgently into his radio; he didn't see Edmond coming. Edmond delivered a swift, sharp blow to the back of the man's head, and Kenneth crumpled, unconscious, into the dewy grass. Edmond crushed his radio with one hand then stripped him of his silver knives, which he handed to Seamus and Andrew.

Ysanne stepped over the fallen guard as if he wasn't even there. Her face was impenetrable, a marble mask.

She led them through the grounds, past the winter-stripped trees that butted against the stone wall and the carefully maintained flower beds, past the oak tree where Renie had once thought June was buried. Renie paused there, gazing at the tree, until Edmond put a hand on her elbow.

"Mon ange?" he said.

Renie tore her eyes away from the tree. For the first time since leaving Fiaigh, real anger burned on her face—that fiery determination that had captured Edmond from the start.

"No matter what happens, Etienne will pay for this," she said.

"I don't wish to alarm anyone, but shouldn't we have encountered some resistance by now?" Caoimhe said, looking around the darkened lawns and hedges. "Some more guards?"

Ysanne was making a beeline for the stone bench that sat in the shadow of the house, close to its soaring walls; at Caoimhe's words she paused and tilted her head, listening.

"I don't hear anyone apart from the crowd at the front," she said.

Edmond didn't, either, and none of his war-honed instincts were prickling or warning him of danger.

"I suspect that Etienne has moved most of the security detail inside the mansion to make sure his little army doesn't get out of hand," Ysanne said.

"Great. More people to hide from once we're inside," Renie muttered.

Ysanne strode over to the stone bench and tipped it over with one hand. It made a soft *thud* as it hit the winter-hardened ground. At the base of the left leg, barely visible beneath the dirt and grass clinging to the stone, was a small leather pouch. Ysanne opened it and pulled out a set of keys.

"What if someone had moved that bench before and found the keys?" Roux said.

Ysanne gave her a withering look. "No one is allowed to move furniture at Belle Morte without my permission."

"No one's allowed to illegally turn people, either, and look how that turned out," Roux mumbled.

Ysanne's lips thinned.

She pulled a key off the small ring and handed it to Edmond. "Here's where we split up. You, Renie, Roux, and Jason take the first door and go after the donors. Do whatever it takes to get them out safely. The rest of us will take the second back door, where we will separate into two groups, led by Caoimhe and me. If the guard rotations have been changed, then we have no idea where Susan will be, so we'll rely on the passageways to help us infiltrate the mansion until we find Susan and get that video."

Ysanne turned to Seamus and the remaining three guards from Fiaigh. "I need you to stand guard by the doors and help get the donors to safety when the time comes. We don't know which exit they'll come out of—that depends entirely on what happens inside the mansion—so two of you will need to man each door."

Seamus gave her a little salute.

"Good luck, everyone," Caoimhe said.

She, Ysanne, Ludovic, Andrew, and the eight vampires from Fiaigh moved farther into the grounds, heading for the second exit on Belle Morte's right side, not far from Ysanne's office.

"Are you ready?" Edmond asked his own little group.

Roux and Jason both nodded. Renie took longer to respond. She was staring up at Belle Morte, strands of auburn hair whisked around her face by the wind, her eyes hard and sad.

Edmond didn't ask her what she was thinking or feeling. He just took her hand, letting her know that whatever was going through her head, he was right here.

"Let's get on with this," said Renie. She smiled at him, but it was tight and tense.

Edmond approached the back door.

"Are we even sure it's locked?" Jason said. "I don't recall the guards ever unlocking it to let us out."

"Etienne has pulled half the guards off their regular patrol. He's keeping everyone else sealed in the house while he, presumably, plans his next move. He'll have locked all the doors," Edmond said.

"But will they still be guarded from the inside?" Renie asked.

"There's only one way to find out."

Renie

My heart felt like it was lodged in my throat as Edmond turned the key in the lock. Could we actually pull this off? Or would we find that Etienne was still one step ahead?

The second the door was open, Edmond moved like lightning. I hadn't even registered that a guard was standing on the other side of the door before Edmond had his arm around the guy's throat, cutting off his air until the guard went limp.

"He's not dead," Edmond said as I stepped through the door. He lowered the guy to the floor and stripped him of his radio and silver-coated knives.

"I didn't think he was," I said.

Edmond had confessed to me that the mistakes of his past had cost people their lives, but he wouldn't murder someone just because they were in his way. A feeding room was directly to our right; Edmond opened the door and dragged the unconscious guard inside, then closed the door again.

The passageway that Ysanne had instructed us to take was located at the back of Belle Morte's little theater—another part of the house that I'd never had a chance to visit. Edmond opened the door and ushered us inside. The theater was all polished wooden floor and paneled walls, with padded seats leading up to a stage, mostly hidden behind a red velvet curtain.

I wondered if June had ever been involved with the theater, if she and Melissa had ever featured in the plays that donors sometimes performed for the House, or even if she'd just been in the audience.

We climbed the small steps that led onto the stage, and slipped behind the curtain.

"This is weird," Roux whispered. "Our whole lives have changed because of Belle Morte, and there's still so much of it that we've never even seen."

"We'll get to see all of it one day," I told her, but I wasn't sure I believed my own words.

Edmond slipped into the wings on our left side, where Ysanne had told us the keypad was hidden, and a moment later, a panel on the wall at the back of the stage swung silently open.

"Let me go first, in case we run into anyone on the other side," he said.

"Hold on to me so you don't trip," I advised Roux and Jason, remembering that there were no lights in the passageways. They'd been designed for vampires, not humans.

We entered the passage and Jason pushed the panel shut behind us. Then Roux put her hands on my shoulders and Jason put his hands on hers, and we started walking. After a few feet, we reached the steps that led up to the second floor.

Ysanne had assured us that no one would hear us inside the passage-ways unless we were being really loud, but my skin still felt tight with unease because every step took us farther into a building that was under enemy occupation. Maybe we were safe in here, but soon we'd have to emerge into the south wing, back out in the open.

The first time Etienne's minions had invaded Belle Morte, the donors had been confined to their rooms for their own safety. With those minions now living in Belle Morte, it was logical to assume that the same safety measures had been taken. Etienne was blaming Ysanne for the fact that donors had died, but he couldn't do that if his minions killed anyone else during the time that he'd seized con-trol of the mansion.

At the top of the steps, Edmond held out a hand to stop us. "I'll go first again, see if the coast is clear. If anything goes wrong, if Etienne has guards watching the south wing, if I'm caught, then you three need to go back the way you came and get out of the mansion," he said.

His voice was soft, but I reared back as though he'd yelled. "I'm not leaving you."

"If necessary, yes, you are."

"I'm really not."

"Renie," said Edmond gently. "Roux and Jason are infinitely more vulnerable than me, and they are relying on you. If we run into trouble, they have to be your priority."

I couldn't speak; I just nodded.

Edmond tapped the code into the tiny keypad on the wall, and a section of wall cracked open, letting light spill into the passageway. Edmond put his ear close to that crack, listening. "Wait here," he whispered.

He slipped out of the passageway and into the south wing, as quick and noiseless as a cat. He was gone for less than a minute, but it felt like the longest minute of my life; my nerves wound tighter and tighter and I found myself holding a breath that I didn't even need.

"We should go to Melissa first," Roux whispered. "I think she might listen."

"She blames me for Aiden's death," I said.

"She'll want the truth. She'll want his real killer to get justice," Roux insisted.

Aiden's real killer was June, but Etienne was as much to blame. He'd created her; he'd turned her loose on the house.

The panel in front of us eased open again, and Edmond appeared in the crack. "All clear," he whispered.

We stepped out of the passageway. The familiarity of the donors' wing rushed over me—had it really only been two days since we'd fled this place? The pre–Belle Morte me would never have imagined feeling anything but suspicion and contempt for this place, but looking around at it now, I felt almost homesick.

Edmond had led the charge up until now, but as we made our way to Melissa's bedroom, Roux took charge. "Renie, you and Edmond should stay out of sight for a minute. Etienne's told everyone that Jason and I are helpless victims, so she's less likely to panic if she sees us."

Obediently, we hung back as Roux knocked on Melissa's door. I heard the door open, but I couldn't see Melissa's face.

"Roux?" she breathed. "What the hell? How are you here?"

"I need you to listen very carefully. Ysanne didn't kidnap us. She didn't kill June. She didn't turn anyone. Etienne and Jemima are behind everything."

"What are you talking about?" Melissa said.

"Etienne turned June. Ysanne and Renie were trying to help her but they couldn't tell the Council because they would have killed June. That's why Renie couldn't tell you what was going on. She wasn't trying to hurt you; she was trying to keep everyone safe."

"Like Aiden?" Melissa's voice was raw and bitter.

"June is little more than a rabid animal. She didn't know what she was doing. But Etienne did. He knew how dangerous she was, and he deliberately turned her loose as part of his plan to frame Ysanne and get her out of the way so he could take over Belle Morte."

"Why should I believe you?"

Roux glanced at me and Edmond. I moved forward so Melissa could see me, and her eyes widened. She tried to shut her door but Edmond stopped it with one hand.

"Please just listen," I said.

Melissa backed away from us, farther into her room, and we all came with her. It was safer than standing out in the hallway. She stood in front of her bed, her arms crossed, her expression hard.

"I shouldn't have lied to you," I said. "I expected you to help me find out more about June, and then I wouldn't help you when you asked me to. I was scared, and I was trying to save my sister, and maybe that's a shitty excuse but I didn't know what else to do. I never wanted anyone to get hurt."

Melissa swallowed hard, her eyes glinting with tears. "And yet my boyfriend's still dead."

"Yes. I wish I could change that, but I can't. But all this started because of Etienne. Aiden's blood is on his hands, and unless you help us, he'll get away with it."

That made her flinch.

The Melissa I'd met weeks ago had been bright and beautiful and stylish, the model donor. The girl in front of me now was exhausted and wrung out, her eyes red from crying, and guilt twisted me up inside, because I'd played a role in this, even if I hadn't meant to.

"Please, Melissa. We're telling the truth. Ysanne is innocent," Roux said.

Melissa's face crumpled. "I just want to go home."

"That's why we're here. We don't know what Etienne's done with June or how much control he has over all those vampires he turned, but we don't think you're safe here, and too many people have died already. So we're getting the donors out," I said.

Melissa looked around her bedroom, as if she was seeing it for the last time. She probably was, I realized. Ysanne wanted to preserve the donor system, but Melissa would never come back here. Belle Morte was no longer the glittering dream it had been when she'd first arrived; it had become the worst kind of nightmare, and she was clearly done with it.

"Okay," she said, "I'll help you get everyone together and then we're getting the fuck out of here."

It wasn't as hard as I'd thought. Melissa wasn't the only donor who'd had enough—even the ones lucky enough to have missed the slaughter caused by June's escape were scared and angry and tired. Their friends had died, the vampires who'd invaded the house were now living here, and Etienne and Jemima weren't telling anyone anything.

When Melissa told the donors everything we'd told her, they jumped at the chance to get out.

"Stay close to us and do exactly what we say," Edmond said.

As we led the donors back in the direction of the secret passageway, a great sense of hope swelled in my chest. Everything had gone smoothly so far, and even though I was aware that it could still go wrong, maybe just this once, things would actually go to plan.

Then we turned the corner and found ourselves confronted by a pair of vampires.

CHAPTER TWENTY-SIX

Renie

Gideon and Phillip stared back at us, and my skin went cold, my mind flashing back to what Ysanne had told us about Phillip's history with Jemima. That didn't mean he was working with her now, but I trusted him less than Gideon. Also, he'd been the one to silver-whip Edmond, so I'd have been uneasy around him even without the Jemima connection.

"What's going on?" Gideon asked, his expression darkening.

Maybe he was the one I needed to be uneasy around.

I was suddenly very aware that Gideon was a big guy. He was about Edmond's height, but larger around the chest and shoulders—a lot more intimidating than Phillip.

I glanced back at the donors huddled behind us. Many of them were older than me, but now that I'd live forever, they seemed impossibly young—too young to be trapped in this situation. We'd been forced to leave them behind once before. It wouldn't happen again.

"We're getting them out of here before Etienne and Jemima kill them too," I said.

Phillip's eyebrows shot into his hairline. "Jemima and Etienne are the ones keeping us all safe," he said.

"Bullshit," I snapped before I could think better of it.

Edmond put a hand on my shoulder, and I swallowed my anger.

"Ysanne would never betray us—you should know that," Edmond said.

"Then where is she?" Phillip demanded. "If she cares so much about us why isn't she here? If she thinks we're in danger why isn't she trying to save us?"

None of us were about to reveal that Ysanne was inside the mansion.

"Ysanne didn't kidnap us. We chose to flee Belle Morte with her and now we've chosen to come back," said Jason, stepping past me so he could face Gideon directly.

The blond vampire's eyes slid to Jason, and I could have sworn that something in his expression softened. But it didn't ease the doubt in his eyes.

"You know that Ysanne and Edmond and Ludovic aren't traitors," Jason continued.

"Etienne turned June. He's behind everything," I said.

Phillip scoffed.

"Between them, they've fucked everything up, and we're trying to fix that. Please trust us. We can *prove* that they're lying," Jason pleaded.

"You're not actually listening to this, are you?" Phillip said.

Gideon hesitated, indecision flickering across his face. He still hadn't taken his eyes off Jason.

"Gideon, listen to me. Jemima is trying to help us; that's all she ever wanted," Phillip said.

"She and Etienne framed Isabeau and had her locked up," I said. Ysanne had said that Gideon and Isabeau were close, so maybe this was what would get him to really listen.

Gideon winced a little.

"They will *kill* her," I added. "Just like they killed me and June, and Rosa, and Aiden and Ranesh and Abigail, and every single new vampire currently shacking up in here. Come on, Gideon, can't you smell the bullshit? Ysanne revealed vampires because she thought it was the best thing for everyone—why would she jeopardize that by going on a deranged murder spree? Isabeau trusts Ysanne with her life, and you know that. What would she do if she was here now?"

"She'd tell me to listen," said Gideon, his voice low and hard.

"She'd be wrong," Phillip said. "Ever since we revealed ourselves to humans, we've been shackled by them. Are you really happy performing for them on demand? Are you happy spending every day in this house, only feeding from donors when you're allowed to?"

"*Yes,*" Gideon growled, his eyes starting to gleam red.

"Then you're a fool too. Jemima can offer us more than that."

"At what cost?" I said.

Phillip didn't answer. Maybe it was easier for him not to think about everyone who'd died during Jemima's quest for power.

Gideon's shoulders were a rigid line, his hands curled into fists. "You betrayed us. You betrayed your House."

The threat of violence coiled through the corridor like a snake, just waiting to strike.

Phillip moved first. I didn't even realize he had a silver security knife until it sliced through the air in a gleaming arc, heading for Gideon's throat, and I opened my mouth to scream, hearing Jason's strangled gasp at the same time.

Gideon's forearm shot up to block the strike, knocking Phillip off balance, and as the other vampire stumbled, Gideon delivered a devastating punch to Phillip's face. There was a horrible *crack*, and Phillip slumped to the floor, his jaw crooked, his eyes closed.

"Is he dead?" Melissa asked, peering over my shoulder.

"No, just unconscious," Gideon replied, glaring down at the prone vampire.

"Thank you for listening," Jason said.

Gideon looked up at us. "Is Isabeau okay?"

"We don't know yet. We didn't have time to go after her, and we don't have time to explain now. We need to get the donors out," Edmond said.

"What can I do?" Gideon said.

"Do you know how many new vampires Etienne and Jemima have brought here?"

Gideon winced again at the mention of Jemima's name, and I reminded myself that he'd known her long before Belle Morte. Her betrayal must cut him like Etienne's had cut me, and I felt a sharp pang of empathy for him.

"Etienne moved them into the west wing, and I haven't seen much of them, but I think there are thirty-four," he replied.

That sounded like a hell of a lot to me, but when I looked at Edmond, there was no sign of worry on his face. Judging from what Gideon had just done to Phillip, he could probably punch his way through them, single-handedly.

Although, if we were getting the donors out of here, then Gideon wouldn't be able to drink from anyone to heal any injuries he might get.

"Is security keeping an eye on them?" Edmond said.

"As much as they can do."

Edmond looked at me, and though he didn't say a word, I knew what he was asking—whether or not we should show Gideon the secret passageways. I nodded. We needed all the help we could get, and if we couldn't stop Etienne and Jemima tonight, then Belle Morte would no longer be safe for Gideon.

"Follow me," Edmond said.

As we reached the door that led back out into the grounds, I felt a swift stab of pain in my chest. Dexter would never guard this door again. He'd never smile at me as he opened the door to let me outside, or good-naturedly ignore Roux's drunken flirting. He'd never talk to me again, never lay down any more foundations for the friendship that might have been.

Edmond pushed open the door and peered outside.

Behind me, the donors shivered in the sudden gust of icy air that swirled in, and I found myself fascinated by the pattern of goose bumps forming on their skin. That wouldn't happen to me again unless I was in the Arctic.

"All clear," Edmond reported.

Seamus materialized through the darkness, his breath frosting white in the air.

"This is the head of security from Fiaigh. He'll get you out of here and reunite you with your families," Edmond said.

"C'mon, kids," Seamus said, beckoning.

One by one the donors hurried out. Melissa brought up the rear, and paused on the threshold.

"Thank you for getting us out," she said.

Impulsively, I hugged her, and she stiffened for a split second before hugging me back.

"I know I can never change what happened, and I can never bring Aiden back, but I promise you that Etienne won't get away with this," I whispered.

Melissa nodded, her Afro tickling the side of my face, then she stepped back.

I watched her walk out of Belle Morte, and I didn't know if I'd ever see her again, but I meant every word. I could never take back the role that I'd played in Aiden's death, but the man who'd caused it would suffer. I'd make sure of it.

As the darkness of the grounds swallowed Melissa up, I felt a great weight lift off my heart. Whatever else happened, at least the donors were safe. That was precious little comfort for the families of the kids who'd died, but we'd done all we could to keep the others safe.

"What now?" Gideon asked as we crowded in the doorway, gazing into the night.

We'd done our part; now we were supposed to get out while

Ysanne, Caoimhe, and the others went after Susan. But we had an advantage that they didn't—Gideon had lived inside Belle Morte during the takeover. He might know which part of the house Susan had been assigned to watch, and where we could find her. Seamus would have said if the others had got to her yet, so they were obviously still in the mansion.

"Do you know where Susan Harcourt is?" I asked.

My voice was so cold that Gideon gave me a surprised look.

"Why?" he asked.

Edmond held up a hand to stop me before I went any further. "Let's talk about this next door," he said, indicating the feeding room, opposite the theater, where he'd dumped the guard.

We hurried inside, keeping Roux and Jason in the middle of our little group. This was another room I'd never visited, and I glanced around, quickly absorbing the white walls, the antique-looking gramophone sitting on top of the equally antique-looking wooden unit painted cream and gold, and the soft gray armchair close to the unit. The unconscious guard still lay in a heap on the floor.

"Right," Edmond said, closing the door and facing Gideon. "We don't have time to explain everything now, so you'll have to trust us. We can prove that Etienne is responsible for turning all those vampires, not Ysanne, but the only person who has the evidence we need is Susan. If we can get to her, we can bring Etienne down."

Gideon lowered his eyes. "You're sure that Jemima's involved?"

I heard the quiet hope in his voice, his need to believe that Jemima hadn't betrayed him the way Etienne had betrayed me, and I wished we didn't have to tell him this. But comforting lies didn't help.

"I'm sorry, but it's true, and you need to be prepared for the fact that Jemima might not give up without a fight." I gave him a second to absorb that before continuing. "Evidence or not, things could get bloody."

Gideon lifted his head, looking away from me and to Edmond.

"Understood," he said, and his voice was simultaneously hard and vulnerable.

I reminded myself that, however hard it was for me to face how Etienne had used me, this was probably much harder for Gideon. I didn't know the extent of his previous relationship with Jemima, but he'd known her for a long time, and now he had to face the bitter reality that someone he cared for was on the opposite side of the battle line.

I couldn't picture Roux or Jason becoming my enemy. I hadn't had many close friends before coming to Belle Morte, but the confident girl with the ruby nose stud and pixie haircut, and the wonderful boy who'd get drunk with me and throw impromptu fashion shows—they'd both set down roots in my heart. Losing either of them would leave a wound that I couldn't imagine healing, and seeing either of them become an enemy was a scenario that I couldn't even contemplate.

"Jemima assigned Susan to stand watch on the front door. She should be there now," Gideon said.

After a few more minutes' discussion, we decided that, rather than trying to sneak around using the passageways, we needed to make a run for it, straight down the long hallway that led to the vestibule. Once there, we could grab Susan and drag her out of the front door. If the new vampires were all in the west wing, they probably couldn't get down to the vestibule in time to stop us, and the original vampires of Belle Morte wouldn't be hanging around in one spot waiting for something to happen. It was a hell of a risk, but it was worth it to save the vampire world from falling to Etienne and Jemima's twisted vision.

I wanted to leave Roux and Jason behind, but they staunchly refused to stay, and we didn't have time to argue. Time was ticking away. If someone discovered Phillip or the unconscious guard or realized that the donors were gone, we'd have to run, and we wouldn't get another chance to break into Belle Morte again. We had one shot, and we had to take it.

Edmond opened the door and peeked out into the hallway. "Let's go," he said.

His gaze rested on me, and there was so much in his face that I could tell he wanted to say—because I wanted to say it too. I wanted to tell him how much I loved him, and how we'd get through this, no matter what happened, but neither of us said anything.

We were halfway there, close to the turning that led to the art rooms, when Caoimhe appeared at the end of the hallway. The light from the chandeliers gilded her curly hair, making her look like an angel, but her face was a mask of cultivated blankness—no warmth, no familiarity, nothing.

My brain registered that something was very wrong, but my feet didn't get the message as quickly, and I would've kept running if Edmond hadn't pulled me back.

He let out a soft snarl that raised the hairs on the back of my neck.

Jemima stepped up beside Caoimhe, a vicious little smirk playing about her lips. A small contingent of Etienne's minions fanned out behind her, blocking us from the vestibule, and I realized with a gut punch of horror that everything had gone to shit.

"I'm sorry," Caoimhe said.

CHAPTER TWENTY-SEVEN

Renie

I knew I didn't need to breathe, but at the same time it felt like all the air had been sucked out of my lungs.

This. Could. Not. Be. Happening.

Caoimhe had helped us; she'd taken us in, helped us formulate a plan, and my brain couldn't comprehend that she'd been a traitor all along.

Once again, someone I'd trusted had been a snake in the grass.

"I wasn't quite careful enough," Caoimhe said, her Irish lilt sounding harsher than normal as she bit off each word.

Wait, what? I blinked at her. *What was going on?*

Caoimhe shifted her weight, and several pairs of hands grabbed her, holding her in place. A silver knife appeared at her throat, and when it touched her skin, it left a burned red line.

"Catherine," Gideon growled.

I swallowed the sting of betrayal as I realized what was really going on. Caoimhe hadn't deliberately deceived us. Somehow, Jemima had caught her, and now Catherine held a knife to her throat. Ysanne had been right about both Catherine and Phillip.

Caoimhe's face was expressionless, even when Catherine pressed down on the knife a little more, and a trickle of blood ran down Caoimhe's pale neck. Caoimhe was older and stronger than Catherine, but I didn't blame her for not fighting back with a silver knife so close to slashing her throat.

Then Caoimhe tilted her head as much as the blade allowed and fixed Catherine with an ice-cold smile. Her eyes burned red. "You treacherous little bitch," she said. "Before this night is over, I'm going to kill you."

Catherine laughed, but it sounded false and hollow. She was right to be afraid. Caoimhe was the Lady of Fiaigh for a reason, and if it came down to a fight between them, Catherine didn't stand a chance. Caoimhe stared at her until Catherine's laughter died away. She glanced at Jemima, who smiled and shook her head.

"Empty threats," she said.

The lethal look on Caoimhe's face said otherwise.

Jemima clicked her fingers. "Let's go to the ballroom and have a little talk."

"Not a chance," I said.

Gideon made an angry noise that I took to be agreement.

My mind raced, calculating our odds. Edmond could handle Jemima, and I could see only ten minions behind her, which might not be more than Caoimhe and Gideon could fight through, but none of us were fast enough to reach Caoimhe before Catherine cut her throat. Maybe she could survive that, but could we take that risk?

What were our other options?

Surrender was out of the question, and if we fled, we could probably make it to the back door before Jemima caught us. But that meant abandoning Caoimhe.

What had happened to Andrew and the four Fiaigh vampires who'd been with her?

"You're thinking about running, but I really wouldn't do that," Jemima said.

"Why not?" I said, before I could stop myself.

"Because," Jemima said, and her face had gone cold and remote, nothing human left at all, "you may be considering leaving Caoimhe to her fate, but would you leave *her*?"

She reached back into the throng of minions and yanked a small figure forward with one hand.

I bit back a moan of horror and disbelief.

Nikki Flynn stood in front of me. She looked so tiny, so fragile compared to the vampires that surrounded her, but she held her head high, and her eyes flashed with anger rather than fear.

Jemima closed her hand around Nikki's throat, and Nikki stiffened.

"I have no particular wish to kill a child, but sentimentality won't stop me," Jemima said, her voice was wintry as her expression. "Ballroom now, or I'll snap her neck."

I knew what was at stake. Ysanne had once told me that the future of the balance between humans and vampires was worth more than the life of one girl—me—but I *could not* stand here and watch Dexter's daughter die.

As long as we were alive, we could fight.

If Caoimhe was the only one they'd caught, then Andrew and the rest of the group were still in Belle Morte somewhere, and even if *they'd* been caught, we still had Ysanne, Ludovic, and the remaining Fiaigh vampires.

"Okay," I said, and held up my hands.

They dragged us into the ballroom, and my heart plummeted when I saw Andrew and the four Fiaigh vampires there, also surrounded by minions, and also with silver knives at their throats. Adrian—the vampire who'd groped me a few days ago—was there, too, lounging against the wall. He winked at me as I came in, and I gave him the finger.

There was no sign of Phillip, so I guessed no one had found him yet.

Where were the rest of the Belle Morte vampires?

What the hell was Nikki doing here?

A security guard I vaguely recognized looked into the room. "The riot outside appears to be calming down," she said. One hand rested on her radio, so I assumed she was getting her intel from the guards outside. Had Seamus and his team managed to persuade the others that they'd been tricked? Or, now that the donors had been released, was everyone packing up and going home? I had to hope it was the former; otherwise the guards outside would have mentioned that the donors had all escaped.

Jemima gave a curt nod. "That will be all for now," she said.

The guard hesitated, her eyes lingering on Edmond, Andrew, and then me. "What's actually going on?" she asked.

"That's none of your concern. You have your orders," Jemima said.

I tried to catch the guard's eye again, to wordlessly beg her to see that something was wrong here, but she was already retreating. I looked around the ballroom, at the new vampires that Etienne had turned. They all looked so proud, like they'd been given the ultimate gift, and they didn't seem to realize that Jemima and Etienne were using them. I truly understood now why vampires weren't allowed to turn people without express permission from the Council, because it was *way* too easy for them to build an army if they were allowed to turn people, unpoliced.

"First things first," Jemima said. She'd let go of Nikki's throat but she still stood in front of the girl, eyeing her like Nikki was a bug that Jemima might crush. "Who are you?"

Jemima was only a slip of a woman but she was still taller than Nikki and much more powerful . . . and Nikki faced her like they were physical equals. But—smart girl—she didn't say a thing.

Jemima grabbed Nikki's chin, squeezing until a small noise of pain trickled from Nikki's lips. But she still didn't flinch.

"Who are you?" Jemima growled.

"I'm no one," Nikki said, when Jemima let her go. "I came with the crowd and I sneaked in behind this lot when they broke into the mansion. Sue me—I wanted to get a look inside a real Vampire House."

I darted a glance at Caoimhe, but her eyes were fixed on Jemima.

The cut on her throat had stopped bleeding, leaving a smear of blood bright against her pale skin and golden hair.

Suspicion still registered on Jemima's face, but clearly she hadn't been familiar enough with Dexter to recognize his daughter.

"Look, I don't know what the fuck's going on in here, but I just came to get pictures." Nikki tapped the shape of her phone in her pocket. "I could make a goddamned fortune from sneaking around all the places that the media don't normally get to see."

Jemima made a soft, dangerous noise. "Have you seen enough now? Have you got close enough to the vampires? We're not animals in a zoo."

A tall woman in security black walked into the ballroom. "Excuse me, Jemima?" she said.

"I told you to watch the vestibule," Jemima said, not even bothering to look at her.

My eyes widened. Was this Susan Harcourt? I glanced at Edmond and, judging from the lethal glare on his face, I guessed it was.

"I know who this girl is," Susan said.

That got Jemima's attention.

"She's the one behind the video I told you about. She got everyone asking questions, and she got that crowd out there tonight. She's Dexter Flynn's kid," Susan said.

Jemima turned back to Nikki with renewed interest. "Why is she here?"

"No idea. Ask whoever's in charge of this lot."

"*Ysanne* is in charge," Jemima said.

"I've got everyone searching the rooms, but there's no sign of her."

"She's here somewhere, I know it. She wouldn't let anyone go to fight for her precious House without her."

A pathetic pulse of hope passed through my chest. Jemima still didn't know about the secret passageways. Ysanne and the others were safe, for now.

Jemima's gaze passed over us, and I fought the urge to recoil. How had I ever *liked* this woman?

"Would anyone like to tell me where Ysanne is, or do I need to employ other methods of interrogation?" she asked.

My skin tingled uncomfortably with the memory of a knife blade slicing through it.

"You don't seriously think we know everything Ysanne plans, do you?" I said, trying to draw Jemima's attention away from Nikki.

"I think that you're here because she wants you to be. Ysanne Moreau does nothing without a plan, and I'd like to know what that plan is," Jemima said.

There was a chance that Ysanne really wasn't in Belle Morte anymore. If she'd realized that our plan had collapsed, she might have escaped the mansion and already be on her way back to Fiaigh. But I didn't believe that. Ysanne and I had butted heads in the past, and probably would in the future, but she really did care about her House and her people. She wouldn't abandon them now. She wouldn't abandon *us*.

I shrugged.

Jemima's eyes narrowed to chips of red ice. "I'm running out of patience. One of you will tell me where Ysanne is, and exactly what you're all doing here, or I'll break the Flynn girl's neck. Do you understand?"

Nikki spat at her.

My blood froze. We should never have involved Nikki with this. I had fulfilled my promise to Dexter, and now I was going to watch his daughter die, and I had no idea how to stop it. I could tell Jemima why we were here, but how many more lives would that cost?

This was the bigger picture that Ysanne had told me about.

This wasn't about me or Nikki.

Jemima wanted humans to remember that vampires were more than pretty playthings—that we were hunters, predators, that we were *dangerous*. But even she didn't want to turn humans against us altogether. That would be catastrophic to the vampires' way of life. If they could no longer coexist with humans, they could be driven back into the shadows, back into the lonely, bloody lives they'd shed when they revealed themselves to the world.

We, I reminded myself. I was a vampire now—I'd be driven into the shadows too. Unless Jemima killed us all here.

I craned my neck to look at the ballroom entryway, but it was empty. The absence of Etienne set alarm bells off in my head.

"It looks like we'll have to fight our way out of this," Edmond whispered.

I glanced up at him; his eyes glittered red with rage.

"We're outnumbered," I said.

"Either we fight or we stand and watch as she slaughters a helpless child."

There wasn't really a choice. If we attacked our captors we'd almost certainly lose, but if we didn't, Jemima would kill us anyway. If we were going down, we'd go down fighting.

"Don't throw this child's life away," Jemima said, looking around the room.

Nikki didn't beg for her life. She didn't tremble or cry; she just stared at Jemima with a steely calm that most adults couldn't have mustered when they were seconds away from death.

"Anyone?" Jemima said.

I opened my mouth, and I have no idea what I was going to say— whatever it took to keep Nikki alive a little longer—but the shout that filled the ballroom wasn't mine.

"Stop!"

Ysanne Moreau stood in the entryway, her eyes flashing.

"If any more blood is to be spilled, it will be yours, Jemima," she said.

Jemima glared back at her, and I thought I glimpsed regret on her face along with the anger. Once, she and Ysanne had worked together to stop a dangerous vampire; How could Jemima not see that she'd become what she fought to stop?

Except in her mind, she hadn't, I realized. Back then, Jemima had done what she thought was best for vampires in general, and she was still doing that. It's just that now she considered a body count an acceptable price to pay for her vision. Ysanne didn't.

"I didn't want things to end up like this," said Jemima, and she actually sounded sincere. "But this is what's best for our kind. It's what's best for this House."

"Except this isn't your House, and you don't get to decide what happens here," said Míriam, appearing beside Ysanne.

My tired heart gave a little leap.

Ludovic stood behind Míriam, and behind them, the vampires of Belle Morte spread out. I couldn't see if everyone was there, but I glimpsed Phoebe and Fadime, Benjamin and Alexandra, and the leap in my chest became a surge of fierce joy.

Some vampires had willingly joined Jemima's side, but far more of them had stayed loyal to Ysanne, and they rallied behind her now, ready to fight for her and Belle Morte.

But how had Ysanne persuaded them that she was the good guy? Susan Harcourt was in the ballroom with us, and she looked as surprised to see Ysanne as anyone, which meant that Ysanne hadn't got that video yet.

The joy in my heart faded. Without that evidence, this was still just Ysanne's word against Jemima's.

Míriam moved farther into the room. "We heard your side of things, but Ysanne and Ludovic have painted a very different picture, and raised a lot of questions that need answering."

"Not the least of which is: Why are you threatening a child?" Ludovic said, and his voice was harsher than I'd ever heard it.

Jemima laughed and I hated how natural it sounded. "Surely

you're intelligent enough to recognize a false threat when you hear one? I have no interest in hurting anyone, but dealing with a danger to any of our Houses has to take priority. If I have to threaten a child in order to flush out a traitor, then that's what I'll do."

"Except Ysanne says that *you're* the traitor," Míriam said.

"Really? Just to reiterate, Ysanne knew that June Mayfield had been illegally turned into a rabid. Rather than dealing with the problem and then informing the Council, she concealed June in the west wing and banned her whole House from speaking of it. Has Ysanne denied any of this?"

Míriam said nothing.

"Doesn't that seem suspicious to you? Doesn't it seem suspicious that she allowed the Council to meet at Belle Morte, only for them to be assassinated? I was there, I know what I saw," Jemima said.

"I was there, too, and you're a fucking liar," said Caoimhe.

"You can understand why we need to get to the bottom of this rather than blindly accepting your version of events," Míriam said to Jemima.

When I'd seen the Belle Morte vampires arrive, I'd assumed they were all dedicated to Ysanne, but maybe that had been naive. Still, they were willing to listen to Ysanne, and that alone was more than Jemima wanted.

"You're forgetting one thing," said a voice I didn't recognize, and two men pushed through the knot of vampires filling the entryway.

My hands curled into fists as thick, black rage poured through me, filled me up.

Etienne looked shell-shocked, and there was a bright smear of blood on his forehead. He leaned heavily on Sanjay, a Belle Morte vampire whose face I recognized—he must have been the one who'd spoken. I'd never heard him speak before.

Sanjay helped Etienne into the ballroom. "Ysanne is controlling the rabid. We all saw it," Sanjay said, giving Ysanne a filthy look. "I didn't want to believe it, either, but I trust what I saw, and you should too."

I couldn't tell if he'd joined Jemima's side because he believed in her vision, same as Catherine and Phillip, or if he genuinely believed that Ysanne was the villain in all this.

"That's not true. *Etienne* is controlling her, he made it *look* like it was Ysanne," I cried.

"Then why is the rabid back?" Sanjay snapped.

Ice ran down my spine.

"The rabid is *here*?" Míriam sounded alarmed.

"It fled the mansion when Ysanne did, and now that she's back, so is the rabid. You expect me to believe that's a coincidence?" Sanjay said.

Etienne put a hand on Sanjay's shoulder and made a show of pushing himself upright. "I only just escaped the creature," he said, touching his bloody forehead. "Ysanne, please, call it off before anyone else gets hurt."

Ysanne looked at him like she was contemplating throttling him with his own intestines. "I do not control June Mayfield," she said.

"She's *in the house*," Sanjay snapped, and there was genuine fear in his voice.

A ragged snarl filled the air, and the vampires in the entryway scrambled to move.

The thing that had been my sister prowled into the ballroom. No one had cleaned her up since the night she'd been released from the west wing, and dried blood matted her hair into thick ropes that hung around her face. Blood still streaked her face, dried to a flaky brown crust, and beneath it her skin was almost pure white, so pale it was almost translucent. Her eyes were like fire. The stench of death and decay rolled over her.

Nikki let out a little squeak, and June rounded on her. My heart leaped into my throat, but June only looked at Nikki with those horrible eyes. She didn't try to attack.

"See?" Sanjay exclaimed. "The creature attacks Etienne but ignores anyone Ysanne brought with her."

Miriam's forehead furrowed, looking from Edmond to June to Ysanne. Maybe she wanted to believe us, but Etienne had made sure the evidence against us was compelling. *Bastard.*

"Please, Ysanne," said Etienne again, not taking his eyes off June. She stalked back and forth, softly growling. "Don't do this."

We hadn't got Susan's evidence.

We had no proof of anything.

Etienne had either given himself that injury or he'd got June to do it, but I'd bet it looked worse than it was, and the seed of a desperate idea formed in my head. When I'd first found June in the west wing, I'd cut my foot on a shard of glass and the smell of fresh blood had driven June into a frenzy.

It was time to find out exactly how much control Etienne had over her.

With June's arrival, the minions had backed off a little—they still surrounded us, but the silver knives that had been held at our throats were drooping. It was still a risk, but one I had to take.

I shoved the nearest minion out of the way and, before I could think about the pain, I slashed my forearm with my own fangs. Blood welled up and splattered the marble floor, and June turned toward me, her lips peeling back from her fangs.

"Renie," Edmond shouted.

I lunged forward, spilling blood across the floor, and June swung around, her eyes blazing even brighter. Sanjay scrambled out of the way, but that was okay, I wasn't after him. I threw myself in front of Etienne and smeared my bloody arm across his face. His baffled expression said he still didn't understand what I was doing, but he would. Unless I'd gambled wrong, and then June would rip me apart.

June gathered herself into a leap, and Etienne's eyes widened as he finally realized what I'd done.

"Stop," he shouted, making a slashing motion with his hand.

June abruptly dropped into a crouch on the floor, still growling like a cornered dog.

The rest of the ballroom was deathly silent.

Edmond was the first to speak. "Do you understand now?" he said. "Ysanne is not controlling June, *Etienne* is. That's how he framed us. He and Jemima are behind everything."

Etienne was frozen in place, and I'd have felt savage satisfaction at the look on his face if it wasn't for the awful tension choking the room, the feeling that we were one word away from everything turning very bloody.

I'd forgotten that Etienne didn't need words to use his most terrible weapon.

He made a sharp gesture with his hand, and June's head snapped up, her red eyes fixed on him. He made the gesture again, and then stabbed his finger at Edmond.

June whipped around and, with a guttural roar, threw herself at the man I loved.

CHAPTER TWENTY-EIGHT

Renie

June clawed at Edmond's face with her nails, her fangs furiously gnashing, and he shoved her back hard enough to send her to the floor. She was up in a heartbeat. This time, Edmond caught both her wrists and held them tightly so she couldn't tear at him with those nails. June growled and snapped, the tendons in her neck standing out like ropes as she fought him.

Again, Edmond pushed her away, and again she fell the floor, but when she scrambled to her feet, she found herself staring at Nikki. Nikki's face was white and her whole body trembled, but she was either too scared to move or was afraid that sudden movements would trigger an attack.

Edmond darted forward. He grabbed a fistful of June's blood-caked hair and hauled her back. June twisted around and sank her fangs into Edmond's arm.

Ludovic immediately charged forward to help, but a swarm of Etienne's minions tried to intercept him, and all hell broke loose. The loyal vampires of Belle Morte rushed in to help one of their own, and for the second time in just a handful of days, the mansion's ballroom became a battlefield.

Across the room, I glimpsed Susan, speaking frantically into her radio—calling the guards who'd been bought off, no doubt. I was about to charge toward her when someone unceremoniously lifted me off my feet and hurled me against the wall. If I'd been human, I'd have broken my back. As a vampire, I was able to bear the pain with a choked whimper. I looked up.

Catherine stood over me, and hatred heated my bones. Humans helping Jemima was a little easier to choke down since it was hardly the first time someone was willing to sell their soul for fame and fortune, but vampires like Catherine had everything—wealth, beauty, prestige—and it still wasn't enough. She was still prepared to betray her friends—to see her friends *die*—in order to get more.

I launched myself at her.

Catherine, being older than me, was also much stronger, but the fury of my attack caught her off guard and she stumbled back. I slapped her, throwing every ounce of vampire strength into it, and Catherine's head rocked on her shoulders. But when I tried to hit her again she batted my hand aside and seized my neck. She lifted me off my feet and threw me again, this time with greater force, and I only had time to think *oh shit*, but instead of smashing into the wall or the floor, I was caught by a pair of strong arms.

My first thought was that Edmond had leaped to my rescue, but just as quickly I registered that the arms were too slim, and the chest pressing against my back was soft and female, not hard and familiar like Edmond's.

Caoimhe set me back on my feet. She didn't look at me; her crimson eyes were fixed on Catherine.

"I told you that I was going to kill you," she said.

The smugness fled Catherine's eyes, replaced by real fear, and she took a step back, but Caoimhe was too fast. In a blur of movement, she'd grabbed Catherine's head with both hands, her fingers curling under the younger vampire's jaw. Superhuman strength flexed in her arms as she twisted—savagely jerking Catherine's head to one side—and kept twisting until skin split, tendons popped, and blood sprayed across the floor. Catherine's body toppled over and hit the floor. Her head was still clutched in Caoimhe's hands, her tongue lolling between bloodied lips. Caoimhe tossed the head away and it hit the floor with a wet *splat*.

Across the room, Jason scrambled out of the way of an enemy attack. I had to get him, Roux, and Nikki out of here before someone was hurt—or worse.

But someone beat me to it.

Gideon was a streak of blond as he launched himself in front of Jason, shielding him from further attack. When an enemy vampire ran at them, Gideon threw her against the far wall so hard that I actually heard bones shatter.

A familiar face met mine across the mass of fighting bodies. Adrian grinned, showing off his fangs, and for a split second I felt the same fear and anger that I'd felt when he'd groped me, when he'd bit into my throat against my wishes.

But I wasn't a donor anymore. Now I had fangs of my own, and I was ready to use them.

I didn't get the chance.

Adrian hadn't taken more than two steps toward me when Ludovic reared up behind him, his face and hair streaked with blood. Adrian didn't even have time to turn. Ludovic knocked him to the ground and stamped on his chest until his ribs caved in. Blood bubbled on his lips. Adrian was the reason that Edmond had been whipped to a bloody mess; Ludovic wanted revenge on the Nox vampire just as much as I did.

Then I heard Edmond's shout of pain and I forgot about everything else.

There were a series of bloody rips in his shirt, and a ragged wound on his arm where June had bitten him. She circled him, her mouth stained with gore, her eyes dilated.

My heart felt like someone had ripped it out of my chest and replaced it with a block of ice.

I'd seen Edmond fight, and under any other circumstances, he could handle a rabid. But this wasn't any rabid. This was my sister. Edmond knew what she meant to me, and he knew how hard I'd fought to save her. The last time he'd faced her, pulling her away from me when she'd attacked me in the west wing, he'd pulled his punches, trying to restrain her without hurting her, and he was still doing that. He *knew* that June couldn't be saved but still he kept himself from seriously hurting her, for my sake.

Bitter, cold reality sliced into my brain like a blade. I'd known this since Edmond had skirted around the subject in Fiaigh, but this was the first time I'd fully understood it.

June couldn't be saved.

I'd tried so hard to bring my sister back from the monster she'd become, but it wasn't possible. June was gone, and this *thing* was wearing her skin.

Blood poured from the wound in Edmond's arm, and unless he really started fighting back, he'd get even more seriously hurt.

June had to be stopped.

I had to stop her.

And I thought I knew how.

I raced out of the ballroom. I was halfway through the dining hall when I sensed movement behind me and looked back to see a tall vampire with close-cropped hair chasing me down.

We were both new vampires, so we were evenly matched in strength, but he was still twice my size, and I didn't like those odds. As he closed in, I snatched one of the chairs tucked against the trestle table and slammed it into his face. His nose burst in a wash of red, and I hit him again, this time knocking him to the floor.

It was satisfying, but I didn't stick around to see the damage I'd caused.

I ran through the dining hall, the parlor, and into the vestibule. Four guards in black uniforms were just coming in through the front door; they gaped at me but I didn't slow down. I tore up the stairs and into the north wing like my feet were on fire. The guards didn't come after me.

When I turned a corner too fast, my feet slipped from under me. The carpet was soft, but the force of my fall caused my hands to skid along the floor, scouring the skin from my palms.

Ignoring it, I scrambled to my feet. Every second was crucial.

Doors flashed past me as I ran—which one was Edmond's? I'd been there only twice: on the day that Edmond had been whipped, and then on the day I'd woken up as a vampire. Both times I'd hadn't paid too much attention to my surroundings.

There—that was the right door, I was sure of it. I flung it open.

The smell of blood still faintly hung in the air, but someone had changed the sheets and made the bed since I was last here. It felt like weeks ago that I'd woken up here, and even longer since I'd been human.

My gaze zeroed in on the two swords mounted on a wooden plaque on the wall. If Edmond hadn't mentioned them in Fiaigh, I probably wouldn't have remembered they were there—whenever I'd been in here, either I or Edmond had been lying in a bloody heap on the bed.

I lifted both swords down. They were simply designed—long blades capped by leather-wrapped hilts—and the edges were nicked and battle scarred, but a single touch of my thumb confirmed how sharp they were.

I understood why Edmond had refused to teach me any sword-play back at the castle, but I wasn't sure I could take June out with my bare hands. It wasn't a question of not being physically strong enough—I couldn't bear the thought of seeing my own hands covered in my sister's blood.

Despite everything she'd done, she hadn't asked to be this monster, and I wanted her death to be clean and painless.

These swords could give her that.

I raced back to the ballroom.

The battle was still ongoing, but I only had eyes for Edmond and June. Edmond was bleeding from two deep slashes to his left cheek but he still hadn't hurt June. If she hadn't been rabid, he could have restrained her or calmly subdued her, but rabids seemed to run on infinite rage and energy. Edmond would tire of the fight before she did, and that could prove fatal.

For a moment I faltered, gazing at the thing that June had become and remembering the girl she'd once been—the girl I'd loved, the girl I'd gone through all this to save.

But Edmond was my priority now, and I couldn't let June hurt anyone else.

I charged forward, barreled through anyone who got in my way, and plunged one of the swords into June's back. But I wasn't prepared for how much force was needed to drive even a sharp object through a person, and June screamed and ripped away, pulling her body off the sword. Blood streamed from the deep wound in her back, but she was still on her feet, still moving.

I stabbed at her chest but June scuttled back.

Someone knocked into me from behind; I stumbled and dropped one of the swords, where it was quickly lost in the scuffle of feet. I didn't dare try to retrieve it—that would mean taking my eyes off June.

Clumsily, I swung my remaining sword at June's head, but momentum carried the blade in an arc that ended dangerously close to my knee. If I wasn't careful, I'd do exactly as Edmond had feared and chop off my own leg.

June hunkered down and edged backward, almost slipping in her own blood.

Most people thought that rabids were mindless monsters, driven only by a need to feed, but Etienne had proved they could be trained, and on the night that I'd died, June had fled from Ludovic after he'd stabbed her in the stomach, proving that some spark of self-preservation still fired in a rabid's brain. That spark must have been firing again now, because as I took another clumsy swing at June's head, she turned and fled.

I'd been in this exact situation before, and the last time I'd chased her, she'd killed me.

It wouldn't end that way this time.

I ran back through the dining hall, but June was impossibly fast; already there was no sign of her. I followed the splashes of blood on the parquet floor through the vestibule and up the stairs. Then I paused. A bloody handprint was smeared across the wall on my right. June had gone back to the place she'd known most as a rabid—the west wing.

I hadn't ever wanted to go back there, and as my brain was flooded with the memory of Aiden's final scream and the awful noise June had made while she'd feasted on the ruin of his neck, the sword in my hand suddenly felt very heavy.

But this had to get done.

Ysanne had once talked about putting June out of her misery, and I'd refused to even consider it. I'd been wrong. Ysanne would have given June a painless, compassionate death. The least I could do was try to give her that now.

Gripping the sword tighter, I strode into the west wing.

Blood droplets were everywhere, and bizarrely, I found myself thinking that Ysanne would have to redecorate when this was over.

I faltered when I reached that short staircase where Aiden had died. Someone had cleaned up the blood, but I could still *see* him lying there, his throat ripped open, my sister crouched over him.

There was no sign of June now, and tension felt like an iron chain around my neck. Had she gone back to the room that Ysanne had kept her in? Slowly, I climbed the stairs, and even though my heart couldn't beat, I swore I could feel it, a phantom drumming against my ribs.

I'd only just reached the top of the steps when a guttural growl sounded in the shadows behind me; before I had time to turn, June slammed into me like a wrecking ball. We both fell to the floor, and June ripped into my shoulder, her sharp teeth slashing through flesh and muscle. I screamed and reared back, pushing myself up and propelling myself and June into the nearest wall. The impact shuddered the paintings that hung around us.

I rammed June against the wall again, and she lost her grip. Her nails clawed at my back as she slid down, and I twisted away from her. June growled, glaring up at me with mad red eyes. The girl she'd been was long gone, and the shell she wore barely even resembled my sister anymore. June was dead, and I had to stop this thing from further defiling her memory.

With a scream of pure rage, I hefted the sword and plunged it into June's chest, hard enough to smash through her rib cage, through flesh and muscle and organs, hard enough for the tip of the blade to sink into the wall behind her, pinning her in place.

June screamed and thrashed, blood foaming from her ruined mouth.

That one blow was supposed to kill her, but I'd missed her heart. June was still alive, still twisting and writhing on the blade that had impaled her.

I felt sick. June had suffered enough—couldn't even her death be quick?

Her cries were so loud that I barely registered the sound of approaching footsteps, and then a fist plowed into the side of my face and the world blurred for a moment.

I hit the floor and promptly rolled over, just in time to avoid the foot flying at my head. Etienne stood over me. His eyes were like fire and his fangs looked like small knives jutting over his lip. A pattern of blood drops—probably not his own—was etched onto one side of his face, and spots of gore darkened his red hair. In one hand, he held the sword I'd dropped.

"You've ruined everything," he snarled, and aimed another kick at me.

I wasn't quite fast enough this time, and his booted foot caught a glancing blow on my ribs. Etienne grabbed my hair and slammed my head against the wall.

I hoped that vampires couldn't get brain damage because my brain felt like it was rattling loose in my skull. Etienne cracked my head against the wall again, and my fangs sliced through my lip, filling my mouth with the copper taste of my own blood. Apparently, he wanted to beat me to death instead of stab me.

"Etienne!"

The beautifully familiar voice cut through the pounding in my head, and Etienne dropped me as Edmond surged up the short staircase. He paused beside June, still snarling and thrashing as she fought to get free of my sword, then grasped the hilt of the sword and sharply twisted it. June made a horrible noise and fell quiet.

Edmond yanked the sword free and June fell to the floor in a bloody, silent heap. My heart leaped into my throat. Was she finally dead?

Edmond deftly swung his sword, the practiced movement of his wrist making it look as if the sword weighed no more than a feather. "I'm not in the habit of stabbing men in the back, but if you don't face me, if you flee like the treacherous coward that you are, then I'll do just that," Edmond said.

Etienne smirked. "A duel? What century are you living in?"

Edmond continued to stare at him, his gaze cold and red, and Etienne's smirk faded.

My heart still seemed to be stuck in my throat, a painful lump that I couldn't swallow down. Edmond had told me that the vampire who'd turned him had taught him to fight, and that he'd been an expert swordsman. He'd also told me that it had been a long time since he'd wielded a sword. How good was Etienne?

I'd told Etienne that he wouldn't dare face Edmond in a fair fight, and this still wasn't fair. Etienne had one small, almost certainly self-inflicted cut on his forehead. Edmond was bleeding in several places from June's attack.

Etienne charged at Edmond with a snarl. Edmond deflected the blow, and the loud clang of metal on metal echoed through the hall. Etienne continued the offensive, hacking and slashing with everything he had.

Watching them, I understood exactly why Edmond had refused to teach me swordplay. This was a brutal, lethal art form—not something that a person with no prior experience could pick up in an hour or two. Etienne would have cut me in half in about two seconds flat.

Edmond slipped past Etienne's defenses, stabbing at his head, but Etienne swayed out of the way, and the edge of Edmond's sword sliced along his cheek. White bone showed through the ragged slash, but Etienne merely grinned.

"First blood," he said. "Good for you."

I hated that all I could do was crouch on the floor and watch, but if I'd tried to intervene, I would probably have ended up on the end of Etienne's sword.

Etienne's blade lanced through the air, sliding through Edmond's guard and punching into his side. Edmond stumbled, and my hands flew to my mouth, holding back a scream. Etienne stabbed at Edmond again, but Edmond parried; the edges of the swords made a horrible shrieking noise as they clashed together. Edmond brought his down in a chopping motion, but Etienne came up under his wrist, slicing Edmond's arm down to the bone.

I flinched.

Edmond fought on, heedless of the injury, but blood was flowing out of his wounds, spraying the walls around him as he and Etienne performed their deadly dance.

Etienne's injuries were minor enough that they wouldn't slow him down, but Edmond's could and did. Finally, Etienne got past another strike and drove his sword through Edmond's shoulder. He twisted the blade and Edmond crumpled to his knees.

"You should have stabbed me in the back when you had the chance," Etienne told him.

Edmond looked up at him, and despite the blood pouring from his wounds, he wore a savage grin. "Never," he said. "I wanted to look into your eyes while I killed you."

He reared up, hurling his body along Etienne's sword while swinging his own sword in a dizzying arc. The blade sank into Etienne's side, smashing his ribs. Blood spurted from his mouth. Edmond wrenched his sword free and Etienne staggered back, his body folding to the floor. Blood pumped from the wound that had almost cut him in half.

Edmond pulled Etienne's sword from his shoulder and tossed it to the floor. Then he held his own sword to me, hilt first. "He killed your sister, mon ange," he said. "The honor is yours, if you want it."

Bracing my hand on the wall, I climbed to my feet. Edmond looked exhausted, and his clothes were soaked with blood, but his expression was calm as he watched me. He'd wanted to kill Etienne for everything that he'd done, and at the last minute, he was handing his victory over to me because he thought I needed it more.

I took Edmond's sword, gazing down the length of the blood-slicked blade.

Could I do it? Could I cold-bloodedly cut down a man who was already dying?

I looked down at Etienne where he lay, gasping with pain. Blood had formed a thick pool around him, and heavier, wetter things were poking out of the wound.

Could I kill him?

Hell, yes.

Hefting the sword in both hands, I swung the blade at Etienne's neck and severed his head.

I dropped the sword, my arms tingling with reverberations. "Oh god, *Edmond*," I cried, and ran to him.

I skidded to a stop before I could fling my arms around him, mindful of his injuries. His face was white with pain, but he managed to smile.

"Did I mention that you're rather sexy with a sword yourself, ma chérie?" he said.

Pain threaded his words. I wanted to slip his arm around my shoulders so I could support him, but I didn't know which arm to take—the one with the bone-deep gash or the one with the stab wound.

When I saw the full extent of what Etienne had done to him, I wanted to kill the bastard all over again.

"He's right, you should have stabbed him in the back," I said.

Edmond gave a strained chuckle. "Not quite my style."

"Yeah, and look at the state of you."

He tried to dismiss my words with a wave of his hand, but the movement made him wince. "It's nothing that can't be healed," he said.

There were no donors left in the mansion, which meant we'd have to rely on security to feed Edmond. It wasn't in their job description, but surely they wouldn't refuse.

Edmond climbed to his feet, leaning on my shoulder, then he stiffened and swore. I followed his gaze and my stomach lurched.

"No," I whispered.

June was gone. I'd been sure that Edmond had killed her, but there was nothing but a pool of blood where she'd fallen, and the notch in the wall where I'd driven the sword through her.

I was so tired I wanted to curl into a ball on the floor. It felt like this would never be over, but I didn't have the luxury of collapsing. June was still loose in the mansion.

"She can't have got far," I said, picking up Etienne's sword.

I wanted to tell Edmond to wait here—he was in no condition to back me up—but I knew that he'd refuse, just as I would have if our roles had been reversed.

We followed the splash pattern of June's blood back out of the west wing, and I'd assumed that she'd have run back down the stairs, looking for a way out of the mansion, but instead, fresh blood drops were spattered along the walls that led into the north wing.

"She's starving, injured, and desperate. She'll be more dangerous than ever," Edmond cautioned.

"I know, but enough people have died. We have to end this."

And I had to end it for June's sake. She may have dreamed of becoming a vampire, but a rabid wasn't a vampire. It was a twisted, blood-crazed mockery of everything June had loved. If any part of my sister had still remained, she'd have begged me to put her out of her misery.

"Edmond! Renie! There you are." Roux jogged up the stairs toward us.

At the same time, a starving snarl split the air, and June raced into view, drawn out of hiding by the promise of fresh meat. Her lips peeled back from her fangs and her hands twisted into claws as she leaped into the air—heading straight for Roux.

CHAPTER TWENTY-NINE

Edmond

Everything seemed to move in slow motion—June's leap through the air was as if she was moving through treacle; Roux was transfixed on the stairs, her uptilted face slack with horror.

But Renie—his fierce, beautiful Renie—she'd reacted faster than Edmond. From the moment they'd heard June's growl, Renie had been running, gathering herself into a leap at the top of the stairs, throwing herself at her rabid sister.

If Edmond had known how this would end, he'd have killed June the first time Ysanne had taken him to her in the west wing, because if June killed Roux before Renie could stop her, Renie would never forgive herself.

Time snapped back into normal speed as Renie crashed into June, midair. They sailed over Roux's head and slammed onto the stairs in a tangle of arms and legs and snapping teeth.

Blood from the wound in June's chest flowed over Renie like paint, and the ruin of her nails scrabbled frantically at Renie's face.

Edmond ran for the stairs but his wounds slowed him down; once again Renie was faster.

She and June rolled down the stairs, the sword slithering down the steps beside them, and as they spilled across the vestibule floor, Renie twisted away from June and grabbed the blade.

June flipped onto all fours, blood and saliva hanging in greasy ropes from her mouth and trailing onto the floor. She hadn't even noticed Edmond on the steps behind her, and if Edmond moved now, he could kill her before she laid another finger on Renie.

But he didn't move.

Renie needed this as much as she'd needed to kill Etienne, and Edmond would not take that away from her.

June scuttled at Renie like some monstrous spider. Renie drew the sword back, keeping the hilt close to her body, then thrust her arm forward with a broken cry.

The sword plunged into June's chest, straight through her heart, and erupted from her back, spraying bits of blood and tissue.

Despite having been a vampire for hundreds of years, Edmond would never understand why puncturing a vampire's heart would kill them when they didn't even need them, but it *did* kill them.

June stared down at the sword sticking through her chest, her mouth hanging slackly open. More blood spilled between her fangs.

She keeled over, and her head hit the floor with an awful finality, the last of the light fading from her eyes and leaving them glassy marbles. Renie reached out to touch her hand, the clawlike fingers that had relaxed in death, but she couldn't seem to bring herself to do it. Instead, she sank back on her heels, staring at her sister's ragged, bloody body.

She looked up as Edmond hurried down the final steps, and a red tear slid down her cheek, then she hunched over, hugging herself, and cried for the sister she hadn't been able to save.

Edmond went to his knees beside her and pulled her into his arms, and she clung to him like an anchor in a storm, her face pressed into his chest.

"It wasn't supposed to end like this," she whispered.

Ignoring the burning pain from his injuries, Edmond stroked Renie's hair, damp and matted with blood, and murmured softly to her in French, the way he'd done in that dank room in the west wing, back when Renie had been trying to bring June back from the brink of madness.

He knew the pain that she was feeling—he'd felt it himself, back when he was human, when he'd watched his entire family fall victim to the plague, when he stood at the edge of the mass grave their bodies had been tossed into. But he'd had hundreds of years to adjust to that, and time had blunted the sharp sting of those losses. Renie's grief was a fresh, raw wound, and it would be for a long time.

"I've got you, mon ange," he whispered.

When Edmond's family had died, he'd been alone.

Renie wouldn't be.

Roux slumped onto the bottom step beside them, tears shimmering in her eyes.

Edmond didn't know how long they knelt there, holding each other, while blood melded their clothes together, and the spreading pool from June's body formed a red sea around the island of their knees.

Eventually, Renie climbed to her feet, steadying herself with a hand on Edmond's shoulder. The bloody tears had made her face sticky, and she scrubbed her cheeks, but only succeeded in smearing the blood around. Her hands were soaked in it.

Edmond rose, too, biting his lip against a wave of pain. He needed rest and he needed blood, but he'd stay standing for as long as Renie needed him, no matter how much it hurt.

"Did we win?" Renie asked Roux.

They must have done; otherwise Roux wouldn't be here with them, unhurt, but Renie obviously needed to hear it—needed to hear that this was over. Edmond needed that too.

"Come and see for yourself," Roux replied.

They shuffled back to the ballroom, slowed by their wounds. The air inside the beautiful room was thick with the stench of blood and meat, and something dripping dangled from a chandelier.

"I'm happy not knowing what that is," Renie said, staring at it.

Edmond gazed around the ballroom. The fighting was over and

it looked as though their enemies were all dead or captured, but Edmond wasn't sure he'd ever be able to look at this room the same way. It was a battlefield now, like the blood-soaked trenches where he'd met Ludovic.

Nikki Flynn bounded over to them. "Hey, you're alive," she said to Renie.

"My girl's tough," said Roux, looking fondly at Renie.

"She certainly is," Edmond murmured, his arm tightening around Renie's shoulders.

"A few of Jemima's minions managed to escape when they realized they were on the losing side, but Seamus is already talking about getting a team to go after them. They can run but they can't hide, and all that," Nikki said.

Edmond narrowed his eyes. The girl's clothes were torn and splashes of what looked like other people's blood marked her cheeks beneath a blossoming black eye.

"Did someone punch you?" Edmond asked.

"Yeah, one of the douchebag guards who sold Ysanne out."

"Who the hell could do that to a kid?" Renie muttered.

"Don't worry, I kicked him in the balls so hard he's probably choking on them," Nikki said.

Edmond's eyebrows shot up and Roux stifled a laugh.

"What's happening now?" Renie asked.

Nikki pointed to the middle of the room, where Ysanne stood, as serene and beautiful as some blood-splattered angel.

"They're deciding Jemima's fate," she said.

"Is this normal?" Renie asked. "Won't they just lock her in the cells?"

Edmond surveyed the ballroom again. All around them, injured humans and vampires leaned on each other or against the walls for support. Some of them openly wept; others gazed at the carnage with stony faces. The battle had been over for only a few minutes, and victory probably hadn't sunk in for everyone yet.

"We've never had a situation like this before," Edmond replied. "But no one will run the risk of Jemima escaping."

Renie edged forward, still leaning on Edmond. Etienne was the one who'd killed June, but Jemima was just as culpable, in a different way. It was little surprise that Renie wanted to know what her punishment would be.

Jemima stood in front of Ysanne, her hands twisted behind her back and cuffed with silver. When she wasn't ripping people apart, she resembled a teenager again, a slim, doe-eyed girl who looked as though butter wouldn't melt in her mouth.

No one believed that anymore.

"Jemima Sutton, you are charged with treason, murder, making unlawful claims on other Vampire Houses, accessory to the illegal turning of a number of humans, and total disruption of the system that has allowed humans and vampires to exist in peace for the last decade," Ysanne said. Her voice was as sharp and as cold as an icicle. "Under usual circumstances you would be taken before the Council, but thanks to your treachery there are only two of us left, so we shall make the final decision regarding your fate. Caoimhe?"

The Irish vampire glided to Ysanne's side. Her hands and arms were coated in blood, like macabre evening gloves, and red chunks were caught in her mass of curls.

"Death," Caoimhe said. No discussion, no defense—just one cold word.

Silence fell upon the ballroom as every eye focused on Ysanne. Jemima's entire future now lay in her hands.

Watching his old friend, Edmond knew exactly what Ysanne was going to do with it.

"Death," Ysanne said.

Jemima nodded, and Edmond supposed she hadn't expected anything else.

"It seems fitting, doesn't it? Our first meeting and our final meeting, both steeped in blood and death." She smiled a little. "I'm glad it will be you."

Ysanne didn't smile back, but her frigid expression softened the barest fraction, an echo of the friendship the two women had once shared.

Then she punched a hand through Jemima's chest and ripped out her heart.

Renie

I'd seen plenty of violence since arriving at Belle Morte, but the casual way Ysanne ripped out another woman's heart chilled me to the bone. Jemima toppled back, and her head cracked on the marble floor, spilling blood. Ysanne stared at the heart in her hand, blood dripping from gore-slippery fingers, then tossed it at Jemima's body. Jemima's heart bounced off her hip and slid across the floor.

"Everyone here, everyone who fought to protect Belle Morte in her darkest hour, has my deepest gratitude," Ysanne said, looking around the room.

Despite the pain and exhaustion that plagued me, despite the fact that Edmond was resting almost his entire weight on me, despite all the death and horror splattered over this room, a warm spark of pride bloomed in my chest. We'd stopped Jemima and Etienne. We'd restored Belle Morte to its rightful owner, saved as many lives as we could, and carried out justice for the lives we hadn't been able to save.

The last few enemy guards and vampires who hadn't died or escaped the mansion were gathered in a knot, surrounded by the surviving Belle Morte vampires. I was unspeakably relieved to see Ludovic and Gideon in one piece.

Ysanne approached her prisoners. "Those of you lucky enough to still be alive will be removed from this house and imprisoned. If I get my way, you'll never see daylight again."

"You can't do that," cried one young woman—a new vampire.

"Did you think this was a game?" Ysanne's voice was soft and deadly. "Have you failed to grasp that you've helped kill people—*my people*? You can't seriously have imagined that you'd escape punishment."

"But you can't just lock us up. We've got rights," the woman protested.

Ysanne stalked toward her, and the woman shrank back. "You wanted to be vampires, and you got your wish. Now you have to abide by our laws. You're lucky to be walking away with your hearts still in your chests." She lifted her bloody hand. "I can change my mind regarding that."

Wisely, the woman shut her mouth.

"Take them away," Ysanne said.

While the prisoners were dealt with, Ysanne approached Nikki, who was still hovering beside me.

"Your father would be proud of you," she said.

"Thanks," Nikki said, standing a little taller.

"Do we know how many of Jemima's people escaped?" Ysanne asked.

Nikki squared her shoulders. Ysanne could have asked Seamus the same question—judging by the way he was giving orders to the surviving security personnel, he'd taken over Dexter's position for the time being. But she was asking Nikki, making it very clear that she valued Nikki's role in this, and saw her not as a child anymore, but someone to be respected.

"We're not sure yet, but not many," Nikki said. "Seamus has that Susan bitch in custody, and once she tells us exactly how many vampires were turned, and once we've identified all the bodies, we'll know who got away."

"They won't get away with their part in this," Ysanne said.

"Hell, no. We'll send a team after them and bring those fuckers to justice."

Ysanne almost smiled. "Even if it takes the next ten years."

"Susan's also going to give us the names of all the humans outside Belle Morte who helped, but I guess it's up to the police to deal with them," Nikki said.

"What about Lamia and Midnight and Nox? What happens to them?" I asked.

Presumably, they were still under the control of Jemima's supporters, and they didn't have lords or ladies to reclaim them.

"I shall arrange for emissaries to visit each house. Jemima and Etienne's supporters will be informed that both traitors are dead, and if their followers give themselves up, they'll be judged fairly."

"If they refuse, we'll liberate each house by force," said Caoimhe, appearing at Ysanne's shoulder. "We'll need to inform the media of what's happened here—the general public knows too much for us to sweep any of this under the carpet now—and we should also contact our allies overseas and let them know of the shadow that nearly overtook us."

"You realize that this isn't over," Ysanne said, looking gravely at us. "The damage that Jemima and Etienne have caused to the balance between vampires and humans may be too severe to repair."

Jason chose that moment to rush over to us and throw his arms around my neck with such force that he almost bowled me over. Without me to lean on, Edmond wobbled on his feet, but Ysanne neatly took his arm, holding him upright.

"Thank god you're okay," Jason said.

When he released me, I noticed a bloodstain spreading around a tear in his shirt.

"You're hurt!" I exclaimed.

"It's nothing serious." Jason lifted his shirt. A long cut ran over his rib cage, but it didn't look deep. It probably wouldn't even need stitches.

"I'll probably have a sexy scar when this is all over. Maybe I can start cultivating a bad-boy image," Jason said.

He didn't mention Gideon, but I noticed the way his eyes strayed in the blond vampire's direction. Gideon had listened to him when we were trying to get the donors out, and he'd protected him during the final fight, but I'd hoped that Jason wasn't reading too much into that. Even if Gideon did feel something for him, it couldn't work.

My own thoughts brought me up short and my gaze slid to Edmond. It had worked for us, hadn't it? Admittedly, it was hardly a traditional romance, what with me having to die for us to be together, but I knew now that we'd have found a way, regardless. It was pretty hypocritical of me to think that Gideon and Jason couldn't make something work the same way. Assuming *I* wasn't reading too much into Gideon's actions.

I slid Edmond's arm over my shoulder, taking back his weight from Ysanne. Right now, I was too tired to think about what the future might hold for other people. I just wanted to focus on my future and how I was going to share it with the beautiful vampire at my side.

An hour later, I sat with Edmond in the dining hall, our chairs pulled close together. Edmond's clothes were still sticky with blood, the folds of fabric turning stiff where the blood was starting to dry, but our injuries were healing. Jason and the remaining members of security had gladly rolled up their sleeves for the Belle Morte vampires, and Edmond had been first in line. Nikki had offered to donate blood, too, but Ysanne wouldn't allow it.

"How hard do you think it will be to track down everyone who escaped?" I asked.

"I don't know yet, but it'll be years before they can be out in the sun for longer than a few minutes. I can't imagine they'll get far."

The Lady of Belle Morte approached us. She'd washed most of the blood from her hands, but flecks of it still dotted her face and hair. "All the donors, staff, and members of security who were killed will be returned to their families, but I'm not sure what you'd like done with June," she said.

"I need some time to think about that," I said.

I'd have to get a hold of my mum as soon as possible. Whether she'd seen the news or not, I needed to tell her exactly what had happened to us.

Ysanne nodded. "There's something else I need to discuss with you." Her gaze flicked to Edmond. "Lamia, Midnight, and Nox have all been left leaderless. New lords or ladies will need to be appointed, and I'd like you to consider a position."

I gaped up at Edmond. I was proud that Ysanne had offered him the role, but at the same time I desperately didn't want him to take it. I wanted us to start a life together, and that didn't involve him being responsible for an entire House. I didn't want him to have to make the kinds of tough decisions that Ysanne had to, or to be in a situation where he had to imprison or punish a friend. But whatever he chose, I'd support him.

"Thank you, but I have to decline. Running a House isn't what I want." Edmond put his arm around my shoulders. "I have everything I want right here."

Ysanne actually rolled her eyes—something I never thought I'd see—but she did it in a good-natured way.

"What's going to happen with Isabeau?" I asked.

"Caoimhe knows where she was taken, and we're organizing a team to go and fetch her," Ysanne said.

"Maybe you should go with them," I ventured.

"There's too much to do here. The team will bring her home," Ysanne said.

She turned and left, the blood-caked ends of her hair swinging with every step.

"I don't think I'll ever truly understand her," I said.

"You've got plenty of time to get to know her better. You're immortal now, and if we stay in Belle Morte, you and Ysanne will see a lot of each other," Edmond said.

That prospect didn't fill me with the same kind of dread that it once had. There was something almost intriguing about the challenge of really getting to know the Lady of Belle Morte.

"Unless you don't want to stay," Edmond said, his voice unusually hesitant.

"If I wanted to leave, would you come with me?" I asked.

"I'll go with you wherever you want to go," Edmond said.

Belle Morte wasn't really such a bad place to live, and Ysanne wasn't the ice-hearted bitch queen that I had initially pegged her for. Maybe we'd change our minds one day in the future—I still wasn't sure I wanted to be cooped up here for the rest of my life, but for now I was right where I wanted to be.

I gazed into the diamond-bright eyes of my beautiful vampire. "My home is wherever you are," I said.

He smiled and kissed me.

Edmond

"What *are* you planning on doing with June?" Edmond asked as they slowly climbed the stairs.

"I know it sounds weird, but I think I'd like to have her buried here. If Mum agrees, of course," Renie said.

Edmond paused, one eyebrow raised in surprise. "Here? But this is where she died." Tactfully, he didn't add that it was also where she'd been turned into a monster, and had spent the rest of her short life suffering.

Renie leaned on the banister, her gaze pensive. "June was a

Vladdict," she said. "Vampires and their whole culture had been her obsession, and applying to be a donor here had been the icing on the fanged cake. For weeks, months even, it was all she'd talked about, all she'd thought about. Before her death, the time she'd spent here would have been the happiest of her life, so if she could have had any say in it, I know she'd want to be buried here." Renie tilted her head to one side. "Assuming Ysanne will allow it."

"I'm sure she will," Edmond said.

Like him, Ysanne knew exactly what it felt like to lose the people she loved.

"Yeah, I think she will too," Renie said.

When they made it back to Edmond's bedroom, Renie made a beeline for the shower. Edmond paused in front of his bed, gazing at the space on the wall where the two swords had been mounted. He'd had those blades for a long time, but he'd never have them on display again, not after what they'd been used for tonight.

A soft moan of relief drifted out from the bathroom, barely distinguishable beneath the sound of rushing water. Heat curled through Edmond. Suddenly he wasn't so tired.

Peeling off his ruined clothes, he headed for the bathroom.

Renie stood in the shower, deliciously naked, her face tilted up, her hair a long, water-dark rope hanging down her back.

She was so beautiful that for a moment all Edmond could do was watch her, fascinated by the way water streamed over her curves, making her pale skin glitter. Then she looked over her shoulder at him, and the heat in her eyes made all the blood in Edmond's body rush south.

He slid his arms around Renie's waist and planted a series of light kisses along the back of her neck. Renie arched against him, hot water sluicing over their bare bodies.

"I never imagined my journey into Belle Morte would end this way," she murmured. "Life kind of jumped out of nowhere and smacked me upside the head."

"Are you glad it did?" Edmond asked.

Renie tipped her head back so it rested on Edmond's shoulder. Tiny droplets shone like diamonds on her eyelashes.

"There's a lot that I've lost by becoming a vampire. I'll never grow old or have kids. I'll never fit in with ordinary humans again, and I'll have to live with all the ways that the world might change in the future. I'll never eat real food again, and any time I want to leave Belle Morte, it won't be easy finding privacy," she said.

Then she smiled, bright as a star.

"But I've gained so much too. I've forged friendships that will last a lifetime. I've tested myself in ways that I've never imagined, and discovered how low I can fall and how high I can climb," she said.

She reached up and trailed her fingertips along Edmond's cheek, catching the water that ran there like tears.

"Best of all, I've found you, and you complete me in a way that I hadn't realized was possible," she continued. "You're the man I can truly say I've given my heart to, the man I can see myself spending every second of the rest of my life with—however many hundreds of years that will be." She smiled again. "I love you. It's as simple as that."

Turning in his arms, Renie looped her arms around his neck and hooked one leg around his hips, pulling him closer. Edmond's eyes locked on Renie's as he slowly slid into her, his mouth closing over hers, catching the gasp that spilled from her lips.

The shower was large enough for two, but the tiles were slick with water and Renie's back kept sliding down the wall, making it difficult for them to keep their rhythm. Finally, with a growl of frustration, Edmond scooped Renie into his arms, his body never leaving hers, kicked open the bathroom door, and carried her through to the bedroom, where he laid her on the bed.

The silk canopy formed a private haven around them, a small space that was uniquely theirs. Without the slippery shower wall getting in the way, Edmond quickly found a frantic, almost desperate rhythm, his hips moving against Renie's until the bed shuddered against the wall, until he felt that perfect moment when she shattered apart, her back arching, her body clenching around him, her head falling back, Edmond's name forming a hoarse scream on her lips.

Edmond followed her over that blissful edge a moment later.

They still didn't know what the future held, or what the fallout from Jemima and Etienne's coup would be. But no matter what, Edmond knew they would find a way to get through it.

CHAPTER THIRTY

Renie

We buried June two days later.

I stood on the grounds of Belle Morte, Edmond on one side, my mum on the other. Roux and Jason stood nearby, with Ysanne, Ludovic, Gideon, Caoimhe, and Isabeau. Nobody wore black, as per my request. June wouldn't have wanted that.

Phoning my mum and confirming that everything she'd seen on TV was true—that I'd died and had come back, and that June had died but was never coming back—was one of the hardest things that I'd ever had to do. Persuading her to come to the house where we'd both died had been almost as hard. At first she hadn't wanted June buried here. She'd been indifferent to Belle Morte before June had come here; now she hated it, which was hardly a surprise. But besides the fact that I *knew* that if June could have chosen anywhere, she'd have wanted to sleep forever in the grounds of her favorite Vampire House, I was terrified at the thought of burying her in a public cemetery. The families of her victims might decide they wanted to vent their grief by trashing her grave. She was safer here.

I still didn't know how the donor system would have to change from now on—currently, Roux and Jason were the only official donors left in the country. Everyone else had been sent home, and I didn't know if they'd ever be brought back or if they even *wanted* to come back. But one thing I'd made very clear to Ysanne was that I would not exist by the same rigid rules that had governed vampires up until now. A lot of them made sense, but typically vampires only left their houses to visit friends or romantic interests in other houses. They were all too old to have human families, but I wasn't. I was not giving up the freedom to come and go from Belle Morte as I pleased—without needing Ysanne's permission—and I needed my mum to have the right to visit the house too.

I'd probably have other requests in the future, and maybe Ysanne wouldn't agree with all of them, but we'd work through it. Once I'd hated her, but after everything we'd been through, we'd reached a new level of understanding and respect for each other.

Andrew and Seamus had organized the survivors of their respective teams to dig June's grave, and the gravesite I'd chosen was the base of the huge oak tree that hugged the garden wall—the tree that I'd once mistakenly believed marked the spot where June's body was hidden. It was a beautiful old tree, and I thought June would be happy here.

There was no coffin; instead, June's body had been wrapped in black silk, and when the guards carried her out, Mum let out a choked sob and clutched my hand. I squeezed back, carefully. I was still coming to grips with my vampire strength.

Ysanne had asked if either me or Mum had wanted to help lower June into the grave, but we couldn't do it. It was hard enough knowing that my sister was going into the cold ground; I couldn't be the one who put her there.

Instead, Edmond and Ludovic took over. Between them, they took June's body from the guards, lifting her as gently as if she'd been sleeping, and carried her to the open mouth of the grave.

Roux curled her fingers around mine, taking Edmond's place at my side.

Edmond and Ludovic lowered June into the grave on black silken runners. The other vampires who'd died hadn't had funerals like this. Rather than burying them, their bodies had been placed outside in the sun until they'd eventually burned to ash. But that had been done outside the grounds of Belle Morte. Etienne and Jemima couldn't hurt anyone now, but none of us wanted any part of them to remain here, not even their ashes.

But June's funeral had needed to be that of a human—or close to, anyway—because she'd never really been a vampire. She'd gone from human to rabid in the blink of an eye, and I needed her to have a grave so Mum and I could come and talk to her.

When June was nestled in her final resting place, Mum stepped forward to say a few words. I looked up at the sky, velvet black and star sprinkled, and thought of the June that I'd known, the dreamer, the Vladdict, the big sister who'd climb into bed with me so we could talk about boys, and who'd always made sure she left me the last bit of ice cream; the girl I'd known better than anyone in so many ways, and yet in other ways hadn't known at all.

Mum finished her speech and moved away from the grave. Now it was my turn. I had no speech; there were no words for what I was feeling. Instead, I crouched by the grave, scooped up a handful of dirt, and gently sprinkled it over the silk-wrapped body lying beneath the cradle of branches overhead.

"I will always love you," I whispered.

It didn't matter anymore that June had made a terrible choice in helping Etienne. It didn't matter that she'd been blinded by her feelings for him. All that mattered was that she'd been my sister and she had died.

I made my way back to Edmond. He held out an arm for me, and I slotted comfortably against his side, resting my head on his shoulder.

Mum didn't want to watch the grave being filled in, so when Seamus and Andrew fetched the shovels, she quickly walked back to the house. Roux and Jason followed, then Gideon, Caoimhe, and Ludovic. Ysanne took a little step toward Isabeau, but Isabeau turned away and followed the others.

Once Caoimhe had told us where Isabeau was, it had taken only hours for a security team to free her and bring her home, but from the way she'd avoided Ysanne ever since, it seemed as though something important had broken between them when the Council had sent Isabeau away.

I hoped that they'd eventually work through their troubles. Everyone deserved to be happy.

The depth of Jemima and Etienne's legacy was yet to be fully understood. In some ways, they'd got what they'd wanted—the world was now painfully aware that vampires were more than pretty celebrities, and everyone was still reeling from that realization.

But I didn't think that the world's obsession had ended yet. The road ahead might be rocky, but it wasn't entirely dark. Maybe donors wouldn't be as keen to sign up—maybe the financial rewards would have to be greater. Security checks would have to be tighter. The lords and ladies of each House, whoever the replacements would be, needed to communicate more with the others—there couldn't be any more secrets.

The vampires who'd escaped the mansion were still at large, and maybe that would cause problems sooner or later, but we'd deal with that too. Things could get worse for us before they got better, but they *would* get better. I had to believe that.

"Are you all right, mon ange?" Edmond softly asked.

I gazed up at him, my eyes taking in his knife-edge cheekbones, the darkness of his hair against the marble paleness of his skin. A huge part of my life had ended in this house, but a huge part was about to begin, and that was the man who stood at my side.

"Not yet," I replied, and took his hand. "But I will be."

ACKNOWLEDGMENTS

Behind every book is a team, and I couldn't have asked for a more amazing team. Deanna, Rebecca, Jen, and Delaney, thank you for being with me every step of the way. This journey has already been so incredible, and I can't wait to see where we go next.

Irina, my creator manager, thank you for being my cheerleader, for every chat, and for our LA breakfast. That was a fantastic grilled cheese!

Ysabel Enverga, thank you for the gorgeous covers. I never imagined my books could look this beautiful.

My family, thank you for always being there. And a special nod to our newest member, little Charlie Bear.

My wonderful friends, who took me out for many, many cocktails when my first book launched. We definitely need to do that again!

My cat, for graciously allowing me to share my desk chair with her and for being my constant companion.

And finally, my readers. I wouldn't be here without you. Thank you to my early Wattpad readers for falling in love with my stories, and thank you to every reader since then. Your support, passion, and excitement are truly humbling.

ABOUT THE AUTHOR

Bella Higgin fell in love with vampire fiction after reading an illustrated copy of Dracula as a kid, so it was inevitable that her dream career would involve writing about vampires. Her works on Wattpad have amassed more than thirteen million reads, including her publishing debut, The Belle Morte series. A collector of swords, books, and TV memorabilia, she hopes to one day have enough money to build a TARDIS in her garden. Bella currently lives and writes full-time in a small English town not far from the sea.

Turn the page for a preview of Book 3
in the Belle Morte series.

A BELLE MORTE NOVEL

HUNTED

BELLA HIGGIN

Coming Winter 2024

CHAPTER ONE

Roux

Standing in the doorway of the dining hall, Roux Hayes couldn't get over how quiet Belle Morte was now. Just a few days ago, this room had been where the mansion's thirty blood donors had eaten meals and filled the huge space with the sound of talking and laughing. It felt like forever ago.

"Do you think it will ever get back to normal?" Renie asked from behind her, and Roux jumped a little.

Renie hadn't yet mastered the liquid, catlike grace of the older vampires but she could move around a lot more quietly than when she'd been human. Roux was still getting used to it.

"Sorry," Renie said.

Roux took Renie's hand and gave it a little squeeze.

Barely a week had passed since Belle Morte had been reclaimed from Etienne and Jemima, the two vampires whose attempted power coup had nearly destroyed the system that allowed humans and vampires to peacefully coexist. But humans—security, staff, and donors—had died in the cross fire, and now none of the vampire survivors knew what future they had with the human world.

"Whatever happens, we'll get through it," Roux said.

Renie smiled wanly. "You don't have to be here."

Belle Morte's remaining donors had been sent home to their families, and though no donors in the Houses of Midnight, Lamia, Nox, or Fiaigh had been harmed, they'd been sent home too. No staff were left, and only a skeleton security detail still patrolled the mansion's hallways and grounds.

The vampires were surviving on bags of donated blood.

Roux affectionately rolled her eyes. "Like I'd abandon you."

Technically, Roux and Jason should have left with the other donors, but neither of them considered themselves donors anymore. They were a part of Belle Morte, and neither of them had any intention of leaving.

Edmond Dantès glided up to them, his dark hair spilling around his shoulders, his shirt open at the neck. Something soft and warm bloomed in Renie's eyes as she looked at the vampire she'd fallen in love with.

"Is no one else here yet?" he asked.

Renie shook her head. "Not even Ysanne."

"We're still a couple of minutes early," Roux said, checking her watch. "Everyone else will be here soon."

She strode into the dining hall and took a seat halfway down the trestle table. The silence and emptiness felt even more pronounced. Belle Morte was a ghost of its former self, and it made Roux's heart ache.

She wanted to believe that the mansion would recover, but there was a real chance that the donor system and vampires' place in the world had been damaged beyond repair. Roux didn't want to think about what that might mean for them all.

Renie and Edmond sat beside her, their hands clasped with each other.

Seconds later, Jason entered the dining hall and threw himself into the chair on Roux's other side. His blond hair was mussed in a style that looked casual, but that he'd have worked hard to create.

"Fashionably early, are we?" he said, then winced as his voice echoed around the huge room.

"Didn't have much else to do," Roux said.

More vampires trickled in, but no one spoke, and the silence grew heavier. Jason sat up a little straighter when Gideon came in, but the blond vampire had his eyes fixed on the floor. Roux was sure she'd glimpsed some sparks between Jason and Gideon when they helped reclaim Belle Morte, but the vampire had retreated into himself since then.

The vampires took their seats; mingled with them were the remaining members of Belle Morte security. Seamus Kennedy, head of security at Fiaigh, sat near the top of the table.

Ludovic de Vauban sat next to Edmond, and though his face was expressionless in the way that older vampires did so well, Roux was surprised to glimpse a flicker of real nervousness in his eyes. She didn't know Ludovic well, but she'd seen him fight, and he was a force of nature when he wanted to be. Now he looked more vulnerable than she was used to.

Edmond leaned over and murmured something to his friend; Ludovic nodded, but his expression didn't change.

Ysanne swept into the room, her high heels clicking crisply across the floor. Her hair was a pale sheet down her back, not a strand out of place, and her sheath dress clung to her lean body. She looked beautiful and regal, a queen once again. But Roux had glimpsed the real person behind the icy mask, and she found it hard to be intimidated by Ysanne now.

A man Roux had never seen before followed Ysanne. Tall and square, his suit too tight across his shoulders, he surveyed the room with a scowl.

"Thank you all for coming," Ysanne said, and Roux blinked in surprise. Usually Ysanne issued orders and expected them to be obeyed. She didn't think to *thank* anyone.

"These have been difficult times for us all, and I'm afraid the storm is not over," Ysanne said.

She started to continue, then stopped, her eyes fixed on something at the end of the room. Roux looked over her shoulder.

Isabeau Aguillon stood in the entryway. Her gaze darted around the room, lingering on every face, before moving back to Ysanne. Roux saw the tiniest crack in Ysanne's icy mask, then it was gone.

"We're glad you could join us," Ysanne said.

Isabeau silently slipped into a chair at the end of the table.

"This is where things currently stand," Ysanne said. "Our prisoners are currently being held down in the cells. I know many of you are unhappy about sharing a roof with traitors, but for now it's better to keep them where we can keep an eye on them. The remaining traitors in the other Houses have been weeded out and imprisoned, and several European Houses are arranging to send over support while we continue to pick up the pieces."

Ysanne waited a beat. "As you all know, two days ago, Prime Minister McGellan issued a press release informing the public of exactly what happened here, except for one detail. During the final battle for Belle Morte, five of Etienne's newly turned vampires escaped the mansion and are still at large in Winchester. The prime minister has decided the best course of action is to keep quiet about this."

"Why?" Renie asked.

"Damage control. The general public is reeling from what's happened, and the last thing we want is to cause further panic by admitting there's anything we still don't have full control over," Ysanne said.

There was something stiff about her words, as if they didn't feel right in her mouth, and Roux guessed McGellan had told her to say all this. Jenny McGellan, currently serving her second term as PM, had a reputation for getting exactly what she wanted, and taking orders from a higher authority must grate on Ysanne.

Her word was still law inside Belle Morte but maybe she no longer had similar clout in the outside world.

"Do you really think that's a good idea?" Renie asked.

"Truthfully, I'm not sure. Before I met with McGellan you told me we should be fully honest with the humans, and I agreed with you," Ysanne said. "But we must remember that the fallout of this catastrophe may affect Houses worldwide. People have glimpsed our dark side, and they won't quickly forget it. We don't want them to lose what shred of faith they might have left by admitting we don't have full control of the situation."

Ysanne paused again, looking around the room. "I shall be honest with you all. Our future is very uncertain. I don't yet know where we stand with the human world, or if there's even a place for us here anymore."

The wide-shouldered man standing a little behind Ysanne shifted his weight and made a noise low in his throat, as if he wanted to say something. But he didn't speak.

"McGellan won't entertain further discussion about our future until those five escaped vampires are caught," Ysanne said.

She beckoned to the man, and he shot her a dark look that she didn't see before he moved closer to her.

"This is Detective Chief Inspector Ray Walsh. He will be working with me to track down and capture our fugitives," Ysanne said.

Walsh's face darkened even more, but he still didn't say anything.

"Working with you how?" Roux asked. Something about the man made her uneasy.

At almost exactly the same time, Ludovic said, "*He* won't be capturing anyone."

"Oh really? Why's that?" Walsh said. His voice was raspy; maybe he was a smoker.

"Because you're human. This is a vampire mess and it'll take a vampire to sort it out," Ludovic replied.

Walsh smiled unpleasantly. "I wasn't planning on handcuffing them. If I had my way, I'd send an armed specialist unit after them."

"That wouldn't make a difference," said Ludovic quietly. "Any human who pursues these vampires will be at risk, guns or no guns.

Vampires can heal from bullet wounds, and an injured vampire is a dangerous one. We're already dealing with angry, grieving humans wanting justice for their murdered friends and family—if we put any more lives at risk it will make us seem even more like monsters."

There was something desolate in the way Ludovic said the last word, and it tugged at Roux's heart. Was Ludovic afraid that the world now saw them as monsters? Or was he afraid they really *were* monsters?

"Ludovic is correct," Ysanne said. "Even uninjured, these vampires will be scared and hungry, and that makes them very dangerous. The best person to deal with them is a much older, more seasoned vampire." Her frost-colored gaze flicked briefly to Isabeau. "That's why I'll be pursuing them myself."

A murmur ran through the room. Ysanne was more than capable of getting her hands dirty, but wading directly into the fray wasn't usually her style.

"You can't do that," Renie said.

Ysanne's eyes narrowed, but it was speculative rather than combative. "Why not?"

"You've worked so hard to maintain positive vampire/human relations, and now that Jemima and Etienne have royally fucked that up for everyone, your House needs you here. There are plenty of people at this table who can go after those rogue vampires, but only you can lead Belle Morte."

Ysanne's mouth tightened. Roux knew as well as anyone that the Lady of Belle Morte liked to be in control, so it couldn't be easy for her to take a step back. But Renie had a point.

Silence filled the room.

"I'll do it," Ludovic said.

Ysanne scrutinized him, her lips pursed. Walsh said nothing, but continued to scowl. Didn't the man have any other expressions?

"Are you sure that's wise?" Edmond asked, and Ludovic gave him a look that Roux couldn't interpret. He slowly nodded, but Edmond didn't relax.

"You realize these vampires are out in the human world, far beyond the reach of this house," Ysanne said.

"I do," Ludovic said.

"And you still think you're the best man for the job?"

Ludovic sat up a little straighter, lifting his chin. Light from the chandelier played over his blond ponytail. "I wouldn't have offered if I didn't think I could do it."

Maybe so, but Roux hadn't imagined the worry in Edmond's eyes. She didn't know much about Ludovic, but his strength and speed suggested he wasn't a young vampire, and Roux had always assumed he was about Edmond's age—somewhere around three or four hundred years old—which should have been plenty old enough to take care of himself. So why did Edmond look so worried?

It suddenly struck Roux that Ludovic, like most vampires, had spent the last ten years sealed in this mansion. Renie had mentioned to her that Ludovic avoided technology even more than most vampires, and despite how strong and fast and brave he was, he had little to no experience of the modern human world.

He was stronger than any of the escaped vampires, but he'd be out of his element in a way that they wouldn't be, and that could put him at risk.

"You need someone to go with you," Roux blurted.

Ysanne cocked an eyebrow. Ludovic's face was a blank mask.

"What are you talking about?" Jason said.

"Ludovic can't do this on his own," Roux said.

"He's a big boy, I'm sure he can handle it."

"I can," Ludovic confirmed.

"Oh really?" Roux faced him. "How well do you know Winchester? What do you understand of the modern world and how it's changed since Belle Morte was built? Do you know how to interact with people without them knowing you're a vampire?"

Ludovic said nothing.

"Do you even know how to use a cell phone?" Roux continued.

A couple of other vampires exchanged uneasy glances.

"That's what I thought." Roux stared at Ludovic, though he seemed reluctant to meet her eyes. "This is the problem with you all locking yourselves away in these houses—the world changes around you but you stay exactly the same. If you jump straight in the deep end, you'll drown. Unless you have a lifeline."

"A lifeline," Ysanne repeated, testing the word.

"Yes. Someone who knows the world outside, who can make sure Ludovic doesn't run into trouble."

"You mean a human," said Ludovic flatly.

Roux nodded.

"And who do you suggest?" Ysanne asked, but the wry note in her voice suggested she already knew.

Roux licked her lips, bolstering her courage. "Me."

CHAPTER TWO

Roux

Renie and Jason spoke at the same time.

"Oh, hell no."

"No way."

"I'll go," Edmond cut in.

"Not without me, you won't," Renie said.

Roux held up both hands. "Neither of you are going. Renie, some of this might have to be done by day so that rules you out. And you"—she pointed at Edmond—"are not charging off on some mission and leaving Renie. You've more than done your bit; you can take a step back now."

"Isn't that for us to decide?" said Edmond.

"Nope, because you'll always try to be a hero. It's okay to let someone else handle this one."

"Hold on," Jason said. "Ludovic already has a human to help him." He gestured to Walsh. "This guy."

"I'm not a fucking babysitter," Walsh growled. "I'm here to track down the five rogue vampires that you all let loose into the city, and the only reason I'm working with any of you is because I'm not stupid enough to try and bring down a vampire by myself."

"You can't even help Ludovic out when he needs to be outside the mansion?" Jason said.

"Not when he'll need to be outside for as long as it takes to catch these bastards."

Jason frowned. "Why would he need to do that?"

"Perhaps I didn't make this clear earlier, but whoever goes after our fugitives will have to leave Belle Morte for the foreseeable future," Ysanne said. "In order to keep all this under wraps we need to avoid drawing any attention to ourselves. With the protestors congregating at the gates and the intense media attention, we can't afford the questions that will arise if Ludovic, or anyone else, is seen frequently coming and going from Belle Morte."

"So what was your plan?" Roux asked.

"I intended to stay at a hotel."

"Then Ludovic and I can still do that."

"Or I can do that by myself," Ludovic said.

Roux gave him an exasperated look but he still wouldn't meet her eyes.

"What will you do when you get hungry? You can't go chomping on strangers' necks," she challenged him.

"I'm perfectly capable of hunting animals," Ludovic said, and a shadow that Roux couldn't interpret flashed across his face.

"Sure, because *that* wouldn't draw attention," she said.

Ludovic shot her a cool look. "I have hundreds of years' experience with hunting in the shadows."

"Yeah, and cell phones didn't exist then. All it would take now is one shrieking fangirl with a camera, and you're screwed."

"She has a point," said Renie.

"You can't be Ludovic's only donor, especially not when you have no idea how long you'll be away," Jason objected.

"I don't have to feed him every day; we can take some bagged blood with us."

"If Ludovic has bagged blood, then surely he doesn't need you."

Roux hesitated, trying to choose the right words. "I know that Ludovic is physically stronger than any of Etienne's minions, but they still outnumber him five to one. He'll need human blood to be at full strength when he goes up against them, and if something goes wrong, if he gets hurt, then fresh human blood will be better for him than bagged blood."

"Then I'll come too," Jason said. "Two donors are better than one."

Roux shook her head. "If we want to stay under the radar, then the fewer of us the better. Less chance of someone recognizing us."

"But this is dangerous," Jason said, frustration coloring his voice.

"What if I go?" Seamus said, running his hand through his tawny thatch of hair.

"Belle Morte can't afford to lose any more security guards right now," Roux said. "Besides, I won't get involved with any of the violent bits. I'll be there to help steer Ludovic through the modern world and to stay in touch with the mansion. I'm guessing we can't rely on DCI Walsh to do that."

"You guessed right," Walsh snapped.

For a heartbeat or two, no one said a thing. Ysanne gazed at Roux, her eyes like drills, and Roux gazed right back. She needed to do this. She and Jason had both joined the fight to reclaim Belle Morte a few days ago, but their contributions had made little difference against angry vampires. This time Roux felt she could be a key player.

"Roux, Ludovic, would you come to my office?" Ysanne said at last. "I'd like to speak with you privately."

Roux sat in Ysanne's office, looking around at the surprisingly modern decor—the leather-and-chrome furniture, and the white carpet that looked even brighter beneath the black desk. The room didn't fit the rest of the mansion.

Ludovic occupied the chair next to her, straight-backed and stiff, refusing to look at her. His hands were tightly folded in his lap. Ysanne sat behind her desk, one hand resting on a slim folder, while Walsh, who'd refused to be left out, hovered nearby, arms folded, eyebrows still twisted in a scowl.

The small room felt thick with tension.

Ysanne opened her folder, took out several glossy photos, and slid them across her desktop.

Roux and Ludovic leaned forward.

"These are the five vampires who escaped Belle Morte after that final fight," Ysanne said. "Stephen Johnson, Delia Sanders, Neal Schwartz, Jeffrey Smith, and Kashvi Patel." With each name, she tapped one of the photos.

Roux couldn't help noticing that Ysanne's nails were unpolished and slightly ragged around the edges. It was a silly little thing, but Ysanne was the epitome of elegance, never appearing in public without being polished and primped and coiffed to within an inch of her undead life. Something like this spoke volumes about the pressure she was under.

Ysanne pulled four more photos from her folder and spread them across the desktop. "And these are the four vampires who never even made it *to* that final fight."

Roux frowned. "I don't understand."

A quick glance at Ludovic's expression told her he didn't either.

"Neither do I," Ysanne admitted. "Susan Harcourt was responsible for helping Etienne gain access to people who'd do anything if he turned them, and she's since provided us with the names of every vampire that Etienne turned. These four were among them. But over this last week, Caoimhe and I have been working out which vampires were killed in the attack, which ones are currently held in the cells, and which ones escaped." Ysanne tapped the photos again. "These four aren't among any of them."

"Wait, so Etienne turned them and then they just disappeared?" Roux said.

Ysanne didn't answer.

"Could they have escaped him after he turned them?" Walsh asked. For once, he didn't sound confrontational.

Ysanne turned in her seat to face him. "All these people agreed to do Etienne's dirty work on the proviso that he would grant their greatest wish—to become vampires. I find it hard to believe that they would have fled as soon as he turned them."

"Even if they wanted to, it wouldn't have been hard for Etienne to catch them. Newly turned vampires aren't as strong or fast as older vampires," Ludovic added.

Walsh's face darkened again. "So what the hell did that bastard do with them after he turned them?"

"That's the question," Ysanne said.

Roux didn't like where this was going. Etienne and Jemima were dead and couldn't hurt anyone else, but that didn't undo the damage they'd caused—the damage that Roux was starting to suspect ran deeper than anyone had initially understood.

"There's more to Etienne's plan than we realized, isn't there?" she said.

"It's possible," Ysanne said.

"So even if we catch the Five, this isn't over."

"The Five?" Ysanne said.

"It's easier to give them a collective name."

"Finding these five fugitives is our top priority. The fact that they were willing to attack Belle Morte means that we must consider them to be the biggest threat."

Walsh looked like he really wanted to say something to that, but he kept his mouth firmly closed.

"Once we have the Five safely in custody, then we can turn our attention to these other missing vampires," Ysanne said.

"Why am I only just hearing about them?" Walsh demanded.

This time Ysanne didn't look at him. "Because I've only just learned about them myself. Etienne turned several dozen vampires, and it wasn't until we'd traced each name to a death, a prisoner, or an escapee that we realized anyone else was missing."

"Does the prime minister know?"

"I shall inform her this afternoon," said Ysanne stiffly.

"Just so I understand this, Walsh's job is to track down the Five and Ludovic's job is to recapture them, but once that's over they have to start again with these four?" Roux said.

Ysanne nodded.

"No pressure then."

Ludovic glanced at her, surprise in his eyes. Maybe she was being too flippant with the Lady of the House, but Roux Hayes wasn't about to change who she was.

Not again.

"Do we have any leads?" Roux asked.

"Yeah," Walsh said before Ysanne could answer. "That's why I'm here. This morning I got a call from Stephen Johnson's family. Apparently, they have some info that could help us, but they're not prepared to discuss it over the phone."

"Why not?"

"The fuck should I know?"

Roux rolled her eyes.

"Walsh is going to visit the family at their home later today, and I intended to go with him. Ludovic, if you're serious about taking this on, then you will go in my stead," Ysanne said.

"I really don't need backup for an interview," Walsh said.

"You will if it's more than an interview. What if Stephen's at his home and he wants to turn himself in?" Roux said.

"Then he won't be a threat to me, will he?"

"Unless he suddenly changes his mind and makes a run for it."

Walsh's expression cleared. "Right, because vampires are untrustworthy."

"That's not what I meant," Roux said, shooting him a hard look that he ignored.

"Vampires are better at discerning lies than humans are. If the

Johnsons aren't being truthful, I'll be able to hear it." Ludovic spoke up.

"Hear it?" Walsh repeated.

"In their heartbeats."

Walsh's lip curled.

"There's another aspect of this we haven't discussed," Roux said. "Ludovic's a famous vampire, and even I'm pretty recognizable these days, thanks to everything that's happened. I get that we're going to a hotel to draw attention away from Belle Morte and vampires in general, but it won't take long for some squealing Vladdict to spot Ludovic. What happens then?"

"We'll have to be careful," Ysanne replied.

Roux shook her head. "Nope, not good enough."

Ysanne's eyes narrowed.

"Look, I don't know how many more times I can tell you this, but you guys are not prepared for the modern world and how intrusive it can be. Way too many people are obsessed with celebrities, especially the undead variety, and one sniff of a famous vampire wandering the streets, and every cell phone in England will be out, trying to capture photos and videos."

"Then what do you propose?" Ysanne said.

Roux studied Ludovic's face, appraising how a little shading and contouring could alter the shape of his eyes, his nose. "We need disguises," she said.

Walsh made an irritated noise. "We don't have time for this."

"Make time," Roux said. "This isn't just about keeping things under wraps. A lot of people are pretty pissed at vampires right now. Did you ever consider that it might not be safe for Ludovic if he's recognized?"

The look that Walsh gave her suggested he couldn't care less. Roux was really starting to dislike the man.

"Roux is correct," Ysanne said. "Compile a list of everything you need and I'll make sure you get it today."

Walsh started to bluster, and Ysanne's expression turned to ice. "Do not ask me to put one of my people in danger, Detective."

"No one would be in danger if you fanged freaks hadn't let this happen in the first place," Walsh snarled.

Ysanne's hands tightened on her desktop, and Roux held her breath. An agonizingly long pause ticked by.

"Roux, how quickly can you get a list together?" Ysanne asked.

"Ten minutes?" Roux said.

Ludovic looked distinctly uneasy. "What sort of disguise do you have in mind?"

Roux grinned.

"Are you sure you know what you're doing?" Ludovic said, warily eyeing the makeup laid out on Roux's dressing table.

"Do you doubt me?"

He didn't answer—a wise move.

"I promise I won't mess up your pretty face. I'll just make you less recognizable," Roux said.

She guided him into a chair and placed a finger under his chin, turning his head this way and that. The tiniest flicker of heat stirred in her stomach.

She'd been attracted to him as soon as she'd arrived at Belle Morte—and who could blame her? Ludovic was six feet of hard muscle, blond hair, and chiseled jaw. His eyes were as deep and blue as the ocean, and more than once he'd come to her rescue during Etienne and Jemima's coup. A bit of old-fashioned gallantry was enough to turn any girl's head.

But this was no time for a crush.

"Can vampires grow beards?" Roux asked, studying the edge of Ludovic's jaw.

"We can, but it takes a very long time."

"Really? I never imagined vampires shaving."

"We have to only very rarely."

"Good to know."

"Why do you ask?"

"Just curious. Facial hair would change the shape of your face, but we wouldn't have the time even if you were human." She tapped her chin, thinking. "I can't give you a beard, but I can pencil on some convincing stubble. Is that okay?"

Ludovic nodded.

"Great," Roux said.

Ludovic's ivory-pale skin was the first thing to change. If they'd had more time she'd push him into a tanning booth but, like the beard, it wasn't an option, so makeup was the answer. Did tanning booths even work on vampires?

Roux applied foundation to Ludovic's face and neck, blunting the lines of his cheekbones and jaw, used subtle eye shadows to alter the shape of his eyes, then carefully penciled on some stubble. It wasn't perfect but it would fool anyone who didn't look too closely.

Seamus had procured everything on Roux's list with impressive speed, including a pair of Clark Kent–style glasses, which Roux slid onto Ludovic's face.

"Almost there," she said.

Reaching one hand around his neck, she released Ludovic's hair from its usual ponytail. He stiffened.

"I won't cut it, if that's what you're worried about," Roux said.

Ludovic said nothing as Roux set to work with wax and hairspray, coaxing his normally straight blond hair into loose waves, giving him a geeky surfer look. Then she took the beanie that Seamus had picked up with Ludovic's clothes and put it on the vampire's head. He still sort of looked like himself, but it was more like a human who vaguely resembled a famous vampire.

"You look adorable," she said, and Ludovic scowled.

He turned in his chair, seeing his reflection for the first time since Roux had started working on him, and gripped the edge of the dressing table.

Roux's voice softened. "I know it's weird, but it's only temporary."

"I look human," Ludovic said, and there was a wealth of emotion in those three words—surprise, disbelief, even regret.

"Are you okay?" Roux said, and he nodded.

Tearing his eyes from the mirror, he turned to her. "Why are you helping me? This isn't your fight."

Roux leaned a hip against the table. "I'm part of this, too, you know."

Even through the thick-framed glasses, Ludovic's gaze was intense. "But why do you care?"

"Because no one in Belle Morte deserves whatever shit might be coming thanks to Jemima and Etienne. Besides, you've saved my life before. Let me return the favor."

"Thank you for caring," Ludovic said quietly, looking away.

"You sound surprised that I do."

"Vampires are facing the possibility that our time in the spotlight is over. Not everyone would care how we feel about any of that."

"Don't jump to the worst conclusions yet. We don't know what'll happen."

But despite her words, Roux couldn't ignore the tight knot of anxiety in her stomach. There was a chance that Etienne and Jemima had damaged vampires' reputation beyond repair, and Roux had no idea how the vampire world could survive that.

CHAPTER THREE

Roux

Roux had told Seamus to get them clothes in dark, solid colors; nothing with noticeable patterns, mostly cheap jeans and long-sleeved shirts—very different to the tailored cuts and luxury fabrics that occupied the wardrobes of Belle Morte.

While Ludovic changed in the bathroom, Roux pulled on the long dark wig that'd lain on her pile of clothes, arranging the thick fringe across her forehead.

"Hmm," she murmured, studying her reflection. It was a very different look to her pixie cut, but she looked damn good with long hair too. She decided to ditch her makeup altogether rather than focusing on a new look—as soon as Ludovic was out of the bathroom, she'd wash her face.

She and Renie knew each other well enough to waltz into the bathroom when one of them was buck naked, but Ludovic probably wouldn't take it so well.

It was a shame really, because she wouldn't mind seeing him naked.

She threw on some new clothes; it felt strange to erase so much of herself.

Jason poked his head around the door, and his eyes widened. "Oh wow."

"Good wow or bad wow?" Roux touched her wig. She'd thought it looked okay, but she *was* biased.

"Roux, my darling, you could shave your head and men would still fall at your feet."

Roux rolled her eyes, but she couldn't stop a smile.

"Where's Ludovic?" Jason asked.

"Getting changed in the bathroom."

"Can we talk to you for a moment?"

"We?"

Renie's head popped around the door, just below Jason's.

"Let's take this into the hall," Roux said. She ushered her friends back, then stepped out of the room and closed the door. "Everything okay?"

Jason smiled, but it was tight around the edges. "We're worried about you."

"Have you thought this through?" Renie said.

Roux suspected they'd rehearsed this. "Guys, it's okay. I know what I'm doing," she said.

"Do you, though?" Jason pressed her.

"Yes. I'm not stupid."

"But this is dangerous. Those vampires won't go down without a fight," said Renie.

"That's for Ludovic to handle. I'll be okay, I promise."

"You can't make a promise like that when you have no idea what's going to happen," said Renie.

"Then I promise to be exceptionally, extraordinarily careful with everything I do from the second I leave the mansion."

Renie's mouth pulled down in an unhappy shape. "This isn't a joke."

"I'm serious." Roux hugged Renie. "Everything will be fine," she whispered into Renie's hair. "It'll be over before you know it."

The second she let Renie go she found herself in Jason's arms, mashed tightly against his chest. "Make sure Ludovic takes care of you," he said.

Roux laughed. "Outside the mansion is my world, not his. If anything, *I'll* be taking care of *him*."

"Taking care of a hot vampire." Jason's expression was wistful. "Sounds like my ideal job."

Roux swatted his chest.

Less than a month ago she hadn't known Renie and Jason, but they'd got under her skin and into her heart and now she couldn't imagine life without them.

"No matter what happens, I'll come back to you both," she said.

Ludovic

Roux was gone when Ludovic came out of the bathroom, but he could hear her voice on the other side of the door. Renie and Jason were with her, and when Ludovic heard his name, he paused, listening.

Bringing down the Five could, and probably would, get bloody, and Ludovic could handle that, but he didn't blame Roux's friends for being worried.

He opened the door. Roux and her friends stared back at him, blatant surprise registering on Renie's and Jason's faces. Self-consciously Ludovic touched his knitted hat and tousled hair. Even when he was human he hadn't looked like this; he felt like a stranger in his own skin.

"Is Edmond in your room?" he asked Renie.

She nodded.

Ludovic felt their gazes on him as he walked down the hallway, but he didn't look back.

Edmond's door was open when Ludovic reached the north wing, but he hesitated on the threshold, suddenly unsure. At any other time in the ten years he and Edmond had lived here he'd have walked in without a second thought. But now this room was Renie's too.

Ludovic knocked on the doorframe.

Edmond, straightening out the bedcovers, looked up, and a flicker of confusion passed across his face. "Are you all right?" he asked, looking Ludovic up and down.

He'd only known Ludovic as a vampire—this human look was as new to Edmond as it was to Ludovic himself.

Ludovic wasn't sure how to answer. Soon he'd leave the place that had been his home and haven and go back out into the world. Leaving Belle Morte a few days and traveling to Ireland didn't count; he and the others had been running for their lives. These next few days—or maybe weeks—would be very different.

"Ludovic? Are you all right?" Edmond repeated.

"Am I doing the right thing, letting Roux come with me?"

"You say it like you have a choice," said Edmond wryly.

He ushered Ludovic into the room and sat on his bed, watching his friend. Ludovic couldn't sit down. He felt agitated, full of nervous energy.

"I could refuse," he said.

"You could, but you can't force her to stay. Besides, she raised some valid points."

"You think I need her."

"I think any of us would."

"But I'll be responsible for her."

"Roux isn't a china doll. She won't break."

"I'm not used to being responsible for anyone," Ludovic muttered.

Edmond was his dearest friend in the whole world, his brother in every way but blood, but if one of them was responsible for the other, it was Edmond who was responsible for Ludovic.

"Are you worried about Roux depending on you, or are you worried about depending on her?" Edmond asked.

That made Ludovic pause. "What do you mean?"

"You don't like depending on people, especially not a human you barely know."

Ludovic sat on the edge of the bed.

"I can still go with you, if you want," Edmond said.

"Renie needs you here."

Once, Ludovic would've seized any offer of help from his best friend, but Edmond had Renie now, and that changed things.

"Maybe this'll be good for you," Edmond said.

"Maybe."

And maybe that was exactly why he'd volunteered in the first place.

"I know you're nervous, but I also know you can do this," Edmond said. His lips twitched. "Even if Roux has made you look so . . . different."

"She's made me look human."

"It's impressive," Edmond said, poking the side of Ludovic's face to check that the stubble wasn't real.

What Ludovic didn't say—but that Edmond had probably guessed—was that he was afraid looking human would remind him how it felt to *be* human. He didn't want that. In the safe cocoon of Belle Morte he didn't have to think about everything he'd seen and done, all the things that haunted him.

"No matter what happens, I'll be here when you get back," Edmond said.

Ludovic pulled off his prop glasses. For most of his life as a vampire he'd been alone, but things had changed when he'd met Edmond in the blasted trenches of the First World War. They'd become friends, inseparable.

No matter how bad things got, Edmond was the anchor that always saw Ludovic through the storm, and now he had to leave that anchor behind and strike out into the world with a girl he barely knew.

Ludovic slid his glasses back on. "We'll be leaving soon."

"I know this is hard for you, but don't make it hard for Roux," Edmond cautioned. "She's trying to help."

"I know."

Before the doorway, Ludovic paused. "I love you, Edmond. You do know that, don't you?"

"Of course I do," Edmond said.

Ludovic heard the rustle of clothing as Edmond got to his feet, and he turned around to hug his friend.

"I hope this is all over quickly so you can go back to normal," Edmond said, holding him at arm's length. "You look unbelievably strange."

Roux

While Ludovic was with Edmond, Roux packed their bags and Renie helped her carry them to the vestibule, where Ysanne waited. There was no sign of Walsh, and Roux was glad. It was easier to breathe when he wasn't looming like a thundercloud in the background.

Ysanne appraised Roux's new look, then looked past Roux to the main staircase, her eyes visibly widening.

Roux and Renie both turned.

Ludovic and Edmond walked down the stairs, and Ludovic's newly human appearance was even more incongruous next to Edmond's ebony-and-ivory vampire beauty. Plus, Ludovic looked awkward as hell.

Roux made a mental note to teach him how to walk and talk a bit more casually. His physical appearance was human but he still moved with the fluid grace of a vampire.

"I see that Roux is already proving her worth. I hardly recognized you," Ysanne said.

Ludovic tugged self-consciously at his beanie.

"There's a car waiting outside for you." Ysanne's lips thinned. "I'd hoped that you could travel with Walsh to the Johnsons' house, but he insisted on meeting you at the hotel. You're staying at the Old

Royal on Romsey Road. Seamus assures me that the car is equipped with the necessary technology to find the hotel without need of a map. The trunk is stocked with enough bagged blood for two weeks, and there's an envelope of money in the glove compartment. I trust you'll use it wisely."

She looked hard at Roux, then Ludovic, and a hint of red crept into her eyes.

"Ludovic, you are to take these vampires alive if possible, but your life comes first. You must kill them if you have no other choice," she said.

"Understood," he said.

Roux peeked from under her new fringe at Ludovic, trying to gauge how he felt about this, but his face was a blank mask. Interestingly, Edmond looked more worried than Ludovic.

"There's one more thing," Ysanne said, and held up a slim black cell phone gingerly between thumb and forefinger. "This is for you. I trust you know how to use it?"

Roux suppressed a smile. "I think I can work it out."

"Seamus has also provided one of these devices for the mansion, and programmed the number into yours. You must call regularly with progress updates."

Roux glanced at Ludovic, who was eyeing the phone with a kind of horrified fascination. He wouldn't be making any progress reports, then.

"Not to sound patronizing, but do *you* know how to use it?" Roux said to Ysanne.

Ysanne lifted her chin, proud as ever, but she didn't pretend that she understood the modern technology.

"Renie shall help with this aspect of the mission. In fact, I shall need her to help the entire House enter the modern world." Ysanne sounded as if Renie was going to teach the older vampires how to swim in sewage.

Roux slid the phone into her pocket. "I guess that's it then," she said, nerves suddenly twisting in her stomach.

Renie gave her a final hug. "Stay out of trouble," she whispered.

"I'll do my best."

Parked close to the front door was a sleek black car—one of the Belle Morte vehicles usually housed in the garage around the right side of the mansion. The keys dangled from the lock of the driver's door.

Tucked away inside the mansion, Roux had almost been able to forget about the protestors who gathered outside the gates almost every day, but out here, the sound of their anger was horribly loud. Roux had faced a lot of scary shit since coming to Belle Morte, but so many voices shouting and raging made her flinch.

"Are you all right?" Ludovic said.

The midday sun was high in the sky, and Roux wondered how long Ludovic could be out in it. It depended how old he was.

"I'm fine," she muttered. "You?"

"Why wouldn't I be?" His voice was flat and inflectionless.

"Don't pretend you can't hear them."

"I never claimed not to."

Roux looked curiously at him, scanning his face for any hint of expression. If this was hard for her, then it was a damn sight harder for him—he was the one these people were protesting against.

"So this is the car?" Ludovic said, eyeing it with ill-disguised apprehension.

"Looks like it."

Ludovic looked at her, his silence expectant, and after a moment or two, something clicked in her head.

"You can't drive, can you?" Roux said.

"Technically, yes, but the last time I drove car was in 1905. I suspect the process has changed somewhat since then."

Roux's lips twitched. "Maybe a little."

Roux unlocked the door, slung her bag into the back seat, and gestured for Ludovic to do the same. There was something monumentally strange about all this. She'd arrived at Belle Morte in a limousine, surrounded by flashing cameras; now she wondered if donors would ever again arrive at the mansion like that.

Ludovic climbed into the passenger's seat, sitting stiffly and uncomfortably.

Roux paused before getting into the car, gazing at the mansion. When she'd first filled out a donor form she'd never imagined that Belle Morte would be anything like home to her. So much had happened here, bad and good, and Roux had become part of the house in a way donors weren't meant to.

"Are you coming?" Ludovic called.

"Yeah."

Turning her back on Belle Morte, Roux climbed into the car.

© 2023 Bella Higgin